The Middle Ages Come to Life . . . to Bring Us Murder.

A PLAY OF LORDS

"Will entertain and confound you with its intricately plotted mystery and richly detailed writing . . . Ms. Frazer knows the fifteenth century and it shows . . . You'll want to rush out and get the previous books in this wonderful series."

—*The Romance Readers Connection*

"[An] amazing wealth of historical detail. While the mystery is compelling, and rooted in a fascinating historical period, it's the details of everyday life that make the story and characters leap off the page . . . Will appeal to readers who enjoy historical mystery and historical fiction."

—*CA Reviews*

A PLAY OF DUX MORAUD

"Deftly drawn characters acting on a stage of intricate and accurate details of medieval life."

—*Affaire de Coeur*

"A meticulously researched, well written historical mystery that brings to life a bygone era . . . Historical mystery fans will love this series."

—*Midwest Book Review*

"Wonderful . . . As always, the author provides a treasure trove of historical detail . . . [G]ood, solid mystery."

—*The Romance Readers Connection*

A PLAY OF ISAAC

"In the course of the book, we learn a great deal about theatrical customs of the fifteenth century . . . In the hands of a lesser writer, it could seem preachy; for Frazer, it is another element in a rich tapestry."

—*Contra Costa (CA) Times*

"Careful research and a profusion of details, especially those dealing with staging a fifteenth-century miracle play, bring the sights, smells, and sounds of the era directly to the reader's senses."

—*Roundtable Reviews*

"A terrific historical whodunit that will please amateur sleuth and historical mystery fans."

—*Midwest Book Review*

continued

THE MAIDEN'S TALE

"Great fun for all lovers of history with their mystery."
—*Minneapolis Star Tribune*

THE PRIORESS' TALE

"Will delight history buffs and mystery fans alike." —*Murder Ink*

THE MURDERER'S TALE

"The period detail is lavish, and the characters are full-blooded."
—*Minneapolis Star Tribune*

THE BOY'S TALE

"This fast-paced historical mystery comes complete with a surprise ending—one that will hopefully lead to another 'Tale' of mystery and intrigue."
—*Affaire de Coeur*

THE BISHOP'S TALE

"Some truly shocking scenes and psychological twists."
—*Mystery Loves Company*

THE OUTLAW'S TALE

"A tale well told, filled with intrigue and spiced with romance and rogues."
—*School Library Journal*

THE SERVANT'S TALE

"Very authentic . . . The essence of a truly historical story is that the people should feel and believe according to their times. Margaret Frazer has accomplished this extraordinarily well."
—Anne Perry

THE NOVICE'S TALE

"Frazer uses her extensive knowledge of the period to create an unusual plot . . . appealing characters, and crisp writing."
—*Los Angeles Times*

A Play of
Treachery

Margaret Frazer

BERKLEY PRIME CRIME, NEW YORK

THE BERKLEY PUBLISHING GROUP
Published by the Penguin Group
Penguin Group (USA) Inc.
375 Hudson Street, New York, New York 10014, USA
Penguin Group (Canada), 90 Eglinton Avenue East, Suite 700, Toronto, Ontario M4P 2Y3, Canada
(a division of Pearson Penguin Canada Inc.)
Penguin Books Ltd., 80 Strand, London WC2R 0RL, England
Penguin Group Ireland, 25 St. Stephen's Green, Dublin 2, Ireland (a division of Penguin Books Ltd.)
Penguin Group (Australia), 250 Camberwell Road, Camberwell, Victoria 3124, Australia
(a division of Pearson Australia Group Pty. Ltd.)
Penguin Books India Pvt. Ltd., 11 Community Centre, Panchsheel Park, New Delhi—110 017, India
Penguin Group (NZ), 67 Apollo Drive, Rosedale, North Shore 0632, New Zealand
(a division of Pearson New Zealand Ltd.)
Penguin Books (South Africa) (Pty.) Ltd., 24 Sturdee Avenue, Rosebank, Johannesburg 2196,
South Africa

Penguin Books Ltd., Registered Offices: 80 Strand, London WC2R 0RL, England

This is a work of fiction. Names, characters, places, and incidents either are the product of the author's
imagination or are used fictitiously, and any resemblance to actual persons, living or dead, business
establishments, events, or locales is entirely coincidental. The publisher does not have any control
over and does not assume any responsibility for author or third-party websites or their content.

A PLAY OF TREACHERY

A Berkley Prime Crime Book / published by arrangement with the author

PRINTING HISTORY
Berkley Prime Crime mass-market edition / December 2009

Copyright © 2009 by Gail Frazer.
The Edgar® name is a registered service mark of the Mystery Writers of America, Inc.
Cover illustration by Brigid Collins.
Cover design by Lesley Worrell.

ISBN: 978-0-425-22333-8

BERKLEY® PRIME CRIME
Berkley Prime Crime Books are published by The Berkley Publishing Group,
a division of Penguin Group (USA) Inc.,
375 Hudson Street, New York, New York 10014.
BERKLEY® PRIME CRIME and the PRIME CRIME logo are trademarks of Penguin Group (USA)
Inc.

PRINTED IN THE UNITED STATES OF AMERICA

10 9 8 7 6 5 4 3 2 1

Chapter 1

The Christmas holidays had gone prosperously for the players. Not needed this year by their patron Lord Lovell, they had spent most of the twelve days passing from town to town along the sheltering river valley of the upper Thames, playing on village greens (a chilly business) and in the great halls of wealthy gentry (a better business).

They were a company of six—Basset, master of the company, Ellis, Joliffe, and Gil, who shared the playing work among themselves; Rose, who saw to their clothing and playing garb and feeding them and was Basset's daughter; and Piers, her half-grown son. There were some bad times behind them, and they all knew better than to look too far ahead because the life of traveling players was nothing if not uncertain, but in this winter of 1435 into 1436, they had good times in hand. Their new play of *Saint George*, with its slaying of the Saracen, the Giant, and the Dragon (not to mention Saint George, too, but he—as always—was brought back to life with a magical pill), and the rescuing of the fair princess at the end, was met with roars of laughter and cheers everywhere they played it, and they had deliberately ended up in Oxford town for the riotous last days of Christmastide, crowning all with a triumphant Twelfth Night performance of the *Saint George* in St. Edmund's Hall.

"For the great and good of town and gown," as Joliffe put it. "Or at least for several score of them."

Basset, as master of the company, declared the next day a day of rest for the players before they took to the road again. "After six days of labor, God rested," he said. "Twelve days of labor and then one of rest for us seems reasonable, I think."

"Meaning you think we're half as holy as God?" Joliffe suggested.

"Ha!" Ellis had said. "Me, maybe. Not you, that's sure."

Joliffe had thrown one of their heavy sitting cushions at him in answer. Ellis had thrown it heartily back, and Rose had said with both threat and promise, "If that rips, one of you mends it."

Ellis had forsaken quarreling with Joliffe in favor of kissing her, while Joliffe quickly made show of checking the pillow to be sure it was whole.

So they stayed one more day in Oxford, and Joliffe took the chance to spend a few hours with the master of St. Edmund's Hall. He and John Thamys had been friends since the long-past time when their paths had first crossed here in Oxford, and despite how wide apart their ways had gone since then. "I having chosen," Thamys said as they sat near his comfortable fire in his comfortable room, "to roam the paths of scholarship while you roam the roads of England."

"I'm rethinking my choice," Joliffe said amiably. "You live warm, you live dry, and this is very good wine."

He raised the polished pewter goblet to Thamys who

raised his in return, saying just as amiably, "You wouldn't last a month at it and you know it."

Joliffe laughed, because it was true. Sitting in Thamys' chamber with a goblet of warm, spiced wine in hand, a quantity of books in reach, a pleasant fire on the hearth, and his and Thamys' talk rich with varied thoughts, it was easy to imagine this was a world he, too, could have had, if only he had stayed put.

It had been that "stay put" part that had defeated him those years ago, and the next day as he left Oxford, walking beside the players' laden cart pulled by their horse, Tisbe, he knew trying to "stay put" would defeat him just as surely now as it had then. The January morning was crisply chill under a winter-blue sky lightly fretted with dawn-cream clouds, the road was firm underfoot, there was no likelihood of snow that day or next and no certainty of where the players would fetch up that night; and Joliffe had no doubts that he had chosen rightly for his life when he walked away from his life in Oxford those years ago. Just as Thamys had chosen rightly for his. To each their own, and to own their each, as the saying was. Each man had to find for himself what his own way was, and today at least, Joliffe's way was the high road to Wantage town.

For one reason and another they did not make it that far that day, but it was no great matter. Toward the afternoon's end, in the last golden light of the fading day, they played *Saint Nicholas and the Thief* on a village's green, earning a few pence by way of halfpennies, plus three half-loaves of bread, and two wedges of cheese. Proportionate to what some wealthier places had paid for their playing, that was very generously done, and Ellis and Piers gave the villagers a show of juggling by way of thanks, while Joliffe and Rose and Gil loaded what little they had taken from the cart for their playing back into it and Basset sought leave from the village's reeve for them to camp on the edge of the common for the night, there being no inn in so small a place, nor even a sufficient alehouse.

Permission was readily given, and in the glowing after-light of sunset Basset and Ellis made quick work of setting up their tent, while Joliffe saw to Tisbe—unhitching her from the cart, wiping her down, tethering her to graze for the night—and Gil built a fire with the bundle of fagots bought in Oxford for just this case (since villages closely protected their wood-rights), and Piers fetched water from the village well, and Rose readied their supper that tonight would be thick slices of bacon (likewise bought in Oxford; it kept well in this cold weather) to go with toasted bread and cheese.

Time had been when they would have had to glean wood from under hedgerows as they traveled along, and bacon would have been a rare treat and the bread and cheese stretched to serve for breakfast as well as supper. But prosperity had come on them when Lord Lovell became their patron, giving them some certainty of income by his favor and a place in a world that could be harsh to landless, lordless men. The boundary between survival and failure was become a little wider, and therefore there was often bacon for supper now and sometimes beef, and they did not have to hoard this evening's pay of bread and cheese; there were coins enough in the company's purse to buy more tomorrow.

So it was with contentment they gathered around the fire to their supper. And it was just then the peddler came plodding out of the last of the gray twilight.

He looked a hale and hearty man but tired, as well he might be after a day walking under the pack he had on his back, and he asked leave to set down by their fire and sleep out there, saying, "I'm not minded to go knocking on doors at this hour, looking for a roof to sleep under. I've my cloak and blanket and was thinking it would be the hedge for me, but if I could share your fire instead, I'd be much obliged."

It was courteously asked, and there was no reason to say him nay. He looked a respectable sort of peddler, the kind who made his living at it honestly, not the kind who used their pack as an excuse to wander in and out of trouble. They welcomed him, he slipped free of his pack and leaned it against a wheel of the cart, took some food of his own from it, and joined them at the fire. While night came on, they sat and ate and talked together, the peddler sharing a sweet cake he had bought that afternoon, the players sharing their ale. With the fire warm on their faces and their cloaks huddled high around their ears against the cold at their backs, they traded news of where he had lately been and what they had heard in Oxford about this and that. He warned them that the next village along their way had little welcome for strangers presently, and they told him the village here was likely to give him good business, being friendly folk. Then the talk turned to telling the kind of stories travelers always had to share, with the peddler able to raise laughter over his own disasters as readily as the players could over theirs, and all in all it was a merry evening, with everyone going to bed later than they would have otherwise and only when the fire was sunk low into its coals.

It was in the frost-touched morning, while Joliffe was hitching Tisbe to the cart, his breath and hers white in the air, that Basset came to him, bringing the peddler, and said, quiet-voiced for the others not to hear where they were packing away the camp, "He wants to talk to the two of us."

Joliffe looked around from the harness buckle he had not quite finished buckling, saw that Basset's face was too bare of any feeling and that the peddler's had lost all its easy, merry lines. With a first shiver of warning, Joliffe turned back to the buckle, finished with it, and only then turned fully to face the two men. "Do you?" he said to the peddler.

"I do," the man said back, meeting Joliffe's gaze straightly. "I'm to say that my lord of Winchester hopes you remember your agreement of last autumn."

Despite something lurched under his breast bone, Joliffe said steadily, "I remember it."

"I'm bid to tell you thus. The fourth day from now, an hour after Vespers, you're to meet a man you'll know in the Crown of Roses tavern in Southwark."

"To what purpose?" Joliffe asked.

"That I was not told." The peddler looked to Basset. "I was told, though, to tell you not to look for him until he comes back."

"He *will* come back, though," Basset said. It was less a question than a half-hidden demand.

"God and the saints willing. That's all any of us can go by. But my lord of Winchester intends it. I was to say that, too, if I were asked."

Basset gave a curt nod, accepting that assurance, with small choice but to do so, "my lord of Winchester" being the powerful Henry Beaufort, cardinal and bishop of Winchester, the king's great-uncle, and a high force in the government.

The peddler said, still to Basset, "You and your company will maybe want to travel other than your usual way for the while he's elsewhere, to forestall questions from anyone who might remember him and be curious about why he's not with you. I'm likewise to pay you for the inconvenience your company will have because of this. What would likely have been his portion in your work for this half year to come?"

"Half year?" Joliffe echoed, in question and almost-protest together.

Both the other men ignored him. "In a good year or a bad?" Basset asked.

The peddler gave him a shrewdly approving look. "A good year. Why not?"

Basset named a sum that was very fair by what Joliffe knew of the company's earnings.

The man raised his brows. "That's in a *good* year?"

"In a good year," Basset confirmed.

"You're not at this to grow rich, are you?"

The question so openly did not need answering that neither Basset nor Joliffe did, merely followed the peddler as he went around to the cart's open back, there took coins from the small satchel hung over his shoulder—rather more whole silver coins than a peddler might be expected to have—and counted out the sum Basset had named onto the high wooden floor's one clear space, where the kitchen box would go when Rose had packed it. Finished, he hesitated, then added a few more coins. "For luck," he said. "Good enough?"

Basset looked up from the coins, his face straight. "Good enough," he agreed.

"One thing," Joliffe said. "How do I find the company again, when I've finished whatever my lord bishop of Winchester wants of me?"

The peddler hesitated as if uncertain he should answer that, but finally said, "Someone will know where they are. You'll be told. After all, I knew where to find you."

The thought that some sort of watch had been kept on them without they had guessed it was discomfiting. That it was no more comfortable to know that someone would go on watching the company, even when he was not there, was in the look that flashed between him and Basset, but Joliffe contented himself with a nod of understanding to the peddler, who nodded back, hefted his pack onto his back, and trudged away toward the awakened village to be about his business of selling this and that, on his way to somewhere else and then to somewhere else again.

Joliffe stood watching him go, then said to Basset, "I feel like a whore that's been sold and bought."

Basset, who had been gathering up the coins, answered

flatly, "You should. You have been. For maybe something worse than whoring, but sold and bought, yes." But his voice went suddenly cheerful as he slapped Joliffe heartily on the back and added, "Still, we got a good price for you. Don't look so dire. It's not as bad as all that. It's what you wanted, and we've all been getting flat and fat and too much used to what we're doing. The shaking up will do us all good. You as well as the rest of us."

Joliffe was not sure how much he believed in Basset's heartiness, but he played back to it, holding out a hand and saying, "If I'm doing you that much good by going away, how if I have some of those coins to see me on the road?"

"You," said Basset, "will have all of them," and held them out.

"No. Enough to see me to London. No more."

Dropping the heartiness, his hand still out, Basset said, serious to the bone, "All of them. You don't know what you're heading into. We're well enough, and there's what we left with young Master Penteney to fall back on if need be, and that's because of you, too. So these are yours. I'm still master of this company, and you're still part of it, and this is what I'm bidding you do—take them."

"Half of them," Joliffe countered.

Basset hesitated, then agreed, "Half then."

Basset made a rough split and still in Joliffe's favor, but Joliffe made no more protest and was tipping the coins into his belt pouch when Piers said, coming with some of the rolled up blankets from the tent, "Hai! If you're handing out coins, where's mine?"

"We get what we earn," Joliffe said. "I've earned some coins. You've earned—" He raised a hand suggestive of a box on the ear. Piers wailed in completely pretended fear, "Mam! He's going to hit me!"

Behind him, Ellis growled as he and Gil came with the rolled, strapped tent, "It's not his turn. It's mine. Shift aside, fryling. You're in the way."

Piers shifted and went with Gil to fetch the kitchen box while Joliffe went to finish harnessing Tisbe, leaving Basset and Ellis to deal with the tent. When all was ready, Basset gathered his company around him, which was warning enough that something had shifted even before he told them that for a certain reason to do with that business in London last autumn, Joliffe would be gone a time, to rejoin them later.

"That's all we're to know?" Ellis demanded. "That he's going to go away and that he'll come back?"

They all knew something of what had happened in London last autumn but not much, because that had seemed safest. Basset, as master of the company knew most, and he demanded back at Ellis, "Do you truly want to know more than that about it?"

"No," Ellis returned bluntly. "I just want to know that whatever trouble he's made for himself, it's not going to turn into our trouble."

Basset beamed at him. "Oh, it's most assuredly going to turn into your trouble. With him gone, we'll be three men and a boy again. We have to change all our plays back to what they were before Gil joined us."

Ellis groaned. Gil grinned. He was as used as the rest of them to Ellis' groans, and besides, these past weeks since London, Joliffe had had him studying the plays as they had been before he joined the company close to a year and half ago and Joliffe had changed them to include him. The several new ones Joliffe had written since then would have to be put aside for the while that he was gone, but there was no help for that, and Gil would do well in the old ones. He was too sensible to ask questions where no answers were going to be given, and although his long look on Joliffe was full of questions, he kept them to himself. It was Piers who refused to accept being told so little, and while the players finished readying the cart he prodded and pried until Joliffe silenced him by promise of a silver penny if he

stopped. In hope of the coin, Piers left him in peace while
Rose gathered a change of shirt and hosen and some few
other things into a sack for Joliffe to carry away with him.
She almost kept to herself her worry at his going, but as she
handed him the sack, in a moment when they happened to
be alone, she started a question to him.

Not waiting for her to finish it, Joliffe said quietly,
"Don't," and she let it go. Worry was too much Rose's share
in the company, and Joliffe was sorry to add more of it to
all she already had, but all he could do was regret, give her
a light kiss on the cheek, and promise, "I'll be well. Truly.
And think—one less of us to trouble you."

"There is that," she agreed, forcing a smile and false
cheer.

The peddler had well-placed his coming to them. Half
that morning's walk brought them, their cart, and Tisbe
to a country crossroads where it made sense for Joliffe to
turn leftward, the others to go onward. Considering how
many years they had been in each others' company, day
in and day out, they made surprisingly short work of their
farewells. Piers remembered to demand his penny, but little else was said on any side beyond, "Fortune's favor on
you" and "Take care." But then, it was maybe those years
of being used to each other that made the farewells short:
knowing each other so well, there was little that needed
saying. It was only when the familiar rattle of the cart and
plod of Tisbe's hooves were gone and Joliffe was left to
only himself and a few birds hopping and chirping in the
leaf-bare hedgerows along the road that the completeness
of what he had done came home to him. The completeness . . . and the lack of any chance of going back to how
things had been.

He had made his agreement with Bishop Beaufort not
because he had wanted "other" than his life as a player but
because he had wanted "more." What he had now, at just
that moment, was neither. Instead, he was standing alone

on an unknown road, going to somewhere he barely knew for reasons he could guess at but not yet know. To get the more that he wanted, he had given up what he had—even if only for a while—and at just that moment, there alone on the road, there was a cold hollow in him that had very much to do with fear.

He was used to fear, though, he told himself. Life was full of things to fear—or at least be wary of. Too many people wallowed in whatever their fear or feelings might be, blindly indulging in them instead of straightly facing and dealing with them. Joliffe—as he did with most things in his life (fear among them)—took, in his mind, a small step back from this present fear and looked at it. Alone on that road between those hedgerows, he straightly faced that for just now he had to do without one of the things he wanted in his life so that, eventually, he could have both the things he wanted. Since that was the way of it and there was no use sorrowing over one hand being empty when the other was full of something good, he hitched his sack to rest more easily on his shoulder and set off along the unfamiliar road with a long stride meant to cover miles.

Chapter 2

Only the next day did it come to Joliffe he could hire a horse, rather than walk his way to Southwark. He had grown so used to walking, he simply had not thought of doing otherwise, but when some of his silver pennies bought him a night's lodging and supper *and* a goodly breakfast at a small, somewhat untidy inn, he bethought himself of how silver pennies could buy other, even less familiar, things, and in the doorway, on his way out to another day of walking, he turned back and asked the innkeeper if there were a hire-stable in town, somewhere he could get a horse for brief use.

The man, probably mindful that he had paid with good silver, said easily enough, "For where are you bound? London, you said?"

"I said London, but it's to Southwark."

"Better yet. Jack Duncell, he has horses to hire, and his brother has a place at the other end, in Southwark, where they can be left—and hired again for coming back, if that's what you want. Mostly it's for folk going back and forth to London, but the Duncells have agreement with other stablemen on to Canterbury for pilgrims and even to Dover for them as are fool enough to go further. Have stables the other way, too, west toward Cirencester and Gloucester, for such as are going the other direction, coming back, as 'twere. Do a good business. You go along that way"—the innkeeper pointed along the street — "and you'll know the place. If he's a horse to hand, he'll see you on your way, will Jack Duncell."

Jack Duncell had several horses to hand and was glumly glad to hire one to Joliffe. "Travel falls off this time of year," he said. "So here they are, eating their way through my purse. I've a good little chestnut gelding will see you to London, right and proper."

Joliffe, finding unused knowledge coming back to him, turned down the chestnut gelding on suspicion of a sore hoof from the way the horse was lifting and setting down its right forefoot, but cheerfully took a black mare with a calm face and sturdy legs.

"She goes steady," Duncell said while saddling her. "But you won't get any turn of speed out of her. There's not much fire to her."

Given how many years it was since he had last done much riding, "fire" was among the last things Joliffe wanted from a horse. "I just need to be in Southwark the day after tomorrow."

"Ah. She'll have you there sometime tomorrow without pushing." He cocked an eye skyward. "Weather should hold that long for you, too."

Duncell proved right about the black mare and only a little wrong about the weather. The next afternoon, as Joliffe rode between the spread of houses, gardens, and orchards that were the outward sprawling edge of Southwark, the first light flakes of snow swirled down from the gray clouds that had been lowering since dawn. A mean wind came with the snow, sharp around his ears, making him huddle deeper into his cloak and pull his hood up over his slight-brimmed cap and welcome when the road became a street crowded between shoulder-to-shoulder houses that gave some shelter from the wind if not from the suddenly bone-biting cold.

His acquaintance with Southwark was slight, but there was not much chance of mistaking his way. Stretched around the southern end of London's bridge, the town's main purpose lay in serving travelers. All the main ways into it drew toward the bridge, and Joliffe had no trouble coming on the swinging sign of St. Christopher that marked the inn where the Duncells had their Southwark stable. In the inn's yard, Joliffe gave the mare over to a man enough Jack Duncell's twin to surely be his brother, and then, with the day getting no warmer and early dark coming on with the swirling snow, he took a room at the Christopher. More than that, he took not just a bed among other beds in some long room—a bed quite possibly shared with someone he did not know—but an actual chamber all to himself. He was spending his pence madly, but not knowing into what he was heading, come tomorrow's meeting, he chose to favor himself this far, and at least the room came with not only a clean-blanketed bed with a sheet, but a small table and even a candle. With the shutter closed over the one window and the candle lighted, the low-beamed room was a haven from the strangeness of the past three days and the uncertainty of whatever was to come, and just now he wanted that haven.

Added to that, the room was warm from the kitchen below it, and he brought his supper of beef and parsnip pottage, rye bread, and spiced wine back to it, to eat and drink in splendid solitude, the wine reminding him of his time with Thamys just—five?—days ago. The shift from that while in Thamys' comfortable room to the next day spent on the road and working had been wide enough but had held nothing unexpected. It was the shift from there to here that was so far aside from anything foreseen that he found he did not want to look at it, instead firmly put aside his thoughts that way and brought out from his sack the small book he had bought, probably foolishly, in Oxford's High Street the other day.

Since everything in a player's life had to be carried either on the cart or on himself, there was little place in a player's life for unneeded things, and for a long time past, books had been among the things Joliffe had not let himself need. For much of that time, too, there had been no money to spare from the company as it barely survived, but now—despite the first still held—the second was no longer true, and the other day after leaving Thamys Joliffe had paused at a scrivener's stall. Just to look, he had told himself, and kept himself away from the more costly books set out to display the scrivener's skill, instead looking only at the plainer works done for such scholars as could afford a ready-written text, rather than have to copy out with their own hand what they needed from someone else's copy of a book.

The particular book that Joliffe now laid on the table was about the length and width of his hand and no thicker than his finger. Small enough to carry easily, he had told himself as he stood at the stall, turning its pages, finding it written in plain black script on moderately good paper stitched into an unadorned parchment cover. It was poems. The first lines his eyes chanced on—

Of long abiding here I may repent,
Lest out of hastiness I at the last
Answer amiss, best be that I leave fast,
For if I among these people step amiss,
To harm it will me turn and to folly.

—had made him want to read more, but with the scrivener's eye already on him—able to tell he was neither stu-

dent nor scholar nor master but unable to place him as a
townsman either and therefore doubly suspicious of him—
Joliffe had given way to that ever-dangerous thing—a sudden urge—and bought the book.

The thing about such sudden urges was that as often
as they could work against him, they could also be to the
good. The trouble there was that by the time he knew which
way the outcome would go, it had already . . . come out.

He supposed the day would come when, full of wisdom
and good judgment, he would make all his decisions in
a well-considered manner, thinking them through before
deciding his way, but that day still looked to be a long way
distant, Joliffe thought with silent laughter at himself as he
opened the book.

This time at least the urge had served him well. He was
in no humour for tavern noise and drinking or Southwark's
famed other possibilities, but neither did he much want to
be alone with his thoughts—his worries—about tomorrow.
Against those, the book served very well, both for compan-
ionship and diversion, and he read by the golden candle-
light until the candle was burned far down and he had worn
out his brain sufficiently that sleep came almost as soon as
the darkness when he blew out the candle and lay down.

With morning came a whole day to be gone through
before he met "a man" in the Crown of Roses an hour after
Vespers. He paid for another night in his room, for somewhere to leave his sack through the day as well as to be
sure of somewhere to sleep, then broke his fast with more
of last night's stew, a small, round loaf of crisp-crusted,
new-baked bread, and some fresh-brewed ale. Ready after
that to face the day, he shrugged his cloak around him and
ventured out. Yesterday's snow still lay in thin lines along
shadowed places close to buildings, and the sky was still
low and gray, but the bitter wind had gone, shops were
opening, people were out and about: workmen carrying
their tools, bound to wherever today's work was; women

with their market baskets, on their way to market and baker and butcher; children to school or—older boys and probably apprentices—on whatever early errand their master had set them. A pair of the town's scavagers were early about their business, shoveling into their cart the waste and rubbish left in careful piles beside doorsteps, a less odorous job at this time of year than at others.

Except that Joliffe knew that Southwark was where the brothels and gambling forbidden in London were gathered, out of the reach of London's laws but not of customers, he could have thought it simply an ordinary town, its prosperity built, like so many others, on serving the monastery in its midst, St. Mary Overy along the Thames. Besides that, there was the added benefit of the bishop of Winchester's palace only a little further up the river, because whenever the bishop was in residence with his large household, all of Southwark's grocers, butchers, and bakers surely prospered. On his own behalf, Joliffe learned, by way of a simple question of the lazing guard at Winchester House's outer gateway, that Bishop Beaufort had spent Christmastide away in Hampshire at one of his other palaces and was not yet come back here. So it was not to have a secret meeting with Bishop Beaufort that he was to meet someone in a tavern this evening. For what then?

Restless with his curiosity, Joliffe spent the day wandering Southwark's streets and alleyways, learning his way around the town from one direction and then another, becoming familiar with more than the main ways on the chance that he would need to know them if Bishop Beaufort had a use for him here. Southwark not being that large of a place, by early afternoon he had done as much as he might without he became too noticeable, and with still several hours to fill, he took himself across London bridge and roamed some of London's streets, to add to the acquaintance he had with London from the players' while there last autumn.

Still, Bishop Beaufort had men enough in London and surely Southwark not to need Joliffe here as well. So why . . .

Try though he did to keep his wondering in check, he could not help his imaginings nor deceive himself that mostly he was no more than filling time to get through the day as best he could, and when bells finally rang out from various church towers for the hour of Vespers in the late afternoon that was gathering early into a gray evening under the day's persevering clouds, he was already crossing the bridge back to Southwark.

As part of his day's wanderings, he had of course made sure to find out the Crown of Roses tavern. Not that that had been a trouble. Its sign of a wreath of red roses thrust out boldly over the wide street that ran along the long side of St. Mary Overie not far from Winchester House. Maybe because it was so near to both the monastery and the bishop's palace, it had looked from the outside to be only a tavern, with no other of Southwark's less desirable businesses part of it. Or maybe, being so near to the monastery and bishop's palace, it merely kept a better front to itself than some other places Joliffe had seen in his wanderings about the town. Either way, the room he came into from the street was welcoming, with long tables down both sides, benches along the wall behind them and more benches scattered in the open middle of the room, all well-lighted by horn-sided lanterns hung along the ceiling beams. The rushes thick on the floor were fresh, neither squishing nor giving out a stink underfoot as Joliffe crossed toward the trestle table set up across the doorway at the room's far end where a woman of middle years, tidily-dressed in a dark gown, with a clean apron, and white starched wimple and head-kerchief presided over several pottery pitchers and an array of vari-sized wooden cups.

Joliffe took up a medium cup, she told him the price, he put down his coin, and she poured a palely gold ale to nearly the cup's brim, no stinting. He thanked her with a nod and turned around, seemingly to decide where to sit. But while crossing the room he had taken an encompassing glance across the several dozen men and a few women already there. They looked to be clerks and small-shopkeepers and their wives, done with their day's work, here for a pleasant while and all of them familiar to one another but equally used to strangers, Southwark being a place that had much coming and going of strangers.

Being a stranger, Joliffe very reasonably went simply to the nearest empty place. It happened to be on the bench set along the room's back wall, beside the door behind the ale-table, at the end of the line of tables and other benches running along the side wall, back toward the streetward door. It also happened to be a few feet aside from another man propped into the corner where the benches along the two walls met. The fellow was pale, as if he did not encounter much sunlight, which went with his plain black robe, as if he were some churchman's clerk, and the wood-rimmed pair of spectacles braced on the bridge of his nose by ribbons around his ears, leaving little doubt that he must spend his life over books—probably account books: he had that look of someone constantly concerned that the record of profits and debts be precisely right lest the world fall apart around him.

As Joliffe sat down, keeping careful distance from him, the man briefly eyed him, very much as if Joliffe were another figure to be reckoned onto an account roll, returned a wordless nod to Joliffe's own with no show of familiarity or any wish to talk, and went back to contemplating the world in front of him. For a few moments Joliffe did the same, wondering if the next move were his to make but not yet decided before another man, come in soon after him, turned from the ale-table with a tall cup of ale in hand and gave a sullen jerk of his free hand to show Joliffe should shift along the bench to make room for him there. Joliffe obligingly shifted, and sitting down, the man grunted, sounding not so much unfriendly as just tired, "Close to the ale here. Makes it easier."

Joliffe made a wordless sound of understanding in answer and turned to the pale man now close on his other side and said, too low for the newcomer to hear him, "Pardon, if I'm crowding you, Master Fowler."

Looking as if Joliffe were a sum of which he did not approve, Bishop Beaufort's private clerk said as quietly, "It's as it should be." He gave a small flick of his eyes to the man on Joliffe's other side. "Nor is there need to worry on him. If it seems we might be heard, he'll begin to sing."

"Ah," said Joliffe, understanding. "What would you have done if I'd not remembered you and not sat down here?"

"Something else. Where are you staying? Not here."

"The Christopher."

Master Fowler showed mild approval, but that might have been only for the sake of making it seem to anyone noting them that they were in easy talk and nothing more, because it was without changing his face or voice that he went on. "At dawn tomorrow you will make yourself known to the master of the bishop of Therouanne's men as they gather in the yard at Winchester House. You will then journey with the bishop and his household to France. There you will be given a place in . . ."

"France?" Joliffe got out on somewhat of a croak.

"France," Master Fowler repeated firmly. "My lord of Winchester has use of you in France."

"But . . ." There were so many things unlikely about that that Joliffe fumbled among them before saying, more in disbelief than otherwise, "Use for me in France?"

"Do you speak French?"

"Somewhat. Not well. It's been years since I did at all."

"Good. That will make you the more believable."

"As what?"

"As a disgraced clerk from my lord's household."

After a pause to take firm grip on himself, Joliffe brought out evenly, "I'm to be a disgraced clerk from my lord bishop's household being sent into France in apparent—exile? punishment?"

"Yes. Both. You drink too much. You have been a disappointment and a disgrace. But you have pleaded for mercy and a chance to do better. My lord sees promise in you of better things and does not wish to cast you out entirely, but this is your last chance to redeem yourself. You will travel to Rouen with the bishop of Therouanne's household. There you will make yourself known to Master Richard Wydeville in the household of the widow of his grace the duke of Bedford, God have the duke's soul in keeping."

Master Fowler crossed himself. Joliffe copied the gesture while his mind played juggle-and-catch with what he knew—or at least half-knew—about any of that. The duke of Bedford had been one of the king's two uncles, and while the younger uncle, the duke of Gloucester, had mis-stirred the pot of politics here in England and quarreled with Bishop Beaufort through these past dozen years and more, Bedford had worked to make good England's hold on Normandy and France. From everything Joliffe had ever heard, it had not been Bedford's fault the odds had been turning against him in the French war before he died last year, but his death had set into play a rivaling among lords here in England for who would take his place as governor of Normandy and France. The whole thing was tangled by King Henry—sixth of the name and son of the hero of the battle of Agincourt—being but fourteen years old and the government not yet in his hands but divided between councils running his realms of England and France, so that these four months on from Bedford's death, no one was yet named to take over the war in France. And by all reports, that war was going badly since the duke of Burgundy had forsaken his alliance with the English and taken up the Dauphin's cause on the French side.

Hesitantly, uncertain how much protest he might be allowed, Joliffe tried, "Uh. Isn't sending me there somewhat like throwing me into a river in full flood before I've learned to paddle in a pool?"

"Very much like," Master Fowler agreed, with an approving nod—whether at the throwing or at Joliffe for seeing it, Joliffe was not sure. "Unfortunately, because of how things have gone in Normandy of late, some of our men skilled at gathering privy knowledge are no longer of use."

"Because they're dead?" Joliffe asked dryly.

"Because they are known by those who are no longer our allies."

"The Burgundians."

"Indeed. So their usefulness is now limited, and while there are still those who are not known, someone new and unknown will surely be of use. More than that, Master Wydeville was spymaster to the duke of Bedford. He will have the directing and training of you, and better you could not have."

"Ah," said Joliffe. That seemed to cover the matter.

"Under the near edge of my robe," Master Fowler went on, "for you to take when you're sure no one is looking this way, there are two letters. They name you John Ripon. You may show openly to anyone the one with my lord's seal. It gives my lord's leave for you to join the bishop of Therouanne's household and go into Normandy. It should be shown to Master Wydeville, too. The other, close-sealed, is for Master Wydeville only. It should be kept on you at all times and seen by no one else. That one is wrapped in oiled cloth for safety. A winter crossing to France is often perilous."

Just what all this was in need of, Joliffe thought—more peril.

At the same time, though, a hot flame of excitement was strengthening in him. This all promised to be not only different from anything he had ever done, but *interestingly* different.

The heavily drinking man on his other side gave a belch and suddenly leaned sidewise, across Joliffe, to say into Master Fowler's face, "Yer one of Winchester's men, bain't you? So when's his mighty lordship coming back to Southwark, eh? There's one of his household knaves owes me three shillings. When's he going to be back here, eh?"

Blocked from anybody seeing what he did, Joliffe deftly slid the packet of letters from under the edge of Master Fowler's robe with one hand while unfastening the clasp on his belt pouch with the other. While Master Fowler drew back from the man, very openly offended by his breath and his demand, Joliffe protested, "Here now!" making as if trying to shove the fellow off him to cover the twist of his body needed to slip the packet into his belt pouch. That safely done and the pouch re-clasped, he used both hands to shift the man back onto his seat while saying good-humouredly, "I'm just in the middle here. Don't add me to your quarrel!"

Master Fowler was sliding away along the bench, to-ward a gap in the line of tables by which he could escape, saying in stiff and indignant protest, "I know nothing of my lord's intents. It might be a week. It might be longer. I don't know." Reaching the gap, he stood up, slid through it, and disappeared beyond several men just come in together at the tavern's door.

The fellow beside Joliffe flung an arm around Joliffe's shoulders and assured him with well-aled breath, "Sorry to have you in the middle. No fault of yours. You don't even know the fellow that owes me, right?"

"My first time in Southwark," Joliffe assured him. Not quite the truth but good enough for now.

"The loins of London, as they say," his companion told him happily. "That what you here for?" He prodded an elbow into Joliffe's ribs. "For the loins? I know a place where there's a woman . . ."

"I'm just here to deliver a horse to my master's cousin," Joliffe said. "That's done and I'm heading home with an early start tomorrow. So an early bed tonight. Alone," he added as the fellow opened his mouth for probably more ribaldry. He made to copy Master Fowler's shift along the bench that was briefly clear, the two men who had sat down there gone to join some friends just seen across the room. Then he paused to lean over and put a coin onto the table in front of the fellow, saying, "Have a farewell cup for me." And, dropping his voice to very low, "This was all to try me, wasn't it?"

"I'll drink to your health," the man said with a hard-drinker's happy grin as he picked up the coin. And added, matching Joliffe's drop in voice and with no sign of drunkenness, "Every bit of it."

Whatever curfew might be in Southwark—supposing it had one—Joliffe guessed he was well ahead of it as he went his way back to the Christopher. More lighted lanterns than need be hung beside and over doorways, that people not be discouraged in their comings and goings, he supposed, and surely the cold night seemed to be discouraging no one from seeking whatever pleasures were promised by loud voices and smoky light beyond open doorways through which sometimes laughter and often singing burst. Other possibilities were offered him as he passed, both by voices out of shadowed alleyways and bolder women in lantern-light beside some of the doorways, but Joliffe passed them all with no more than a smile and a shake of his head and was glad his own inn was a quieter place, turned to plain travelers and pilgrims rather than other ways of income. Coming into the place's main room, he found perhaps a dozen folk among the various tables there, all in easy talk over their wine and ale while the landlord wiped down a cleared table and said friendliwise as Joliffe crossed the room toward the stairs, "Early back, sir."

"Early back," Joliffe agreed. "Early back, early to bed, and an early start tomorrow."

"That's the sensible way of it," the landlord agreed. "A good night's sleep is always the thing before taking to the road."

Joliffe cheerfully agreed again, no matter that he doubted how much he would sleep tonight. He had too many thoughts running around and into each other in his head. Almost the strongest was: France! He was going to France!

But stronger, if no more insistent, was: in the name of all the saints, what had he got himself into?

Chapter 3

Only the first streaks of color were showing in the east as Joliffe passed through Southwark's darkened and nearly empty streets to Winchester House, to find the palace's courtyard lantern-lighted and bustling with servants and horses. By questions, he found the master of the bishop of Therouanne's household among it all and presented himself. He was pointed toward the one baggage cart in sight and told to get himself on it. He did, scrambling over the tail-board as the cart lurched forward toward the gateway. Sitting himself on the nearest of the long chests roped in place there, he grabbed hold to one of the curved half-hoops of the canvas tilt to keep from being pitched about as the cart swayed into a turn outside the gateway, the carter snapping his whip over his horses' backs.

From the back of the cart, Joliffe could not see where they were going, only where they had been, but he chose not to shout questions the cart's long length to the carter or try to make his way forward over the chests and piled bundles. For worry his sack could be lost among them, he

kept it slung over his shoulder, made himself as comfortable as might be—which was not much—and waited to
see what happened next. Supposing the bishop—where in
France was his bishopric of Therouanne, anyway?—meant
to go by the pilgrim's road to Canterbury and on to Dover,
to take ship there for France, Joliffe expected a southward
turn into the high street but it did not come. That confused
him until the cart lurched to an unexpected stop, and with
its rattling no longer in his ears, he heard waves slapping
a wall and guessed where he was even before he thrust his
head from under the tilt and found the cart was standing on
a quay, the river lapping high against its pilings and at its
end the masts and rigging of a ship standing black against
the graying sky.

Along the quay and on the ship, men were going back
and forth by lantern-light, doing things with ropes that Joliffe did not understand, but he did grasp that, rather than
to the Canterbury road, the cart was come to the Thames
and he was going to have a sea voyage some days sooner
than he had expected.

He climbed from the cart. At the front of it, a man was
asking the carter, "This the last of it, then?"

"'Tis. The rest get loaded right?"

"Long since." The man nodded his head sidewise at Joliffe. "Who's that?"

The carter shrugged. "He was told to get on back at the
palace. That's all I know of it."

Joliffe went forward as the other man said at him, "You
supposed to be here?"

"I'm bound for France with the bishop of Therouanne's
household," Joliffe said, with a shrug to show none of it
was his fault at all.

"This is where you should be, then," the man said. "Get
aboard and keep out of the way."

Joliffe got. He did not much like the plank he had to
cross, but was ready when the man on watch at its other

end demanded, "What're you doing here?" and answered lightly, "I came with the baggage."

"Then stand yourself over there and stay out of the way."

The man pointed, and Joliffe went, into a corner beside a steep stair up to the raised rear of the ship. From there, he watched the final readying of the ship and the bishop's arrival among his rather scant household of hardly more than a score of men. In Joliffe's experience over the years, lords too often made fluster beyond reason at whatever they did, as if their dignity required making other men's lives difficult, but the bishop of Therouanne, dressed simply and plainly for travel, made no trouble whatsoever about dismounting, giving a coin to the man who took his horse, then coming onto the ship, his men gathering to follow him. On board, he paused long enough to give his blessing with raised hand over the ship's master and crew as they all knelt to him, caps in hand—Joliffe matching them—before moving toward the forepart of the ship, as well out of the way as Joliffe was.

His men, too, cleared out of the sailors' way; orders were shouted; sailors scurried; ropes were pulled in and wound up; the ship was shoved from the quay with poles, away into the river, and began to gather speed as the tide took it and a sail was raised. The most that Joliffe had ever had to do with boats was sometimes crossing a river by ferry. He knew this was a ship and never to be called a boat. Beyond that, all was surprise, beginning with how fast the quay slid away behind them, and then the buildings lining the shore. In barely more than moments he was further from land than he had ever been. A light wind began to shove at the sail; the ship swung further out into the river. Forgetting to stay where he was, he stepped to the railing. The ship was steady enough underfoot, but with his hands on the railing, he could feel the tremble of it, like a live thing, and now the land was gliding past faster than a horse could gallop, faster than Joliffe had ever gone in his life.

Held by seeing the world in a way he never had before, he stayed there at the railing, forgetting all else, until after the day was fully come and distracted then only because a man came to fetch him to the bishop, seated in the forepart of the ship on a curved and cushioned wooden chair.

Last night Joliffe had summoned to mind everything he could remember having heard about Louys de Luxembourg, bishop of Therouanne. His family was Burgundian nobility of some sort. There was a brother—Sir Jean de Luxembourg—famous for his victories on the English side against the Dauphin and his claims of French kingship, and another brother who held the family's lordship, whatever it was named. The bishop himself was presently chancellor for the English government in Normandy and had been in England these past months because of the angry break between the English and the duke of Burgundy, their erstwhile ally. Last autumn, when Joliffe and the other players had been in London, rumor had been running that the bishop had come at his brothers' urging, to see if some manner of agreement and peace might after all be made between Burgundy and England despite Burgundy's treacherous desertion to the Dauphin. So far as Joliffe had heard—but how likely was he to hear if agreement had been made behind surely very closed doors? he thought dryly—the English government was just as furious with the duke of Burgundy as they had been last autumn, and that meant the bishop was going back to Normandy in failure.

If he was, it did not show on his wide-boned face as he held out his gloved hand for Joliffe, kneeling, to kiss. Rather, he regarded Joliffe with cool, stern interest for a long moment, not bidding him rise but saying in French, "You are in disgrace with my lord of Winchester, yes?"

"Yes, my lord."

"You have been given into my household, to go into France, for chance to redeem yourself."

At a guess, the bishop was somewhere in his forties, maybe twice Joliffe's age, and beyond doubt a man both certain and comfortable in his power and place. Under his heavy gaze, Joliffe had no trouble bowing his head and saying again, very humbly, "Yes, my lord."

"Good. I will ask no more of you at this time, merely bid you keep from trouble now you are in my household."

"Yes, my lord."

The bishop sketched a cross in the air between them. "Go with God, my son."

Joliffe went. If not with God, at least back to his corner by the railing and to watching the land flow past the widening river.

When night came, they were still in sight of land, but it was altogether gone when Joliffe uncurled from his cloak the next dawn, stiff and unrested from a night of barely sleeping on the hard deck. No one had offered him anywhere else or even a thin straw pallet between him and the plank flooring, but he had joined the line for the supper of stew and bread, and this morning he shuffled to have a share of the bread and cheese being given out. No one objected.

But his stomach did. During the night he had felt the ship change under him, taking on a lift and dip and sway it had not had before then. There had been a busyness among the sailors, an opening of more sails to a stronger wind, and Joliffe had understood they must be leaving the Thames and going out into the Channel. He also gathered from overheard talk and the way all lantern-light was kept low and shielded that there was worry over being seen by enemy ships. French. Breton. Burgundian. Any of those, let alone plain pirates, would have at any English ship they happened on. He also gathered from someone's half-whispered talk—mixed with oaths—to someone else not

far from him that Bishop Louys had been waiting nearly
a month for a chance to return to Normandy and that this
was the first favorable weather. There being no certainty
how long it would hold, the captain was set on making a
straight run for Honfleur.

"Why not Calais?" his fellow had protested. "It's nearer.
Nearer his bishopric, too. We wouldn't have so long to
worry about being seen at sea."

"Because there's a whole swathe of double-damned
Burgundy's territory to ride across between Calais and
Normandy, and wouldn't the cursed, mighty duke love to
get his hands on the bishop, eh?"

"Saint Andrew cramp Burgundy's guts," the other man
had muttered as they moved off, leaving Joliffe to drag
himself down into another shallow doze for a little more
of the night.

He had thought to go on picking up bits of talk like that
today, to understand as much as might be of what he was
going toward, but found all his interest held by his uneasy
stomach. Not until he saw a green-hued man in the bishop's
livery stagger to the railing, lean well over it, and vomit into
the sea did he realize what he was feeling himself was sea-
sickness. Except it was not quite sickness with him yet, he
thought, studying the feeling. It was more as if his stomach
was surprised. And his head. That was gone slightly giddy,
too, as it sometimes had when Rose had tried to teach him
tumbling tricks in his early days in the company, before
everyone decided he was too bad to go on bothering.

So rather than eating, he took his bread and cheese back
to his corner and sat down, still holding his food but settling to loosen his body to the rise and fall and sway of
the ship, to the sway of the masts against the low sky of
gray clouds, to persuading himself to accept it all instead
of resist it.

He was succeeding when a man in the bishop's livery
colors came to stand over him and say, "If you're going

to be sick, want I should take your breakfast off your hands?"

Joliffe looked up and grinned. "No, I think I'll keep it for myself." He stood up. "My thanks for the kind offer, though."

"This is your first time crossing the Channel?" Somewhere in years between Joliffe's and the bishop's, he seemed simply friendly, and glad for the chance to talk, Joliffe said, friendly in return, "First time, yes."

"You are not going to be ill?"

Joliffe leaned back against the railing and tore off a piece of the bread. "I don't think so."

The man nodded as if pleased for him. "That is good." He leaned beside Joliffe but facing outward. "If you are fortunate, this weather and wind will hold. We purposed to be back in Rouen well before Christmas but winds were against us. It has been hard to have news come from France but be unable to send any back, or any of the aid that's needed."

Joliffe paused in his eating to ask, "What *is* the news from France?"

The man gave him a curious look. "What have you heard?"

"Nothing of note. The duke of Burgundy is angry and there is fighting." At the man's surprise-widened eyes, he added, defending his ignorance, "I've been out and away from London for weeks. If there's more to know, it's missed me."

The man's laugh was short and bitter. "There's more to know, but likely it hasn't spread far yet. To begin, the Armagnacs are north of the Seine now and have taken most of Caux. Do you know what that means?" He changed the question. "Do you know *where* that is?"

"No."

"Somewhat roughly, the Caux is the part of Normandy between Rouen and the sea and also a goodly way north toward Burgundy's Flemish lands. It means," he said grimly, "that for now the Armagnacs are on—"

"Armagnacs?" Joliffe asked.

The man paused, then said slowly, "You know there are those who claim the Dauphin is king of France, instead of King Henry, yes? That the war these thirteen years and more has been for that? Those are the Armagnacs."

"Ah!" said Joliffe. "Dauphinists."

"That I have not heard them called, but yes. So now they are swarming where they should not be, because the duke of Burgundy is letting them, and meanwhile that same Philippe, duke of Burgundy is complaining of how the English have wronged him."

Joliffe choked on a last bite of bread, swallowed, and said, somewhere between a cough and a laugh, "How the English have wronged *him*?"

The man shrugged again. "Well, it could not be that his most Christian grace and mighty lord the duke of Burgundy did anything amiss. Nor his shining new friend, the Dauphin Charles against whom he had sworn eternal vengeance."

"Having now chosen," said Joliffe, "to measure eternity in a hands-count of years, rather than as 'forever.'"

The man tched his tongue and said mockingly, "A hands-count of years? But no. It has been at least fifteen years, even sixteen, since the Dauphin saw to the murder of Burgundy's father. Surely that suffices for eternity?"

Matching the man's mockery, Joliffe granted, "It must. At least with Burgundy. I'm John Ripon by the way."

"I am Guillaume Cauvet. "

"You're French, then," Joliffe said as if taken by surprise. He was not, but he supposed it was time "John Ripon" came into being, and he had decided that "John Ripon" was not deep-witted. He did not think he could sustain playing stupid for the weeks—for the months?—this might last. Nor would a stupid man be of sufficient worth that Bishop

Beaufort would have taken this much trouble to give him chance to redeem himself. So John Ripon would be sharp-witted and competent but not deep: one of those men who have not yet learned they are not as forceful of wit as they think they are, and—being John Ripon—Joliffe went on, "Your English is very good. Better than my French, that's certain."

"I am my lord bishop's English secretary," Cauvet said. Meaning that any correspondence or other matters in English that came to or went from the bishop were in his charge.

Now leaning on his elbows beside Cauvet, watching the white-capped waves stretching into the gray distance, Joliffe feigned hesitancy. "Well . . . my French is none so good." Which was true enough. "Could we talk in French, to help mine along? It will help to know French in Rouen?"

"*Oui. Bien sûr,*" Cauvet assured him, and went on, still in French, "You will find there are a great many French in Rouen."

Joliffe pretended not to hear the mockery in that but merely said earnestly, "I suppose there are. Yes." He paused, then tried, slowly, "*Je pense.*"

"*Bon,*" Cauvet said, and went on in French, slowly enough for Joliffe to keep up, "What is taking you to Rouen?"

Joliffe allowed himself to grimace. A John Ripon grimace at the world that was not behaving toward him as it should. "I, um, fell out of favor with the bishop of Winchester. I was a clerk in his household." Trying to say it in French became too much. He went back to English. "Instead of casting me off entirely, he's given me over to your bishop, to be a clerk in his household. I gather that if I can keep from disgracing myself, maybe I'll be moved on to the lord governor's household. If ever a lord governor is decided on."

"Oh!" Cauvet said with surprise and certainty. "It is the duke of York who will be governor."

"York?" Joliffe echoed in plain surprise. Since the duke of Bedford's death almost four months ago, the governing of Normandy and whatever of France the English held had been in the hands of the Normandy council in Rouen while the royal council in England had stayed undecided on his successor among the various possible lords. The last Joliffe had heard—admittedly two months and more ago—the duke of York had been thought too young and too inexperienced to be seriously considered. "When did York get into the running?"

"When no one was willing to anger either my lord bishop of Winchester or my lord the duke of Gloucester by choosing one or the other of the lords they preferred."

"Ah," said Joliffe. In the autumn, when he had last been in London, the open talk had been over who among the lords might be chosen, and why, and which way loyalties most strongly lay in the on-going struggle between Winchester and Gloucester, uncle and nephew, for highest power in England's government. If Cauvet had it right, compromise must have finally twisted around to settle on York as after all the only lord acceptable to both sides. Or should that be "all sides," Joliffe wondered, knowing something of how many sides were rivaling against each other in the matter.

Was the duke of York their final choice *because* he was indeed too young and inexperienced, and everyone had hope of swaying him their particular way?

And how much of all that did York himself understand?

On the raised rear of the ship someone shouted a string of words that seemed to be English but made no sense to Joliffe. They made sense to others, though, because sailors all over the ship burst into movement.

"What is it?" Cauvet shouted in English to no one and anyone. "Have we been seen?"

"No," a sailor shouted back, hurrying to do something with a nearby rope. "Squall coming."

"*Merde*," Cauvet muttered. "I'd better pass word along to my lord to keep below deck and be ready."

Not asking Joliffe to go with him, he disappeared through a doorway the other side of the stairs.

Since Joliffe had not been alone in sleeping on deck last night, he had supposed there was not space inside or below for everyone, and now that looked true enough as the men left on deck crowded out of the hurrying sailors' way and into what shelter they could. Deciding everyone knew more about squalls at sea than he did, Joliffe joined two other men in crowding under the open-stepped stairway near him. He had to crouch down on his heels to fit and doubted the open stairs would give much shelter, but they were better than no shelter at all, and he was glad to be able to brace himself against the ship's heave and tilt as first the wind hit and then the rain pelted down.

From walking England's roads, he was used enough to being wet, and he had been growing used to the ship's lift and dip and sway, but now, suddenly, it was tilting and plunging and heaving, and for the first moments he was starkly afraid. But fear was of no use, would make no difference nor do him any good, and he let it go; instead gave himself up to the ship and the storm and found delight in the wildness of it.

But being only a squall, it soon passed, and a squat, covered brazier was brought out on deck and a coal fire made in it, for passengers and sailors to gather around to warm and dry themselves a little. That gave Joliffe chance to strike up talk with others of the bishop's household beside Cauvet. Some were more ready to talk with him than others but no one was particularly unfriendly, and shortly showed willing not only to laugh at Joliffe's French but help him to better it, not simply then but on through the day.

With the good ear and practiced memory that came

with being a player, and much of the French he had once
known beginning to come back to him, Joliffe was soon
doing better than he let show. As Master Fowler had said,
a seeming of ignorance was good cover for learning things
if men thought he could not understand. Not that he heard
or overheard anything among the bishop's men that was
anyone's secret. Their talk was mostly of being home, but
there was also half-angered wishing the English council
would hurry with naming a governor for Normandy and
get him and a new army to France *immédiatement,* and
that told Joliffe that what Cauvet had said about the duke
of York was not openly known yet.

Then why had Cauvet seen fit to tell *him* about it? It
could be Cauvet simply had a loose tongue—not a desirable thing in a bishop's secretary. Or—had he been test-
ing to see if Joliffe knew more than he might rightly be
expected to know?

If the latter was the way of it, Joliffe trusted his true
ignorance had been convincing, while making note he
should sharpen his skill at seeming ignorant, on the chance
he would have more use for it should he ever, in time to
come, indeed learn things he "should not."

After all, he had to suppose that was why he was being
sent to the late duke of Bedford's spymaster—to learn how
to learn things others meant to keep hidden.

Chapter 4

Besides the bishop's men, Joliffe took what chances came to talk to the sailors, who were mostly English and as willing as most men to talk freely about what they knew best. By late the next day when they came in sight of the walls and harbor of Honfleur, having met neither storm nor enemies along the way, he knew more than he had about ships, including that they did not have front and rear; they had prow and stern, with amidships between. All the ropes—the rigging—had their particular names, too. He had not got so far as learning those or the differences among the guns set along the ship's sides, but he knew starboard from larboard, which some of the sailors seemed to think was a grand accomplishment.

He also knew for a certainty that Bishop Louys was well-thought of by all his people here. Given that they had been in England longer than any of them had wanted to be, that no one thought their purposes there had gone well, and that now they were making a winter crossing of a rough sea, the fact that their displeasure did not spread to include the bishop spoke very well of him, Joliffe thought. There was no one could dislike a man as much as those who lived nearest with him.

On his own part, he had no other encounter with Bishop Louys, and after the household's landing in Honfleur, he was treated as not much more than a piece of baggage, hurried off the ship along with the bishop's traveling chests and loaded with them and most of the household men onto another ship, not so different from their English one but crewed by men familiar with the river they would be following to Rouen, Joliffe gathered.

Then they all waited.

From the talk around him as he sat on one of the traveling chests, Joliffe learned that Bishop Louys was gone to meet briefly with the captain of the Honfleur garrison and certain important citizens, to give them letters and greetings from King Henry and the royal council in England, and that in the usual way of things, the bishop would have celebrated Mass here in Honfleur, in thanksgiving for the safe crossing from England, but the river—the Seine, Joliffe heard it called—was as tidal as the Thames, and if the bishop left now, he would have the tide's advantage to speed the beginning of his upriver journey. So the boatmen were ready, and when someone shouted the bishop was approaching, they began to loose ropes holding the ship to the quay.

Besides his accompanying dozen household men, six men-at-arms and a dozen archers came with the bishop along the quay, and boarded, and while the bishop took a seat on his traveling chair under a tilt amidship, they shifted about to find places out of the way as the last ropes were cast loose, freeing the boat to the current. Not until some sort of cooked cold meat, bread, and cheese were being handed out for supper did Joliffe make chance to say to one of the few Englishmen in the bishop's household, with a twitch of his head toward the soldiers, "What's that about, then?"

The man answered, not totally hiding he thought Joliffe was an idiot not to know it, "They're our guard. These days the French are ramping and trampling in and out of Normandy like someone left a gate wide open. It's why we're going by way of the river instead of straighter across country. Safer."

Just as coming to Honfleur instead of Calais had been thought to be safer, Joliffe thought.

He looked around him at the men-at-arms with swords and long daggers casual on hips, and the archers with their bows and quivers of arrows slung easily over shoulders or at hips. They were variously garbed in padded surcoats and canvas jacks, some with well-linked mail shirts, others with breastplates, all with other armor for arms or legs and a variety of helmets, some simply pot-shaped, others close-fitted, some even visored. What all their clothing had in common was obvious hard wear. What all their weapons shared was how well-kept they were. These were not some men pulled from their plows to serve their handful of duty-days for their lord and intent on going back to their plows at the end of it. These were men hired to the war; men who made war their livelihood and at ease with knowing there would surely come a time when they would have to kill. Or be killed.

Joliffe, watching them, started to find that *knowing* there was war in France was a different thing from being *in* the war in France, and he did not like the difference. Hopefully he was well away from any of the fighting. Even more, he hoped he would be able to stay that way.

Their first night upriver from Honfleur, with the river wide around them and the weather clear, they sailed all night. The next nights, when the river had drawn in between high, steep-sided hills, they spent ashore, behind the walls of fortified towns. Bishop Louys sent a messenger from both places, to let the council in Rouen know he was coming, and Joliffe, still speaking French haltingly but understanding more of what he heard than he let on, gathered that these overnight stops were as much for the bishop to learn what was happening across France and Normandy as for safety's sake. Precisely what he learned, Joliffe did not know, but he saw no joy of homecoming lightening the bishop's face from one day to the next.

The weather remained gray but not so cold as it had been. Warm enough in his cloak, Joliffe kept well-occupied with watching the land and the many other boats on the river slide past. Sometimes Cauvet would join him at the railing and tell him things, such as that most of the barges and lesser boats to be seen were carrying supplies to the garrisons in the towns and castles along the river, and that the English presently held most crossing places along the Seine from Honfleur to somewhat above Paris. "Because we need to control the river, both to move supplies and as a barrier against the Armagnacs. Until lately, fortified bridges at walled towns kept them mostly, much of the time, south of the Seine and from our throats. What my lord of Bedford hoped was to make the Seine serve as the moat of Normandy." Cauvet gave a grim half-laugh. "For a while, a few years ago, the hope was to make the Loire our 'moat.' If that could have been—if we could have shoved the Armagnacs beyond the Loire and kept them there—things would be far different now. But the French witch spoiled that six, almost seven, years ago, and the land south of the Seine, all the way to the Loire, it is desolate from being fought over so many times. They say it made the duke of Bedford weep to see it. Now we look to see the same all over again in Normandy. Thanks to god-cursed Burgundy opening the eastern ways to them, the Armagnacs are north of the Seine again, burning and killing across Normandy as they have not been able to do for years. The duke of Bedford must be writhing in his grave. He gave Normandy peace. The people had begun to have hope. Now Burgundy has ended all that, and if Burgundy ceases to play his waiting game of the past few months and sets his men to join openly with the Armagnacs in the field—" Cauvet shrugged his shoulders high and left the thought for Joliffe to finish, saying instead, "God and Christ and the saints willing, he'll turn all his heed against Calais instead."

He crossed himself. Joliffe copied the gesture, readily willing to invoke any and all help there might be.

The strange thing was how at peace the river seemed to be, whatever was passing in the world beyond its banks. Twice, Joliffe saw black smoke columning into the sky north of the river, telling that somewhere something large was burning. Once one of the men-at-arms barked a warning that brought all his fellows to their feet and the archers into a line along the north side of the boat, their bows at the ready. With everyone else, Joliffe stared where they were staring, up the steep slope of the winter-pale hillside above that stretch of the river to where a line of horsemen were black-shaped against the sky, a double-pointed pennon carried above them.

"Can you see whose they are?" someone of the bishop's household asked.

The soldiers' captain shook his head. "Can't make out the arms. French, though, most likely." He amended that. "Armagnacs. But anyway no trouble at this distance." But neither he nor his men eased their watchfulness until, a while later, the riders swung away from the river and out of sight.

Joliffe carried away two thoughts from that. One was that rushing all your men to face an open foe on one side left your back to anyone waiting to come at you from the other way. The other was that he heartily wished England's King Henry V had not taken up his great-grandfather's claim to the French crown—or else that when France's King Charles VI had been brought to grant the French crown should go not to his son, the Dauphin, but to King Henry as husband of King Charles' daughter, the Dauphin had then died. The intent was to join the two kingdoms under a double crown. What neither king foresaw was that King Henry, still in the full flourish of his manhood, would die of disease something like a month and half before old, mad King Charles, leaving the crowns of France and England to King Henry's infant son, King Charles' grandson.

Only now, fourteen years later, was that child nearing an age to rule in his own right—a right opposed all these years by his disinherited uncle, the Dauphin, so that along with his double crown, young King Henry VI had inherited this war, begun seven years before he was born and showing less sign than ever of coming to an end.

Unless this new alliance between the Dauphin and the duke of Burgundy proved able to defeat and drive the English out. Which it surely would not.

Not while I'm in the middle of it anyway, I hope, Joliffe thought wryly.

But among other things he had learned in his player's life was that the only moment possibly under his control at any time—and even then assuredly not always—was the moment in which he presently was. Plans and hopes could be made and had, but there was no certainty of what would come, not even from one moment to the next; and he stood gazing at the river's swirl and flow, and at the—just now—peaceful-seeming countryside, and knew that he had been set into the swirl and flow of matters he did not much understand, with probably a great many unfamiliar and presently unseen dangers all too near. More all the time, he was wondering into just what Bishop Beaufort had sent him.

A change in the rhythm of men about the ship told him when they were nearing Rouen, even before a yards-long standard streamed out from the mast, bright against the clouded sky, showing a red lion rampant and what Joliffe supposed were the heraldic arms of the bishopric of Therouanne. So near to Rouen, it was safe to let the world know the bishop was here, aboard this very ship, and to give warning ahead to any sharp eyes on watch from one of the towers in the city appearing now below the high-rolling hills that curved to make a wide bay of land along the river's north side. There, behind a stretching town wall fattened here and there by towers, a thick scatter of church towers and spires rose above steep house roofs. From their midst, higher than them all, were the long stone intricacies of two massive churches, while on the city's side toward the hills the higher walls and close-built towers of a castle bulked huge.

Something that promised to be as large was being built this downriver side of the city, and as Cauvet joined him at the railing, Joliffe pointed and asked, "What's that to be?"

"That would have been King Henry's new castle."

Joliffe sorted out the verb's tense and said, "Would have been. It will not be?"

"Work on it has gone on for more than a dozen years. Or it is maybe better to say work has mostly *not* gone on. Building is costly. So is war." Cauvet made a gesture of balancing one hand against the other, then sank the left one lower. "When choice is made where the taxes will go, war wins."

The river here was busy with the coming and going of other ships, with barges and vari-sized boats. The bishop's ship was slowing among them, heeling in a long turn toward the low quay that ran along all of the riverside of the town wall, and Cauvet said, spreading an arm outward, "But there she is. Rouen. The queen of Normandy. In all of France, only Paris can claim to be greater, and that is Paris, and Paris is not in Normandy. Normandy is Normandy. But you are missing one of Rouen's wonders. Look there."

He turned, making another wide gesture, this time

to the ship's other side, upriver, and was probably well-satisfied by Joliffe's sharply in-taken breath. The river here was wider than even the Thames at London and with the same treacherous tidal flow, and yet there was a stone-built bridge of—how many arches? More than London's, anyway. Joliffe tried to count them but settled for "many."

"Five hundred years it has been there," Cauvet said, proud as if he had built it. "Five hundred years. Made by a great queen for her people. It is a marvel, no?"

It was, and Joliffe said so. For him, France had always been a place simply talked of. It had been words in his mind, not sights. Through these past few days his mind had been spreading to take in all the new he was seeing, and here, with more than ever to take in, he stayed at the railing while Cauvet went away to whatever his duties presently were at the end of Bishop Louys' travels.

Others, elsewhere, were busy at their duties, too. By the time the ship had been brought around and to the quay, with ropes thrown and tied and the landing-plank run out, a swarm of liveried servants and several saddled horses and a white mule with purple saddle and trappings were waiting on the quay. Most of the men were in ecclesiastical black with the bishop's badge on their doublets, but there were others in green with a black band of cloth worn over one shoulder and slantwise across their chests, and it was one of the latter who stepped forward to greet the bishop with a deep bow as he descended from the ship. Joliffe was too far away to hear what few things were said between them, but their brief exchange ended with the bishop making a gracious bow of his head, the man bowing deeply in response, and the mule being brought forward for the bishop to mount while the man and several others took the horses and rode away, surrounded by a flow of liveried servants and at least some of the men who had been to England and back.

Left behind with the baggage and those who were to see

to it, Joliffe got himself off the ship and aside from the ordered hurry of unloading the many boxes, bags, and chests,
unsure what he should be doing with himself. Should he
have gone when the bishop did? Or . . .

Cauvet paused in passing with a small, locked chest
that must contain something of particular worth, and said,
"You look lost."

"I don't know what I'm supposed to do."

"Come with us. We're away to Joyeux Repos."

Joliffe picked up the sack he had set at his feet, slung
it over his shoulder, and asked as he joined Cauvet in the
flow of laden men toward the nearest gateway through the
town wall along the quay, "That's the bishop's place here
in Rouen?"

In England at least it was common for bishops to have
not only their episcopal palace in their dioceses, but a
house in London where the government was centered. Here
in Normandy, Rouen was the government's center, and
Bishop Louys was the duchy's chancellor; so never minding where his bishopric was, he had more reason than most
to have a place here.

But Cauvet said, "Joyeux Repos? No, it was the duke of
Bedford's hotel. Though little joy or repose he had there at
the end, God keep his soul. After his wife, the Lady Anne,
died—Blessed Mary have her in keeping—he hardly could
bear to be there. Now it is his widow's place, and she is
my lord bishop's niece and very young. It was understood
before we went to England that my lord would move in
there, both for her good and as the duke himself wished as
he was dying."

"Wait. Wait." In his confusion, Joliffe forgot to keep to
his attempt to speak in French. "The duke's wife died, but
his widow . . ."

Cauvet threw him the pitying look of a man hardly able
to believe another man's ignorance. "He married again,
yes? The Lady Jacquetta. My lord bishop's niece. It was

not a marriage that pleased the duke of Burgundy, but I
think that by then my lord of Bedford was past thinking
there was any pleasing the duke of Burgundy."

Joliffe had lately written plays making sport of the
treacherous duke of Burgundy, and Basset's company had
acted them everywhere, from village greens and gentry
houses to the great halls of high lords, always to much
laughter. But that had been there and this was here, and Joliffe was rapidly finding how very differently things looked
to him now he was on this side of the Channel instead of
the other. Until now, everything here had been happening
somewhere else for him. He had felt no great need to think
over much about whatever he happened to hear about it. But
now that he was here, not comfortably somewhere else, he
did not like he knew so little. He had vague remembrance
of knowing that the duke of Bedford's first wife had been
the duke of Burgundy's sister. If his widow was Bishop
Louys' niece, that meant . . .

He found he did not know what that meant. But great
lords and ladies did not marry for simple reasons, nor was
the duke of Burgundy likely to have been displeased about
this marriage for any simple reason.

There was no time now, though, to think about it or
to ask Cauvet. They were to the gateway, and the guards,
accepting they were among the bishop's men leaving the
quay, let them pass without question into the wide, stone-
arched passageway between the gateway's towers, to come
out the other end into daylight again. If Joliffe had been
alone, he would probably have paused then, to give himself
chance to take in that for the first time in his life he was
somewhere that was not England; but Cauvet kept onward
and Joliffe did, too, assuredly not wanting to be left behind. Basset had taught him early on to take in quickly as
much as he could about any place the players came to, to
judge what the welcome there was likely to be and whether
they should ply their trade or simply keep on their way to

somewhere else. As a traveling player, he was use to being in "foreign" places, because in England, folk used "foreign" as readily for a neighboring village as for Constantinople, but as he kept among the bishop's men along a street running with surprising straightness between tall, narrow houses, the feeling grew in him that he was come to somewhere foreign in a wholly new way. He had known Rouen would be foreign in a way different from foreign among English villages, but somehow he had not expected Rouen to be *this* foreign. It was more than that he was not hearing English words anywhere around him. The townspeople moving out of the way of the bishop's men had somehow a *look* to them that was not English. Was it a subtly different cut to clothing? Something in the way they moved? Those were things that, as a player, he was trained to note, knowing the difference they made, but just now he lacked chance to look long enough at anything or anyone to tell for certain. By the time the street opened into a wide marketplace in front of what had to be Rouen's cathedral, all he had managed to acquire was the queasy, growing certainty that he was somewhere more foreign than anywhere he had ever been.

Uncertainty at all the strangeness began to twist toward fear in him, only to be suddenly overtaken by silent, saving laughter. The uncertainty was much the same feeling that came when he was about to stride out into some barely known place to make a play for some great gathering of unknown onlookers and that familiarity steadied him. At such a time there was nowhere to go but onward. However far larger beyond usual this present playing-place was, he was after all here to play a part. He was to be—already was—"John Ripon," and he had long since decided that John Ripon was a man full of self-consideration and no deep awareness. So for John Ripon, it was Rouen's problem that it was foreign, not his.

"Eh," Cauvet said as somewhere ahead the straggling

line of the bishop's men began to come to a halt that spread unevenly backward until they were all standing still, while at the forward several men argued about something.

"What is it?" Joliffe asked.

"Robert is arguing we are to go where the bishop lived before. Jehan is insisting we are to go to Joyeux Repos. Robert, he never listens and always thinks he knows better. Here." Cauvet shifted the box into Joliffe's hands, then went to join the other men now joining in the arguing.

Joliffe, having made certain he had good hold on both the box and his sack, used the pause for the chance to look at the cathedral huge in front of him across the market-place, its front of fretted stone flanked by towers, one of them stunted as if unfinished, but also looking as if it had not been worked on for some time, being bare of scaffolding or anything else that showed it was on its way to going higher. While he considered what that neglect meant, one of a pair of men passing by burst into laughter and said in English to his fellow, "You never!"

"Sure as sinning, I did," the other returned.

Joliffe gave them a swift look. By their padded jerkins, and the helmets slung by straps over their shoulder, and the sword as well as the usual dagger each wore at his waist, he judged they were men-at-arms, probably of the English garrison here. Not on duty, though. That was plain. But wearing their swords nonetheless, and with their helmets ready. Joliffe was not used to men going that heavily armed in the ordinary way of things. Was there such constant likelihood of trouble here the men felt obliged to be so ready for it? As the bishop's men started moving again, he added that unsettling thought to the others he was gathering.

Cauvet stayed ahead, not returning to reclaim the box, so Joliffe made sure to keep well up among the others, not wanting to lose them by any chance. The line of men swung rightward, skirting and circling the cathedral's yard and finally turning into another straight-running street, this one angled eastward. Joliffe guessed that, just as the other straight street had led inward from a gateway, this street ran outward toward another gateway, and he had a spasm of worry that—unlikely though it seemed—this Joyeux Repos was outside the city's walls. From what he had seen so far of France and by all he had heard, Joliffe knew he would much prefer to have city walls around him, not open countryside.

It was a fine street, though—wide and stone-paved like the other, flanked by houses mostly stone-built, rather than of timber-and-plaster. At one point, the bishop's men were passing what Joliffe took for a long, stone, two-storied housefront standing flat and blank to the street, until ahead of him, the other men were turning through what proved, when Joliffe reached it, to be a gateway high enough for a horseman to ride through without bending, wide enough for a large cart to pass through easily, but its pair of metal-banded gates showing it could equally be closed against the world.

Beyond those gates, Joliffe found himself in a court-yard of irregular shape, four-sided, and larger than he had thought it would be, with buildings on all sides, but the one directly ahead of him across the yard catching and holding his startled gaze. The blank wall along the street had not readied him for—the *hôtel*, Cauvet had called it. Certainly it was more than only a house and other than a castle. Long and of three tall storeys, its pale-stone front was fretted with elaborately carved stonework and surprisingly many windows. A steep roof of blue slates with sharp-pointed windows gabled out from it made it all the taller, while at one end a wide round turret reached even above roof-height and there were lesser turrets elsewhere along its front. For richness of detail and grace Joliffe had never seen a building more lovely.

Cauvet, rejoining him, said unnecessarily, "Joyeux Repos."

Chapter 5

Bishop Louys and the others must have arrived well ahead of them; there was no sign of him or them or mule or horses in the yard. In truth, just then there was no one in the yard but Joliffe and the men around him, all come to a stop just inside the gateway, and he asked of Cauvet, "What now?"

Cauvet shrugged. "Now we wait to see how we're to be fitted into here. Joining my lord's household with that of her grace the duchess will be none so simple, no matter there's been time to consider it."

His tone implied he doubted anyone *had* troubled to consider it, but he was proved wrong when a pair of servants with the bishop's badge on their doublets came out a lesser door toward one end of the long *hôtel*-front and to them. One gave orders in rapid French while the other shepherded them toward the door like an over-eager dog among a flock of sheep. Not understanding anything that was being said, Joliffe kept close behind Cauvet through the doorway, into a stone-floored passage leading to somewhere in the house. But the servant was shooing the men to the left, up a narrow, twisting stairway. Cauvet paused to protest, making a gesture with the chest, "This is for my lord's chamber."

"Your chamber first," the servant said. He added something else too quickly for Joliffe to catch and then, "Go. Go."

Cauvet went, and Joliffe followed him, asking, "What did he say?"

"We go to our chamber first. After that, we will see."

The stairway curved upward, first past a closed door and then, higher, past an open doorway through which Joliffe glimpsed a high-ceilinged room and a tapestried wall. Cauvet, probably recognizing the tapestry, said with satisfaction, "Ah. My lord's bedchamber. Good."

Their climb brought them finally to another open doorway, the men passing through this one into a long space of bare floorboards and slanting rafters that told it was directly under the roof. Wooden bedsteads with thin mattresses were lined along one side, a heap of bedding on the foot of each. Except for an unlighted candle on a wall pricket beside the doorway, that was all. Without being able to make out exactly what was being said among the men, Joliffe guessed from their voices there was some grumbling as they spread along the dormer to the various beds. Perhaps they had had it better at the bishop's palace? Or was that properly also called a *hôtel* here?

What he did not catch quickly enough was how the men were choosing their beds. Cauvet, abandoning him, joined another man in claiming the two beds at the far end, near the brick wall of a chimney that would give out warmth rising from the fires in rooms below. Joliffe belatedly guessed the other men were sorting themselves according to their greater or lesser place in the household, and he found himself left to the bed nearest the door—and also nearest a screen in the corner there, behind which were the pottery pots of the dormer's necessarium, to give the polite name.

Resigned, and ignoring the sniggering glances of the nearer men, Joliffe set his sack on the floor and shoved it under the bed. Just so he was not the one who was supposed to empty those pots, too, he thought, and copied the other men in spreading a coarse linen sheet and then a thick woolen blanket of undyed wool over the straw-filled mattress. If he laid his cloak over the top of that, he thought he might sleep warm enough. If the weather got no colder, he silently added, looking up at the laths between the rafters and the roof slates held to them by wooden pegs, all there was between the attic chamber and the wind. He had slept with less between him and the weather often enough, and he silently laughed at himself because he had hoped for better while in a bishop's household.

With nothing else to do and unable to join in the general talk around him, he sat down on the bed to wait for whatever came next. Used as he was to doing almost all the time—even if the "doing" was simply walking along the road toward wherever the players were next going or, on board the ships coming here, taking in all there was to see and learning what he could—idleness felt strange, the more so because everyone else seemed to have some thought of what they should be doing next. Cauvet, for one, had already disappeared down the stairs, taking the chest he had brought from the ship. After him, the other men went, too, one by one or several together, none giving Joliffe heed, until as the last several of them went past him, he decided it was pointless to stay here alone and stood up and followed them. Master Fowler had said he was to make himself known to Master Wydeville and he would never do it by staying here among the rafters.

The men he followed descended first to what Cauvet had said was the bishop's bedchamber. Wide and long, it had windows at one end that must overlook the courtyard, and at the other end the bishop's bed, raised above the floor on a low dais and enclosed by tall carved posts holding up a canopy of white and red striped cloth that matched the bed's coverlet and the curtains drawn back to the bed's four corners. The wall-hung tapestries around the room were woven with tall, vividly colored figures of undoubtedly allegorical men and women that Joliffe supposed he would have chance enough to look at, because besides bedchamber, the room was furnished—as was common—at the end opposite the bed for the gathering of men to attend on the bishop and, guessing from the low desk in one corner, for some secretary's work.

Joliffe could guess that because Bishop Louys' journey to England had been half-secret—in other words, no secret at all but kept as low-viewed and little flaunted as possible—the bishop had traveled with very little of his household and none of the rich flourish a bishop's travel usually entailed. Because so little of the bishop's goods had been with him, there was not the fuss and flurry of much unpacking and readying the chamber there might have been. The shift of his goods from his *hôtel* to here having been already done, the chamber was complete, simply waiting for his presence. Only the tall-mantled fireplace on the chamber's far side told this had been someone else's place: across the pale-stone surround were carved, over and over again, the image of a long-rooted tree-stump. A woodstock—a badge of John, duke of Bedford. So this had, in all likelihood, been the duke's great bedchamber and, presumably, his duchess'. She must have moved—or been moved—to make way for her uncle. Joliffe wondered to where.

And what she thought of being so displaced.

At any rate, Cauvet was not there, and when the bishop's men, having milled about purposelessly, admiring the chamber but lacking reason to be there without the bishop, began to leave through one of the room's several other doors, Joliffe went with them, wanting to see more of the place and hoping to find Cauvet along the way. At least one of the men was clearly acquainted with the *hôtel*, leading them through a series of lesser rooms and down a stairway to another large chamber as if he knew where he was going and from there into the great hall, coming out just below the dais where a brace of servants were spreading white cloths over the high table there in preparation for whatever welcoming feast was to come. Behind the table, several men on ladders leaned against the wall were putting up a long-hanging tapestry beside another already there, with a canopy extended forward from it over one of the two tall-backed chairs set there at the table, turning it into a chair of estate—the duchess', presumably, with the other likely to be Bishop Louys'.

Below the dais a scattering of men stood about in talk with one another while an intensity of more servants thumped through the business of setting up the trestle tables lined down either side of the hall's length where lesser members of the household would sit to eat. The hall was not as large as some Joliffe had lately been in. Not so great-sized, surely, as the one lately built in London by Bedford's brother, the duke of Gloucester. Rather than somewhere newly-made, here looked more as if it were an older place that had been changed and added to, but what had been added was splendid, with at the dais' far end a stone-traceried window from floor to rafter-height curving boldly outward, paned below in clear glass but resplendent above with bright-hued heraldic shields and beasts. Further down the hall, one long wall was emboldened by a wide fireplace with a surround even more richly carved than that in the ducal bedroom, while facing it across the hall was a long sideboard whose four stepped shelves rising up the wall were draped in black cloth, probably in sign of the household's year of mourning for Bedford's death but surely showing to perfection the display of gold and silver

dishes, goblets, basins, and ewers set out there. Joliffe had
never seen such an array even in London, either at the gold-
smiths' shops in Cheapside or any lordly household where
he had played.

All too often, the world judged a man's worth by the
wealth he showed to his fellows' eyes. The display there
on the sideboard served to assert the duke of Bedford had
been a very worthy man indeed. From what little Joliffe
knew about the late duke, though, that was an assertion
that might well have been made less from Bedford's pride
than out of plain necessity. Placed as he had been in the
world—regent of France and Normandy for his young
nephew in England and therefore perilously balanced between a war that would not end and the governments and
politics of two kingdoms—Bedford had had every need to
display his wealth, and thereby his power, as one more way
to constantly impress on powerful men that he was an even
more powerful man, with both right and might to rule here
in his nephew's name.

Or, if it had come to it, to rule here in his own right, because Bedford had been his as-yet childless nephew's heir.
If it had been young King Henry who had died last year
instead of the duke, Bedford would now be king of both
realms, and his duchess a queen.

But it was Bedford who had died, and all that right and
might must of necessity fall to someone else, while his
wealth would presumably go to his widow.

Joliffe looked forward to seeing this wealthy, widowed
duchess.

He had slowed while taking in all there was to see there
in the hall and fallen behind the men he had been following; was starting after them again when he saw a man, just
come from the hall's other end, pause one of them and, by
the look of it, ask a question, because the man he asked, and
several others who had heard, searched around, found, and
pointed toward Joliffe. The man gave a quick bow of his

head in thanks and came onward. Joliffe stayed where he was, letting the man come to him, and was not altogether surprised when the man asked him in French-touched English, "You are John Ripon?"

Joliffe, trying to judge the man's place in the household—his black clerk's gown was without a badge but of good cut and cloth; the question was abruptly but not rudely asked; the man had made no bow; did he expect one to be given?—chose to follow Basset's advice that you could not go wrong giving a man more respect than might be due him; and knowing that "John Ripon" was no one in the household yet and this man surely some manner of superior servant or clerk here, he gave a respectful bow, said, "I am, sir."

"The chamberlain of the household, Master Wydeville, has asked you be brought to him. Pray, come with me, Master Ripon," the man said and started away, not rude, merely a man very busy.

Suddenly sharply aware of the sealed packet tucked between his doublet and his shirt all these days from London, Joliffe went with him down the hall toward its further end. Halfway along it, though, the man paused and turned to look back toward the dais, and Joliffe copied him. The servants there had the second tapestry up now, were rigging its canopy to thrust out beside the other one already hung there, making both the tall-backed chairs into chairs of estate, as Joliffe had thought; and from here he could see that the newly-hung tapestry showed Bishop Louys de Luxembourg's heraldic arms—those of his bishopric impaled with that of his family—while the other hanging showed the Luxembourg arms again but here impaled with those of England—the royal gold lions on scarlet and gold lilies on blue, differenced by a five-pointed label of ermine and fleur-de-lis to show they were not the king's but the duke of Bedford's. That would be the duchess' arms, then, showing both her family and her marriage, Joliffe supposed.

This was going to be a complicated household if, as it seemed, she and her uncle the bishop were going to share equal honors here.

The man beside him gave a sharp nod, as if satisfied at what he saw, and moved on. Joliffe perforce went with him, leaving the great hall through one of three broad doorways at its far end, all three leading into a wide passageway floored with squares of green and white tiles that at one end opened to the courtyard through a broad, stone-framed doorway—the way into Joyeux Repos for its lord and lady and other great folk, Joliffe did not doubt—while a scuttling of servants through doorways at the passage's other end made him guess the more serviceable parts of the place—kitchen, pantry, butlery, and all—lay that way. His own way, in the man's wake, was partly along the passage toward the outer door, then up a wide stairway well-lighted by windows as it curved upward through a turret to come out one floor up into a gallery that looked to run the length of the building here.

Along one side, several windows with cushioned benches below them overlooked the courtyard. Joliffe could only guess to where the several shut doors along its other side led. Not to anywhere he was presently going, it seemed. His guide continued his brisk way to the gallery's far end and through a doorway there to another stairway. Far narrower and darker than the other, it twisted tightly both downward and up, but Joliffe followed the man upward and then aside through yet another doorway into yet another room.

Given where it was in the house, so high and aside from the great hall and lordly chambers, the room was well-sized—space to swing a cat around, as Ellis would likely have said—but with bare floor-boards and plain-plastered walls. A place meant for work, not ease, with several closed chests and an ambry with shut doors standing against one wall, a single window in the wall facing those, and where the light would be best, a slant-topped desk beside a shelf fixed to the wall holding various small boxes and some books. Joliffe's guide bowed to a man standing there and said, "John Ripon, sir."

As the man laid the book he had been holding back on the shelf, Joliffe bowed, too. He had worried how he was to come to Master Wydeville quietly, supposing it would be best to make no particular show of it. He had not been ready for it to happen this soon, this openly, and by no effort of his own; nor had he given much thought to what a duke's spymaster would look like. Not "ordinary," at any rate, but the man in front of him looked only that. Somewhat past his middle years, with his quietly furrowed face beginning to be dragged down by time and his remaining rim of fair hair gone mostly white, he was dressed in an ordinary three-quarter-long, high-collared black robe in keeping with the household's mourning, with black hosen and low-cuffed leather shoes and no ornaments except a ring on either hand. He could have been a modestly prosperous merchant or landed gentleman rather than what he was—a well-placed officer of a noble household.

"Master Ripon," he said in the ordinary voice of a man from the southeast of England, something welcomingly familiar after all of the unfamiliar foreign talk around Joliffe these past days.

"Sir," Joliffe responded, slightly bowing again, remembering to keep the rounded shoulders and uncertain, cowed-dog look he thought John Ripon might well have in front of anyone so much his better.

Master Wydeville raised a hand, dismissing the man who had brought Joliffe.

"Sir," the man said and went onward, into the next room, closing the door behind him while Master Wydeville said at Joliffe, "I'm told you are sent by the bishop of Winchester to serve in my lord the bishop of Therouanne's household. That you are leaving some disgrace behind you."

"I fear so, but hoping to redeem myself and regain my lord of Winchester's good opinion," Joliffe answered while shifting quickly through surprise that Bishop Louys in the short while since coming here should have already spoken with—or else had troubled to send a message to—Master Wydeville about him. From there he passed to a wary wondering why the spymaster, knowing nothing of the packet Joliffe carried, had wanted to see him so immediately. That mix of wariness and uncertainty held him from slipping the letter from his doublet and presenting it, while Master Wydeville went on, "What was the nature of your disgrace?"

Joliffe bent his head with Ripon's shame and muttered toward the floor, "Drunkenness, sir."

"Just drunkenness? Or gambling and women, too?"

Joliffe lifted his head as if stung and said with the earnestness of a man who feels himself wronged, "No. Never either of those! Just . . ." He looked down at his toes again and muttered as if in shame, ". . . drinking too much. Too much and too often."

"How is your French?"

Joliffe raised his head again, blinking at Master Wydeville with a simple man's surprise at the change of questioning. "Poor, sir, I'm afraid."

"Do you write a fair hand in English?"

Judging it was time for what little pride John Ripon might have, Joliffe said sturdily, "I do."

"And your Latin is satisfactory."

That was statement rather than question, but it gave Joliffe pause. He had let Bishop Beaufort believe he knew no Latin, but a clerk in a bishop's household would surely have it, and he admitted unwillingly—but truthfully—"I can do plain Latin. No one would want me to translate Virgil, though."

"I will not," said Master Wydeville. "Nor I doubt will anyone else. My lady of Bedford is in need of an English

secretary. I have leave to offer the place to you. I advise
you to take it."

Master Wydeville seemed not a man who trifled over
things. Neither would he be a man who appreciated trifling
in return, and Joliffe grabbed hold on his surprise, mixed
as it was with dismay at the suddenness of all this, and
stuttered out with what he thought would be John Ripon's
blinking uncertainty, "You do? Uh, yes. I do. Yes. Thank
you. I will. Gladly. Thank you." He added a half-bow for
good measure.

Straightening from it, he found Master Wydeville regarding him with a shuttered, unreadable look. A silent
pause drew out between them, with Joliffe waiting for his
next cue to what he should say or do, but Master Wydeville
not giving him any, until with sudden wild surmise, Joliffe straightened his shoulders and said in more of his own
voice, putting a hand to the front of his doublet, "By your
leave, I've something here I was told to give you."

Giving not even a flicker of surprise, Master Wydeville slightly bowed his head, giving leave to give it. Joliffe, deliberately not hurrying lest he betray how much
the man's silence unnerved him, undid his doublet at the
waist enough that he could slide in a hand and bring out
the packet. It was crumpled and creased from its hard
passage, the wax seal cracked but still mostly there. He
held it out to Master Wydeville who took it, broke the last
of the seal away, unwrapped the cord it had held around
the packet, then unwrapped the oiled cloth from around a
folded parchment likewise held closed by a wax seal. This
one was intact, and Master Wydeville gave it a close look,
holding it to the window's light to see it the better—not for
sake of whatever the image on it was, Joliffe guessed, but
trying to tell if it had been meddled with—before he broke
it, unfolded the parchment, and read whatever was there
with what seemed to Joliffe painful slowness. Only when
Master Wydeville set the parchment aside on the desk did

Joliffe glimpse there were no words on it, only a jumble of letters.

Cipher, he thought.

Master Wydeville, his hands now folded together in front of him, regarded Joliffe with narrow-eyed assessment through another long moment of silence, then asked, "What were you told about me?"

Guessing he was not asking that of John Ripon, Joliffe answered not as Ripon but as himself, "That you were the duke of Bedford's spymaster. That you are to have the training and directing of me." He paused, then went on, "Which says that you are still someone's spymaster. I would guess Cardinal Beaufort's. Or the bishop of Therouanne's. Or more likely the both of them, since they share interests, Cardinal Beaufort being high in England's government and Bishop Louys head of the Council here until the duke of York comes as governor."

He added that last very deliberately, to see how his knowing that would count with the spymaster.

Master Wydeville's eyes slightly widened, not with surprise, Joliffe judged, but approval before he asked, his voice nonetheless level, "You know that by what means?"

With matching level voice, Joliffe said back, "Men talked on the journey here. I listened."

"Then you have one of your first lessons well begun. Pierres."

Master Wydeville had barely raised his voice on the name, but Joliffe's guide came immediately back into the room. His look still on Joliffe, Master Wydeville went on, "Pierres, Master Ripon has accepted a place as my lady's secretary. It will be several days before Master Strugge will leave us. Give Master Ripon over to him, to be shown where he will sleep and to learn such of his duties as he may in the while before Master Strugge takes ship." Then, to Joliffe, "Let me see 'John Ripon' again."

That was so near to something that Basset might say—

"I'm not seeing the comic baker. I'm seeing Joliffe *pretending* to be a comic baker."—that Joliffe with all of Basset's training behind him immediately shifted, rounded his shoulders forward again and sank his head a little, his eyes going all uncertain and shying aside as John Ripon might well do in front of someone who knew his shame. He held the look under Master Wydeville's assessing gaze, until Master Wydeville said, "Good. You look like someone I can only barely approve of for service to my lady. We'll suppose your confidence will grow as you settle into the household, but for now craven uncertainty is good."

On the advantage of that approval, Joliffe dared ask, in Ripon's slightly whining voice, "Won't it be thought odd you've taken such interest in getting Lady Jacquetta a secretary? And so promptly after my coming here?"

Without pause, as if granting Joliffe had a right both to question him and to have an answer, Master Wydeville said, "I was chamberlain of the duke of Bedford's household. Mostly I gave these duties over to a deputy, but since my lord's death, I have taken more on myself, claiming age as reason to stay here in the household, continuing as chamberlain for her grace Duchess Jacquetta. It's only reasonable that her uncle the bishop is concerned how his niece has faired in these first months of her widowhood and that he should wish to hear from me immediately how she has been during his absence and how her household fares. It's also reasonable I would speak of my lady's need of a new English secretary and that you, having been added willwo nill we to the household and something having to be done with you, should be named as sufficing for the place and be immediately provided to it. All that should settle any question of 'oddness' in the matter. Pierres."

Pierres bowed to Master Wydeville and held out a hand to show Joliffe should follow him. Joliffe made his own bow to Master Wydeville and did.

Chapter 6

For Joliffe the next two days were a stern jumble of learning his way about the *hôtel*, the household, and his duties. Or rather the house*holds*, since it seemed Bishop Louys' and Lady Jacquetta's were to be kept separate from one another. Uncle and niece did indeed dine together in formal estate and apparent amiability at the high table on the day of the bishop's return, and certainly members of the two households met and mingled easily in the great hall, both at mealtimes and when they were not needed to attend in chamber or elsewhere on their respective lord or lady, but however it had been before the duke of Bedford's death, Lady Jacquetta and her people now kept to the side of the *hôtel* where Joliffe had met Master Wydeville, while all the *hôtel* beyond the great hall was become the bishop's.

Joliffe's own shift from one household to the other was as simple as collecting his sack from the chamber he would after all not be sharing with the bishop's men and being led by Pierres back to Lady Jacquetta's part of the house and up to the slot of a room, under the rafters there, that he would have to himself once William Strugge, the present English secretary, was gone. After that, the most he knew of Bishop Louys was that there was much coming and going of various men on business to him and that he sometimes rode out among a clutter of attendants to other places in Rouen. Joliffe meant to have talk with Cauvet when there was chance, but for the while he had more than enough else to take in, with William Strugge so eager to be away that he gabbled hour by hour, pouring into Joliffe's ears a mix of what his duties would be, household gossip, and his own readiness to be safe back in England, as he kept saying.

He was saying it yet again as he wrapped one of his three books in a clean shirt and thrust it down into the bag he was packing early in this afternoon, readying to go on board a ship that would sail on the evening tide.

"Safe back in England. In Gloucestershire. That's from where I come. That's to where I'm going back. The other side of England from Normandy and all of France, and not far enough at that."

Joliffe was sitting high-kneed on the low three-legged stool in the corner, as out of the way as he could be in the short, narrow room. By now familiar with Strugge's theme, he suggested with deliberate ignorance, "I'd think you'd feel safe enough here in Rouen, what with the walls, the Seine, and the whole of England's army to hand."

"What have I told you?" Strugge snapped impatiently. "These past two months the Armagnacs have been swarming everywhere the length and breadth of Normandy. Yes, Lord Talbot and Lord Scales have been scouring them out of the Caux since Christmas, but that will go for nothing when the duke of Burgundy finally comes down on us with all his force. He's going to. It's only a matter of time. I am beyond glad I won't be here when it happens. That's what I keep telling you. Don't you listen?"

Joliffe had been listening, but had long since learned that the different ways someone told the same thing several times over could add much that had not been there in the first or even the second telling. Not in Strugge's case, however, and the tedium of listening to him was become painful. But since John Ripon had not shown himself over-clever to Strugge, Joliffe whined, "I know. You keep saying. But with the river and walls and army and all, Rouen has to be safe if anywhere is."

"Just so!" Strugge turned from his packing, a fist set impatiently on one hip and aggravation in his voice. "There's not likely anywhere safer in Normandy, and I've told you what happened four years ago. The French broke into the castle itself! Took it by surprise in the night, let in by a traitor. Lord Maltravers and a handful of his men skinned out just before too late. We had to turn the city's guns on our own castle. If the French hadn't surrendered then, we would have had to batter down our own castle walls. You call that safe?" He turned back to his packing. "Huh."

"It was four years ago," Joliffe protested. "It's not something that will happen again."

"Until it did, I would have said surely it would never happen at all. What I'm saying now is that I'm glad not to be staying around to see what the French do next. Or the god-cursed duke of Burgundy." Strugge swung around again, pointing at Joliffe in accusation. "There's where your Seine won't do you any good. It's to the south. It was Burgundy who kept the Armagnacs from coming at us from the east and north. Now Burgundy is welcoming them through, God damn him." Strugge grabbed up his cloak, started to fold it fiercely, probably realized he would need it soon, threw it aside, and took up something else to stuff into his bag, muttering, "Not that the Burgundians have been that much use to us of late anyway. May they and their duke all rot together."

Joliffe murmured protest, "But Lady Jacquetta is Burgundian."

"The Lady Jacquetta is *not* Burgundian. Nor is her uncle this bishop of Therouanne or her brother the count de Saint-Pol. How often must I needs say that to you? They—are—not—*Burgundian*."

"But . . ."

"They're of Luxembourg. Which is one of the very many counties, duchies, lordships, and territories the duke of Burgundy has gobbled up, taken over, claimed lordship of—however you wish to say it—one way and another over these past years. Just because the duke has a grip on a place doesn't mean it's Burgundian. That's why Bishop Louys was in England. Because his brother and his nephew don't want to give up their oaths to us. So they were hoping some manner of peace could be patched up between god-damned Burgundy and King Henry."

"It's tangled," Joliffe-as-John-Ripon whined.

Strugge gave a heavy sigh. "Yes. It's tangled, and I can't tell you how glad I am to be getting out of it."

On the contrary, he had told Joliffe often and in detail how glad he was to be getting out of it, and now he began on another of his favorite themes. "It was different when my lord of Bedford was here. *There* was a prince worth the name. Not the best-looking of men. And devil-awful tall. Seeing him together with my Lady Jacquetta, you had to wonder. Beast and beauty. It was his first wife matched him best in years and all. God keep her beautiful soul." Strugge crossed himself and shook his head. "My lord was never the same after she died. Then he married into the Luxembourg alliance. There was no one who doubted that would set Burgundy against him. Not but what everyone was all sure-to-a-safe-bet by then that Burgundy was set on foreswearing all his oaths anyway and going over to the Armagnacs. Though the bastard could have waited until Bedford was dead before he did it. I wish you joy of the duke of Burgundy and all his treacheries, that I do. It's Gloucestershire for me."

Just for mischief, Joliffe asked in seeming-innocence, "But that's close to Wales, isn't it? Trouble can come out of Wales, too, you know."

"Huh. Where I mean to be, there's the wide Severn to keep the Welsh away. Nor will I be near the coast either. The French have come a-raiding along there before now, and the way things are going, they will again, and I mean never even to see another Frenchman if I can help it."

Joliffe suspected that any French who knew Strugge probably felt the same about him.

What Joliffe would have liked to hear more about was Lady Jacquetta herself. So far, he had been no more than presented to her by Strugge, had bowed low to her, and had her say to him in careful English as he straightened, "I am pleased you are come to join my household, Master Ripon."

"As am I pleased to be here, my lady," he had answered.

She had smiled, given a small nod that was agreement and dismissal together, and that had been that.

Beyond it, he had only been able to draw out of Strugge that she was "not a difficult lady." Whatever that might mean. Certainly, Joliffe had been surprised at how young she was. Could she be even twenty years old? If so, how young had she been when Bedford married her? She did have the fair-haired, fair-skinned, fine-boned loveliness that looks young "for an unfair number of years," as he had once heard an envious woman say, so he was maybe ill-guessing her age, and he could not bring himself to ask Strugge outright.

"Mind you keep a wary eye for old Wydeville," Strugge was reminding him again. "I've shown you there's not so much work that you'll be sent cross-eyed by it. But you have to look busy enough you don't get saddled with other work. Wydeville doesn't think a man's time should be his own."

Joliffe suspected his time would indeed not be his own once Master Wydeville took him in hand, but meanwhile he did indeed wonder how there was enough work as secretary to spin into even the appearance of being fully busy. His main dealing would be with the letters and account rolls from the English properties that had come to Lady Jacquetta as her dowry at her marriage and her dower at Bedford's death. Income and properties had been settled on her as part of the actual marriage agreement, but by law, at Bedford's death, one-third of his other properties became hers for life as his widow. In the case of a royal duke, that one-third was considerable, but with the duke hardly four months' dead, and the winter's bad weather making cross-Channel travel uncertain, the details of precisely what was now Lady Jacquetta's were still being worked out among the late duke's executors and officers in England and in Normandy, Lady Jacquetta's own household officers here, and several of Bishop Louys' officers, the bishop rightly taking an interest in his niece's welfare since no other of her near-kin were to hand. "Except a cousin," Strugge had warned. "M'dame. Old enough to be my lady's mother and acts like an old hen with one chick. If it has to do with the household or my lady's person, M'dame has the say, even over old Wydeville. Nor don't go giving love-eyed looks Lady Jacquetta's way. M'dame will rap more than your knuckles if she sees you at it." Strugge had paused as if hearing what he had said, then added, "I've seen her do it," to show, unconvincingly, that it had not happened to him.

For his own part, Joliffe rather thought he could avoid being foolish over a duke's widow. His years as a player had given him a very firm understanding of the perils of pushing beyond his low place in the world's way of things. The understanding had not always kept him where he ought to be, but it had made him wary of being more of a fool than need be, and he did not think he was fool enough to fall into any pointless longing after a duchess, no matter how young and lovely and gracious she might be. If nothing else, dust-dry account rolls, stiff letters of business, and whatever Master Wydeville was going to require of him should be sufficient safe-guard against time for idle indulgence in pointless languishing over the fair and unobtainable.

"Oh," said Strugge now as he strapped shut his bag. "Sometimes her grace will want you to read to her in English and talk English with her. My lord of Bedford spoke French like a Frenchman, but he wanted her to know English, too. Seems a waste of time now. It's not likely she'll go to England anymore. But she sometimes keeps it up. Just so you're warned."

Joliffe thanked him.

Strugge hefted his bag off the bed, looked around the small room, said, "That's it, then. I wish you good luck with it all."

"And to you good luck with your travel and homecoming," Joliffe answered.

"I get seasick," Strugge said glumly and left.

Feeling no need to see him through whatever other good-byes he might want to make, Joliffe stayed sitting on the joint stool for a few long moments more, partly waiting to be certain Strugge was truly gone but mostly savoring being alone for the first time in days. Then he rose and, by way of claiming the place for his own, emptied the sparse contents of his sack into a small chest beside the bed and shoved the sack down beside them. His cloak already hung on a wall peg beside the wall-pole where his daily clothing would hang at night. He had so far spent his nights on a thin straw-filled pallet on the room's rush-matted floor. Minded now to try the bed, he lay down on it, to find its somewhat thicker straw-filled mattress on boards not much better, but being off the floor would be warmer, and given he had spent most of his nights these past years sleeping on the ground, he hardly had reason for complaint about boards; and the blankets were good. He would be comfortable enough, he supposed as he looked around this place that was now "his." As high in the house and close under the roof as the dorter for the bishop's men, the dorter here at least had board walls between the beds, and rough-woven gray curtains across their outer ends, giving the lesser men of Lady Jacquetta's household a sort of privacy. If not a room—given its length and narrowness, it was more like a stall—at least it was his own.

He sat up. He could not expect this kind of ease after today, and he saw no use in wasting it lingering here in utter idleness. Tomorrow would be soon enough to take to Strugge's desk—*my* desk, Joliffe reminded himself—in the small chamber the English secretary shared with the duchess' French secretary and several other officers and clerks of the household, just beyond the room where he had met with Master Wydeville. What he needed was to learn more about this part of the *hôtel*. Strugge had led him over much of it yesterday afternoon, but had balanced fairly evenly between complaint and vagueness with very little detail in between: "That way goes to the kitchen. You shouldn't ever have to bother with that," and "The privy on this floor is along there," with a vague pointing, as if that were sufficient for someone else to understand everything. Joliffe had never decided if people who did that simply supposed that if they knew a thing, then you must know it, too, or that they took a private delight in feeling superior because they knew a thing and kept you from knowing it.

Either way, now looked the best time to learn at least this half of the *hôtel* better than he yet did, before either Master Wydeville or Lady Jacquetta had need of him. Without Strugge, he might still be unfamiliar enough to be challenged, but he had his loose black over-gown that made him plainly a member of the household. It was part of his pay, this robe. They had been given out to much of the household after Bedford's death, to make an outward show of mourning to match the inward there should be. Plain servants, such as had come to the quay, had to settle for wearing a black band across their usual livery, but Joliffe, being higher in the household, had the gown. As befitted his moderate place in the household, it was of well-dyed wool of medium weight and went to somewhat below his knees. The collar, standing high under his chin, and the long sleeves, close-fitted to his wrists, hid his far less worthy shirt. His own hosen were satisfactorily black, but the clerk of the household's wardrobe, having given him the gown, had eyed his travel-worn brown leather shoes with disfavor and handed him a pair in black leather, made of finer leather than he was used to and meant for house-wear, not days and miles of solid walking. They still felt unfamiliar on his feet. Not uncomfortable. Just unfamiliar.

So did the gown, come to that. He was only used to wearing fine garments when he was playing a part in a play that needed them, not when simply being himself. But he was not being himself here, he reminded himself as he left the dorter by the same spiraled stairs that led down past the offices. Here he was being John Ripon, a disgraced clerk who—while not worth much himself—was at least used to being around life's finer things. Whatever unease Joliffe might have, John Ripon, having been in Cardinal Beaufort's wealthy household, would not be uncomfortable here. He had to keep that in mind.

As it happened, no one challenged his right to be anywhere in the while he roamed down and up and around Lady Jacquetta's part of the *hôtel*. He did not waste time going all the way down the stairs from the dorter. Strugge had showed him that at their bottom a door opened into a corner where the forward courtyard and the stableyard met. "But you're not likely to be riding," Strugge had said. "My lady has ridden no further than the cathedral these months since my lord of Bedford died. Things haven't been safe enough outside the walls, and that doesn't look like changing."

Since Joliffe had no desire to leave the safety of Rouen's walls, that suited him well enough. He had noted, though, in the brief moment he stepped outside the door, that it was angled so that whoever came or went that way through the stableyard would not be readily seen from almost anywhere in the foreyard—something surely useful for the subtle coming and going of anyone Master Wydeville wished to come and go subtly, Joliffe had thought as Strugge turned back into the *hôtel*, saying, "If we were going to the gardens, it would be from here, around through the back gate from the stableyard, but it's not the weather for gardens."

Nor was it today, to Joliffe's mind, and he chose instead to wend all the way down to the cellars instead, where a clerk was counting off the gallon pitchers of cider several servants were carrying out, undoubtedly drawn from a barrel somewhere among the stores of wine and foods and other goods stored vault-high among the thick stone pillars and cold shadows. After there, the warm, well-smelling, busy kitchen was welcome, but he no more than looked in, to avoid the likely irk of the cooks, their kind never pleased to have someone of no use to them in their way. He went on to try various stairways and put his head cautiously around open doors. He found both ways into the minstrels gallery that looked out on the great hall from above the screens passage, and roamed the three great chambers—outer, solar, and bed—off the long gallery that in the duke of Bedford's lifetime were only somewhat less public than the great hall itself and intended to show his wealth and power to such lords and others as were granted the favor of coming there. Glass, both plain and colored, was in every window, and high-set hooks showed that ceiling-high tapestries had once hung on almost every wall, but the chambers were empty now, tapestries and furnishings gone, and undoubtedly the rooms—this whole side of the *hôtel*—were older and less fine than the side Bishop Louys now had. Joliffe had asked about that while Strugge was taking him briskly through them.

With a shrug and not much interest, Strugge had answered, "This side is what was here when my lord of Bedford bought Joyeux Repos. He had it made over and used it while the new half was built, but Lady Anne died about the time it was finished, and he went cold toward it. When he married Lady Jacquetta, he gave it over to her, and she lived there without he ever really did. He always kept more to this side when he wasn't at the castle or altogether gone from Rouen. Now that she's his widow and living quiet in her widowhood, it's better sense for Bishop Louys to have the finer side, and for her to shift here. Not these rooms of course. There's no sense to having them opened, while she's still living so private in her mourning. That's why she has those lesser rooms above here. Where I made you known to her." Said as if Joliffe might have somehow let slip from mind being shown to Lady Jacquetta the day before. Strugge's voice had turned pious. "She has those, and her uncle has the fine new side of the *hôtel*, and the duke lies in the cathedral in that small room we all come to at the last. There's the turn of Fortuna's wheel for you."

John Ripon had murmured solemn agreement with that piece of commonplace piety that Joliffe could have done without. What he wanted was to know more about how matters had been between the duke of Bedford and his apparently neglected young wife. He had held back from asking because the less Strugge had to remember or mention about John Ripon, the better, and the less John Ripon asked or said, the less there would be left about him in Strugge's mind.

Always supposing Strugge didn't forget John Ripon and everything else about Rouen as soon as he was safe in Gloucestershire again.

But Joliffe's curiosity remained, and having seen as much as he freely could around the *hôtel*, he thought that perhaps time was come for John Ripon to betake himself deliberately into the Lady Jacquetta's presence, to see if she might have any present use for him—and maybe to satisfy some of his curiosity.

The January day being gray, cold, and blustered by a strong wind, Joliffe supposed the duchess and her ladies were not in the gardens; and since there had been no bustle of them going altogether out from Joyeux Repos or even down to the great hall, they must be in her rooms. Those were reached by a stairway from a corner of the outermost of the three great chambers and were, yes, less fine, but to Joliffe, in the brief while he was there, they had seemed ample of space and comforts, being originally intended less to impress the world than for the more private living of Joyeux Repos' lord and lady, he supposed.

The household yeoman on guard at the head of the stairs shoved forward from the wall where he had been leaning and said, "You're on your own today. Strugge is gone?"

Joliffe remembered he was Foulke, that he had been at duty here the other day, and that Strugge had been haughty at him. So Joliffe grinned and said, "Well and truly gone and expecting to be sick as soon as the ship sails."

Foulke grinned back. He was hearty English, part of the thorough mix of English and French the late duke had preferred for his household, and ready to be friendly if Joliffe was. "You want to see my lady? I'll ask," he said and opened the door to what Joliffe remembered was Lady Jacquetta's parlor.

It was a pleasant room, with a long window overlooking the gardens, and the walls hung with tapestries woven in wide bands of blue and white and red emblazoned with the gold-crowned red lion of Luxembourg and the golden woodstocks of the duke of Bedford. When Joliffe was here with Strugge, the duchess had been seated on the window seat with two small white dogs nested in the trailing hems of her skirts. Her half-dozen ladies had been sitting here and there on cushioned chests or else cushions on the floor, and an older woman he had supposed was the dragon M'dame had had a chair near the hearth. One of the women had been reading aloud in French from some book. The others, including Lady Jacquetta and M'dame, had had one manner or another of sewing in hand. In their black mourning gowns, they had been a drift of darkness around the otherwise bright chamber, but all had been ordered, quiet, and gracious.

Today it was not. Today, although Lady Jacquetta again sat at the window, her ladies were in flurry about the room, turning over cushions and looking under things in seeming search for something. One of the chests stood open, its contents disemboweled onto the floor beside it, M'dame was not to be seen, and the dogs were scampering and yipping into everyone's way.

Joliffe's first instinct was to retreat, but Lady Jacquetta saw him and said, "Ah! You. You are Master Ripon, yes?"

The flurry in the room stopped, everyone—even the dogs—pausing to look at him.

Joliffe bowed low. "Yes, my lady."

She gave a graceful beckon for him to come to her. As he obeyed, Foulke closed the door behind him and the two dogs leaped toward him, shrilly delighted to bark at someone new. Lady Jacquetta said quietly, "Ryn. Kywaert. Enough." And to her ladies, "Search on. It must be here somewhere."

The dogs went mercifully silent. The women flurried back to their task. Joliffe, crossing the chamber as when Strugge first presented him here, was again taken with Lady Jacquetta's loveliness. She was young and slender, her face delicately boned and pale and made all the more pale and delicate by her tight, face-surrounding widow's wimple. A hint of golden-fair hair showed at her temples, but all the rest of her was lost in the yards of her black widow's gown and the veil trailing from her wimple, save for her white hands graced with various golden and gemmed rings.

Now in front of her, Joliffe bowed again, and she gestured for him to kneel there. In the bustle of the room, they had to be near to talk together, but to talk with him standing over her would have been awkward for her neck, and to have him sit beside her would have been unseemly. He went down on one knee, the dogs began to circle him, sniffing interestedly, and she asked him in English, "Strugge is gone?"

"Yes, my lady."

"Good." She patted the seat beside her and ordered at the dogs, "Here." They jumped up, one beside her, the other onto her lap. "He was a tedious man. Are you going to be tedious, Master Ripon?"

"Should I prove so, I trust your grace will tell me, that I may improve."

Lady Jacquetta laughed at him. "Good. Already you have less tedious than he did."

Her words were made the more charming by the French glide she gave to them, but Joliffe made bold to say, "Your grace may mean 'you are less tedious than he was.'"

"What? Oh." Momentarily, she was not pleased to be corrected and showed it. Then her face cleared and she said, "Good. I need to know. We will talk English, and you will tell me what I say wrong." Then, in French, she snapped impatiently at everyone else, "Oh, let it go! If we stop looking for it, we will find it. That is always the way." As the flurry fell away, she added to Joliffe, "We came here a week ago and still everything is not found out and in its place." She looked around, and Joliffe could not tell what her deeper thoughts were as she went on, "Where I lived as my lord of Bedford's wife is too splendid for his widow, yes. So that is now my uncle's, and I am here." She nodded firmly. "Yes. It's well. Even though my lord husband had there built, I think he always liked here better. I think I do, too. These are quieter rooms. Except"—her voice sharpened and rose— "my women still cannot find everything."

Then she smiled on Joliffe, and her brief tartness was immediately nothing against her sweet, young loveliness.

Add that loveliness to her wealth as the dowager duchess of Bedford, thought Joliffe, and her powerful Luxembourg relatives would have no trouble finding another marriage for her. Which was surely what they had in mind: she was not someone to be wasted in widowhood when she could bring another useful alliance to her family.

Just now, though, her smile was on him as she made a small lift of her hand to bid him rise, and said, while he did, "I would hear how you read. Better than Master Strugge, I hope. Tonight come here after supper. You will read to us. Monday we will begin on my accounts my uncle brought from England for me. The Michaelmas accounts, yes?"

Joliffe bowed. "As it pleases you, my lady."

Understanding he was dismissed and aware of her ladies brightly watching him, he retreated, only belatedly noting M'dame now standing in the room's other doorway, likewise watching him. Strugge had said, "M'dame watches over my lady like a dragon over its hoard of gold." Which Lady Jacquetta indeed was. And being "a hoard of gold" wrapped in a woman's fair body, she was surely in need of such a dragon as M'dame, to keep all safe against thieves.

But of course this was a "hoard of gold" with a mind of its own, which might make the dragon's task more challenging and the dragon that much fiercer; and Joliffe made sure he looked no more than very humble as he bowed at the parlor's outer door and escaped.

Chapter 7

Done with seeing what he wanted of the *hôtel* and with no thought of what better he might do, he changed his mind and decided to venture a little acquaintance with his work. After all, he had to do better than *seem* Lady Jacquetta's English secretary. He had to *be* her English secretary, and if she did indeed intend to make a beginning on the Michaelmas accounts the day after tomorrow, he might do well to look at them today.

When he passed through Master Wydeville's chamber to reach that shared by the secretaries and clerks of the duchess' household, Master Wydeville was standing at the desk beside the window, talking to Pierres over some papers there. Joliffe gave a brief bow of his head as he went by them, but neither man gave even a glance his way. In truth, Master Wydeville had shown no interest at all in him these past days. Joliffe was waiting with mingled curiosity and wariness for when that would change, but for now facing the men at their desks in the next chamber, all of them looking up from their work at him as he came in, was sufficient challenge.

Save for Henri, who oversaw Lady Jacquetta's letters of business in Normandy and France, they were clerks of the ducal household, charged with keeping record of everything the household bought, spent, gave, and got day by day—from how much bread, meat, and other foods were provided at the day's meals, to the hay for horses in the stable, the bundles of firewood used in ovens and hearths, and how much spiced wine was taken to the duchess' bedchamber each evening. Strugge had brought Joliffe here long enough to show him his desk, name him to his fellow clerks and all of them to him, and say how to go about getting ink, pens, paper, and parchment when need be. Afterward he had bothered to add, "You may do well enough with George. He's English. The others, well, they're French. You'll have to decide for yourself," making it plain his own decision had been unfavorable.

Joliffe suspected his fellow-clerks were probably as glad of Strugge's going as Strugge was.

With all of them looking at him, he paused, smiled brightly, and said, deliberately clumsily, "Good afternoon. Er. Um. *Bon jour?*"

Jacques and Bernard frowned as if trying to remember who he was. The secretary Henri frowned as if remembering him but not much pleased about it. Only George gave him a friendly nod and said, "He's gone, then, is he?"

"He's on ship by now and waiting for the tide," Joliffe said.

There were general nods in answer to that—of satisfaction, Joliffe thought—before they all bent back to their pen-scratching. Taking his cue from their diligence, he went to the desk that he had to think of as his. The rolls of papers and parchments and the sealed letters that were now his duty were in the small locked chest beside it, and with the key Strugge had given him, he knelt, unlocked and opened the chest, and took out not the leather bag on top but the strap-bound gathering of parchment rolls below it.

The label hanging from it told they were last year's records, and he thought that beginning with those would help him better judge what this year's records had to say. With perfect awareness that he knew very little about what he was doing, he sat at the desk and began to read.

Lady Jacquetta's dower properties from her marriage were a small part of all the duke of Bedford had held, but not far through these reports of her lands' and other properties' worth, and her income from them, Joliffe began to be overwhelmed. As a player, he was used to eking out his days on pence, with some days very few of even those. At present, all that he owned was on his body or in the chest beside his bed in the dormer or else in the back of the players' cart, wherever that might presently be. Except for the wits between his ears, that was all his full worth, while here in front of him was record of income reckoned in pounds and shillings to the point where the pence and ha'penny of the sums seemed hardly worth the bother of writing them down. As he worked his way through enough of last year's rolls to begin to understand them, he did not know whether he admired or was appalled by her receivers' skill in apparently missing nothing that was due—or overdue—to their lady and recording all of it in careful detail. The figures he was reading from the parchment were only ink, but his imagination was more than sufficient to translate them into acres of land, scores of buildings, and hundreds of people owing rents and other payments, all to the profit of the black-gowned girl he had lately bowed to. And these were only her English lands. How much more was hers in France?

Deep into his work, he hardly knew how far the afternoon's gray light had faded, until Henri straightened on his stool and said, "There," with the air of someone putting an end to his day's work. "Is anyone doing anything that needs lamp-oil wasted over it?"

He was answered by a general shaking of heads and

chorused *"Non"* as everyone else straightened from their desks, with Joliffe surprised to find how near his nose had come to the parchment he was reading.

He could have copied Jacques in groaning and pressing a hand to his back, but simply joined his fellows in a general rustling of papers and parchment, tidying work away into chests to be locked up for the night before they went down to the great hall where there would be warmth and light and others of the household gathering in the way of the hall-servants readying the long tables for supper. His brief wrestling with his own unfamiliar lock and its key made him last to leave, finding in the outer chamber that Pierres was gone, the shutters had been closed across the window, and a pair of oil lamps hanging on a tri-footed stand lighted, giving warm light to Master Wydeville standing at the open door of a squat ambry beside his desk, not looking up from the paper he held as Henri and the passing clerks, one after the other, gave quick bows of heads and murmured "Sir," toward him as they passed. But as Joliffe did the same, he said, "Master Ripon. I'd speak with you."

Joliffe stopped sharply enough he would have slid if on a slippery floor. George, just ahead of him, looked backward over a shoulder and grimaced with apparent sympathy before disappearing into the stairway after the others. Joliffe stayed where he was. Master Wydeville went on looking at the paper in his hand the few moments more until the men were far enough down the stairs to feel free of their work and gave way to talk and someone's loud laughter.

Master Wydeville put the paper back in the ambry and said, "Close the door."

Joliffe obeyed, then turned to him, carefully blending courtesy and curiosity on his face. He had long since learned that *some* look on the face was better than trying for bland or blank. Bland or blank suggested an effort to hide something and was therefore best not used when indeed trying to hide something. Or when having nothing to hide, as presently.

"You are settling into your place here, I trust?" Master Wydeville asked.

"I am, sir."

"Master Strugge gave sufficient explanation of your duties?"

"I believe so. I'll be better able to say in a few days."

"Surely," Master Wydeville agreed. He had turned to a silver pitcher standing at one corner of the table by the window and was pouring deeply red wine into two silver bowls. "You have also seen Lady Jacquetta. Her dogs did not bite you, so that went well."

For a moment, Joliffe thought Master Wydeville had made a light jest, then decided by the look on his face that he was serious.

Oh.

Master Wydeville set down the pitcher, took up one of the bowls, and held it out to Joliffe. Joliffe took it, his fingers curving around its graceful shape. Too long used to the clumsiness of wood cups and alehouse pottery, he had a moment of awkward uncertainty before memory came back, and as Master Wydeville took up the other bowl and drank, Joliffe raised his own with the needed graceful bend of his wrist and drank, too. The wine was fulsome; he gave an admiring nod as he lowered the bowl.

"Burgundian," Master Wydeville said. "Not something we'll be having more of any time soon. Not from Burgundy itself anyway."

He drank again. Not so deeply as he seemed to, Joliffe thought, and drank very slightly himself, minding how quickly wine this rich and unwatered would fuddle his wits.

As they both lowered their bowls again, Master Wydeville asked as evenly as he had commented on the wine, "What did Master Strugge tell you of matters here in France and Normandy?"

"Mostly that he was more than ready to be away from them."

Master Wydeville said with a slow and serious nod, "Yes. However uninteresting a man he is, he is not a fool."

He looked at Joliffe as if waiting for more. Watching Master Wydeville in return, Joliffe went on warily. "He seemed to think that on the whole, matters presently look ill here. He did not think either the Seine or Rouen's walls were likely of much use, should things go as far to the bad as he thought they might."

"Did he give you some thought on how badly things are presently gone?"

Still warily, Joliffe said, "The Armagnacs are across the Seine and north of Rouen, where they haven't been for years. Or at least not in force like this. They're being swept out again by Lord Talbot and—I think he said Lord Scales—but there's nothing to keep them out. Some crossing of the Seine near Paris was lately lost?"

"Charenton, yes. We have *baleniers d'armée* on the Seine from Honfleur to Meulan, to keep the river open to us and bar the Armagnacs crossing, but that's small use if they hold too many of the bridges. What else have you gathered from Master Strugge or others?"

"He seemed to think that the Armagnacs taking of the castle here four years ago showed how quickly things could fall apart."

"Many of us think the same. Although some of us knew it well enough before then." Master Wydeville raised and turned his bowl so that the lamplight caught and shone on its polished silver. Seeming to take up another thought, he went on, "Those of us who have prospered here in France have lived more richly than we were ever likely to have done in England. My lord of Bedford once said that we're living richly on dead men's bones."

He paused, as if considering that thought along with the sheen of the lamplight on the silver bowl, then said,

"But then don't we all live on what's been made and left by those came before us? But in our own case"—he turned the silver pitcher to show Joliffe the bright, enameled heraldic arms affixed to it—three gold fleur-de-lis on deep azure with a silver label of three points—"my lord spoke in the closer sense of gnawing on the very bones themselves. This pitcher and these bowls were the duke of Orleans'. After the battle at Agincourt, they were plundered from his tent. He was taken prisoner at that battle. Is still a prisoner these twenty-one years later and likely to be so for the rest of his life, while we drink wine from his bowls and lay claim to his lands. The tapestries that hang in the great council chamber here were taken from duke of Bar's *hôtel* in Paris. Here in Rouen I live in a house I bought for a pittance of its worth because its owner, once a wealthy merchant, was broken by King Henry's siege that gained us Rouen. Many and many English here in Rouen and other towns we've taken have come by property that way. There are men who slept on straw in England who now sleep on feather beds they never would have had if they'd not taken them from Frenchmen."

Certain that none of this was mere idle talk on Master Wydeville's part, Joliffe said cautiously, "That's the usual way in war, isn't it? Those who win, plunder?"

"The better way to say it," Master Wydeville returned, "is that, whichever side they're on, men plunder as the chance comes to them. War is profit for some, ruin for others. The trouble here has been that, having plundered, we then sat down to govern those we had plundered. Our late King Henry, God keep his soul, claimed the duchy of Normandy and the crown of France as his by right of blood. He proved his right in war, then confirmed it by treaty and marriage. What folk forget now is that—right of blood or not—he never could have done it except the French lords were too busy ripping at each other's vitals to join together against him. You will likely hear, sooner or later, how all the ills in France and Normandy are because of the English, that the English have robbed and ruined Normandy with war. What you will have to listen harder to hear is the truth that France and Normandy were well on their way to ruin before ever the English came. The French lords had been rending the government and people to pieces for years, and would be at it again the moment there were no English here to hate."

Joliffe, to show he was listening, said into the pause then, "But meanwhile there *are* English here to hate."

"There are. And every lord, petty thief, and brigand who wants to make trouble uses us as an excuse to make it. Before we came, they used each other for excuse. Now they use us, and the outcome is the same. Ruin for the common folk and countryside. Most folk wouldn't care who ruled them so long as they could live in safety and their taxes not be too heavy. We haven't been able to give them safety, and their taxes are high because of the war. So they hate us the way they hated their French lords, forgetting their quarreling French lords were the cause of their troubles before we came, are the root cause of their troubles now, and would go on being the cause of trouble if every Englishman left France and Normandy tomorrow."

Disgust had darkened Master Wydeville's voice. Maybe at the follies of mankind. Maybe only with the frustrations of dealing with those follies. Maybe with both.

He nodded at the bowl in Joliffe's hand. "More wine?"

Joliffe had drunk very little, had noted Master Wydeville had drunk even less, and shook his head. "Thank you, not yet. Is Master Strugge right, then? Should anyone who can, scuttle out of here now, rather than later?"

Master Wydeville frowned, maybe less at the question than at how to answer it, before saying, "My lord of Bedford wore himself into an early grave trying to firm Normandy to peace. He died knowing he had failed. But he succeeded well enough that I doubt Normandy is on the verge of being lost."

There was a gap in that assurance. After a moment Joliffe asked, very quietly, "But France?"

Master Wydeville gave him a nod of bitter approval for the question and answered, "My lord of Bedford doubted we could keep hold on Paris if Philippe of Burgundy turned against us. Now he has, and if Paris slides away, our hold on France goes with it. With Paris and France slipped away, the keeping of Normandy becomes a harder business for a time."

"For a time?"

"Until Burgundy and the Dauphin fall out with one another again. Despite all their present love-fest, sooner or later they and their factious lords will go back to what they do best—snapping, snarling, and tearing at each other. Then we'll be able, just as we've done before, to return into France through the gaping holes they've made in her sides. That was the way my lord of Bedford saw it and said it. It was the only hope he found in the matter—that if we could not hold onto France and Paris now, we would recover them later, and meanwhile firm our hold on Normandy. Supposing we do indeed lose France. Which is not altogether certain," he added sternly and set a hard, assessing look on Joliffe. "I tell you all this because that is the purpose you are here to serve. A double purpose. To do what can be done to lessen the likelihood of losing France, while safeguarding against stabs-in-the-back that might lose us Normandy. Do you understand?"

Joliffe took time over his answer, putting together what he knew for certain with what Master Wydeville had been saying, before he offered, "I understand the purposes and the need of them. I don't understand what my part in it is to be."

"Nor do I," Master Wydeville said bluntly. "It will de-

pend on what skills you are found to have, and then on how
I decide to use you. From what I've been told and what
I've seen, you have sharp wits, are good with words and
at deceiving in your seeming. All that is to the good with
what we do."

He paused, looking at the wine in his bowl. Joliffe
waited. Still regarding his wine, Master Wydeville finally
went on, with words that Joliffe sensed were again the late
duke of Bedford's, used now as his own. "In this world
there are matters that powerful men talk over face-to-face
in broad daylight, with great ceremony and the fanfare of
trumpets, to let the world know their doings. When talk
fails, matters are given over to men wielding weapons in
open battle, their praises afterward sung for the world to
know their bravery. But there are also those matters that
can only be done well if the world and all know nothing of
them. Secret questions asked. Hidden messages passed. No
one's praises are ever sung for it. But the powerful men's
talk, and maybe the fighting afterward, often come because of those secret questions, those hidden messages."
He looked at Joliffe and said, probably seeing it in his face,
"You understand."

Joliffe understood. Understood, too, that this unseen
work could be as tangled and deadly as any open battle.

"There will be skills you need to learn," Master Wydeville went on. "Not here, nor openly, but fitted in around
your given work, to keep suspicion aside from you. Tomorrow being Sunday, you will go to Mass with my lady and
the rest of the household in the chapel here. Then you will
have time to yourself for the day and will go to the cathedral and wander in it. A usual thing for someone new to
Rouen. In one of the chapels someone will offer you the
favors of a black-haired woman. You will accept and then
be led to somewhere that has nothing to do with any black-
haired woman. There you will begin to learn your needed
skills. Repeat what I have just said."

Joliffe had been listening as closely as if for his cue in an unfamiliar play and repeated not all the actual words Master Wydeville had said but many of them, and all the meaning.

Master Wydeville nodded as if sufficiently satisfied. "Meanwhile, you are to read to her grace this evening. You will read well, I trust?"

Sure of his skill, Joliffe almost answered, "I will," but instead asked warily, "Do you wish I should?"

"Yes. She did not like Master Strugge and had him rarely around her. If it can be otherwise with you, I'd have better thought then how matters are with her."

"You mean I'm to spy on her."

"I mean you're to see what everyone else around her sees and then to tell me of it. Less spying than a passing on of common gossip. The tittle-tattle any of her women might share among themselves. Let you understand the present difficulties around the Lady Jacquetta. You've maybe heard jibing talk about my lord of Bedford marrying a girl so much younger than himself."

There had indeed been ribaldous talk and laughter about it in English alehouses and taverns at the time. Joliffe gave a small nod.

"Her youth and that he married so soon after his wife, the Lady Anne, died, gave talk. As he knew it would. More than that, Lady Anne was the duke of Burgundy's sister and a bond between Burgundy and my lord of Bedford. Burgundy saw this new marriage as an insult, worse for being to the daughter of one of his own vassals. So it's been easy for many to see the marriage as a foolish, unpolitic, unwise indulgence on my lord of Bedford's part, gaining England nothing except the duke of Burgundy's anger. But it was neither foolish, unpolitic, nor unwise. Burgundy had long been looking for a way to slip free of his alliance with us. His fondness for his sister was nearly the only thing that held him back. With her dead, it was sure he would shortly give way to treachery, whatever my lord of Bedford did or did not do."

And so Bedford had said be-damned to Burgundy and married to suit himself, Joliffe thought.

But Master Wydeville went on, "Not all in allegiance to Burgundy think as he does, though. Among those who would rather hold with England are the Lady Jacquetta's family. Her father who was count of Saint-Pol. Her brother who now is count. Her uncle the bishop of Therouanne. Her other uncle who has been one of our best war-captains against the Armagnacs. They've all been long wary of Burgundy's interest in Lady Jacquetta, worried he would urge a marriage for her they could not refuse. The trouble is that marriages that Burgundy has 'urged' on other people seem always to work—through one way and another, including the deaths of other heirs—to Burgundy's advantage. Lady Jacquetta's father, brother, and uncles thought they would rather she was married out of Burgundy's reach. Besides that my lord of Bedford was the only man with power enough to stand out against Burgundy's displeasure, he also owed Bishop Louys and his brother Sir Jean a great deal for their loyalty and service, often done in despite of Burgundy. The bishop in the government here, Sir Jean in the war. There being no hope of any longer keeping Burgundy either pleased or loyal, and with possibly much to be gained by allying with her family, my lord of Bedford married her. Despite how it looks to those who do not know his reasons, the marriage was neither unpolitic nor foolish."

Joliffe started a question but stopped, unsure if he was allowed questions.

"Say it out," Master Wydeville said.

"But wasn't marrying her too much like slapping a bear across the muzzle? If it wasn't angry before, it surely would be then."

"If the bear is already on its hind legs with a paw pulled back to sweep at you, you've little to lose by hitting it first," Master Wydeville said grimly. "Too, the marriage meant the Luxembourgs were a little more able to stand out against Burgundy's demands for treachery when the time came. They had somewhere else to be than altogether under Burgundy's thumb."

"How much of all this did—does—Lady Jacquetta understand?"

"Her father, her uncles, and my lord of Bedford made certain she understood the why of their marriage. She has likewise had her uncle the bishop to guide her much of the time here in Rouen. Now that her father is dead, her brother is count of Saint-Pol, and while he and her other uncle perforce serve Burgundy, as the duke of Bedford's widow and with her nearer uncle presently chancellor of Normandy, her fortune and future are with England. I'm taking time to make all this as clear to you as may be, that you be able to make better sense of whatever you see around Lady Jacquetta. Do you have any questions about it all?"

Joliffe considered before saying, "Not now. But later, surely."

"Until later, then. If anyone asks why I've kept you so long in talk, best say I was making harangue at you about your duties and what your place here is. No one will doubt I do that."

Chapter 8

Because of Master Wyderville's talk at him, Joliffe took several new layers of curiosity with him as he returned up the stairs to Lady Jacquetta's parlor that evening. Another man than Foulke was on duty outside the door but let him in without question, only for him to find no one was there, the soft light of a single candle on a table showing all the chaos tidied away, the shutters closed across the window. Beyond the slightly open door to the next room, though, there were voices and light and he crossed to it. Under several people's sudden laughter, his uncertain tap on the doorframe went unheard, and rather than try again, he eased through the gap into the room that clearly served—as was usual in great houses—as both withdrawing room and bedchamber for the duchess. Brightly woven tapestries showing lords and ladies riding and walking in flowered fields covered the walls, and on the wide hearth of a stone-mantled fireplace a fire burned among thick logs, denying all winter's creeping cold, while a dozen candles in a polished golden-brass candlestand spread warm light over the gathering of black-clad young women and men of varied ages standing and sitting here and there between him and the red and white canopied-and-curtained bed on the room's far side.

As heads and stares began to turn his way, Joliffe was suddenly, unaccustomedly, uncertain what he should do next. If he had been summoned there as himself, he would have known his part and how to play it—a smile, a low and flourished bow, a grand greeting to "My lords and ladies," and a bold announcement of why he was come. Come as John Ripon, he was less certain what he should do, how he should be. Then one of the women, vaguely familiar to him from this afternoon, said happily, turning toward the bed, "It's the secretary, my lady. The new one. He's here as you bade him be."

There was a small shifting aside among the women and men, and Joliffe saw Lady Jacquetta sitting on a long, low, cushioned chest at the foot of the wide bed. Two men were sitting at her right side, one beyond the other. She had been in talk with them, or listening to them, it seemed, because it was away from them she looked toward Joliffe.

"Master secretary," she said and raised a hand in slight beckon for him to come to her.

Joliffe made a low bow, crossed to her, and went down on one knee in before her, doubting it was possible to show too much respect here. She had changed her gown since the afternoon. She still wore black, of course—there were months of mourning left to her—but her present gown was of cut-velvet, its curving patterns sumptuously black on black, its fullness gathered in by a wide belt just below her fine, high breasts, between which the deep-veed neckline of the gown was open to show her undergown of black silk embroidered with gold and silver flowers. She no longer wore the throat-covering surround of her widow's wimple or the heavy-hanging veil of this afternoon. Instead, a veil of black gauze floated lightly behind her, pinned with silver-headed pins to a band of black gauze that curved softly under her chin and left her white neck bare, swan-smooth against her outer gown's wide collar of thick sable fur.

It was the finest display of wealth and young loveliness Joliffe had ever seen, let alone been close to—close enough that the drift of her flowered scent reached him as she asked, all this afternoon's sharpness gone from her voice, "You are ready to read to us, master secretary?"

"I am, my lady, if you please."

"We please, do we not?" she asked, smiling, of the two young men beside her.

Like everyone else there, they were in mourning-black, their fur-trimmed surcoats open-fronted to show well-cut doublets and close-fitted hosen, but it was the men themselves Joliffe most noted. Both were comely beyond the ordinary. The man favored to be nearest Lady Jacquetta had deeply red hair and a long and oval face, made handsome by its strong bones and sharp eagerness. The other man was—Joliffe forced himself away from staring at him—perhaps the most beautifully-faced man he had ever seen, golden-haired and with a confidently easy air as he joined the other in assuring Lady Jacquetta they were as pleased to be read to as she was. Surely knowing they would have assured her of anything she asked, she laughed at them and said to one of her women, "That book, then. The one I chose." She gestured for Joliffe to rise. "Master Ripon, choose where you wish to stand."

Joliffe chose to stand where the candlelight fell well. He understood how William Strugge might have been a poor reader when brought to stand to it with a roomful of eyes on him, but Joliffe was used to doing words in front of people, usually straight from his memory and with the added tangle of pretending to be someone else while he did it. Simply to stand and read words from a book was nothing to unnerve him, even as "John Ripon" because he saw no reason why John Ripon should not be a good aloud-reader. Especially if Master Wydeville wished him to be.

More than that, when the lady-in-waiting gave the book to him and he saw what it was, he doubted he could have resisted the urge to read well. *Reynard the Fox* was too great fun to spoil.

There were many tales of Master Reynard the Fox, made over no-one-knew how many years by no-one-knew how many tellers. The fox was a cheat, a liar, a villain, and a murderer, yet was always able to convince King Lion of his good-hearted innocence and end with himself free and his victims both unsatisfied and often laughed at, if not actually dead. Mostly the stories were passed aloud, teller to teller, changing as they went, but now and again some were gathered together and written down, although Joliffe had never seen them in so fine a book as this one, with its straightly ruled lines of very black ink on pale parchment, a gilded letter at the first tale's beginning, and an array of bright-garbed animals doing various things along the bottom of the page among curved and gilded foliage.

Rather than give those the close look he would have liked, he looked to Lady Jacquetta and asked, "Which tale will you have, my lady?"

"We have not heard any for a time. Begin at the beginning."

Talk fell away through the chamber. As everyone turned his way, he tried to stand as if at least a little abashed at being the center of that much attention, but when he began to read and found the first tale was the one where various animals came to King Lion to complain against Reynard for tricks and wrongs he had done them, he let the story take him. His voice changed from animal to animal—from King Lion's deep and rolling tones to Isegrim the Wolf's growling malice, to Bruyn the Bear's slow grumbling, to Tybert the Cat's meowling, and finally Reynard's own quick, sharp charm.

Holding the book limited Joliffe's gestures but he stood straight with head proudly raised when it was King Lion's words he was reading; moved as if wanting restlessly to pace when he was being Isegrim; hunched his shoulders and lowered his head as Bruyn; twitched his hips as if swinging Tybert's tail; shifted restlessly from foot to foot when Reynard was thinking hard about how to escape the consequences of his mischief. Laughter rewarded him, and when he ended the tale and looked toward Lady Jacquetta to see if she wanted another, she clapped her hands together twice and exclaimed, forgetting her English in her delight, *"Bon! Bon! Merci, maître!"*

That was chorused through the room. Joliffe bowed to her, and she gestured for her lady that had brought him the book to take it back from him. Talk was starting up again around the room, and as the lady took the book, the red-haired gallant said something that drew Lady Jacquetta's heed. Joliffe moved to take himself quietly away, able to tell that they were done with him for the evening, but two of Lady Jacquetta's ladies came into his way, smiling. One of them, holding out a goblet of pale wine, said in French, "You are thirsty after that?"

He made a bow to them both, smiling back at them. "I am," he granted and took the offered goblet. He was used enough to drawing women's eyes—and sometimes more— to him, but had not expected such particular notice here. So far, either in Strugge's company or this afternoon and evening, he had allowed himself no more than passing looks at Lady Jacquetta's ladies, knowing how far above him such high-blooded girls and women were. There were seven of them, all near their lady's own young years and all of them variously lovely in the ways that youth and wealth-bred care made possible. These two in front of him looked to be the youngest, and now a third joined them, a little older and probably there to urge the others away, Joliffe thought. But she joined in talking with him, still in French, until he stumbled badly over a word and one of the younger girls laughed. Joliffe smiled, acknowledging his foolishness, but the third girl chided, "Guillemete, that is unkind."

Guillemete shrugged prettily, prettily pouted, said, "Pooh," then immediately smiled again and said in English, "We shall speak English, and he will laugh at *me*." She leaned a little toward Joliffe and said as if sharing a secret, "Alizon always wants to be correct."

It was Alizon's turn to shrug prettily. "Just as Guillemete never wants to be."

The third girl laughed at them both. They were all gowned in black of course, but unlike Lady Jacquetta, their long hair flowed loose down their backs in token of their maidenhood. More than that was alike between Guillemete and Alizon, though, and Joliffe said in discovery, "You two are sisters."

Guillemete merrily admitted they were, while Alizon agreed more mockingly, as if it was wearisome burden. Then they laughed together.

Joliffe was finding the advantages of being a secretary. Lowly though a secretary might be in the general way of things, he was assuredly better placed than a player. As a player, he would have been seen immediately out at his work's end, a hireling who had done his work and was expected to leave, with a coin put in his hand by some servant on his way into the night. Neither wine nor talk with demoiselles would have been offered.

He thought he could get used to the difference.

Certainly these three were ready with their welcome, happily telling him about themselves—the third was named Marie—until Guillemete said sadly, "All was better here before my lord of Bedford died. Everything has been all black since then. Even Christmas. We've had more laughter tonight than in weeks and weeks." Plucking discontentedly at her skirts, she added glumly, "Now, soon, it will be Lent."

"Even in Lent we will have Master Ripon to read to us,"
Marie pointed out.

"And you all look lovely in black," Joliffe offered.

Guillemete dimpled at him, but then gave a heart-deep
sigh and, "But M'dame will have him read only holy books
in Lent."

"We are all still in mourning," Alizon pointed out. "It is
not even a half year since my lord the duke died. My lady
still feels her loss."

Joliffe took the chance to ask, trying to make it seem
more like simple curiosity than unseemly probing, "Was
there true affection between the duke and duchess, then?
Enough that her mourning is from the heart?"

The girls looked at one another as if each thought the
other would have the better answer, before Alizon said,
"The marriage was to take her from the duke of Burgundy.
That everyone knows. To take her from whatever plan he
might make at her. With her." Alizon gave a small shake
of her head, impatient at her search for the right word.
"Around her. You see."

"I see," Joliffe agreed.

"She seemed content enough with it," Marie said. "She
never wept or complained."

"My lord of Bedford gave her lovely gifts," Guillemete
sighed. "*I* would have been content. Even if he was so old."
She brightened. "But now she's a widow and very wealthy.
Once the mourning year is done, all will be good again."

"Guillemete," her sister said despairingly and added
something in French that Joliffe did not follow.

Guillemete rolled her eyes.

Before they could go further that way, Joliffe said,
"There's a young man glowering at us."

"Glowering? That is what?" Guillemete demanded.

Joliffe shifted his eyes sideways without turning his
head. "That is glowering."

The three demoiselles turned their heads to look at a

slight-built, dark-haired youth standing alone near one of the tapestried walls. Marie gave a light laugh. Guillemete made an impatient sound and turned her back deliberately toward him, while Alizon said, "Glowering. Yes. That is Alain. Master Queton."

Marie waggled fingers at him. Scowling more, he turned away. Alizon said, "He glowers whenever Guillemete talks to a man not him. We wish my lord bishop would take him into his household. Then, like these others, he would not be here so much."

"These men aren't of Lady Jacquetta's household?" Joliffe asked.

"Most of them, no," Alizon said. "My lord her uncle likes such of his young men who are not to be priests to learn their manners in the company of ladies as well as in that of churchmen. So they spend some evenings here."

"Also to spy on Lady Jacquetta," Guillemete said with a confiding nod. "Some of them. For her uncle."

"Guillemete," Alizon sighed. "That is not to be said."

"But it is truth."

"Truth is not to be said when it is something we are not supposed to know."

"But everyone knows it!"

"Guillemete!"

Guillemete rolled her eyes. Marie laughed.

Joliffe ventured, "He was glowering at the men sitting with Lady Jacquetta, too."

"He would be," Guillemete said. "When he is not sighing for me, he is sighing for her. He is not faithful."

"What of those men sitting with Lady Jacquetta? Are they her uncle's, too?"

"Remon Durevis is," Alizon answered. "Sir Richard was of my lord of Bedford's household and is come into hers because his father . . ."

A hand clapped down friendliwise on Joliffe's shoulder. He looked around and said, pleased, "Master Cauvet!"

"Well met again," Cauvet said. "I've seen you now and again these past days, but had no chance to speak to you. You look to be doing well enough, spending an evening in talk with my lady's ladies."

"He came to read to us. He made us laugh," Guillemete said, and added to Joliffe, "You are better at the reading than Master Strugge was. He did not make us laugh at all. Except when he had to speak French. His French made me laugh."

"And she did," Alizon said despairingly. "To his face."

"He did not even try to make it better," Guillemete went on. "But then he did not like being here. He was afraid." She gave a shrug of one shoulder. "As if we are not more safe in Rouen than anywhere."

Joliffe, to rescue Alizon from her sister's burbling, jibed at Cauvet, "So have you come, like the others, to learn manners among the duchess' ladies?"

"No. I've come to collect my lord's young men and take them back where they belong, before the dragon breathes fire and burns them all to a crisp nothing." Cauvet shifted his eyes sideways toward M'dame sitting in the shadows beyond the bed, unnoted by Joliffe until then, her gimlet gaze surely taking in all details of what passed, even if she could not overhear everything.

"Just as we will be, for having been too long in talk with only Master Ripon," Alizon said.

She laid a hand on her sister's arm to draw her away. Letting herself be drawn, Guillemete said cheerfully, "Oh, we shall blame it all on me. M'dame will believe that."

Cauvet, his eyes on them as they went away to join a laughing pair of other girls and several youths—the glowering Alain not among them—shook his head. "A household of children. That's what we have here."

"M'dame would be pleased to be thought that young," Joliffe observed.

"She would not. Poor woman. His grace the duke of

Bedford did not want his young wife to take up all a wife's cares and duties before she had done being a child. He let her keep many of her young companions this while. But they're of an age that time is come for them to be married away. My lord her uncle purposes to give her older companions in their place. The dragon will have an easier time of it then."

"If the Lady Jacquetta agrees to these changes," Joliffe murmured, half in doubt, half in question.

Cauvet answered both the question and the doubt with, "She understands her place as the duke of Bedford's widow, and all that she owes her uncle. She will do as she is bid."

Joliffe supposed she would. After all, doing as she was bid was part of the price a high-born woman paid to live in such comfort and safety.

Chapter 9

The morning brought the cascading call of Rouen's church bells from all over the town, summoning people to Sunday Mass and prayers. Lady Jacquetta and all those of her household and of the bishop's not needed at immediate duties elsewhere went to Joyeux Repos' own chapel, as they did every morning. It was a beautiful place, not over-large but delicately made, with slenderly fluted pillars of pale stone arching to a stone-vaulted ceiling painted gold and cream. Tall windows full of deepest-blue glass curved behind the altar in an apse whose ceiling was of a matching blue flecked with heaven's golden stars. It was a place that graced the eye with beauty while minds and hearts were graced with God's word, and for added measure, there was a choir of several well-voiced clergy and half a dozen boys who sang their parts of the service with angelic purity. More than that, today Bishop Louys himself performed the Mass, with added prayers of thanks for his safe return from England and much incense.

By the time it was done, Joliffe had had quite enough

of holiness, and in the general leaving from the chapel, he wove his way through the lesser household folk with whom he had stood, trying to move quickly without seeming to, but nonetheless among the first away. Passing through the great hall, he took a share of the bread and cheese set out there on a trestle table for everyone's breakfasting but kept going, eating as he went, all the way back and up to his sleeping place where he snatched his cloak from its peg and immediately pelted back down the stairs to the yard. He finished the bread and cheese on the way and swung his cloak around his shoulders as he went out into the morning cold that was even colder once he was through the gateway and into the wind cutting along the street, pushing him into a huddled rush among the huddled rush of other folk as ready to be out of the cold as soon as might be.

He found his way to the cathedral easily enough, spent no time admiring it from outside but hurried in by the first open door. He did not expect the cathedral's stone-vaulted vastness to be noticeably warmer than the outside, but to be out of the wind was something, and he found that braziers were burning here and there along the nave and transepts, making small islands of warmth. He unchilled his hands at one of them, then set to wandering. The place was well-worth wandering in, but he saw less than he might have, centered too much on the very many chapels there were, all of them feasts of color with their painted screens and the stained glass windows, the richly embroidered altar cloths and kneeling cushions and painted pictures of each chapel's particular saint, all bathed in the light of many prayerfully lighted candles.

He happened to be in St. Nicholas' chapel, standing considering the retable showing St. Nicholas in his bishop-robes working his series of miracles for young women, schoolboys, and sailors, when a woman sidled to his side. He was surprised. For no good reason, he had been expecting a man, and certainly not a woman who looked a respectable housewife of middle years, pleasantly plump, her wimple and veil clean and white, her cloak anonymously gray. Her voice was plain, too, as she asked him in English, "Is this the only sort of beauty you've in mind, good sir? Or might you be interested in a warmer kind?"

"A warmer kind?" Joliffe returned. "What warmer kind might that be?"

"A black-haired woman warmer kind? With soft curves and willing ways?"

"Yourself?"

That surprised a laugh from her, quickly curbed, although her eyes were still merry as she answered, "No. You just come along with me, young sir, and you won't be disappointed. I promise you."

He made a small gesture of acceptance that bade her lead the way.

She said, "Best you keep some paces behind me and don't keep looking about to see if we're followed; just come," and walked away from him.

He stayed where he was a few moments longer, head bowed in apparent prayer. It unexpectedly turned into true prayer. St. Nicholas was after all protector of sailors in peril, and Joliffe was sharply aware that, in a sense, he was about to embark on a new and probably perilous course on an unknown sea, so to say. A prayer to St. Nicholas seemed reasonable, and he briefly made it, crossed himself, and left the chapel.

The woman was standing not far away, gazing up raptly at one of the nave's high windows glowing azure, crimson, and gold against sunlight briefly escaping the day's clouds. As Joliffe neared her, she gave a great sigh, as of pleasure or satisfaction at so much beauty, and without seeming to see him, turned away and joined the come-and-go of other townsfolk through a near transept door. Joliffe, not seeming to see her any more than she had him, followed.

The wind was tattering the clouds away, but the sunlight

had no particular warmth and no one was lingering anywhere in the streets. The woman hurried, too, but Joliffe
had no trouble keeping her in sight the short way they went
from the cathedral, along one street and then another. He
saw when she turned into an alleyway and turned into it
after her. She was waiting in its shadows, lingered only
long enough to say, "Learn this way," and went on.

The alley ran narrowly between head-high plank fences
of rear yards. Since it apparently did not matter if he were
seen here with the woman—not that there was anyone else
here to see them, and only a few windows in the taller
houses might give view over the high fences—Joliffe kept
close behind her, avoiding the refuse heaps beside some of
the back-gates and paying heed to the various turns they
made, until at a blank-faced gate where the woman rattled
a latch open, went in, stood aside for Joliffe to pass her,
then shut the gate behind him while he stood aside to let
her lead on, up the path between straw-covered garden
beds to the back door of a tall and narrow house not different from any of its neighbors.

That back door opened into a long, stone-floored passageway that looked to lead straight through to the front
of the house, but the woman said, "Wait here," and turned
aside, into a kitchen where a girl was stirring a pot hung
over low-burning coals on a wide cooking hearth. From
where he had been left in the doorway, Joliffe could smell
it was a meat-rich stew in the pot and saw the woman take
the spoon from the girl, give a firm stir, give the spoon
back with an approving nod, and open the door of a bread
oven for a quick look at whatever was there. She must have
approved of that, too, because she immediately closed the
door and turned back to Joliffe, saying as she rejoined him,
"This way now," and led him on along the passageway to
a narrow stairs.

"You go up those," she said. "When he's done with you,
come back to the kitchen and you'll be fed."

With the good smell of the stew in his nose, Joliffe would have preferred to be fed now, but he only nodded, and started up the stairs as she went busily back toward the kitchen. He had had no clear thought about what he would find, but the stairs brought him simply to an ordinary room, long and narrow like the house, with the plastered walls painted a pleasant yellow and thick-woven rush matting on the floor. At one end, a wood-framed window overlooked the street, a long table set under it. At the other end, blue curtains were closed around a bed. A small fire burned in the fireplace of a brick chimney rising from the kitchen, and a short settle and a barrel-backed chair, both cushioned, stood angled to the fire in homely comfort.

A man was just rising from the chair. He was as lean as Joliffe, somewhat taller, and a good number of years older, with white edging his dark hair. The full cut and gray-furred edging of his dark-gray surcoat over his plain dark doublet told he was prosperous, but there was nothing else to show what his place in the world might be, only that it was surely higher than Joliffe's, and Joliffe took off his hat and bowed as the man turned toward him and said in English, "Master Ripon."

"Yes, sir."

"Will you be able to find this house again, by the way you just came?"

"Yes, sir."

"You're certain?"

"The alleyway is between the fourth and fifth houses on the left-hand side when coming from the cathedral. There's a deep notch cut hip-high into the corner post of the houses on each side of the alleyway, to mark it. After ten paces, the way splits to right and left. A notch is cut in a fence there to show you go right. After that, your gate is fifteen paces along, with a deep notch cut on the left-side post of the gateway to make it certain." He hesitated before adding, "I'm not sure if there's something particular needed to loosen the latch."

"There is, and you'll be shown it," the man said. He smiled. It was a warm and ordinary smile that went with the warm and ordinary room. "You're settling well in the duchess' household?"

"I seem to be satisfactory. No one has complained yet about my work or seems suspicious of me. Last night I read aloud to the duchess and her people and think I'll be asked to do it again."

"What of your French? Is it good or ill?"

"It's acceptably poor, I think. I understand it better than I speak it, but haven't admitted to how much I understand, except to Master Wydeville."

The man made a sudden right-handed slap at Joliffe's face. Without thought Joliffe threw up his left arm, blocking the blow. At the same time, equally without thought, he grabbed low for the man's left wrist coming with a fist for his stomach. For an intense moment they stood frozen in that pose of block-and-grab, staring into each other's eyes, before the man smiled, eased, and drew back a step at the same moment Joliffe smiled and let him go. The man nodded his approval. "Good. Not slow. Not over-driven to strike back. We'll go upstairs now."

Another steep, narrow rise of stairs against one side of the room took them to the floor above. Joliffe expected there would be another room there, if the house were that tall, or else simply the sloped place under the roof where servants would sleep. Indeed, there was a room there, and it was directly under the slope of the roof, but only because the ceiling that might have been between it and the attic had been removed, leaving an unexpectedly tall space, the purpose of which Joliffe immediately understood as he saw the various weapons racked along one wall.

"A training place," he said.

"It is. With what weapons do you think yourself skilled?"

Joliffe held in a smile at that "think yourself" and answered, "What I've used most is a club."

"Have you done much dagger-work?"

"Not enough to say I'm good at it."

"Good. Knowing what you don't know is a fine place to start."

Joliffe gestured sideways. "Won't we be heard?" The walls of plaster and wattle shared with the houses on either side would hardly be sufficient to muffle any great noise of clashing weapons.

The man nodded to one side. "There the house is empty and will stay so. To the other side—that happens to be Master Wydeville's own house and he's a solitary man whose few servants ask no questions."

"Is it"—Joliffe considered how best to ask this—"well done to have somewhere like this at next door to the spymaster's own house? Given there's been trouble of late over spies being too known?"

The man made a small nod, not so much answering the question as approving the asking of it as he answered, "What's known about me is that I've been in France for twenty years, come upward from plain archer to prosperity and no longer a soldier; that I give training here to anyone willing to pay to better their weapon-skills; and that I've long been a friend of Master Wydeville. I can't help what else may be suspected. You will, in the next few days, let people know you're becoming very uneasy at all the talk of Armagnacs and Burgundians and war. Someone will, where others can hear it, recommend me. I'm well known as a weapons master. Then you'll be able to come in by the front door here once in a while with no one taking heed. Other times you'll come by that back way, for lessons in other than weapons."

"You'll be teaching me those, too?"

The man gave a grin that showed his dog-teeth. "No.

Weapons are what I do. Master Wydeville prefers his spies be subtle enough to need no use of dagger or sword, but there's always the chance, and if it comes, best they be good at it. That's what I'm for. I'm Master Doncaster, by the way. So. We'll begin."

They began not with daggers, as Joliffe expected, but— stripped to their shirts and hosen—with wrestling.

"Your body is as much a part of the fight as whatever weapon you have in hand," Master Doncaster said. "You need awareness of it."

The man who had taught wrestling to Joliffe years ago had said much the same. Since then, Joliffe had not much used the skills he had learned; he was thrown more than once before a particularly jarring fall seemed to shake them all back into his head, and at his next grappling with Master Doncaster, he hooked a leg around one of Master Doncaster's and with a twist and a shift of his balance he had forgotten until then, he had the man down. After that, they traded one fall apiece, and Master Doncaster said he was satisfied that sometime, somewhere, Joliffe had had some manner of good training at it.

He did not ask when or where, and Joliffe did not offer to say.

They went to wooden practice daggers, balanced and weighted to the feel of true ones. As with the wrestling, his training with weapons was long past, but with his once-skill probably reawakened by the wrestling, Joliffe did "not so badly as you might," according to Master Doncaster at the end of trying him for a lengthy while. Joliffe nonetheless knew by the ache on his thigh when he had downward-blocked a thrust away from his ribs but not far enough aside to miss his leg that he would be bruised there when he looked.

When they were dressed again, Master Doncaster asked to see Joliffe's own dagger, looked at it carefully, tried its balance, and said, "A fine one. Sheffield steel, I think. Somewhat misused but still sound. In need of right sharpening, though." He showed how a fine blade should be wooed by a whetstone, as he put it, then polished the blade with a soft cloth and handed the dagger back to Joliffe, warning, "It will cut the wind now, as they say. So be careful of it. Best, too, you put it away for now and get a different dagger the first chance you have. Some hearty pig-sticker with a fool's hilt, to go with your talk of being worried over the war. That will make plain past questioning your need to be sent to me for lessons."

Joliffe nodded that he understood, keeping to himself his resolve to oblige Master Wydeville's desire that his spies be subtle enough to avoid the need to use dagger or sword—devoutly adding his own hope that no one would ever have desire to use dagger against him, either. Or—saints forbid—a sword.

A while later, he left Master Doncaster's with a bowlful of the good stew inside him, followed the alley back to the street, and strolled along it, meaning to see if he could tell which were Master Doncaster's and Master Wydeville's houses but finding it no challenge because of the sign painted with crossed swords hung above what had to be Master Doncaster's door. Ah, well.

Then, on the chance someone might ask where he had been for so much of the day, he set to briskly walking as much of Rouen as seemed reasonable to allow for his absence if he had been merely strolling all this while. For good measure, he spent time in a tavern near the quay, to be able to name somewhere particular he had been. But he returned to Joyeux Repos to find clusters of angrily talking men crowding the great hall, and seeing his fellow-clerk George was in one of the near clusters, Joliffe edged up to him to ask, "What's amiss? What's happened?"

"Where've you been, to miss the uproar? Taking a nap?" George returned. "It's Burgundy, damn him. All the bishop's going to England in hope of making a peace was a farce and a waste. Damned Burgundy never meant anything but war from the first."

One of the other men protested, "That's not altogether the way of it. He maybe meant it when he asked Luxembourg to ask his brother to go. It was the letters from England that threw it all to nothing."

"Ha!" George threw back. "Burgundy was playing for time, nothing else. He'd have found one excuse or another whenever he was ready."

"King Henry didn't have to give him such a fine one on a platter," another man grumbled.

"What excuse?" Joliffe asked.

"There's that," George granted, agreeing with the man, not answering Joliffe. "The royal council had no business sending off those letters."

"It wasn't the council," the second man countered. "It was King Henry signed them."

"Don't be such a simple-head," a third man snapped. "It's been King Henry's name on the council's orders since he was nine months old. This wasn't his doing any more than anything has been since then."

"Lay you odds that it was," George said. "King Henry's of age to take things into his own hands, and aren't these letters more surely a youth's throwing of a gauntlet at Burgundy's face than something the old sober-sides of the royal council would do?"

"What letters?" Joliffe persisted.

"Letters to the Zealand towns," George said. "Letters out of England urging them to rise in revolt against their rotten duke, saying England would back them if they did."

The second man laughed. "They're saying Burgundy fair foamed at the mouth when he heard about it."

"Would he would choke on his own bile," the first man said.

"It's wiped out any good might have come from our

lord's time in England, that's sure," said the third man gloomily. "Burgundy will settle for nothing but war now."

To Joliffe, George said somewhat grimly, "Report is that he's swearing vengeance and destruction on everything English."

"That's all he's wanted from the beginning, I tell you," one of the other men said, which brought the talk back to where it had been when Joliffe joined it. As it started through the same round again, he drifted off, to hear what else was being said around the hall but, finding it all fairly much the same, the only variation being, "Would to God the royal council would choose a new governor and get him here," which told him word was not yet open about the duke of York.

When he had heard, several times over, everything there was to hear, he went away, up to the dormer. The wrestling, dagger-work, and walking had somewhat tired him. So had the swirl of anger and talk. Wrapped in his cloak for more warmth, he lay down on his bed. At this hour, the dormer was blessedly quiet, giving him chance to think for a while. Not that he much liked his thoughts. These Zealand letters looked to have set the bad blood between England and Burgundy even further to the bad, and that could not be good for Normandy or what England held in France. Not that anybody had seemed to deeply expect anything else in the long—or maybe even short—run of things, but the Zealand letters had exploded Burgundy's false front of wanting peace, meaning whatever was going to happen was going to happen all the more soon.

To the good, Joliffe thought, it all gave him open reason for proclaiming his "fears" to the world and getting that pig-sticker dagger. Beyond that . . .

He longed for home.

The thought came from seemingly nowhere and surprised him. He had, by his own deliberate choice, left what had been his home a good many years ago. To find himself missing it now made him look hard at the feeling, distrusting it. Was it only wariness about where he was now, not truly a missing of "home," that he was feeling? But a closer look showed it was not a place in particular he was missing. What he missed was the familiarity of belonging. In truth, if belonging was "home," then the other players had been his "home" this while past, and it was them he was missing. Basset, Rose, Ellis, Gil. Even Piers. No matter the changes that daily came with being traveling players, these last few years there had always been them, a familiar core to his life. Now there was no familiar core. There was only change and strangeness. There was only himself.

He stared at the wood grain of the blank wall beside him. Was he lonely? Was that it? Why should he be? After all, no matter where or with whom he ever was, he had always been alone with himself. At the core of everything there *was* only himself. Once he had come to understand that, having only himself for company had never been a particular trouble to him.

Was this maybe more a matter of *where* he was alone— that he was more completely a stranger here than anywhere he had ever been?

Players, of necessity always on the move, were used to being constantly strangers, with anyone on the lookout to make trouble willing to turn on them if no one else was to hand. It was simply something players faced, along with days of walking roads and occasionally going hungry—familiar troubles. Here in Normandy, in Rouen, the troubles were unfamiliar ones, and he had the very bad certainty that he barely understood many of them, and the worse certainty that he had not even begun to guess at what some of them might be. More than that, here he was not simply a stranger—to some people he was an outright enemy simply because he was English.

And today he had begun to learn how to kill men.

That was part of his deep unease, too. He had never

doubted he could kill if he had to, if it came to living rather than dying for himself or a friend. But to learn to kill as a skill . . . To learn it very deliberately . . .

He did not like the thought of learning how to kill. Of course he liked the thought of *being* killed even less. But the two went together, didn't they? He was going to learn how to kill because someday someone might want to kill *him*, and then he would . . . know how to kill instead of being killed.

He got abruptly up, dropped his cloak across the bed-foot, and headed for the stairs. Warmth, light, company, talk, and soon supper—those were what he wanted just now. Not thinking.

Chapter 10

Because neither Bishop Louys nor Lady Jacquetta came to supper in the hall that evening, there was no ceremony to the meal. The servants served, people ate, and it was done. Through it, the talk was still about Burgundy and what was likely to come next, and minding Master Doncaster's bidding, Joliffe showed himself very ill-eased and unhappy, even muttering that Strugge knew what he was doing, taking himself back to England.

"Strugge is an old woman!" George declared. "We're in Rouen, for God's sake. There's no place safer!"

Other of the men chorused that, but at the meal's end, when George and some half-dozen other of them were for going out to a nearby tavern, Joliffe said he should see if he was wanted by Lady Jacquetta. He was jeered at good-humouredly for being afraid of the dark, with a squire claiming, "He's afraid the French are already in the streets," then saying with mock surprise, "But wait. They are! This is Rouen. It's full of French!"

That sally of wit and accompanying laughter carried

George and the others out the foredoor on a swirl of ice-touched wind. Content not to be going out into the cold dark with them, Joliffe went upward, expecting there would be more talk of the news from Burgundy among Lady Jacquetta's people, but that her rooms would be warm, brightly lighted, and less loud than any tavern.

What he did not expect, as he came into the outer chamber, were raised voices from the bedchamber beyond, and the demoiselle Guillemete and two others of the ladies whose names he did not yet know clustered tightly just inside the bedchamber doorway, either for protection or in readiness to retreat from Lady Jacquetta, who was out of sight but declaring furiously, "Because I'm weary of it! Weary and *sick* of it!"

Or maybe their wariness was of M'dame, answering with equally raised voice, "Your weariness does not matter in this! You are barely four months into your mourning. You . . ."

"Four months! Yes!" Lady Jacquetta cried. "And eight more before I am to wear anything but black or do anything but sit like a dull old woman."

"A year of full mourning is what you owe his grace the duke your husband. At the very least. For your own honor as well as his, you owe him that!"

By now Joliffe was close behind the demoiselles, able to see over their shoulders into the bedchamber. Rather than last evening's gathering, there were only Lady Jacquetta's women there, a lone older man, M'dame, and Lady Jacquetta standing with her arms folded fiercely across herself, saying angrily, "But to have no sport at all! All Christmastide was tedious with doing nothing. A few card games. A little dull music. Nothing more. No dancing. No sport. Nothing! Now you say Shrovetide must be the same. Then it will be Lent, and Lent is always tedious, and this year it will be worse. I will have *something* at Shrovetide!" She turned sharply toward the man. "Master Fouet, say something! What can we do? I want more than card games and prayers at Shrovetide. What can you offer?"

Master Fouet had Joliffe's instant sympathy. He vaguely knew the man was choirmaster of the chapel, which meant that, among other things, he had charge of training and overseeing the boys who sang in the household chapel. Now it seemed he was also expected to be the household's revel-master, and caught between Lady Jacquetta's demand at him and M'dame's gimlet gaze warning him off any rash offers, he looked back and forth between them, his mouth opening and closing with no words coming. Joliffe, out of pity and with pure folly, edged past Guillemete, saying as he went, "What of a play, Master Fouet? A psychomachia? Sins in battle against Virtues?"

He did not know from where that thought sprang—or why he then let it spring out of his mouth—but as M'dame turned her narrowed gaze upon him, he hurriedly added, "Nothing riotous. No outright fighting. A debate and a formal dance." He was making this up as he went and gained himself a moment by his low bow to Lady Jacquetta, who did not look taken with any of that, until he straightened from the bow and added, "You could of course be no part of the play itself, my lady"—that was to forestall M'dame—"but some of your ladies might dance, and there would be their lessons to, um, watch, and their dresses to make," he ended somewhat lamely.

He thought Lady Jacquetta was showing a spark of wary interest, but Master Fouet protested, "I have no such play!"

"I can write you one," Joliffe said before he could stop himself. Gone too far for going back and with everyone looking hard at him, he outright lied, "I did one once for my lord of Winchester's household. A small one. One year at Shrovetide."

Master Fouet's dignity kept him from outright pleading, but he was near to it as he said toward M'dame, "A thing suitable for the cardinal bishop of Winchester's household at Shrovetide would surely be seemly here."

"Surely!" Lady Jacquetta agreed, glaring at M'dame.

Giving no sign she noted her lady's glare, M'dame eyed first Joliffe, then Master Fouet, then said at Joliffe, "I would need to read this play before I agree to it, Master Ripon."

Seeing too late the very large flaw in what he had said, Joliffe said quickly, "I have no copy of it here. Not the one I wrote. But I can write it a-new, for you to approve. If it please you, my lady."

Master Fouet said worriedly, "We're not that far from Shrovetide."

"The speeches are short. Easily learned," Joliffe promised. "I'll make as quick work of writing it as my duties allow."

"Your other duties can wait. Begin at once," Lady Jacquetta ordered.

Resisting any look toward M'dame—knowing Lady Jacquetta would resent it and equally certain that if M'dame had objection she would make it—Joliffe made a low, acknowledging bow.

Far too late, he was remembering the proverb that warned against digging a pit with your mouth and then falling into it.

As he straightened from the bow, Lady Jacquetta gave a sharp clap of her hands and said, "Even before reading the play, we can decide who of my ladies will play which Virtues."

Master Fouet began, startled, "I had thought the play would be for the boys of the chapel to . . ."

"There are only six of them," Lady Jacquetta said with gleaming mischief. "There are seven Sins and seven Virtues. Now, how would it be if all the Sins were played by my gentlemen and all the Virtues by my ladies? Yes. I like that thought. Yes."

Master Fouet turned to Joliffe as if to an ally. Which

they now were, Joliffe supposed. At least, they had *better* be allies, if they were to survive this. And in answer to the choirmaster's silent plea, he said with a bow to Lady Jacquetta, "It might be best to wait until the play is written before we choose, my lady." And added, to win Master Fouet and himself more respite, "Would my lady have me read to her again this evening? It being somewhat late to begin taxing my wits with writing tonight."

Lady Jacquetta hesitated, then accepted that graciously, and while one of her ladies fetched *Reynard*, Master Fouet bowed himself out, so that it was only to the ladies Joliffe read, and at the end he escaped with an honest plea of tiredness as the ladies began to talk of which Virtue they would like to be. Although Guillemete said happily that she would rather be one of the Sins. To them all, trying not to let his retreat seem like the flight it actually was, Joliffe smiled and said, "We'll have to see," and got himself away.

But morning inevitably came, and while Joliffe lay listening to the scuffling, moaning, and griping from the other men along the dormer, putting off crawling from under his own blankets and cloak, he considered what he would do. He had once thrown together a play about Sins and Virtues. That much was true. But it had been a farce for mad-cap scholars rather than something fit to play in the bishop of Winchester's household, and it would not serve for here.

So.

A play about the seven deadly Sins and the seven soul-saving Virtues sufficient to divert a bored young duchess while not offending M'dame, and simple enough to be practiced and performed in a very short time before Lent began. Joliffe encouraged himself with the thought that, to the good, once the thing was written, his part in it would be done, the rest of the problem all Master Fouet's. With that comfort, he finally got himself out of his bed's warmth and into the morning's cold, to dress and hurry down to the hall, among the last of the household taking a share of the breakfast ale and bread.

Being too low in the household to be required to attend every morning's Mass with Lady Jacquetta and her ladies, he chose not to today and went up to his desk, thoughts about Sins and Virtues twitching in his mind. He found word of his new duty was there ahead of him and that no one seemed to envy him for it. Henri said right out, "I'm glad it is not me."

Jacques, clerk of the kitchen accounts, asked, "Is it to be in French or English?"

Joliffe had not thought that far about it yet but answered immediately and from the heart, "If it's to be played in French, someone will have to turn it from my English, that's sure!"

The others laughed at him and returned to their work. Among the scratching of pens that was soon the only sound among them, Joliffe's was the least as he played with thoughts. The matter seemed straight enough. After all, there was only so much that could be done with a psychomachia. The Sins—Pride, Envy, Wrath, Sloth, Avarice, Gluttony, Lust—and the Virtues—which were various, according the purpose of whoever was making a list, but for this would be Humility, Kindness, Patience, Diligence, Liberality, Temperance, and Chastity—had to present themselves, quarrel against each other, and the Virtues be victorious at the end. That was all. What each Sin and Virtue had to say for themselves and to each other was fairly well set out in any number of treatises and other works. All Joliffe need do was write out short verses of no particular original thought for each, and leave it to Master Fouet to put dances or whatever else around them. No, not even verses, since surely the play would be turned to French. Short speeches, then, and anyway it would be the dancing that people most wanted to watch, rather than listening to badly delivered speeches by giggling girls and stiff young men, if this went like every household-done play Joliffe had ever seen in his younger days. Besides, he should not write it too well. Among the last things he needed was for people to fix in their minds that he had skill that way, because if they did, there might be no end to what was asked of him.

By late morning he had a number of random-seeming lines scribbled down on paper, but the whole shape of the thing was in his mind, and by late afternoon the Sins' opening speeches were well toward being finished, and he doubted the Virtues would give him much more trouble. His one worry through supper was that he would be summoned to Lady Jacquetta that evening, and when George slapped him on the shoulder at the meal's end and asked if he wanted to join some of the fellows at the Crescent Moon tonight—"I've heard they've opened a cask that's not so bad."—Joliffe agreed more readily than he might have otherwise.

Besides, it would give him a chance to play up both John Ripon's insistence he must not drink too much and his worries about the war, and he started while he and George were crossing the yard toward the gateway by asking, "George, while we're out—that fellow that's said to teach sword-work—the one someone was talking of yesterday— could you show me where he lives? Maybe recommend me to him?"

"Saint Agatha's breasts! I don't know the man," George protested. "I've only heard of him. You're not truly set on this, are you? You're in Rouen, not out in the bleeding countryside!"

"Strugge didn't think here was all that safe," Joliffe said with an edge of stubborn whine. "This Master Doncaster is good?"

"Experienced, anyway. Fought at Agincourt and all that."

"Ha!" someone said, coming up behind them. "Like every other old soldier in Normandy, he was at Agincourt. Ha!"

George slapped a hand on the newcomer's shoulder and said to Joliffe, "Estienne, clerk of the chamber to his grace the bishop, and a right good drinking companion. Coming to the Crescent with us?"

Estienne was a short, bustling man, perhaps a little older than George, dressed in a dark clerk-gown much like their own, and he said he would most willingly go to the Crescent with them, adding scornfully as they passed through the gateway, "If every Englishman who says he was at Agincourt had truly been there, your King Henry's army would have been double the size of the French and his victory none so glorious after all."

George laughed, and Joliffe kept to himself his thought that Master Doncaster had too much the straight feel of true steel to be other than he said he was.

The Crescent Moon proved to be a clean-kept place, the strewn straw on the floor none too old and the benches and tables well-scrubbed. The men whom George and Estienne led him to join looked to be, like George and Estienne themselves, middling clerks of the respectable sort or else journeymen in one craft or another. Joliffe gathered as they talked that none of them had wives waiting at home; gathered, too, that George and Estienne were seen as somewhat above the rest of them, given the households they served, and that same reflected worth came Joliffe's way, too, and the more so because it was already generally known among these men that he had been in the bishop of Winchester's service. That he was here because of disgracing himself there seemed not to count.

Joliffe reminded himself never to under-guess men's ability at gossip, for all that women had the worse reputation for it.

Unfortunately, these men's gossip this evening was

mostly of Rouen folk and matters, until the stationer's journeyman commented grumpily that the latest shipment of paper from Paris, needed by his master, was being held up by Armagnac raids along the Seine. That brought on general head-shaking and obviously familiar muttering about taxes being wasted on garrisons that didn't do the work they were paid for, and Joliffe took the chance to bring up John Ripon's worry over how dangerous things might be, even here in Rouen.

Just as George had done, everyone jibed at him for his worry, with George adding to the jesting by saying, "He's so worried that he wants to learn how to fight. Does anyone know where that Englishman lives that teaches swordwork?"

That brought a rude jest from someone about knowing where some "swordwork" could be done that needed no teaching, and Estienne asked didn't he want a Frenchman to teach him since it was the French he was afraid of.

Joliffe protested, "It's just that everyone says it's going to come to fighting, but what do I know about fighting? Nothing! I just want to know more than I do about what to do with a dagger, that's all."

That brought an array of rude suggestions, and the stationer's journeyman called him "an old woman." Playing John Ripon, Joliffe got a little sullen, and that brought more laughter at him, until finally the cutler's man took pity on him and recommended not only Master Doncaster but another man, and several of the others gave him jumbled directions to both.

"But you're not going there now," George said. "So drink up."

Joliffe muttered he had had about as much to drink as he should, but Estienne beside him poured more wine into his bowl from the pitcher being passed around and said, "This wine is too watered to do anyone's head any harm."

That was not true. If anything, the wine was surprisingly

good, but Joliffe pretended to take Estienne at his word, drinking deep and then asking, as if somewhat drunkenly suspicious, "This isn't Burgundian wine, is it?"

"It's Gascon," the stationer's man assured him.

"Good old Gascon," Joliffe said. "We used to get tun-fulls of Gascon every year. Comes into Southampton with the autumn wine fleet. For my lord of Winchester's house-hold." He blinked owlishly around him at the other men. "We don't want Burgundian anything, do we? Not their wine. Not their duke. Not anything."

The others agreed to that with general head-noddings and varied mutters and oaths at Burgundy. As Joliffe had hoped, their talk turned to the war. He was surprised at how little any of the men seemed worried by Burgundy's new rage over the letters to the Zealand towns or had any doubt that Rouen was safe enough.

"The Armagnacs already threw their best at us these past two months, and Talbot and Scales put them back where they belong," one of the men said. "They'll do the same for Burgundy if it comes to it."

"We'll have to take the treacherous bastard down sooner or later anyway," one of the men said. "Might as well be sooner."

They all drank to that, but afterward the talk slid away to how old Bremetot had proposed marriage to a widow and been accepted. "Although I've heard he proposed something else first," the mercer's clerk said. "But she threatened him with a fry-pan for it, and he changed to marriage to save his pate."

"More than his pate will need saving if he marries her," George said. "Did you hear . . ."

The talk went on to some quarrel between merchants in Rouen's court and then to taxes, none of it any interest to Joliffe. What did interest him was how, under cover of the talk around them, his bowl was kept full by Estienne beside him while the clerk asked him questions about what was said in England about matters in France and Normandy. Most especially what was said in the bishop of Winchester's household. And then more questions about the bishop himself. Since Joliffe had never been part of Winchester's household, there was little he could accurately tell Estienne. He made do with oddments he had heard in the players' travels, telling them as if learned in the household itself and embroidering where possibility suggested itself to him, mostly because Estienne's interest was somewhat too-intense and gave Joliffe questions of his own that increased as the clerk's questions began to go deeper, trying for more particular information about Bishop Beaufort himself. How did matters presently stand between him and his nephew the duke of Gloucester? Who among the English lords did he seem most to favor? Was he much around the king? Who *was* much around the king?

John Ripon, not too sharp-witted to begin with and increasingly fuddled with wine, was unlikely to wonder much about Estienne's insistent interest, but Joliffe was *not* fuddled with wine and he *did* wonder. As he ran out of answers he wanted to give, he retreated into Ripon's ignorance, grumbling he did not know anything about any of that, all he had been was a clerk at one of his grace's godforsaken palaces in god-forsaken Hampshire, and if he had been given some place worthy of him, he wouldn't have been driven to drink and he wouldn't be here. He kept up his weak man's whine that his life was all someone else's fault and none of his own doing, slumping lower on the bench, his nose closer to his wine bowl while he did, until Estienne lost interest in him.

Along the bench a corn merchant's clerk was complaining about the lack of good grain because of last year's poor harvest. Someone else was going on about a ship supposed to be bringing pine planks from Norway but still not come in. The stationer's journeyman brought up his master's troubles with paper again. And suddenly Joliffe had had enough. It was a long, long while since his life had been so bound into a single place as these men's lives were. The smother of that life had helped to drive him to become a player, and it was that same sense of smother that now brought him to his feet like a man with a sudden need for an outside wall. The laughter of his erstwhile companions followed him as, somewhat staggering, he left the tavern.

He kept his walk wavering until he was around a corner and away from anyone maybe watching him from the tavern's doorway. Night was fully come but curfew was a while away. The cold was a welcome slap to his heated face after the crowd-warmth of the tavern, and he was not minded to go back to the *hôtel* yet. The streets' darkness was eased by lighted lanterns hung beside doorways—town laws must require that here, as in England—and there were people about, so he felt safe enough to wander a while, and for something to do, tried the directions he had been told to Master Doncaster's from here.

He was surprised to find they did indeed bring him into a street where he recognized the sign of the crossed swords hanging among the uncertain lantern-shadows. Other than a man and a little boy hurrying toward and past him, hand in hand and homeward bound, he guessed, he and a cloak-wrapped woman ahead of him had the street to themselves, leaving him space to be surprised when she stopped at the door below the sign of crossed swords, stepped up onto its step, and knocked—must have knocked, although Joliffe did not hear it, or else she had a key, because the door opened readily to her and she disappeared inside without pause for speaking to anyone there. So she was probably the housekeeper or else the kitchen girl he had seen there yesterday, late home from some errand. But as he came abreast of the door half of a moment later, meaning to pass by, it was still standing

open, and with his inevitable curiosity he looked in and
saw in the shadowed passageway, by uncertain candle-
light coming down the narrow flight of stairs, the cloaked
woman stretched out motionless on the passageway's
stone floor, and a man crouched over her.

Chapter 11

oliffe had just time for his stomach and heart to lurch before the man stood forcefully up, demanding, "Who—" with a dagger in his hand that Joliffe would have sworn was not there an instant earlier.

But in that same moment he and Master Doncaster knew each other, and the dagger disappeared.

"Come in," Master Doncaster ordered. "Shut the door. Drop the bar. Help me. I need her into the light."

By the time Jolilffe had swung the heavy wooden bar down across the door and turned to the hall again, Master Doncaster had the woman turned onto her back and was lifting her shoulders from the floor. At the weapons-master's sharp, wordless nod, Joliffe took her legs, bundling her cloak and long skirts around them, and followed as Master Doncaster backed along the passageway and into the light and warmth of the kitchen, where the woman and girl who had been there before were at the hearth and table. Looking around, they both made wordless exclaims, but as Master Doncaster started, "Matilde—" the woman said

sharply at the girl, "Get your pallet. Here. Before the fire."
And to Master Doncaster, "You hold her half a moment
more. Who is it?"

"Perrette."

The woman made a distressed tching noise but was already swinging a kettle on its iron arm from the side of the
hearth to over the fire as the girl pulled the thin mattress
that must be her night-time bed from behind a tall cup-
board and threw it on the floor in front of the hearth.

"There now," Matilde said, turning from the kettle.
"You put her down there. Gently. Jeanne, your blankets,
too. And mine."

Both men laid the woman down as gently as might be.
Not that she gave any sign of feeling anything; she was
as limp as if maybe already dead. Joliffe was careful of
her nonetheless and at Master Doncaster's order unclasped
her cloak at her throat while the weapons-master fumbled
to take off the white veil and wimple she wore. Matilde
tched again and elbowed him aside, deftly pulled out pins
to loosen the veil and, under it, the wimple that circled the
woman's face. By then Master Doncaster had shifted to the
woman's side and thrown open her cloak. She was dressed
in a plain, long-sleeved gown of russet-brown wool that
might well hide a bloodstain from first glance, and he demanded at Joliffe kneeling on her other side, "Do you see
where she's hurt?"

"No."

Greatly careful, Master Doncaster eased her limp body
far enough onto one side for him to see her back, said,
"Nothing. No blood there either," and eased her gently
down again. "You must have been coming along the street
when she was. You saw nothing? No one?"

"I was maybe three houses behind her as I came. I didn't
see anyone near her or anything wrong. She seemed to be
walking strongly enough."

"She would. Up to the point where she couldn't anymore," Master Doncaster said, then added in a mutter, "And probably past when she should have given up." His hands were questing along both her sides. "There has to be something. If she's been hit with a club maybe—if she's bleeding inside—" He had his dagger out again. "We have to get this gown off her."

He was moving with the clear intent to slice the gown open when Matilde stopped him with a hand laid on his wrist, saying, "She won't thank you for ruining her gown. You leave it to me."

"But . . ."

"I'm saying," Matilde said, elbowing him away and reaching out for the thin-bladed kitchen knife Jeanne was already bringing her.

Master Doncaster let himself be elbowed. Joliffe copied him in shifting aside, leaving Matilde to turn up the gown at the hem, prick loose some threads of the gown's front seam there, then quickly, skillfully, cut her way up the full length of the seam to where Jeanne was pulling free the lacing that closed the gown between the woman's breasts, so that when Matilde reached there, the gown fell open from throat to feet, showing the white linen shift beneath it.

"Gently now," Matilde said to Jeanne, and together they lifted Perrette enough to slip the gown from her shoulders and free her arms before laying her carefully down again, Matilde saying while they did, "Whatever else is wrong with her, she's gone hungry a while, too."

"What?" Master Doncaster said blankly.

"Look at her face," Matilde answered with the sharp impatience of having to point out what she should not have had to. "That's hunger-sunk. She needs food."

"Why would she have been going hungry?" Master Doncaster asked, more of the air than of anyone, which was just as well because no one answered him.

The linen shift was sleeveless, and Matilde was unpricking the short shoulder seams as deftly as she had undone the dress. There was still no sign of any wound or wounds, the woman was still breathing, and her face did not have the odd graying that came with approaching death. All that was to the good, and even in his distraction Joliffe thought her face was not uncomely. Somewhat thin, surely, and no saying what it would be like when not slack in unconsciousness, but even-featured. Her hair was dark brown where it showed at the edge of the close-fitting coif Matilde had not taken off her, and there was nothing wrong with her breasts, Joliffe saw as Matilde and Jeanne turned down her shift, baring her to her waist.

He was instantly ashamed of the thought, as if he were no better than one of the Elders secretly, shamefully gazing at Susanna in her garden. He as instantly argued to himself that his response to a woman's nakedness was against his will, wasn't it? It was not his fault that he was male and she was female and that it was in the natural way of things that he would take a certain heed of . . . things.

Then he saw what Master Doncaster had already seen, and Matilde, too, to judge by her sudden intake of breath.

A black-blue bruise as big as a man's outspread hand darkened the side of the woman's lower right ribs. Something large and blunt had surely struck her there and, "Those have to be broken," Master Doncaster said. He began to feel for the bones beneath the flesh.

The woman flinched. Her eyes opened. She stared upward at the ceiling beams, a little startled for the moment before she slid them to one side and the other, taking in the faces clustered over her. Uncertainly, her right hand moved to touch her side, and she said, a little thickly, as if her mouth was dry, but quite clearly, "You had better have good reason why I am undressed in front of you all."

As directly as if to a stricken soldier, rather than to an injured woman, Master Doncaster said, "Perrette, you've taken a hard blow to your ribs."

She silently considered that, than said, "That would be why they hurt so badly, I suppose."

"I need to learn how bad the hurt is."

She closed her eyes. "Best that you do so, then."

Matilde took her hand, and as Master Doncaster began to feel firmly along her side, Joliffe saw the woman's fingers tighten around Matilde's; but she made no sound, and except that her lips pressed together with pain, her face remained still.

Master Doncaster finished and said while covering her with her shift, "No bones are broken. How bad the bruising is, how deep it goes, it's too soon to tell."

Perrette's hold on Matilde slackened, along with her whole body that Joliffe had not realized was lying so rigid against the pain of Master Doncaster's hands. "It was my cloak," she said, opening her eyes. "It's loose and thick. It muffled the force of the blow."

"Who was it?" Master Doncaster asked. "Where did it happen?"

"Not far before I came to the bridge. I don't know who. If you ask, you may find out something from the watch. There'll be his body."

Master Doncaster touched her left forearm. "Your dagger?"

For the first time Joliffe saw the sheath of pale leather strapped there. An empty sheath.

"He staggered me," Perrette said, explaining with the care of someone tired almost past talking. "He did not stop me."

"His mistake," Master Doncaster suggested quietly.

"Yes," she agreed, and closed her eyes.

Joliffe in pity and worry would have let her rest then, but Master Doncaster laid a hand on her shoulder and asked, "Had he followed you, or was he waiting for you?"

Perrette's eyes stayed closed. "I don't know. I thought I

had no one behind me. Maybe he was waiting. Maybe he knew me."

She could not see the grimace Master Doncaster made then, but Joliffe did and understood it. Far away and what felt like long ago in Southwark, Master Fowler had said the present agents were all too well known in Normandy now and that was one reason Joliffe was wanted there. But he had also said no one was being killed for it, and if the attack on this woman had not been meant to kill, it had certainly been meant to cripple. And *she* seemed certain she had killed, whatever her attacker had meant to do.

The kitchen's warmth did not stop the chill that moved through him.

Matilde, who had gone away for a moment, came back to kneel beside Perrette again, holding a cup that—having gentled an arm under the woman's head enough to raise it a little—she put to her lips. Perrette sipped, paused as if to gather strength, sipped more, then more again before shaking her head slightly to let Matilde know she was done and smiled her thanks. Whatever had been in the cup had brought faint color back to her face. She shifted her hand to take hold on Master Doncaster's wrist and said with new-awakened need, "Not the Armagnacs next. The Bretons. Richemont with a large force out of Brittany. That's what they intend."

Master Doncaster's free hand closed over hers. "Richemont," he repeated. "Out of Brittany. When?"

What little strength the drink had given her was fading. Her certainty and her grip on his wrist lessened together. "As soon as may be? When the weather turns? That I did not learn. They may not know themselves. It's Richemont after all," she added, faintly scornful and as if that explained much. To Joliffe it did not, but Master Doncaster made a wordless sound of understanding and agreement; but Perrette's eyes had closed nor did she stir as Matilde covered her with a blanket brought by Jeanne.

Master Doncaster stood up and moved away. Joliffe went with him, followed by Matilde who said almost accusingly at Master Doncaster, "I'll make a poultice for her side. She must rest and eat before you have more from her. By her look, she had done neither for a long while."

"She maybe could not," Master Doncaster said. "She maybe had to move too fast and too secretly."

"For what good it did her," Matilde sniffed.

"It did her well enough. She made it here," Master Doncaster returned. He turned to Joliffe. "Come to it, why are *you* here?"

Joliffe explained.

"Was there anyone else in the street as you came along? Anyone who saw her and you come in at my door?"

"No one that I saw."

"That's the best we can hope for. Now, about you."

Joliffe eventually made his lone way back to Joyeux Repos, only remembering as he came to the gateway and was let pass by the guards, that he had left the Crescent Moon supposedly well on his way to being drunk. With that in mind, he crossed the yard and entered the great hall like a man working hard at walking well and failing. George, in talk with Estienne and several other of the men idling here and there about the place, saw him almost at once and beckoned him into the group, demanding, concern mingled with laughter, "Where did you get to?"

"Was sick," Joliffe said. "Got lost. Went looking for that sword fellow."

"You went wandering through Rouen muddled with drink?" Estienne laughed.

"Got lost," Joliffe insisted sullenly with John Ripon's offended, somewhat drunken dignity. "Found the fellow, though. He said he'd take me on. He said he'd teach me some dagger-work will serve me well."

Estienne grinned. "Well enough to get you into trouble."

The other men laughed. Joliffe swayed, looking befuddled, and George threw an arm around his shoulders, saying, "Come on, then. Early to bed for you, don't you think?"

"Um," Joliffe agreed.

"You. Master Ripon," said someone behind him.

Joliffe turned unsteadily from under George's arm to find Lady Jacquetta's squire Alain there. "Sir," he said in answer.

"Her grace required you to read to her tonight. You couldn't be found."

Back on John Ripon's unsteady dignity, Joliffe gave the bow needed to show his respect not to Alain but to the high place of the lady who had sent him and said, "I was out. I can come now."

Pretending drunk in front of Lady Jacquetta was not something he wanted to do, but as he had hoped, Alain said, albeit curtly, "No. The hour is too late now. She was hoping, too, to hear how her play goes."

"It goes well. I should be able to share what I've done with Master Fouet after another day or two, to see if it meets his need."

"My lady will wish to hear it as soon as may be."

Joliffe drew himself up, standing straightly as he said, firm voiced like someone sure of his ground, "She will be more diverted if she does not hear it until it is performed. I will give the completed play to Master Fouet. He will, of course, take counsel with her, and if he chooses to share it with her, that will be his business." Joliffe intended that once the play was written, everything about it would be altogether Master Fouet's business, with himself out of the middle.

Alain stared at him, seeming taken aback, perhaps at Joliffe's tone that said he expected no contradiction. Joliffe's thought was that if Alain did not like his tone, the squire should try a different one himself.

Finally, coldly, Alain said, "I'll tell her grace," turned, and walked stiff-backed away.

"What was that about?" asked one of the gathered men, someone of the bishop's household.

Joliffe explained about Lady Jacquetta's desire for a Shrovetide diversion. The men began immediately to jest about which sins they wanted to be. Lust was the main choice, although Estienne put his hand to his hip as if to the hilt of an imaginary sword and declared he wanted to be Wrath, while George first declared for Lust but changed to, "No, I want to be Sloth."

"Alas, no Sloth for me," Joliffe said. "If I'm to have this play done, I'd best to bed tonight, to have my wits back come the morning."

No one could gainsay that excuse for him to leave, but George said, laughing, "At least you'll be ready then to write against the sin of drunken Gluttony, yes?"

Joliffe made the pained sound of a man who did not want to think about that and went away, leaving their laughter behind him.

Chapter 12

The next days were ordinary. Or what passed as ordinary for Joliffe just then. The psychomachia gave him little trouble. Everything a Sin or Virtue might say was so known to everyone that he went to no great lengths to be clever about it, suspecting it was more important the little speeches gave the same number of lines to each Sin and Virtue, to keep happy those who judged their part's worth by how many lines it had. Unhappily, those who did so were usually better at counting their lines than saying them.

When he gave Master Fouet the roll of the completed play, he pointed out the short speeches and equal lines, and the choirmaster said gratefully, "My many thanks for that. My lords and ladies will care more for what they wear in the play than what they say, but for a certainty every one of them will know if they have more or less to say than someone else."

He also asked that Joliffe stay while he read through the play, and as he came near the end, he asked, "But this?

They dance their battle against each other, yes. But who are this Lord Justice and Lady Wisdom that come in and end it before the Virtues have triumphed?"

This being the one thing Joliffe had added beyond the necessary, he answered readily, "It seems to me the Virtues have yet to win full victory over Sins, and unlikely they would have one now. Thus, Lord Justice and Lady Wisdom appear in splendor to put an end to it."

"With Lady Wisdom taking the Virtues to her, and Lord Justice driving the Sins away before him. Yes." Master Fouet nodded. "Good. Good. But who shall play them, to be so much more splendid than the rest?"

"That I must leave to you," Joliffe said, beginning his retreat. "Nor," he added, "can I put it into French for you."

"That will be something for my scholars to do. That, and copy out the separate parts." Because no one but Master Fouet himself would have the whole play. Except for the last line of the speech before theirs for their cue, everyone else would have only what they had to say themselves. Master Fouet was nodding, pleased, saying, "Yes. This will go well enough," as Joliffe escaped.

With the play done, Joliffe turned back to his right duties. Writing on the play had set him behind with the English accounts and letters but not kept him from becoming more familiar with Joyeux Repos. Although "Joyous Rest" seemed increasingly a less-than-apt name. From what Joliffe was able to see from the fringes of it all, Bishop Louys certainly had little rest just now. As chancellor of Normandy, he was often gone to council meetings and constantly beset by men, messengers, and fellow-councilors coming and going. Joliffe gathered from the general talk that neither the hoped-for soldiers nor any new governor were on their way from England yet, that every report concerning Burgundy continued ill, and that a present lessening of Armagnac raids was taken to mean their men were being gathered into a single force for something large to come.

"Paris, most likely," Cauvet said one evening. "It will be Paris they're after. Then they'll move west into Normandy, and if we're truly ill-fated, Burgundy will move on us from the north at the same time."

Cauvet was rarely in the hall, but Joliffe always welcomed the chance of talk with him when it came. Not that Cauvet often had anything comfortable to say. Besides the war, he had become caught in the bishop's efforts to lessen Lady Jacquetta's household. Officers of both households were supposed to be dealing together toward that end, but from the few things Cauvet said about it, Lady Jacquetta was not submitting with the seemly quiet suitable to a young widow grateful for her uncle's care. Joliffe, going to her rooms one day to ask her mind about a letter just come from England, found her ladies sitting rigidly silent in the parlor, intent on voices in the bedchamber. Several raised warning fingers to lips at him, but Guillemete, nearest the bedchamber's open door, beckoned him forward. Willing to be curious, Joliffe went, keeping aside to be unseen, and heard Bishop Louys saying with patient firmness, "There is too little for them to do. You will be paying them to do nothing."

"Then I shall pay them to do nothing," Lady Jacquetta answered with matching firmness. "It is, after all, my money, and so my choice."

"You are young. These are choices . . ."

"I am the widow of the duke of Bedford, who was a good and wise man who trusted me to do rightly for his people. If he did not, he would have said otherwise in his will. Did he say otherwise in his will?"

"No. But . . ."

"You are here to guard my good name, yes. But this is my house and household, and I want my cook in my kitchen, and my cook wants his own people with him, and therefore so do I. What happens to your cook is no concern of mine. *My* cook stays where he is. *Your* cook will stay away from him."

In the pause that came then, Joliffe sorely wished he could see the bishop's face and was surprised when he finally went on, stiffly, "Well, then. The stables."

"The stables?" Lady Jacquetta sounded caught by surprise, too, as if she had expected a longer argument. But she rallied quickly and said evenly, "I do not ride out much anymore, true. Good enough. You may send some of my horses away."

"I was thinking some could be sold, and some stablemen dismissed."

"No. No horses sold. No one dismissed."

"You will keep your mare, surely, and some others. But not all. Merrak, for one, can . . ."

"Merrak? Part with Merrak? My lord husband's favorite? No!"

"Jacquetta . . ."

"His warhorse, yes. Merrak, no."

"Jacquetta!" For the first time, Bishop Louys sounded openly impatient. He probably saw as bad enough he had to take time away from greater matters because his niece resisted other persuasion without she defied him to his face.

"No!"

From somewhere in the bedchamber, M'dame said, "My lady," so evenly that Joliffe could not tell whether she was warning or chiding.

Whichever it was, after a silent moment Lady Jacquetta said coolly, "Some of the horses may be sold if you think it needful, my lord. Not Merrak, though. As for dismissing anyone, if any of my household wish to leave, I will not insist they stay. Even those who have not served their agreed time. So. Will that do well enough?"

Bishop Louys must have decided to settle for what he had. He granted, "For now, yes. Thank you, niece."

The demoiselles became busy with whatever tasks they had in hand, and Joliffe moved well aside from the doorway in hope of going unnoticed as Bishop Louys swept out a few moments later, accompanied by two of his gentlemen, one of them Cauvet, carrying several parchment scrolls tucked under an arm. Joliffe, feeling that now might not be the best of times to ask more decisions from Lady Jacquetta, gave them time to be well away, then matched their retreat, but encountering Cauvet in the great hall at suppertime, he asked, "What was that between my lord bishop and Lady Jacquetta today?"

To his surprise, Cauvet not only answered readily but smiled widely while he did, "That was my lord bishop discovering his niece is not the biddable girl he might wish she was. How much did you hear?"

"Just the end, I think. About cooks and stables and people leaving if they wish."

"That was most of it. You missed where he explained how the mingled households were making it difficult for the clerks to keep the household accounts accurately. She answered that if the accounts were difficult, she would surely need all of her present clerks who 'understand what needs to be understood better than you or I could do.'"

"He surely pointed out that if her household was reduced, she'd not need so many clerks," Joliffe said.

"He did. She answered that when her household was sufficiently reduced, then they could decide about the clerks, but for now, from what he had said, surely they were needed. She then refused almost all his other suggestions."

"Is he badly displeased with her for it?" Joliffe asked.

"But no! I think he is pleased to find she was able to hold to her own but willing to bargain fairly. It would hardly suit him to have a fool for a niece."

Joliffe would have preferred to stay in talk with Cauvet, but Cauvet's gaze went past Joliffe, his face stiffening a little, just before Estienne slapped Joliffe on the shoulder and said, "Some of us are away to the Crescent Moon. Come, too."

As John Ripon, Joliffe went all rueful and regretful. "No, I think not. Not tonight. My thanks, but no."

Cauvet, without having greeted Estienne, murmured excuse and left them. Watching him go, Estienne said, "A dry stick, that one. You're sure you won't come?"

John Ripon was hesitant, but Joliffe quite surely did not feel like pretending to be even slightly drunk tonight, or having more of Estienne's too many questions about Bishop Beaufort and matters in England. The man seemed to think every small piece of English gossip he might have out of John Ripon was valuable.

"Then what of some of Rouen's other pleasures?" Estienne offered. "A certain house I could show you, where the women are willing? Eh? You know. After supper maybe?"

Joliffe had the sudden but very certain feeling that among the last things he wanted was any more of Estienne's company. He was shaping a refusal when Sir Richard—the fair-faced knight of Lady Jacquetta's household, so often close-companioned with her in the evenings—came up to them and said to Joliffe, with no sign he saw Estienne at all, "Lady Jacquetta wishes for you to read to her this evening after supper, Master Ripon."

Joliffe promptly bowed as if to Lady Jacquetta herself. "It will be my pleasure."

Estienne, apparently determined to be acknowledged, said with a bow, "Sir Richard."

Sir Richard, already turning away, paused long enough to say "Master Doguet," acknowledging his presence but showing no pleasure at it, then walked off.

Estienne watched his departing back with an open twitch of distaste and said, "Our Sir Richard Wydeville is somewhat over-proud for a nothing-knight, I think."

"Wydeville?" Joliffe echoed in surprise. "He's kin to Master Wydeville?"

"You don't know? He's Master Wydeville's son and heir.

Knighted when still a child by the hand of King Henry VI himself."

"Master Wydevill's son is a knight and he's not?"

"By Master Wydeville's own choice, so it is said."

"But how did the son come to be knighted then?" Joliffe asked, thoroughly puzzled.

Estienne shrugged. "There was a great peace-making between angry lords, years ago, in England. The king's uncles—the duke of Gloucester and your bishop of Winchester—had been quarreling. My lord of Bedford brought them into accord, and there was a great ceremony of knighting as part of the celebration of it. Several dozen sons of noblemen and others were knighted. Master Wydeville's son was one of them, making him *Sir* Richard." Estienne's scorn matched Sir Richard's distain toward him.

Joliffe failed to see why either one should matter to the other at all. Or was it that Estienne had a hidden desire to be a knight himself, instead of a clerk, and resented the squire's son's easy knighthood?

But that did not explain Sir Richard's cold rudeness toward him. What was the cause of that? Joliffe found he was not curious enough about it to keep in Estienne's company and soon pried himself loose of it.

Later that evening, he had his answer anyway. Finished reading more of Reynard the Fox's adventures aloud to the duchess and her companions, he was in talk with Alizon and two other demoiselles, all of them watching Lady Jacquetta trying, hand in hand with red-haired Remon Durevis, to teach a circling dance to several of the bishop's young gentlemen partnered with others of her ladies, including Guillemete. To judge by the general laughter, the effort was effecting more hilarity than success, and Sir Richard, wandering the sides of the chamber rather than joining in, paused beside Joliffe to say, smiling, "Alizon, Ydoine, Michielle, shouldn't you give your companions relief? I think Isabelle is about to kick Thierry if he steps on her skirt again, and James almost sent Blanche to the floor there."

Joliffe supposed James was the youth who had just confused slide-slide-turn with cross-step-turn, entangled his feet around each other, and lurched into the girl beside him. Alizon, Ydoine, and Michielle laughed agreement and went. Joliffe supposed Sir Richard would go, too, but instead he stayed and said, his gaze on the re-sorting of partners and his voice low, "You'd do well to stay as clear of Estienne Doguet as possible."

Joliffe was surprised into saying, "Willingly." Then added lightly, to see where the talk would go, "I haven't decided yet whether he's a mere mischief-maker or some brothel's way-man. Either way, I'm not taken with his company."

"He is a nasty little French spy who's no good at what he does."

Joliffe tried to keep his smile, to seem as if he and Sir Richard were no more than speaking of the dancing, but said, startled, "He's what?"

"A French spy."

"He's known but he's allowed to stay?"

"Bishop Louys prefers a spy who can be spied on to a spy we don't know of. So he stays. But you'll do well to keep away from him."

"And if he insists on my company, I tell him nothing. Not that I know anything a spy would care about anyway," he added.

"You have it," Sir Richard said.

How much did he know of his father's work? If anything, he was not giving it away, simply went on, raising his voice for the benefit of Guillemete and Alain, come aside from the dance, "We're all curious who shall play which Sins and which Virtues. Her grace charged me to find out, if I could."

Joliffe spread his hands to show helplessness. "I can't tell what I don't know. The matter is all Master Fouet's now."

"He shall be laid siege to, then," said Guillemete merrily. "We are perishing to know who we are to be." She caught Sir Richard by the hand and drew him forward. "Lady Jacquetta says you know this dance and must come to help."

Sir Richard went with her, leaving Alain behind, but Lady Jacquetta gave Remon Durevis over to Guillemete and took Sir Richard's hand herself, saying, "Here. Help me to show how it should be done."

Joliffe, left with Alain, asked him, "You're not joining again?"

Alain shook his head. "I'm not needed. It's enough that I may watch her."

"Her?"

"The prize of all prizes. The loveliest of the lovely. The . . . the . . ." Alain fumbled, invention failing him.

"The rose of all roses?" Joliffe suggested. "The jewel of all jewels?"

"*Yes*," Alain agreed, fervently.

"And she is . . . ?" Joliffe prompted.

Voice low and throbbing, Alain declared, "My Lady Jacquetta."

Yes, it would be, Joliffe thought dryly, and said, carefully keeping mockery out of his voice, "You hope high."

"No." Alain drew out the word on a trembling sigh of infinite melancholy. "I hope not at all. No more than I would hope to hold the sun, a star, the . . ." Invention failed him again.

"The moon?" Joliffe offered.

"The silver-shining moon!" Alain agreed eagerly.

Dear Saint Valentine, he has it badly, Joliffe thought, fighting to keep his face schooled to sympathy.

"But still I may gaze upon her," Alain sighed. "If nothing else, I may gaze upon her."

"Feeding your soul, despite your heart languishes," Joliffe offered and immediately wished he had bitten his tongue instead as Alain turned to him, wildly grateful.

"You understand. You *know*."

Unwillingly, Joliffe granted, "I have, um, loved in my time." Although never so pathetically or poetically, thank the saints. But Alain, convinced he had found a fellow-sufferer, wanted to know more, that they might suffer together. Joliffe resisted, claiming that even to speak of his supposed lost love was too pain-filled for him, and finally escaped.

Admittedly in flight, he went up to the dorter. Several of the household men were sitting on the floor between the sleeping stalls, playing at dice by a candle's light. They invited him to join them, but he said he preferred bed just now, which was no lie. He would also have preferred to fall straight to sleep, but his bed was cold, and he lay awake for a time, wrapped in his blankets and under his cloak, thinking.

So. Estienne Doguet was a French spy. A French spy tolerated here because he was known to be a spy.

Master Wydeville had surely considered Estienne could be a blind for an unsuspected French spy among them, but did Sir Richard Wydeville's warning come from the open dislike between him and Estienne or because report had been made to Master Wydeville of the interest Estienne was taking in John Ripon's company, and Sir Richard been given order to warn Joliffe away? Joliffe little liked the thought that he was being particularly watched, but he equally supposed Master Wydeville would be a fool *not* to have him watched while he was still such an unknown quantity in the household. But did Sir Richard know of his father's work? Was he part of it? Probably. Possibly. Perhaps not.

Joliffe was briefly diverted by the thought that maybe he would only know he was fully trusted—or as much trusted as Master Wydeville likely trusted anyone—when he was asked to spy on someone else in the household, rather than be spied on himself.

Or was it less a matter of trust or distrust than that Master Wydeville simply found it useful to have his spies spy on each other, to know what they were doing?

Joliffe had found little in his right work as secretary to hold and interest him, but he was increasingly curious about what he was coming to understand of the households here. In them, lives were layered onto each other, from the lowly kitchen scullions up through the higher and yet higher servants to the middle order where he himself was, on to the gentlemen and ladies attending and serving most closely on those for whom the households existed at all— Bishop Louys and Lady Jacquetta. Ordered and orderly though those layers might be in theory, they were made of people, and there were cross-currents, under-currents, even over-currents constantly running, and from what he was starting to see of them, he was fascinated. And wary. Because it would be a bad thing for him to be caught the wrong way into any of it.

That slid his thought away to foolish Alain and from there to wondering about Lady Jacquetta and her strange place at the center of so many other people's lives and plans but with such little final say in any of all that swirled around her. Thought about what was to become of her had to be very much to the fore of her mind. Widowed so young, she was unlikely to stay unmarried. In the common way of things, her family would reclaim her, to make use of her in another marriage, but there was nothing common in the matter. A return to her family would put her back in reach of the duke of Burgundy, something neither her family nor the English were said to want. Come to it, would the English let her go back to her family even if they wanted it, if it meant she would come under Burgundy's control? Very possibly not.

Joliffe noted that the one thing he was not asking was what Lady Jacquetta might want. To be a widow immured in Joyeux Repos by her widowhood was surely not all she wished for herself, but bound as she was by her blood and her wealth, her choices were few. Her family and the English had made use of her to their own ends so far, and would go on doing so, and what she might wish would probably count for very little in the end. At best, she could, in theory, refuse to marry anyone again, could live a widow all the rest of her days and win a measure of freedom that way. But even though today she had fairly well fended off her uncle's attempt to lessen her life, she had had to give way on some of it, and would surely be forced to give up more as time went on. Was she likely to be content with widowhood forever?

Still, she had time. There were eight more months of her year of mourning to be gone through before any great changes could be made for or by her. She had that much time, at least.

Ah well. Her life was not a problem he had to solve. Most likely sooner or later after her year of mourning was done a satisfactory marriage would be urged on her and she would take it. That was the usual way of things.

With the blankets finally warm around him, and the rattling of dice on floorboards and men's swearing and laughter not troubling him, his final thought as he drifted to sleep was a vague wondering—not for the first time—how the woman Perrette was doing at Master Doncaster's.

Chapter 13

The next day was some French saint's day, and so half a holiday for the household. Joliffe had thought before now that giving holidays on holy days was the surest way to have people remember saints with thankfulness, and although he was not able to make out this saint's name, he did give grateful thanks when he was able to slip away unnoted from the *hôtel* after the mid-day meal, not having need to make excuse for his going or refuse anyone's company as he went. With an hour before he was expected at Master Doncaster's, he wandered roundabout for a time, seeing what the various shops open-fronted to the streets had to offer and taking the chance to buy a particularly vile dagger—the blade not bad but the hilt and sheath cheaply gaudy with badly dyed red leather and pewter bits pretending to be silver. The cutler was as glad to be rid of it as John Ripon was pleased to have it. Joliffe thought he could get tired of John Ripon.

It was as he left the cutler's shop that he glimpsed the fellow in the bright blue cap for the second time. Glimpsed

once, pausing at a neighboring shop at the same moment Joliffe had paused to look at a first cutler's display of knives,
the man had been nobody. Glimpsed now a second time,
again paused at a neighboring shop and the same distance
away that he had been before, he caught Joliffe's heed,
and after that, Joliffe found him always the same distance
away, always pausing when Joliffe paused and still there
even after Joliffe had turned in to several different streets.
Joliffe briefly considered how to lose him but doubted he
could, since the man probably knew Rouen better than he
did.

His watchfulness told him something else, though, and
he was holding in a smile when he finally took himself to
Master Doncaster's street, pleased that he found it easily
but paused by sight of a large hand-cart at the next door to
Master Doncaster's. Master Doncaster had said that house
was kept deliberately empty, but two—no, three—small
children chased out of its door, ran laughing around the
cart and the men unloading a large wooden chest from it,
and darted back into the house. Distracted from thought of
the blue-capped man, Joliffe knocked at Master Doncaster's door, hoping he could be heard over the shrieks of the
children racing out the neighboring door again and around
the men now carrying the chest into the house, leaving several wicker hampers waiting their turn.

Jeanne answered his knock. "You're to go up," she said,
and he did, to find Master Doncaster standing at the table
by the front window, in company with Master Wydeville
and a man whom Joliffe did not know.

Because of the third man, he slipped into being John
Ripon, took off his cap, and said, bowing, "If now is not a
good time after all, Master Doncaster—"

"Now does very well," Master Doncaster returned. "You
see I'm getting new neighbors?"

"With children," Joliffe agreed.

Master Doncaster nodded his head toward the unknown

man. "They're Master Roussel's. He serves in our Chambre des Comptes in Paris. He wished to have his family away from there, and here they are."

"What does that tell you?" Master Wydeville asked crisply.

Joliffe had a moment of blank puzzlement that he tried to hide, before a thought took him so by surprise that he said, "Oh!" He paused to straighten the thought, then said, "That Master Roussel wanted his family somewhere safer than Paris. Which means the rumor that the Armagnacs are going to move against it is—likely more than a rumor."

"Somewhat right," Master Wydeville granted. "He does want his family away from Paris. But he wanted that before there was word yet of the Armagnacs' likely move against it this spring. What does *that* tell you?"

Unwilling to believe what it told him, Joliffe said slowly, "That matters were already bad enough in Paris, even without word of the Armagnacs, for Master Roussel to want his family away." Watching the men's faces, he added even more slowly, "Bad enough that he thinks there's strong chance it's only a matter of short time until Paris is lost."

No one made answer aloud to that, but Joliffe thought he saw the answer plainly enough in Master Roussel's face. Having traveled with small children could account for the taut tiredness there, but Joliffe thought the strain went far deeper than that. To uproot and shift a family was no small thing at the best of times, but to do it this way, with fear behind it . . .

A small child's wail of outrage rose from the street. Master Roussel made a sound both impatient and resigned as he started for the stairs, saying, "If you'll pardon me—"

Scant moments later he could be heard below the open window saying, "Madelaine, what did you do to your brother?"

Master Doncaster pulled the window closed. Joliffe used the moment to say, "I was followed to here."

Both men looked sharply at him, but it was Master Wydeville who asked, "What makes you think so?"

Shortly, clearly, Joliffe told of the blue-capped man, ending with, "But then, you were hoping I'd see him, weren't you?"

"Why do you think that?" Master Wydeville asked blandly.

"That cap was too bright a blue for someone who wanted to go unnoted," Joliffe said. Carefully watching both men, he added, "Spotting the fellow in the tan cap took me longer."

Master Doncaster laughed. Master Wydeville went so far as to smile and said, "You have a suspicious mind and some cleverness, Master Ripon. That's to the good. A suspicious, clever man is likely to live longer in this game. Martin, I leave him to you. Good day."

Joliffe was still taking in that "live longer" as he bowed to Master Wydeville's departure, then watched, surprised, as Master Wydeville went up the stairs instead of down. As his footfalls crossed the floor above, Joliffe looked his question at Master Doncaster who answered, "There's a door between the houses up there. People who come in at one of his doors can go out one of mine if need be. Or the other way around. Or lets us meet without anyone to know of it."

Joliffe nodded toward the lately empty house on the other side. "What of that way?"

"That way will have to be blocked now there are children there. It's not to the best to have them there, but Master Roussel needed somewhere for his family quickly, to set him free to return to Paris as soon as might be."

"Does Master Roussel know about"—Joliffe made a vague gesture—"all of this?" Meaning not simply the houses.

"He knows. But talk is not what you're here for," Master Doncaster answered. "Come."

This time they wrestled only a little, by way of warming up. Then Master Doncaster had him put on a padded surcoat. That served to blunt the blows that too often got past Joliffe's guard. Toward the lesson's end, fewer blows were getting through to him, but he guessed that he should not begin to think himself skilled until Master Doncaster felt the need of padding, too.

At the lesson's end, still warm from the effort but dressed again and come down to the parlor, he was surprised to have Master Doncaster not dismiss him but set him at the table near the streetward window, give him a rolled parchment, and say, "By rights, this should be someone's business to show you, but Master Wydeville thinks you may do well enough on your own. You're to learn it."

That was all he offered in explanation. He went away downstairs, and Joliffe unrolled the parchment, weighed it open across the table with the little, bright-painted lead bars kept to hand for just such work, and found the parchment patterned with what might have been called a spider web of black lines, if one accepted the spider was drunk when it made them. Along the lines, small, red-inked drawings of walls and towers with names beside them marked towns, and with a little study, Joliffe determined this was a map showing at least some of Normandy and France. He found Paris and Rouen because of the numerous roads spidering from—or to—them, and he was able to trace the Seine from Paris to the sea, and then the roads that went outward from Rouen, taking in the names of the towns along them. He doubted the map showed the distances between them anything like rightly, and while some vaguely sketched lumpy hills here and there probably meant uneven land, for the most part the map only showed the general way to all the places on it and what rivers might have to be crossed.

After a time Master Doncaster came back from wherever he had gone and asked, "Questions?"

Joliffe put his finger on a town near the coast. "Caen. I've heard the name but know nothing else. Do I read the map rightly? There's a castle there and it's a port?"

"You have it. There are also two great abbeys, founded by the Conqueror himself and his wife four hundred years ago. My lord of Bedford worked to start a university there, to be a rival to the arrogant scholars in Paris who think it's their right to weigh in on every trouble that comes up and that their word should be the last in any contest. What will come of Bedford's hope now, I don't know." He shrugged and tapped a finger on another town. "Could you get from here to there if you had to?"

"Honfleur?" Remembering what he had heard about Armagnac raiders through that part of Normandy, he said, "Not without a good-sized armed guard around me."

"Huh." Master Doncaster's grunt was appreciative. "Good enough for now, then. Time you left."

Setting aside the weights to let the scroll roll up on itself, Joliffe took the chance to ask, "One thing. How is it with the woman who was here and hurt?"

"She's gone on about her business," Master Doncaster said, easily but as if that was all he meant to say, and Joliffe warily left it at that.

he was working at his desk the next day when a servant summoned him to Lady Jacquetta. He welcomed the escape, not so much from the work itself but from the low-voiced worrying among George, Jacques, and Bernard over what would come of the dealing between Bishop Louys and Lady Jacquetta over her household. Given how many people had overheard what had been said between them yesterday and how word spread through any household, there was no wonder at talk about it being everywhere by now, but because no amount of talk and scrabbling worry by those with no power in the household was going to affect what those above them decided, Joliffe had soon tired of listening to them and left his work willingly.

The servant who came for him did not say why he was wanted, and Joliffe chose not to ask, so he walked unprepared into the duchess' parlor and chaos. But a bright and happy chaos, with Lady Jacquetta's women scattered, laughing and talking, among a dozen or more bolts of cloth set around the room on stools and tabletop, with many of the bolts partly unrolled, their rich cloth falling and flowing in vivid heaps of bright colors. Joliffe thought of the delight Rose would have taken in having such cloth to sew, rather than the rough-and-cheap with which the players mostly made do. Certainly, the women here were taking delight in the wealth of it. Several had swathes caught up to themselves, held against their black gowns, or draped over shoulders, or held out to see at arm's length. Lady Jacquetta's little dogs were nowhere to be seen, a mercy for the cloth-merchant, who was likely the man standing with his gaze twitching uneasily around the room, not far from where Lady Jacquetta stood beside the table, stroking a shining blue satin and looking thoughtful, while across the table from her Master Fouet stood looking much like a man barely holding back from wringing his hands.

While Joliffe was still bowing to her, Lady Jacquetta said at him, "It was Master Fouet who requested you come. We are not agreed about your play. Since it is yours, he said you would be best able to say. I agreed you might be."

Joliffe took special note of that "might be." As with her household, Lady Jacquetta was giving no ground until she had to.

Master Fouet, a man embattled, said, "You see, Master Ripon, I came here to try out her ladies' voices, to choose who would do well for which Virtues. But I found this. The Virtues are to be gowned in shining white, to show . . ."

"Then I don't want to be a Virtue," Blanche declared.

"No," said Marie. "I want to be Envy and wear this green!"

An outcry of counterclaims and laughter from the others answered that, while Master Fouet said desperately, "No, no. The Sins are to be played by men. For ladies to take on any seeming except of virtue . . ."

Indignant, laughing outcries and exclaims interrupted him, Lady Jacquetta's the most firm with, "It will be Mardi Gras. *Carnaval*! Everyone takes on seeming then and it means no more than sport."

Master Fouet looked ready to continue his protest, but from a corner where she was sitting much like a watching black crow, M'dame said, dry-voiced, "Given that the Church teaches insistently that women are the fount of all sin, to have the Sins played by women does not seem unreasonable, Master Fouet."

That was the last opinion Joliffe would have expected to hear from M'dame, and it surely brought Master Fouet to startled silence, staring at her. She turned her look on Joliffe. "So. Can the speeches you gave to the Sins be done as well by women as by men?"

Lady Jacquetta took that up eagerly. "Yes! Could the Sins be played by women and the Virtues by men?"

Warily, Joliffe granted, "There's nothing in the play that says they could not."

Glad exclaims among the women and a few hands clapped met that answer, before he added (lest Saint Genesius, patron of players, strike him down), "*But* it is also every player's duty to obey what the master of the play tells them to do. The play is in Master Fouet's hands. It is for him to determine how it is to be done."

That was true as well as fair, although Master Fouet probably little appreciated having the problem handed back to him. But it *was* his to determine, and showing only a little desperation, the choirmaster looked around at all the young, eager gazes fixed on him and finally at Lady Jacquetta to whom he bowed and said, "If my lady gives her permission that her ladies be Sins rather than Virtues, I can but gladly obey."

Joliffe thought that "gladly" was a deft touch. While seeming to give complete surrender, it meant that if Master Fouet hereafter suggested something counter to Lady Jacquetta's wish about anything, she should see him doing it only as someone careful in his work and duty, not as a resentful foe. Certainly Lady Jacquetta's smile and accepting nod were his reward now as she said, "I do give my permission, Master Fouet."

General merriment among the women answered that, and across the room Guillemete, who had been standing with a long swathe of rose-pink draped over her shoulder, did a happy twirl, moving from in front of the woman who had been kneeling behind her.

Perrette.

Or was she?

For a moment Joliffe was unsure, the difference was so great between the woman at Master Doncaster's, strong even in her pain, and this mouse in a dull gown and apron, a simple headkerchief over her hair, and her lips pursed around several pins as she put out a protesting hand in perforced silent protest after Guillemete.

"Guillemete," Lady Jacquetta said. "Stay still for Perrette. How can she work if you dance about?"

Laughing, Guillemete twirled back into Perrette's reach, and a thin, aged woman Joliffe had not noted before among the welter of cloth and other women said, "Thank you, your grace."

At a guess, she was the sempster who would oversee the coming gown-making, Joliffe supposed. Then Perrette was . . . ?

Master Fouet made a small gesture toward the doorway

and said, "My lady, I will want a different speech to try your women's voices on. If your grace will pardon me, I will go for it."

"Of course," Lady Jacquetta said graciously. "Pray, go."

"And might Master Ripon come with me?"

Lady Jacquetta waved them both away with a smiling nod and was turning to the cloth merchant, saying, "Now, Master Labbat . . ." as Joliffe followed the choirmaster out of the room.

He was half-glad to be out of there, half-wary of Master Fouet, and indeed once in the gallery and well away from being overheard, the choirmaster turned on him, pointing a shaking finger back toward the parlor while exclaiming, "That's what I found when I came there. They were already planning all those colors for *Virtues*!"

"Why shouldn't a Virtue be colorful?" Joliffe asked, honestly curious. "Virtues have a hard time enough holding out against all the delights of Sins without being dull to look at, too."

"But they aren't going to be colorful now! Now the women are going to be Sins!"

"But that means you can have the Virtues all in white after all, just as you want," Joliffe pointed out. "Or—" He stopped himself. He did not mean to become part of this. It was not his business to become part of this. But the words kept coming. "Or they could be all in white and *gold*, carrying golden spears. And if there were some way to have the points of the spears flaming . . ."

Master Fouet went from harassed to suddenly excited. "Yes! Flaming spears. That would be something. Yes." His hand clamped down on Joliffe's arm. "Have you any thought about Lord Justice and Lady Wisdom? Here's what seemed possible to me—"

Joliffe had the sudden and terrible sense that he had yet again opened his mouth one time too many.

He finally escaped from Master Fouet's eagerness by claiming need to return to his rightful duties, and the rest of his day went well enough. Except for the tedium of it, his work was not burdensome; he had time to think of other things while he did it, and the woman Perrette was among his thoughts, although he did not know what to think of her, the difference was so great between his first seeing of her and today's. But then look at the difference between what *he* seemed, sitting here at this desk, and who he was. Except he was both, because he was not *seeming* to do a secretary's duties; he was doing them. So he was the Joliffe who walked England's roads as a player, and the Joliffe who was learning a spy's skills here in Rouen, *and* the Joliffe who was sitting at this desk, quietly at work over letters and accounts. As with music, someone who was a single note would be a dull thing. But—as with music— the mingled notes should make a pleasing whole. Else they were a pointless jangling.

It was all very well to be curious about the woman Perrette and the seeming jangle between the two ways he had seen her, but he was not yet sure even about his own notes—whether or not their present jangling would some- day make a whole.

With that uncertainty in mind, he gave the day's end over to thoroughly being John Ripon, refusing George's and Estienne's efforts to persuade him out to a tavern with all of John Ripon's regret and hesitance, and instead spending the evening playing games of draughts with Cauvet and several others in the great hall. He made a point of complaining about how sore he was from his time with Master Doncaster yesterday (although he was not so sore as he claimed to be) and showed off John Ripon's new dagger. That drew laughter and jibing about having a "pig-sticker" of a dagger, and his feeble protest that, "Well, better to have it than not," brought more laughter at him.

All in all, he thought that by evening's end John Ripon was considered quite a fool, if not an outright coward. Poor John Ripon, he thought as he was going bedward. If the fellow did not annoy him so much, he would have felt very sorry for him.

Chapter 14

The days after that were an unsettling mix of ordinary and not. Mostly, it was work at his desk, with occasional need to consult with one or another of the household officers over some small matter or, more rarely, with Lady Jacquetta herself. He avoided doing the latter when he could, wary of being drawn into anything about the play that seemed to have taken over her chambers and her demoiselles' lives. Twice when he went to her, both parlor and bedchamber were over-filled by the necessities of the Sins' bright gowns, the sempster there with scissors and pins, and Perrette on her knees, basting the hem of Ydoine's gown the first time and Marie's gown the next.

Each of the ladies now had her Sin, while the youths chosen from both households to be Virtues seemed to have been let off most of their other duties so they might learn their parts, which seemed to require they keep close company with Lady Jacquetta's demoiselles. At least they certainly were one afternoon when Joliffe went with a question about a plan to drain some Northamptonshire acreage, wondering how Lady Jacquetta was expected to make sensible decisions about land she knew nothing about—although he understood why her steward in England was hesitant to make them completely on his own—and found Sins and Virtues sitting in their pairs around the parlor, heads close together as they supposedly memorized their speeches with each other under M'dame's sharply watchful gaze from the bedchamber doorway.

Catching words being said by a sandy-haired youth near him, Joliffe judged he was Generosity, which meant Blanche, now answering him, was Greed; and away in a corner, Guillemete was waving a fist in a way that suggested she was Wrath, so Alain, there with her, must be Patience, the unsuitableness of both momentarily diverting Joliffe. The only pairing he knew without guessing was that of Sir Richard and Alizon as Lord Justice and Lady Wisdom, and he was somewhat surprised to see they were not sitting together. Instead, she was with the squire Remon Durevis and just putting a hand over her mouth, to cover laughter at something he must have said, while Sir Richard sat with Lady Jacquetta at the window, where she looked to be helping him learn his words. She was watching a paper on her lap, and he was muttering toward the ceiling, his eyes tightly shut as if his words might be written on the inside of his eyelids.

Sitting on cushions near the hearth, the demoiselle Marie and the well-favored youth with whom she was partnered leaned nearer each other with a shared warm look that had nothing to do with anything Joliffe had written between a Sin and a Virtue. As M'dame glided forward from the doorway, Marie and the youth sat back from each other, abruptly intent on the pages they held, and M'dame shifted her course to come to Joliffe. "You have need to speak with my lady?" she asked quietly.

"If I may. The matter is not urgent."

"Neither is any of this," M'dame returned.

At the window, Lady Jacquetta reached out a forefinger and gently touched the back of Sir Richard's hand. His eyes flew open and to her face, his own face going scarlet.

M'dame, who maybe saw it from the corner of her eye, left Joliffe, crossed to Lady Jacquetta and said something at which Lady Jacquetta immediately beckoned for Joliffe to come forward. He did, thinking M'dame did well to keep her sharp-eyed watch here in the close-confines of a young and widowed duchess' household, where too much could grow that should not.

In his own time, he continued to avoid Estienne's attempts at "friendship" as much as he might, and once found chance to ask Master Wydeville about the possibility of a more skillful spy hidden behind Estienne, but for answer got only a level look and, "That would be something for you to find out," leaving him uncertain whether such a finding out was a challenge to discover the unknown or a test to see if he could learn what Master Wydeville already knew.

Either way, it gave an edge to his growing awareness of how much happened under the smoothly running surface of things among the double households' scores of people that he did not understand and probably altogether missed.

What no one could miss was the steady flow of reports and rumors of what was happening—or said to be happening—or feared to be happening—in the rest of the world beyond Rouen's walls. None of it was good, so far as Joliffe could tell, although he did hear someone among the men gathered to dinner one mid-day in the great hall dismiss the rumors that Paris was dangerously full of unrest with a laugh and, "It's Paris! It would hardly be Paris if there weren't troubles there!"

One evening during those days he went openly to Master Doncaster's house for a weapons lesson. Somewhat early, he found the loose-limbed son of a Rouen craftsman having his own lesson. Joliffe gathered it was far from the youth's first, but Master Doncaster set them to try each other's skill with wooden daggers, and Joliffe's first wariness turned to pity as it became quickly plain the youth had no instinct at all for fighting nor much grasp of what Master Doncaster had surely tried to teach him. Despite that, at the end of their short bout, the boy said, panting and pleased, "That went well, didn't it? I did well, didn't I? Did better, anyway."

"No," Master Doncaster returned bluntly. "You did not. Nor do I think you ever will. Tell your father there will be no more lessons."

The boy's face darkened into scowling anger. "I'll tell him," he snapped while snatching his doublet and cloak from the bench, and flung over a shoulder as he started down the stairs, "Then I'll make him send me to Master Walters. *He'll* be able to teach me since *you* can't."

Master Doncaster waited while he thundered down the stairs and slammed out the front door, then said grimly, "If he ever goes into a true fight, he'll be dead before he's struck three blows. Unless he meets someone as bad as he is. Then he may last six or seven." He turned a hard eye on Joliffe. "You, on the other hand, went into that fight warily. Why?"

"Because I didn't know how well he fought. I thought I'd best learn before I gave my own skill away."

"Not so bad a way to go into a fight, yes," Master Doncaster granted. He took up the youth's abandoned wooden dagger. "Now let's see to getting you good enough you won't have too much worry that way because you'll have your man dead before he's trouble."

A few days of good weather brought a messenger from England with general news including, finally, word the duke of York was to be the new governor. "Young for it," was about half of what Joliffe heard. That was balanced by those who remembered when he had been in Normandy for the king's French coronation six years ago, and how well Bedford had thought of him then.

Either way, on the whole there was simply plain relief to have the matter settled and, "All we need now is for him to get here, with a sizable army at his back," George said.

Among the letters in the messenger's bag were several concerning Lady Jacquetta's English holdings. Those came to Master Ripon, and after consulting the account rolls in his keeping, Joliffe went to see if he could have word with Lady Jacquetta about some matters in them. He found her in the chapel, watching practice for the play, and he knew he should withdraw, bring his question to her later and elsewhere. But he stayed, watching, too, envisioning how Basset would have made a shining, living whole out of the wealth of words, people, and rich garb that Master Fouet had here. The choirmaster was doing well enough, from what Joliffe saw, but did he really think the Virtues were such dull things they should move with the dignity of wooden poles on stiff legs? Speaking for himself, if he were a Sin, Virtues like that were the last things in God's creation to which he would give way. And if the demoiselle Isabelle giggled one more time when it was her turn to speak . . .

Better this was Master Fouet's task than his, Joliffe thought, and went away. He would after all consult with Lady Jacquetta later.

By the morrow's mid-afternoon he had all the letters' business sorted to satisfaction and the rough drafts of the answers made, and when he was summoned to Master Wydeville, he left his desk with alacrity, hoping Master Wydeville had something of interest for him to do.

Unfortunately, it seemed not. Master Wydeville merely asked for report of how he—how Master Ripon—was doing with his work and if he was become at ease in the household and in Rouen. Joliffe, on John Ripon's behalf, answered that he was doing well, was well content.

"And keeping sober?" Master Wydeville asked.

Joliffe hung his head. "Mostly," he muttered. "All but—once." If only the time he had feigned it at the Crescent Moon was counted and not the twice he had deliberately become somewhat "unsteady" in the hall.

As if to be beyond hearing of his clerk Pierres pen-scratching across paper on the chamber's far side, Master Wydeville gestured for Joliffe to come aside to the window. There, as far from any door as from Pierres, Master Wydeville said very quietly, "You're doing well, both at seeming John Ripon and at your lessons at Master Doncaster's, both with weapons and the maps. Tell me the way from here to Honfleur."

Joliffe did.

"From here to Paris," Master Wydeville said.

Joliffe did, with only one confusion that he sorted for himself.

"And from Dover to Winchester?" Master Wydeville asked, because a map of England had become part of Joliffe's lessons, too.

Joliffe answered that most easily, and when he had done, Master Wydeville nodded in moderate approval and said, "Good enough. You will continue that learning. This evening, though, I'd have you go to Master Doncaster's to begin your study of ciphers. Can you get away to that without trouble?"

"I'm to go out after supper with George and some of the others, now Shrovetide is started. There'll be crowds in the street here as much as in England?" These being the last few days before Ash Wednesday, folk generally crammed as much excess into them as might be before Lent with its fasting and penance began.

Master Wydeville nodded agreement, and Joliffe said, "Then I should be able to 'lose' myself and go to Master Doncaster's."

"By the back way, not the front this time."

"Yes."

Master Wydeville turned away from the window, raising his voice to normal pitch as he said sternly, for anyone to overhear who might, "Then see to it you remember it, Master Ripon, and keep better rein on yourself hereafter. Her grace is pleased with your work and with this play you made for her. I do not want her *dis*pleased by anything otherwise you do."

Joliffe gave a jerking bow suitable to John Ripon's chastened unhappiness, muttered, "Yes, sir," and at Master Wydeville's dismissing gesture hurried—head bunched between his shoulders—back to his desk.

He did not in the least mind losing his companions that evening. George and Bernard were not the most diverting of men, and Estienne was tedious. Nor was losing them any harder than he had thought it would be. People—many already masked—were out in milling crowds, looking for sport and pleasure by flaring torchlight and pole-hung lanterns. Shops were open and all manner of pastimes were happening at every widening of a street as well as in the marketplace below the cathedral's west front where rough booths were set up for the selling of festive foods and, most especially, much ales, beers, and wines.

That was where George and the others headed first, and there that Joliffe chose to lose them, becoming apparently so interested in watching a juggler of firebrands that he seemed not to note being left behind. He trusted that when he looked around and around, unable to find them, he gave the seeming of someone somewhat alarmed to find himself abandoned. On the chance they might yet see him, he pretended to look for them while carefully going other than the way they had disappeared into the crowd. He twisted in and out of the crowd and between and around booths until he was certain no one could have kept him in sight and only then made for the back way to Master Doncaster's.

Even along it a few lanterns had been hung tonight, but Master Doncaster's gate was in shadow. The latch gave in well-oiled silence to his pull and he let himself into the garden, shut the gate silently behind him, and went up the path through darkness to the rear door. His careful tap there was shortly answered by someone who barely opened the door and asked, "Who?"

"Master Ripon," he said back softly and was let into another darkness, until the door was shut behind him and whoever was there put aside a curtain hung across the passageway perhaps a yard in from the door. He understood that was to lessen the escape of light that would mark anyone's coming or going from the house, and saw now it was the servant girl called Jeanne who had let him in.

Smiling, she led him to the kitchen, where warmth and the hearthfire's leaping light met him. Matilde was scrubbing the top of the worktable with the vigor of a woman devoted to cleanliness, and Jeanne returned to the pot she had been scrubbing in a basin of water set on a low stool. Beside the hearth on another low stool, Perrette sat, her long hair loose over one shoulder, her head bent to one side to let the dark, damp fall of it hang free almost to the floor, the firelight shining auburn through it while she slowly drew a wooden comb down it.

Matilde was laughing at something Perrette must have just said. Both women were smiling as they looked toward him. "Ah!" Perrette said lightly, "The duchess' English secretary who wrote the play that is giving us all so much trouble."

The still face and downcast eyes she had at the *hôtel* were gone, and as he shed his cloak and cap onto the bench beside the table, Joliffe met her light mockery with a bow and, "Ah! The sempster's humble helper, who works to cover in beauty the error of my ways."

She laughed. "My cousin does indeed kindly let me work for her when I am in Rouen."

"Nor asks no questions when you suddenly take away to parts unknown," Matilde said comfortably.

"An excellent cousin," Perrette confirmed.

"How does your side?" Joliffe asked.

Perrette narrowed her eyes, considering him with sudden sharpness. Then her face cleared. "Yes. That's why you are familiar. You were here that night. I remember." She seemed unbothered by how much of her he must have seen that night. "I do well as long as I remember not to move much or suddenly. The bruise fades. How goes your dagger-work?"

"I have my own bruises now," he said ruefully.

"He will have more," Matilde said. She was rubbing the table dry with a towel now. "Master Doncaster means to try him with long staffs next time they work together."

Joliffe made the pained sound expected of him, and all three women laughed at him, as he had meant them to; but an uncle had taught to Joliffe and his brothers the use of the long staff as a weapon, so he had hope he might not gather too many bruises while relearning his lessons.

Jeanne was setting the pot to dry on the hearth as Matilde finished with the table. "There," said Matilde. "Time we should be gone, Jeanne. Otherwise we are like to miss all the sport." Which was a jest; high merriment would go on in the streets until dawn, likely, curfew forgotten. The two of them took their cloaks from pegs by the door. Perrette and Joliffe bade them farewell, and when they were gone, he went to sit on his heels at the other end of the hearth from her, holding his hands out to the fire and trying not to watch her combing, combing her shining hair.

She was watching him, though, and smiled sideways at him as she said, "I took this chance to wash my hair. It's nearly dry. Then you'll have your cipher lesson. Do you object to being taught by a woman?"

He did not hide his surprise. "No. Not when she knows things that I do not."

"You think I know things you do not?" she asked lightly.

Remembering the pale leather sheath empty on her forearm and her simple acceptance that she had probably killed a man, he said, "Yes." Then added, to shut out that thought a little, "How to learn Richemont is bringing Bretons against us, for one thing." Emboldened by the twitch of a smile from her, he added, "But—um—who is Richemont?"

She laughed outright, lifted and turned her head, swung her hair to hang over her other shoulder, and went on combing it while she answered, "He is a little man, both of body and soul, but he struts big and talks bigger, and there are those who are fooled by that. He is brother to the duke of Brittany, and a betrayer of oaths. Once upon a time he was England's ally for a while, but he quarreled with the duke of Bedford when Bedford would not give him command of English troops at Richemont's demand—Bedford was no fool, you see. So now he is the Dauphin Charles' constable for all the Armagnac armies."

"Why hasn't he yet invaded out of Brittany?"

"Probably because there has been an unexpected great strengthening of Norman garrisons along the Breton border. Unhappily, that likely accounts for why he has turned all his heed and the Armagnacs toward Paris."

Her easy knowledge impressed him. He would have liked to ask more, but she straightened, tossed her hair behind her, and looked at him while asking, "So. How do you like the rich life of a duchess' clerk?"

"I might die of screaming idleness if that was all I was doing."

Merriment gleamed in her eyes. "As I would if I were only a sempster's helper. You were a player before?"

Although he kept his voice light, he answered with a vehement urge to protect that part of himself, "I'm still a player."

"Of a different sort, yes," Perrette agreed easily.

"Of both sorts," Joliffe said, maybe more firmly than the moment needed, because Perrette regarded him in considering silence for a moment, before saying, "Time to begin your lesson, I think," and gathered herself to stand up.

Joliffe rose more quickly and held out a hand to help her. She paused as if in surprise, staring at his hand, then took it and let him pull her to her feet. Nor did she let loose of his hand immediately but stood gazing into his eyes for a thoughtful moment before loosing him and turning away to the table, leaving him shaken without being certain why.

From that moment, though, she was entirely business, and his lesson in ciphers—both the making of them and the reading of them—went quickly and well in the candle-light. But she left her hair unbound, and the lavender smell of it wafting to him whenever she turned her head was a distraction against which he had to set his mind. As she well knew, he thought.

But time came when she straightened from the table and began plaiting her hair while saying, "There. That is enough for tonight. You do well. Master Wydeville will be pleased. Now I say we should forget work and see what mischief and bonchief we can join in the streets."

He could think of somewhere better than the streets to go with her, but since he had no idea where her bed was and assuredly could not take her to his, he asked, "Should we be seen together? Being what we are and you . . . being known?"

Still plaiting her hair, Perrette slid from the end of the bench and went to one of the shelves on the shadowed wall. She paused to tie the end of her plait with something waiting there, then took other things from the shelf, one in each hand, and turned back to Joliffe, holding them up and saying with laughter, "That is what masks are for."

Chapter 15

Perrette proved excellent company for *carnaval*. With her for his guide, Joliffe doubted they missed many of the better pleasures possible in Rouen that night. Toward the end they even joined in a long line of other mostly-masked merry-makers snaking in clumsy-footed dance along streets until the dance fell apart from its own weight and weariness, leaving the merry-makers to stagger, stroll, or stumble their own ways away. He and Perrette, laughing, swung together into a shadowed corner where two house-fronts met unevenly, and all unplanned—although not un-thought of—he pressed her back against the wall, and his mouth found hers below the edges of their half-masks. She hotly returned his kiss, pulling him tightly to her with her arms low around his hips so that surely she felt his swelling desire for her. He slipped a hand free to find one of her breasts, and she did not resist that either.

It was when he slid that hand down, wanting to fumble her skirts up and out of his way that she freed her mouth from his and said, "No." Not with the weak, unwilling protest of a woman who would rather say "yes," but firmly like someone who meant "No. And don't make me say it again."

He drew back, both because he had never forced a woman and with the wariness of knowing the sheath along her forearm was no longer empty. But he asked, "Is that 'no' forever? Or 'no' only for now?"

He took it as a hope-filled sign that she laughed, answered, "'No' for tonight," and lightly kissed him.

Then she whispered in his ear, "Name for me the towns between here and Caen."

His lust-muddled, wine-fuddled brain did a body's equivalent of stumble and fall on its face, but he picked it up, dusted it off, and answered, and for a wonder answered right, so that Perrette smiled at him and said, "Well done. It is good to know you can keep your wits about you under, um"—she gestured delicately toward his groin—"pressure."

"That," he returned with mock sternness, "is cruel."

"It is," she agreed lightly. "Now I will see you in sight of the *hôtel*'s gateway and leave you there."

He did not trouble to protest that, and they parted as she had chosen, with a final kiss to warm him the last lonely way to his bed.

Curfew held no more for household than for town during *carnaval*; he was not among the last among his fellows to come stumbling to bed in the dormer. Nor, judging by the groans, was he the only one to awaken with aching head and too little sleep in the morning. It was just as well that today and tomorrow not much in the way of work was expected of most of the household. These last days before Lent were the time for eating and doing all the things that would have to be given up until Easter. Or should be given up—there being a strong difference between "should" and "did," and he had noted often enough before now that those who made the most of Shrovetide's license were all too often those who least troubled themselves to heed Lent's prohibitions afterward.

On his own side, he had yet to decide what he would give up this year. A player's life was usually lived so scant of food and other things that there was little left that could be given up for Lent. This year, living in plenty as he was, he would have to decide on something to forego, he supposed.

Then there was the matter of confession. When time for it came, what was he to confess? His lust toward Perrette was straight-forward and ordinary enough, but the constant lying he had been living in since answering Bishop Beaufort's summons was another matter. These past weeks he had been living by lies but could hardly confess to them here. Was lying maybe not a sin if done at a bishop's order and for good, not ill? Or if it was a sin nonetheless, would Bishop Beaufort give him remission for it later, and would that suffice to compensate for failing to confess it now?

All that was a problem for later, Joliffe decided. Today and tomorrow were holiday and not to be wasted. Because surely waste was a sin, too?

Having had enough of the streets for a while, he chose to stay in the *hôtel*. Still in the year's mourning for the duke of Bedford, it was quieter than it would have been in other years. Bishop Louys had even ruled against card games, but the long tables in the hall were left up, for chess and other games on boards to be played, and rich foods and drink in plenty were being constantly set out, although George did object to a sugar subtlety shaped into the likeness of a fish. "We'll see enough of fish in Lent," he complained.

In mid-afternoon, about the time practice for the play began in the chapel, Joliffe's late night and short sleep caught up to him. Tired of talk and games and even of eating, he retreated, with a bowl of wine, from the great hall up the stairs to the long gallery. It being chill and without pastimes, he had the place to himself. Content with the wine and the white fluffs of cloud drifting across the winter-pale sky for company, he was just settled on a wide windowsill when M'dame came out of the great chamber. For respect's sake, he immediately stood up.

He did not suppose she was looking for him, but she said sharply, "Good. That saves finding you. Come."

She turned back through the doorway. Surprised but perforce obedient, Joliffe followed her. She led him back up to Lady Jacquetta's rooms. Foulke, on duty at the door there, looked a surprised question at Joliffe as he passed. Joliffe could only answer with a shrug and a shake of his head.

"Close the door," M'dame ordered.

He did, then followed her across the parlor and into the bedchamber. With everyone gone to the practice in the chapel and only Lady Jacquetta's dogs there, curled together on a cushion near the hearth, the rooms were strange in their emptiness. "You must go to my lady at once," M'dame said, still sharply. She snatched up a cloak lying across a chair and thrust it at him. "Here. She's in the garden. Go to her."

Catching the cloak awkwardly one-handed, Joliffe repeated, bewildered, "Go to her?"

Already going away from him toward a door in the chamber's far corner, M'dame snapped, "In the garden. Yes."

Joliffe set the wine aside on a chest and followed her, more confused by the moment. "What? Why?"

"She must come back here. Immediately. You are not to say that, but you are to bring her back here. Without delay. Go." M'dame jerked the door open to shadows and a tight curve of stairway. *"Go."*

Joliffe went.

The stairs—only a little lighted through a few narrow windows—went both upward and down. Up would be to a roof-walk, Joliffe supposed. The first door he came to downward had to be to the grand chambers, and he guessed the next would be to the gardens, then found that it had better be because the stairs did not go beyond it, and let himself out, onto a graveled path and into the cold cut of the wind. Driven by M'dame's urging, he had moved fast but stopped now, both to put on the cloak and to take chance to look around him. He had never been in the gardens, only seen them from upper windows, enough to know they were large and beautifully made. Besides the graveled, open paths between presently winter-bare beds, there was an ever-green laurel arbor along two sides, giving cool privacy on warm summer days but now probably chill and dank under its thick-growing leaves. Along it, on the garden's far side was a greensward that in summer was surely a daisy-meadow where ladies would sit on cushions and pluck flowers from the grass to make flower-crowns; or it could be used for ball-games of various sorts, or strolling, or dancing. It ended in a small grove of slender trees between it and a high brick wall of what Joliffe guessed was an enclosed smaller garden, meant for lords' and ladies' particular privacy.

Whatever the garden was like in summer, today with the wind and cold it was no pleasant place to be. Was it fear for Lady Jacquetta's health that had M'dame so urgent? Or . . .

Joliffe saw the more likely answer. Well away across the garden, their backs to him, walking along one of the paths, were a woman and a man. They were both in long cloaks, but she surely had to be Lady Jacquetta, while the red hair showing under the man's hat told almost as surely he was Remon Durevis.

Only the two of them and no one else.

While all her ladies and most of the squires of her household were playing at being Sins and Virtues, Lady Jacquetta had taken this foolish chance to walk alone with a man. No wonder that M'dame wanted them interrupted.

Joliffe had never supposed Lady Jacquetta so attached to
her much-older husband that her heart might not turn to
someone nearer her own age, given the chance, but that
did not lessen her foolishness in inviting scandal this way.
M'dame's alarm was justified. Probably she had been ordered not to accompany her lady and was using him instead to interrupt this indiscretion.

Joliffe made a wordless, angry noise in his throat, not
liking to be in the middle of this—or anywhere near it,
come to that—and set off after the pair. With the wind
blowing from them to him, they did not hear him behind
them on the path, but as he neared them, Remon's voice
was carried to him clearly, insisting with incautious force,
". . . a thing you must share with someone. You have to
know I'm your heart-friend in this."

"There is no 'this' to share," Lady Jacquetta answered,
somewhat sharply.

"My eyes tell me differently."

"Your eyes need care then," Lady Jacquetta said more
sharply. "Remember, there are those who warn me against
what they see about you."

"My lady." Remon's voice was suddenly melting with
warmth. "If I thought there was any hope . . ."

Joliffe, so near that he had to say something, threw himself forward into a headlong walk just short of a run and
called out, "My lady! I must speak with you. Before it's
too late!"

Lady Jacquetta and Remon jerked around. Joliffe pulled
up barely in time not to run into them, gasping for breath as
if he had been running. He hurriedly bowed and burst out
as he straightened, "It's Master Fouet, my lady! He's ruining the play. You must stop him. I pray you stop him!"

"Master Ripon," Lady Jacquetta said coldly. "Control
yourself. What are you saying?"

"Master Fouet. I didn't know all he was doing! The
words, my lady! With all he's done, no one will heed my

words. The dancing and . . . and . . . and flaming spears . . . and . . . and . . . everything!" Joliffe, out of invention, let John Ripon's frustration break down from fumbled words to helpless hand-waving.

Lady Jacquetta snapped, "Master Ripon, it is somewhat late to be finding fault with what Master Fouet has done. It is *very* late. It is *too* late."

"But I did not see until now," Joliffe protested. He went down on one knee, the better to plead. If he had had a cap, he would have snatched it off and wrung it between his hands. He wrung his hands instead, protesting, "With all the music, all the dancing, no one is going to hear my words at all!"

"By Saint Denis," Remon burst out. "Who cares about your words? My lady has the right of it. It's too late to do anything. Let it go, you fool."

Lady Jacquetta took a step forward, laid a hand on Joliffe's shoulder, and said, suddenly mild, "Master Ripon, *I* care about your words. But indeed it is too late. You must let it go. I am sorry for it. Will it help if, while we watch it tomorrow, you sit beside me?"

Honestly moved by that kindness, Joliffe bowed his head and murmured, "To be so honored would wipe away all my griefs, not merely for the play."

Lady Jacquetta took her hand away with a light laugh. "You are on your way to being more a courtier than a secretary, Master Ripon. Please, stand up."

As he obeyed, Remon said to her, mildly chiding, "You've given him M'dame's place. Will she mind?"

Her voice sharp with sudden malice, Lady Jacquetta replied, "No. Because it is *your* place I've given him."

To judge by Remon's abruptly widened eyes and immediate scowl, that was a thrust that went home. Lady Jacquetta, seeming not to see, went on, calm again, "It's time we went in. Master Ripon, you should not have come out without a hat. You will take a chill."

But she did not bid him return ahead of them to the house, instead let him follow as she and Remon went the straightest way back to the house, up the stairs, and into her bedchamber, where M'dame was sitting on the chest at the bedfoot, an embroidery frame standing in front of her and a threaded needle in her hand. But Joliffe would have wagered that until a few moments ago she had been at the window, watching. As it was, she stood up as they came in, said to Lady Jacquetta, "You endured the wind longer than I thought you would, my lady," then with surprise, "Master Ripon?"

"He came to me with worry over his play," Lady Jacquetta said easily. Her two little dogs woke and came running to her, the smaller one yipping its delight. She loosened her cloak and let it drop. Remon caught it as it fell, while she scooped up dogs, one on either arm, and went on to M'dame, "Sadly, I could give him no comfort except promise he might sit beside me when we watch his play tomorrow. Now I think I will rest a while."

To that more-than-hint, she added a dismissing nod at Remon and Joliffe. They both bowed, Remon laid the cloak on the bed, and Joliffe stood aside from the door to the parlor for Remon to leave first. With neither look nor word at him, Remon did, and Joliffe took his time shutting the bedchamber's door behind them both, giving the squire time to be well away, wanting no word with him if he could help it. Remon seemed to be of the same mind; he had stalked across and out of the parlor by the time Joliffe turned from the door.

Joliffe took the chance to leave the borrowed cloak draped over a chair before leaving the room in turn, almost wishing the questions he had gathered in the past half of an hour were as easily left behind him. Oddest among them was an almost-certainty that Lady Jacquetta had been pleased at his interruption. Pleased—or relieved? But if she had not wanted to be with Remon, why had she been?

Or had her displeasure come after she and Remon were alone together? From something the squire had done or said? If her displeasure went deep enough, M'dame would be relieved to know it.

He encountered Lady Jacquetta's demoiselles in the gallery, returning from their practice. He stood aside with a bow to let them pass, grateful they were too busily talking happily among themselves to spare him a word. He was about to start down the stairs to the great hall when he had to stand aside again, this time for Alizon and Sir Richard, coming well behind the others and in head-close talk, Alizon saying as they passed him, ". . . if we were hand in hand, to show better we . . ."

Something about the play, Joliffe thought as he went down the stairs, intent on finding wine in the great hall.

he went out that evening with George and the others, and this time did not lose them in the joyous streets, so that the next day he and his head were glad to lie a-bed as long as might be, it being the last of Shrovetide and full holiday. Once he was up, though, he had full share of Shrovecakes and all else, and then it was evening and time for the play. In other years there would surely have been an array of guests—lords and officials whom the duke of Bedford wished to honor or whose company he enjoyed—but this was a mourning household, its pleasures subdued and the company lessened even more by Bishop Louys having gone with many of his men to dine with the archbishop of Rouen, afterward to join his fellow-churchmen for the evening's ceremonies at the cathedral.

Lady Jacquetta had dined in the hall, though, and lingered on the dais afterward while the trestle tables were cleared away. To the eye, it was a glooming gathering there—all that black mourning garb—but judging by the busy garble of talk and bursts of laughter among those waiting for the play, humours were high. Bright-burning torches were being brought in and set in the high holders along the walls, blotting out the last faint glow of sunset beyond the hall's tall windows. Lady Jacquetta's ladies had disappeared at the meal's end, along with their counterparts in the play, leaving her unaccustomedly alone as she settled again into her tall-backed chair that had been brought forward to the dais' edge. Two lesser chairs were set on either side of it, for those privileged to sit beside her. Other people allowed the dais would stand, while most of the household would draw back against the walls, to leave the center of the hall clear for the players.

Until yesterday, the best Joliffe had expected was to stand on the dais. Now, though, as the household's musicians began to gather at either side of their gallery above the screens passage at the hall's far end, Lady Jacquetta settled into her chair and gestured graciously for M'dame to sit on her right and Joliffe on her left. He was aware of stirrings and whispers as he bowed and obeyed; managed not to see Remon Durevis despite knowing he was near, but glimpsed Master Woodville raising questioning eyebrows at him from beyond M'dame.

Unable to answer, Joliffe settled for sitting stiffly, to seem as if John Ripon were both aware of the honor done him and uncomfortably uncertain what to do with it. Which fairly well matched what Joliffe himself felt about it.

Master Fouet entered the hall through the screen's wide doorway below the minstrels' gallery. He carried a staff tall as himself, and several paces into the hall stopped and rapped the staff's end sharply against the stone floor. All through the hall, talk and laughter rippled to silence, save for some shuffling of feet and a few brief coughs. Master Fouet made a bow toward Lady Jacquetta and declared, his voice clear and carrying, "My great lady, my lords and ladies, gentlemen and gentlewomen all, we come tonight —"

Joliffe had not troubled to write this opening, supposing Master Fouet knew best the greeting for such a company, and surely the choirmaster did it gracefully, asking briefly for everyone's good will for the play, then drawing aside and rapping his staff on the floor again, sign for the musicians to break into lightsome music and the Sins to sweep into the hall, three pairs of lovely demoiselles in bright gowns, each carrying a gold-shining wand, their long hair loose, their heads crowned with narrow bands of gold. Tall Ydoine as Pride came alone and last, with a somewhat larger wand and crown and little bells hung from her sleeves. The other Sins stood aside to let her pass between them, curtsying to her as she did, to show Pride's preeminence among Sins.

After that, they made their speeches while weaving through a simple dance. Then the six young men as the Virtues entered, again two by two, likewise crowned but with bigger golden bands, and carrying tall spears. They were wearing their own bright doublets of the household's non-mourning days, with sleeveless tabards of white samite over them, cut very full and gathered at the shoulders to fall in wide folds to almost the floor. Only Humility, as Pride's opposite, was robed entirely in white.

Joliffe could not help thinking that keeping all those yards of white cloth clean must have been a challenge right up to the moment the players entered the hall.

The Virtues danced and made their speeches more solemnly than the Sins had. With everything turned into French, Joliffe could not be sure how much was as he had written it, but what he understood sounded close enough, and while Basset might have done more with all of it, what weaknesses there were in the devising were well-countered by the splendor of gowns, crowns, spears, and wands sheened and shining in the torchlight. And all the dancing was gracefully done. If nothing else, these high-born young were able to move with a confidence and grace through the dances' careful patterns, and somehow Master Fouet had convinced them of the need to say their words clearly and loud enough. Surprisingly, Guillemete as Wrath was best among the Sins, playing her part with better seeming than anyone else. Alain as her opposite was somewhat too stiff, but in the almost-ritual of the play it hardly mattered. The Sins confronted the Virtues, and they "battled" in graceful dance, striking wands and spears—that after all did not flame, Joliffe was relieved to see—together in careful "fight," until abruptly two trumpeters stood up at either end of the gallery, swung up long, straight trumpets, and played a flourish that brought the Sins and Virtues all to a frozen halt, staring up at them.

From the shadowed rear of the gallery a man and woman came forward into light so suddenly much brighter that Joliffe guessed somewhere up there lanterns had just been unshielded toward them. They were robed all in cloth-of-gold that shone as if with inward captured fire, wore tall, jewel-flashing crowns, and held between them—the woman's hand above the man's—a single, heavy, ornate scepter. The trumpets ceased, and with surely every gaze in the hall fixed on them, the man declared in boldly ringing voice, "I am Lord Justice, come to end this fray."

Lighter-voiced but as bold and clear, the woman declared, "And I am Lady Wisdom, come to bring peace beyond this day."

They were only Sir Richard and Alizon, but in the wonder that sometimes came when the playing went true, for the on-lookers they had in that moment the true seeming of Lord Justice and Lady Wisdom speaking from high heaven, and while Joliffe silently acknowledged Master Fouet's skill at spectacle, Lord Justice spoke at the Sins, condemning them. With heads bowed in humiliation they sank to the floor, bright skirts spreading around them. The Virtues, straight as the spears, their white robes shining in the torchlight, stood over them, triumphant.

And some slight movement from Lady Jacquetta made

Joliffe slide his eyes sideways without shifting his head. She had leaned a little forward and her gaze was fixed, rapt, on the gallery. On—Joliffe tried to match her gaze—on Sir Richard. Not on "Lord Justice." No. No one had ever looked at Justice, or even justice, in the way she was looking at Sir Richard, and beyond denying he was exceedingly fine to look on there in the torchlight, in the shining splendor of his crown and golden robes.

Who, Joliffe wondered, had been foolish enough to allow such a man into the household of a young widow?

Lord Justice ended his condemnation. Lady Wisdom gently and firmly bade the Sins take the Virtues for their guides and teachers, not their foes. Pride and Humility acknowledged peace with one another and on behalf of all their followers. The Virtues helped the Sins to rise and joined hands with them in a dance of accord out of the hall, while Lord Justice and Lady Wisdom drew back into shadows and vanished, ending the play.

Chapter 16

By all the praise afterward, there was no doubt the play had been a success. For Joliffe, appreciation came foremost from Lady Jacquetta by way of words and a small but well-weighted embroidered purse pressed into his hand before she turned to Master Fouet, come to kneel in front of her. While she thanked him with another coin-weighted purse, Joliffe slipped into the shifting of household folk out of the way of servants setting up tables down the hall's middle. On a usual Shrovetide evening there would have been drinking, dancing, and loud games now. This year would of course be quieter and without dancing, and when Lady Jacquetta retired to her chambers in a while, people would be away to better merriment elsewhere; but presently the drink and food-heaped platters being set out along the tables would give merriment enough.

Having joined the elbowing toward the food and drink, Joliffe was just drawing back with a cup of wine when he caught a man saying to another as they elbowed forward in their turn, "There'll be hell to pay when my lord bishop hears about those robes."

Joliffe would have liked hearing more but was pressed away from them in the crowding, and now the Sins and Virtues were returning to the hall. Someone had seen to having the white tabards off the Virtues, leaving the men to party in their own doublets, colorful like the Sins still in their bright gowns among all the mourning-black. Sins and Virtues alike were merry with their success and ready for everyone's praise, making Joliffe smile at how openly they shared every player's belief that he was the world's center. But after all, every player *was* the world's center while he played, at least for all the lookers-on whose eyes and minds were fixed on him. The hard part was to grasp that when the play was done, the world's eyes—the world's center—shifted elsewhere. As Basset had had to point out to him in his young days as a player, "You're only of worth to them while you're being someone else. Think on that, my fine-strutting fellow. Once the play is done, you're back to being you, and you're not the center of anything. Except to yourself, of course. So if I were you, I'd make that self someone worth your while to be with and not count on the world and all."

A sharp missing of Basset panged through Joliffe. Aside from having been mad enough to become a player, Basset had been the most centered-in-the-world man Joliffe had ever known.

He caught himself up sharply. Not *had been*. Not *had known*. Somewhere Basset still was. And Rose and Ellis and Gil and Piers. Where they were or how they were he had no way of knowing, but surely they were somewhere and making merriment for someone. They still *were*, and for an unsteady moment Joliffe wished he was with them wherever they were, whatever wearily familiar work they were playing.

Someone's little finger crooked around his free hand's

little finger. Little finger to little finger was the way a pair of lovers might walk properly together, and he jerked his head around to find it was Perrette making so bold with his hand and smiling at him. She wore a plainly cut but beautifully dyed crimson gown, its neckline curved somewhat over-low, showing her white shoulders and subtly making plain the soft swell of her breasts. Only the narrowest of wimples curved under her chin, leaving her slender throat bare, and the light veil over her hair floated gently as she tilted her head, watching him enjoy all he was seeing.

Happy to let his enjoyment show, he said, "The evening has been blessed with Justice and Wisdom. Now you doubly bless it with Beauty." And more practically, "You're here to help your cousin have the players in and out of their finery."

"I am, and with the tabards folded and safely packed away, I have this while to enjoy . . ." She paused, her eyes daring him to finish the thought.

Not about to be led into libidinous hopes, Joliffe said, "My company and some ducal wine."

Perrette laughed at him and turned toward the tables. She had let go his finger, but he kept close behind her as she wove in reach of wine and a platter of meat pasties. She passed a pasty to him, took one and a cup of wine for herself, and with food and drink in hands, they drew away to a lee corner beside the screens, where they ate and drank and Perrette said, "So. Your play went well."

"It did. But why did I just hear someone say there would be hell to pay when Bishop Louys heard about the robes. Which robes? Justices's and Wisdom's?"

"Those robes indeed. They were planned to be blue embroidered with golden stars. My cousin had four women madly stitching to finish them this morning when word came that Lady Jacquetta had provided otherwise."

"Provided otherwise?" Joliffe echoed.

"Provided otherwise." Mischief sparkled in Perrette's

eyes. "Those cloth-of-gold robes they wore instead—those were the duke of Bedford's and his late wife's. Their robes of estate."

Joliffe felt his jaw start to drop and pulled it firmly closed. Robes of estate were something to be worn at a coronation, or for the reception of a king, or at a royal wedding. Not . . . Almost choking on his surprise, he asked, "Who was mad enough to let her give them to use in a play?"

"The question you need to ask is how she kept it secret from her uncle. Secret from everyone until it was done and too late. And how persuaded M'dame to it, too. Because M'dame would have had to know." Perrette laughed. "I would much like to hear what her uncle says to her when he does hear of it. He's here to keep everything seemly around his niece's widowhood, and yet she slides this past him easily as anything."

"If he's wise," Joliffe said, "he'll say nothing to her at all."

"True. She's galled by her life at present, I think. He'd do best not to rub the sore, lest it worsen."

Joliffe looked toward the dais. Lady Jacquetta was standing, M'dame beside her, in talk with Sir Richard and Alizon. They were no longer in the cloth-of-gold robes, only their own clothing, but the glow of the play's other-world was still on them. And on Lady Jacquetta, too, it seemed, because while Alizon and Sir Richard looked to be answering something M'dame had said, Lady Jacquetta was looking at Sir Richard in a way that made the thought cross Joliffe's mind that maybe Master Wydeville should be warned.

Of what? That Lady Jacquetta had twice now looked at his son in a way that might not be—safe? Master Wyde-ville, standing not far away on the dais with several other household officers, could see as much for himself if he looked. And if he did not see for himself, would he want to be told?

As the saying went: least said, soonest mended.

Or as Basset had once snapped at Ellis, "You can break more with your mouth than you can mend. So think before you say."

He was distracted from his thoughts by Perrette saying, "We should not be seen long together. So I am going to laugh at you and go away." And just that abruptly she did.

To anyone watching them, it would seem Joliffe must have said something that offended her. Joliffe, on his part, had no trouble looking momentarily startled at her suddenness, before shaking his head with a show of apparent disgust and heading back to the table in quest of more food and drink. Encountering Master Fouet, he took the chance to congratulate him on the play's success. Master Fouet, with the giddy air of relief at having the thing over and done with, thanked him and congratulated him back. That was all there need have been, but Joliffe took the chance to say, "You were especially fortunate in Lord Justice and Lady Wisdom. Was this their first time at such playing?"

"For the Lady Alizon, yes. But Sir Richard, no. He has done this manner of thing before now, here in the household."

Feigning light puzzlement, Joliffe said easily, "Oh. For some reason, I thought he was new to the household."

"Sir Richard? But no. He was in my lord of Bedford's household from boyhood."

Which changed the question from who had been foolish enough to let him into the young widow's household to who had been foolish enough to leave him there.

"His father being my lord of Bedford's chamberlain and all, you see," said Master Fouet.

"Ah," Joliffe said, and because someone came up then with more congratulations for Master Fouet, he slipped aside, saying no more. He looked for Perrette but she was gone, and although through the next few hours he joined in various of the games and ate and drank as well as anyone, he was glad enough when time came to go to bed.

The next day was the first of Lent, the beginning of its weeks of fasting and penance, a humbling time for considering one's sins in preparation for Easter's glories, and Joliffe went with the rest of the lesser household folk to take turn at making confession to a priest in the chapel. As usual, he found himself regretting how petty his sins of the past year had been. True, a soul could be nibbled away to damnation by many, many little sins as surely as by one or two great ones, but on the whole Joliffe thought he would prefer—if he were so stupid as not to repent at the end and be saved—to go to Hell for some great soul-shattering sin than for a clutter of small, dull ones. The trouble was that, thus far, he had never been tempted to any great sins, only paltry everyday ones, and those not so much from temptation but simply because they were almost impossible not to stumble over, being constantly in the way, like being unable to avoid every stone on a rocky road, where no matter how carefully you went, you could not help stubbing a toe once in a while. Groveling to God for the equivalent of every stubbed toe seemed hardly worth his bother.

Or God's, come to that.

But maybe that was Lent's purpose—to gather up all those toe-stubbing sins in one heap, do penance for them, and go forward with life.

Which unfortunately, inevitably, included promptly beginning to accumulate new sins. And unfortunately his present great, daily, on-going sin of lying was one he could not yet confess. Telling a priest might be safe enough, but forgiveness could not be had for a sin he meant to continue committing, and he expected to go on with his daily lying.

So he admitted to Lust, unfulfilled though it presently was, and Gluttony, which must be a common enough sin from Shrovetide, and then, for good measure, to Pride in having written last night's play. He was shriven for all

of that and given the penance of saying a rote number of
prayers on his knees in front of Saint John's altar here in
the chapel between now and Palm Sunday. Thus cleansed,
he knelt in the chapel to have a priest draw a cross in ashes
on his forehead, signifying Lent was well and truly under
way.

The while after that was, on the whole, dreary. The
short, chill days and long, cold nights gave no clear promise
that spring would ever trouble itself to come. The humours
of both households darkened, and while Joliffe was still
sometimes summoned to read aloud to Lady Jacquetta, it
was from books of devotion and saints' lives suitable to the
season. Those, being mostly meant to deepen the listeners'
sense of sin and need of penitence, did nothing to raise
anyone's spirits.

If anything passed between Lady Jacquetta and her
uncle concerning the cloth-of-gold robes, they kept it private between themselves. Likewise, Joliffe came to doubt
he had seen anything that mattered in her look at Sir Richard the play's night. He saw no more sign that anything
was changed between them, anyway, just as there was no
trace of displeasure at Remon Durevis despite her anger in
the garden that one day—unless it was that he seemed less
often at her side in the evenings and most often at Lady
Alizon's.

In like wise, Guillemete and Alain were much in each
other's company. Somewhat too much, Joliffe thought.
From what he had seen of Alain, the youth was far too
given to feeling passion for the sake of feeling passion,
rather than in anything like a true loving of the supposed
beloved. As for Guillemete, young and foolish did not always go together, but Joliffe suspected they did with her.

Still, it was for M'dame to deal with as she saw fit.
Certainly, the triflings that had grown among the other

demoiselles and youths while they played at being Sins and Virtues were faded away quickly enough under her sharp watch, and the saints knew there were matters of more urgent interest in the world than Guillemete and Alain. Despite the days remained dreary, the year was on the turn, and with the winter's harsher weather waning, no day went by without news or else rumors foaming through the household of what was going on in the wider world. The autumn-into-winter surge of Armagnacs through Normandy that had made Joliffe's arrival perilous had long since been pushed back, but it had left behind a scum of brigands infesting the countryside beyond Rouen's walls. Now, word of brigand troubles was increasing at the same time there were more reports of Armagnac raids in the east and that the Armagnac force south of the Seine was still growing, definitely swelled by Richemont and his men out of Brittany. Mixed with all that were endless rumors of troubles in Paris, although common opinion was that, at the most, the Parisians would roil up, butcher each other in the streets for a while—"the way they're always doing there," as George said—and then settle down long before any Armagnac attack came, supposing any ever did.

Generally more troubling was sure report that the duke of Burgundy was still enraged over King Henry's winter letters urging the Zealand towns to an uprising, and had sworn to siege and take Calais. For Rouen that was better news than that he meant to turn on Normandy, but it was nonetheless not good. The port of Calais, close across the Channel from Dover, had been England's wool-port and foot-hold on the continent for the reigns of five kings now, but was surrounded on its landward side by Burgundy's lands, making his threatened siege easily possible. Tavern talk had it that, "He'll be sorry if he tries it, see if he isn't," but reports varied wildly of what would be done to counter him. Either a massive force was being raised in England to come to Calais' relief, or else the lords around the king were locked in discord, with nothing going forward. There was fear the duke of York and the men he was supposed to bring into Normandy would be sent Calais-ward instead, but there was talk, too, that King Henry himself might go. Being fourteen years old, it was time he was bloodied, and why not against damned Burgundy?

Whatever happened, though, everyone agreed that men must not be drawn out of Normandy. Whether the Armagnacs meant to attack Rouen, or sweep toward Paris, or move against the Channel ports to cut off English help coming up the Seine, Normandy needed all the men it had. The most hopeful thought was doubt the Armagnacs could gather enough men to the Dauphin's impoverished cause to be a true threat in *any* direction, but when George said as much in a tavern-gathered group, someone else said, "You forget *la Pucelle*," and the silence that followed told Joliffe that no one had forgotten the witch who had nearly broken England's hold on France a mere hand's count of years ago. Finally captured, she was found guilty of heresy by a church court, but most folk knew her greater guilt lay in having brought the Dauphin's dying claim to France's crown back to vigorous life— in having united his wrangling lords and roused them to a fierce string of victories before she was captured and her madness shown for the devil's work it was. After her death, the war had settled back into its duller ways, but parts of France lost then were not yet recovered, and memory of "the Maid" was plainly still sharp. In truth, Joliffe realized as he shifted his gaze among the faces around him, some of these men had probably seen her burn at the stake here in Rouen's marketplace.

All the while through those uneasy days, his lessons that were no part of his household duties went on. He was now become too familiar in Lady Jacquetta's household to be of particular interest to anyone—even Estienne no longer troubled him with undue questions—but he could believably have only so many weapon lessons from Master Doncaster, and he learned to say sometimes, tipping a wink, that he was off to read in St. Ouen's library. That brought winks and knowing laughter back at him from his fellows, "reading in St. Ouen's" being off-talk for dice-play and whoring. To keep it the more believable, he complained of his losses or strutted a little about his wins, and avoided talk of the supposed whoring by saying that those who "did" had no need to "talk," which got him laughter and fewer questions.

Laughably enough, among his lessons with maps, ciphers, and weapons, he *was* coming to know Rouen's gambling holes and brothels. As Master Doncaster put it, "Where men are being most stupid, that's where you're likely to learn what they ought to keep secret," and led by Ivo, a rough-mannered, scar-faced man-at-arms, Joliffe gambled some ("Be sure to quit while you're losing. You'll be the more welcomed when next you come.") and whored not at all but sat listening to how much Ivo could learn in easy talk with a whore over a pottle of good wine in her room—in her room but not in her bed. ("And mind that it's good wine. They know the difference, don't think they don't. You'll get quality for quality, don't think you won't.")

Likewise from Ivo, he learned a rough French of a sort not to be picked up in the ducal household—or to be used there either, once he learned it. He did, though, take George and Estienne gaming one evening at a place where John Ripon was known, and was satisfied to hear them laughing about it to others in the household afterward, but it gave him an odd feeling to know that, for them, John Ripon was real and he—Joliffe—did not exist at all.

He might have settled for thinking that was the base of the unease he increasingly felt in himself, or accepted that his years of being constantly on the move as a player had made him unused to being tethered so long in one place, so that with the newness of everything here worn off and his household duties become familiar, he was simply grown restless. There was more to his unease than that, though. When he looked closely at it, he knew it came from his deepening sense of the households' undercurrents, even if he still could not clearly read them all. Taut worries over which way the world was going to jump were plain enough. Others, grown out of the likes, dislikes, ambitions, weaknesses, subtle alliances, and close-kept angers common to any household, were beyond Joliffe's French to lay hold on, so that he had a feeling much like sitting in a kettle of water up to his chin, unable to see the fire beneath it but feeling the water getting hotter and closer toward boiling all around him with no way for him to get out. And there were moments when he very much wanted out, or else for something clear and sure to happen, to break the bonds of all the unsure waiting.

At the same time, he knew that when that something happened—as it surely sometime must—he would probably not be pleased about it. It was all very well to moan for "a change, a change," but all too often when change came, the refrain altered to "not *this* change, not *this* change."

Time with Perrette might have helped, but of her he saw and heard nothing. He once asked Matilde about her, but Matilde only answered, unconcerned, "She's about somewhere. Comes and goes."

He was left with his duties as Lady Jacquetta's secretary and whatever lessons Master Wydeville set him and to listening to men's talk in tavern and hall, with their mix of news and rumors of the wide world and reports of which Rouen alehouse had the latest brew of ale.

Some change came early in March, when Sir Richard, Remon Durevis, and others of the young men of both households left, to take their turn riding guard for the supply wagons going out of Rouen to the castles and lesser fortresses through Normandy and to do some brigand-hunting along the way. As Joliffe had foreseen, the change was not to the good. Their going lowered the humours of everyone left behind, not only among the few youths, like Alain, who did not go, but Lady Jacquetta's, too. Joliffe was summoned more often to read to her and her demoiselles out of the solemn, suitable books, and in apparently casting about for new ways to occupy herself, she took more especial interest in her English properties than she had. Because of that, late one morning Joliffe was at his desk going through letters come with the latest messenger from England, to be ready when she would send to him to know about them, but rather than the expected summons, he heard her chamberman Foulke saying hurriedly to Master Wydeville in the outer office, "My lady has been summoned to her uncle. She wants you to come to her. She's gone to him."

"Do you know why?" Master Wydeville returned.

"It's about something from the king's council in England? An oath?" Foulke said uncertainly. "I didn't hear it all, but she ordered I was to say you were to come to her as soon as might be."

"Master Ripon," Master Wydeville called. "You're her English secretary. Best you come, too."

More than willing, Joliffe sprang to his feet and obeyed. Master Wydeville had already started down the stairs. Joliffe caught and kept up with him only by long-legged effort, all the way down from Lady Jacquetta's side of the *hôtel* to the great hall and beyond it to the richly tapestried room that was Bishop Louys' great council chamber. The bishop was there, standing with perhaps a dozen of his officers and men, Cauvet among them. Lady Jacquetta, attended only by M'dame, stood facing him—a slight, lone girl all in black among the men and the tall, bright figures of lords and ladies that filled the ceiling-high tapestries. She should perhaps have seemed small, but the tapestried lords and ladies were caught in the stillness of their woven moment while Lady Jacquetta—if Joliffe read her rigid

back and raised chin a-right—was in a fury, while her
uncle was saying at her with forced soothing, "It's no great
matter. It's an oath often asked of widows."

"I doubt that," Lady Jacquetta snapped. "It's asked of
me because I am the duchess of Bedford."

"Of course it is!" her uncle returned.

Lady Jacquetta lifted her chin a defiant inch higher.
"Then you should say it is a common enough oath to ask of
a duchess of Bedford. Not of 'widows,' as if we were all of
a piece." She looked sharply aside to Master Wydeville as
he and Joliffe bowed to her uncle and her. "Good. You've
come. My uncle asks something of me that I do not think
he should. I wish to hear what you advise, so long my husband's friend."

"This oath is not my doing," Bishop Louys said with
thinning patience. "The king's council in England has
asked—"

"Demanded," said Lady Jacquetta bitterly.

"—*asked* for her vow never to marry without the king's
consent. She objects to it."

"Because the matter is not the king's council's concern.
It is mine," Lady Jacquetta returned.

"You are the king's uncle's widow. You have considerable dower land in England. The council is concerned that
you—"

"That I will be a fool and marry someone who will use
my English wealth against England here in France," Lady
Jacquetta interrupted. "Why should this council in England think I would so dishonor my late husband by making
such a marriage? They have no right to think that!"

"Niece, it is their duty to think of all things. The oath is
as much to keep you safe as anything else."

"Ha! To keep me safe as a prisoner is kept safe!" Lady
Jacquetta scorned at him. "Master Wydeville, of everyone
here, you knew my husband longest. Would he have wanted
me to swear this oath?"

Was there pleading behind her defiance and demand? Joliffe was not sure, and whether there was or not, Master Wydeville paused a long moment before answering slowly, "I do not see that the king's council will be satisfied without your oath in this, my lady, nor that my lord of Bedford would see any dishonor in you swearing never to marry from this time forth without the king's or else the council's consent."

Lady Jacquetta stared at him for a long moment with narrowed, considering eyes, then gathered herself with a long in-drawn breath and turned back to her uncle. "On Master Wydeville's advice, I will swear. What he said, I swear to. Will that suffice?"

Her tone suggested it had better. Bishop Louys, more than ready to be satisfied, said back readily, "Yes. That will suffice."

"*Bon*," Lady Jacquetta declared. She bent her head to him in courtesy, turned away with a wide swirl of her skirts, and swept out of the room.

M'dame made quick curtsy of her own to the bishop and followed.

Bishop Louys looked at Master Wydeville and said, "I had thought to have her swear it in the chapel at the altar."

"That might be making too much of the matter. Do we want to make more of it than she already has?" Master Wydeville asked.

"No." The bishop said with great certainty. "No. She has sworn in front of witnesses and will surely keep her word, now that it's given."

"Surely she will," Master Wydeville agreed. He bowed. "By your leave, my lord, I'll return to my duties."

Leave was given, and Joliffe followed Master Wydeville away, until in the long gallery Master Wydeville stopped, faced him, and asked, "What did you learn from that?"

Joliffe paused. Wary of saying all that he thought, he finally said, "Lady Jacquetta believes in your continued loyalty to her late husband and trusts you to advise her well."

"Yes. When you're questioned about what passed between her and her uncle, you can say that, and that he asked this oath of her on behalf of the English council, that she doubted the rightness of it, asked my advice, then gave her oath. That's all that need be said of it. The less talk of it the better."

Joliffe bent his head to show he accepted that. But "less talk" was not the same as "no thought," and Joliffe was thinking several things as he returned to his desk.

Chapter 17

Joliffe's learning of weaponry went on. Much of it he enjoyed, but one evening Master Doncaster showed how to use cord or hands to throttle a man—"Or woman," Master Doncaster said grimly—into instant silence and quick death, and Joliffe found he felt befouled at having that knowledge in him. Sword and dagger and quarterstaffs could all be used at least sometimes in sport, for the pleasure of the skill. With throttling, the skill was for nothing but killing, and while Joliffe was grappling at the lesson's end with the dark thought that he now had that skill in his hands, the badly painted wall hanging on the wall of the practice room moved suddenly and oddly and Master Wydeville side-stepped into sight from behind it.

He was not a man much given to smiling at any time Joliffe had seen, but was so grim-faced now that Master Doncaster immediately asked with a worried edge, "What is it?"

"A fresh warning from Roussel. Support for Burgundy is running higher than ever in Paris."

He was not merely grim, Joliffe realized. He was angry, too, and Master Doncaster swore one of the rawer oaths Joliffe had lately learned and added with furious disgust, "Paris! The dukes of Burgundy have seen to buckets of blood being shed in Paris streets, then more than once have all but spit in the people's faces instead of helping them when they could have. But every chance it gets, Paris cheers Burgundy through the gates like he's Christ himself. I say let the damn place go, instead of draining men and grain out of Normandy to it, trying to keep it 'loyal.' "

"Come to it, there are plenty in Normandy would sing *gloria ad deum* if we gave up and left here, too," Master Wydeville said with a bitterness Joliffe had not heard in him before this.

"They've forgotten it was their own lords ripping the guts out of the country well before we came," Master Doncaster returned. "Master Ripon, I think we're done here for tonight."

Joliffe would have been willing to hear more, but he bowed to both men and made for the stairs, catching up his cloak from a stool on the way and hearing, as he started down, Master Doncaster say, "I'm thinking of following Fastolf's lead."

Joliffe did not know who Fastolf was or the why of the dark layer of unsaid things in Master Doncaster's voice, and he was at the stairfoot before Master Wydeville answered, level-voiced, "Are you?"

"Aren't you?" Master Doncaster returned as levelly.

Joliffe stopped at the stairfoot to swing his cloak around his shoulders, holding quiet through the pause until Master Wydeville said slowly, "For one reason and another, yes."

"There then," Master Doncaster said.

"There then," Master Wydeville answered, flat-voiced.

Not daring a longer lingering, Joliffe went on, taking their words' discomfort with him. Were matters really so desperate that Paris could be lost? Master Wydeville, who likely knew matters best of anyone, seemed to think so. And if Paris could be lost, how secure was England's hold on all the rest it held here?

Through the next few days the weather at last began to gentle into enough hope of spring that Lady Jacquetta took to walking with her ladies in Joyeux Repos' greening gardens some early afternoons, cloak-wrapped and hooded though they still needed to be, but although Joliffe watched and listened sharply, he heard nothing of what Master Wydeville had said about Paris, nor anything new about the war at large, and finally, to satisfy at least a small corner of his curiosity, in the hall one evening he asked Cauvet who Fastolf was, saying vaguely he had heard the name.

"Sir John Fastolf, yes," Cauvet answered readily. "One of our best captains in the war. A knight of your Garter and all. But of late he sold away his lands and rents and all he held here in Normandy and France, and went home to England, a very rich man, it's said."

And a man whose example Master Wydeville and Master Doncaster thought they well might follow.

The next day the usually gray sky gave way to fat drifts of white clouds across a sky scrubbed to a shining blue by a cold-gusting wind that kept at bay any feeling of spring; but something was different in the air, and Joliffe knew he was not alone among the secretaries and clerks in being restless. They were so obvious at it that perhaps a full hour before sundown Pierres put his head through the doorway from the outer chamber and said in his sober way, "Master Wydeville has gone out, but he gave me leave, if you were plainly doing your work badly, to give you leave to end early, while there was still sun to enjoy."

George and Jacques whooped and made quick work of shuffling papers away, closing inkwells, and cleaning pens. Henri and Bernard were less headlong about it, yet not far behind them in being done and out of the office, while Joliffe, having told George and Jacques he would catch them up at the Crescent Moon, took time over his going, thinking maybe he would not catch them up but wander on his own for a while, minded to be out of walls and into the open for a time. Not outside Rouen's walls and into the countryside, surely, but maybe to the quay, for the wideness of river and sky there.

He went up to the dormer for his cloak and hat and was coming down, headed for the foreyard, when he had near-collision with Foulke coming through the doorway from the long gallery. Crowding behind Foulke was Alain, who burst out over the chamberman's shoulder, "Have you seen Lady Alizon today?"

"Or at least since early in the afternoon," Foulke said more temperately, drawing back from the doorway into the gallery, making Alain back away, too.

Joliffe followed them, answering, "I've not."

"No one has," Alain fretted. "Foulke said we had to ask everywhere before starting an outright search. We're to the clerks the last thing." He was trying to edge around to the stairway, but Foulke kept resolutely in his way.

Not shifting either, Joliffe said, "They've been set free for the rest of today. They're all gone."

"Then we're away to search the gardens," Foulke said. "Lady Isabelle and Lady Blanche say maybe she went out to the gardens sometime while Lady Jacquetta was at the chapel. I'd say that's nonsense, in this cold and wind, but we have to look since she isn't to be found elsewhere. You'll come, too, to make it go the faster?"

With no real reason to refuse, Joliffe said, "If you will."

"We won't need to find someone else, then. Three's enough," said Foulke.

Alain spun around and led the way, jigging with worried eagerness, through the unused great chambers to the private spiral stair by which Joliffe had gone down to the gardens from Lady Jacquetta's bedchamber the day M'dame had sent him after Lady Jacquetta and Master Durevis. Beyond the door at its foot, the wind instantly found way through Joliffe's cloak, gown, and doublet, and he echoed Foulke with, "It's surely too cold for her to be out here," while sweeping a long look over the garden.

"We looked from my lady's windows but didn't see her," Foulke agreed.

"But Isabelle and Blanche said she went out," Alain insisted. "If she's in the laurel walk or the small garden, we wouldn't see her. That's where we must look."

"I'll take the laurel walk," Joliffe said, because the thick ever-green leaves would give some shelter from the wind.

Foulke gave him a dour look of understanding, but agreed with a nod and, "The small garden for me then. Alain, you cut straight through the center, looking along all the paths, on chance she's fallen and is lying somewhere."

That was well thought. The garden beds were raised. If the angle of sight was wrong and Alizon was lying somewhere, she might well be hidden from the windows.

Leaving Foulke and Alain to go their ways, Joliffe went aside and into the laurel walk. It did indeed give comfort from the wind, but because it was deep in late afternoon shadows, he would have to walk its length to be sure Alizon was not there. If she was, she would be sitting on one of the sheltered, shadowed benches along it and very likely unwilling to be found, because even out of the wind, the day's chill bit deep, and she had to have some deep reason to be still out here, if she was. Or ever had been.

He did not find her along the first arm of the arbor and had just turned its corner to follow it along the garden's rear side when a desperate shout ahead of him stopped him between one step and the next, then broke him into a run toward the arbor's far end.

There, he came out onto a narrow path between the arbor and an open-work wrought iron gate in the high brick wall of the small, enclosed garden he had only seen from a distance until now. From other such gardens he had known, he could guess there would be turf-topped benches around the inside of the high walls, probably with flowering vines—climbing roses very likely—spread over trellises behind them. There would be smooth-kept grass and perhaps a fountain. There might be . . .

Foulke was in the gateway, hands braced to either side of it as if to hold himself up, staring into the garden and moaning, "God. God. God. God."

Alain, just arrived at the same hard run as Joliffe, cried out, "What? Is she there?" and tried to crowd past him.

Foulke swung around, stumbling from the gateway, shoving Alain back and out of his way while gasping, "There's blood. Oh my god and saints! There's blood! We have to tell someone."

Alain twisted past Foulke and into the gateway, but froze there as Foulke broke into a run toward the *hôtel*. Joliffe let him go, went instead to see past Alain's shoulder into the garden. Then could have wished he had not.

There was indeed blood. A wide spread of it. Red on the pale gravel path between the gate and a white stone fountain burbling clear water quietly in the middle of the garden. And Alizon, lying there on her side, her back against the fountain's low curb as if she had rolled backward out of the blood and come to rest there, her left arm stretched out across the blood-pool, her right arm hanging limply across her body. Her head was cast a little back, her wide-open eyes staring upward into a long, low slant of sunlight that gave them a glint of the life they no longer had.

Alain made a sound between cry and howl and made to go forward. Joliffe caught him by the arm, saying, "Best we wait for . . ." He did not know what French officer matched an English crowner or sheriff. Or would it be the marshal of the household who came first?

"She might be alive," Alain protested.

"She isn't," Joliffe said flatly. Not with that much blood

gone out of her. Not with those staring eyes and slack-hanging mouth. She was dead. Had died where she lay, with her life's blood draining out of her.

But then whose blood was that?

Against what he had said about waiting, Joliffe put Alain aside and went forward, circling wide from Alizon's body and the blood, going leftward part way around the fountain and then a few steps toward it, close enough to be certain there was indeed the red—the bloody—print of a man's hand on the white stone curb of the fountain.

Probably a man's hand. Although there were large-handed women. But beyond doubt far too large to be Alizon's. Nor was it near her body, and Joliffe saw no sign she had ever moved beyond where she had fallen. Instead, he could imagine Alizon's murderer, red-handed with her blood, kneeling there to wash it from his hands. The fountain's flowing water would have briefly whorled with red, then flowed clear again in its unceasing soft burble and whisper, its purling probably the last thing Alizon heard as her life left her.

Except the handprint faced the wrong way.

A man kneeling to wash his hands and thoughtlessly putting a hand down there on the white stone—a singularly careless thing to do anyway, if he was aware enough of his bloodied hand or hands to want to wash them—would have done it facing the fountain. The handprint looked more like that of someone leaning one-handed on the fountain's rim as he went past.

But the curb was low. Not even a foot high. To put a hand down there, the murderer would have had to be passing on his knees?

Alain had disappeared from the gateway, probably unable, after his first urge to go forward, to bear what he saw. Joliffe partly wished he could retreat with him, but even sickened and angry as he was, he was coldly considering what was there and raised his gaze from the bloody handprint, for the first time taking a hard look around the garden.

The place was square with—as he had supposed—a turf-topped bench running around most of its sides with trellises grown over with bare, thorny stems that would be rose-covered come summer and fill the garden with scent on warm days. The fountain itself was a short stone pillar down which the water ran into the low-curbed pool around it, with the graveled path from the gate parting around it in a wide circle. Otherwise the garden was close-cut grass, winter-dulled now but probably like green velvet in the spring and through the summer. In the waning afternoon, the southern third of the space was already in shadow but not darkness deep enough to hide anything or anyone.

Joliffe took in all that with a swift, sweeping look before he turned back to Alizon's body. Keeping well away from the blood, he circled the fountain to come close to her head. Little though he wanted to touch her but wanting to know how cold she was, he leaned over and touched her white cheek. White not merely because she was young and fair. White not merely in death. White because so much of her blood had drained out of her as she died.

There was still, faintly, warmth in the white flesh.

Joliffe flinched his hand back from that fading evidence there had once been life in this dead, dead body. But it told him she could not have been killed so very long ago. In the chill day, her flesh would have cooled quickly.

He would have liked to touch the blood, too, to tell how much it had congealed, but given how quickly men could jump to fool conclusions, keeping his hands clean of blood was probably better.

He reached out again, this time to close Alizon's eyes, holding the eyelids down until they stayed.

It was as he made to draw back that he saw the footprint.

Or what might be a footprint.

The slant of sunlight and that he was bent over let him see it. Or think that he saw it. He straightened and saw—now he was trying to—how someone's foot had been put down partly in the outer edge of the pooled blood sometime after the blood had dried enough to keep the shallow shape of the front part of a soft-soled shoe. Or of something shoe-shaped, but what else could it be but a shoe? A shoe that afterward had blood on it, surely.

Unfortunately, gravel was not a surface to take and keep footprints, even bloody ones. Joliffe thought he saw smears in two other places on the pale stones that might have been made by a slightly bloodied shoe, but they only let him guess that maybe the murderer, after stepping in the blood, had taken a step or two backward.

Or had Foulke come that close, then backed away? Not by the way he had been braced in the gateway and crying out, sickened even from that distance. But if not Foulke . . .

Questions began to gather in Joliffe's mind. Why had the murderer still been there so long after the murder, to put his foot into the drying blood? Was it that he had gone away and then come back? Had he stabbed her and fled, then come back to be sure he had killed her?

Joliffe shifted to stand almost where the murderer must have stood to put his foot into the blood—if that was what that mark was. The sun was starting to slide below the top of the wall; the garden would soon be all in shadow and then in darkness. In the failing light there were going to be things he did not see, but he was seeing more than he had in the first moments of mind-blurring horror. By the look of it, Alizon had fallen face-downward. Had she, in her last moments of living, pushed herself onto her side, the way her body now lay, trying to rise?

Joliffe doubted it. He thought he saw, now he was looking more carefully, a drag mark through the blood that made him think it more likely she had been dead before she was moved, had been lying with one arm outflung, and when her murderer, standing here, had bent over, taken her body by the near shoulder, and rolled it sideways against the fountain's curb, the outflung arm, that now lay slack across her body, had trailed through the drying blood.

He wished he dared lift her hand, to see what the blood on it might tell. He also wished he could see the wound that had killed her, but between the failing light and her gown's black cloth that hid the darkness of blood on it, he could not tell anything and was not going to touch more than he already had.

He moved away to the gateway. Where were Foulke and Alain gone? For a few moments the only sound in the quiet was the fountain's burbling to itself, until at last—although it had not been that long—a burst of people came out of the *hôtel*, their raised voices loud to each other. Joliffe closed the gate and put himself in front of it. If he knew people, most of those coming fastest wanted more to see a murdered body than to do what needed to be done. He meant to keep them out if he could, and indeed the jostle of the three men who first reached him objected to him being in their way and craned necks to see around him. But by good fortune Master Wydeville came next. With his authority as Lady Jacquetta's chamberlain, he ordered the men aside, saying, "The household's marshal has been sent for. This is his business, not yours."

He kept saying that as more people came. To the questions thrown at him, he sometimes added, "I don't know. I haven't gone in." He did take a single long look over his shoulder, through the iron scrollwork of the gate, and asked Joliffe, "Foulke had it right? It's murder?"

"It's murder."

Lady Jacquetta's coming brought a sudden falling away of all the questions and demands. The clutter of people shifted to either side, making way for her, and for M'dame, Ydoine, Guillemete, and Alain. Master Wydeville stepped forward, blocking them from coming nearer the gate, saying with firm respect, "My lady, you need not be here. Best you wait inside, out of the cold, until your marshal and the coroner have been here."

Lady Jacquetta stopped but not as if she intended to be turned back, and asked, "Is it truly Lady Alizon? But she's not dead, surely?"

"She's dead, my lady. It looks to be murder."

He had kept his voice low but there was no way to keep the words from Guillemete, who cried out with sharp pain and started forward. Even as Joliffe said urgently, "She should not see," Master Wydeville reached out to stop her, while M'dame and Ydoine took hard hold on her arms from either side and Ydoine asked, "She was not . . . . Was Lady Alizon . . . Was she . . . dishonored?"

Dishonored more than having a dagger thrust into her heart? Joliffe thought sharply. But he knew what Ydoine meant, and at Master Wydeville's glance silently bidding him answer, he said, "There is no sign that her . . . skirts . . . were touched. Or that there was any struggle."

"Thank the Virgin!" someone in the gathering said.

Joliffe held back from snapping, "You mean, give thanks for a clean kill?"

"I want to see her!" Guillemete cried. She was not in tears yet, but Joliffe thought wild breakdown was close.

Lady Jacquetta questioned Master Wydeville with a look, and when he shook his head, she ordered, "Ydoine, take Guillemete inside. Alain, help her."

Alain took M'dame's place and hold on Guillemete. She gave a single great sob and would have sunk to the ground without his and Ydoine's hold, and together they more carried than guided her away, toward the *hôtel*.

Not troubling to watch them go, Lady Jacquetta said steadily at Master Wydeville. "Now I am going to see her. She was of my household. This is my duty."

Master Wydeville looked past her to M'dame as if asking for her help. M'dame, stony-faced, gave none. Lady Jacquetta, pale but certain, started forward, and Master Wydeville moved aside. Joliffe unlatched the gate and stepped backward, opening it ahead of her. M'dame followed her in. Master Wydeville, after giving order to someone for lights to be brought, followed them both, and Joliffe—because no one said he should not—moved after them, to one side of the path to be quiet-footed on the grass, telling himself that if either of the women collapsed as Guillemete had, Master Wydeville would need immediate help.

The sun was now below the top of the garden's wall, but there was still light enough to show all that needed to be seen without the women went too near the blood or body, and they did not but near enough that Lady Jacquetta made a small sound that brought M'dame and Master Wydeville immediately beside her. She did take hard hold on M'dame's arm but did not sway or look away from Alizon.

M'dame, after one swift look at the body, stood staring at the far garden wall, stiff as an iron rod. Lady Jacquetta, after a moment, said in a small voice, "They say the dead are asleep. She does not look asleep. She looks empty. We hear—we always hear—about the killing. There is so often—among the men—someone who does not come back, because they're dead. We hear they're dead. But we don't see death. Not death like this. Death with blood and—suddenness."

"My lady," M'dame said, not lowering her gaze from the wall. "You should come away now."

Lady Jacquetta looked at Master Wydeville. "Is there pursuit of who did this?" she demanded, and under her disciplined quiet, Joliffe thought he heard anger like his own at so wrong a death.

"My lady, no one was here when she was found, so there's no one to pursue," Master Wydeville said, then asked, his tone measured, "Do you know why she was here? Was it to meet someone?"

"I do not know why she was here. She *did* meet some-one, though. That is plain. Someone who did this and left her." Lady Jacquetta's head snapped around. She stared toward where the *hôtel* was out of sight beyond the brick wall. "Left her and went back to there?" she said in a hor-rified half-whisper.

"Or else through there." Master Wydeville made a grim nod toward the far wall of the garden.

Forgetting, in his surprise, to keep silent, Joliffe echoed, "*Through* there?"

The garden's far wall was of stone, rather than brick. Directly opposite the gateway there was a gap of perhaps two feet in the turf bench, with branches of rose bush trellised on the wall there like everywhere else. With the half-thought Joliffe had given it, he had vaguely supposed that in summer a large pot of something—a lily or maybe irises—was meant to be set there in the space, but now Master Wydeville went toward it, saying grimly, "Come and see."

Joliffe followed, heard the click of a latch as Master Wydeville touched the wall, and was startled by Master Wydeville swinging inward part of the wall and some of the trellis with its vine.

"See," Master Wydeville said. "Here the wall is wood, painted to seem stone unless someone looks closely." Painted very skillfully and with the trellis and rose branches serving to further obscure it.

Joliffe went closer and saw there was a drop of sev-eral feet beyond it—with no steps down—to a somewhat grass-grown pathway running along a wide, clear-flowing stream. On the stream's other side were what looked to be the backs of other gardens, some walled, some not.

Level-voiced, Master Wydeville said, "My lord of Bedford had the door made when the garden was. He said no sensible man put himself into a place from which there was only one way out." He started to shut the door. "So you see . . ."

Joliffe put out a hand to stop him, then pointed to the broad board that was the door's frame and said, "There."

A few more moments of gathering twilight would have hidden it, but he and Master Wydeville bent together for a closer look.

"What is it?" Lady Jacquetta demanded from where she still stood beyond Alizon's body.

Master Wydeville straightened. "I'd judge it to be blood, my lady."

"Alizon's?" Lady Jacquetta asked.

"She never moved from where she was stabbed," Master Wydeville answered.

"And up here," Joliffe murmured for only Master Wydeville to hear, slightly nodding toward a lesser smear higher up on the frame.

Master Wydeville nodded that he saw it, too, finished shutting the door, and answered Joliffe's questioning look toward the latch with, "Yes. It only opens from this side. Not from the other at all."

Chapter 18

Lady Jacquetta left the garden, M'dame going with her. Beyond the gathered gawkers outside the gate, someone was coming with the lights Master Wydeville had ordered. Surely a priest was on the way, too, and probably the household's marshal, but in the few moments he and Master Wydeville were alone, Joliffe took the chance to point out the handprint on the fountain's edge and the possible footprint. Master Wydeville said nothing about the first and had to bend low and lean a little to one side and another to see the footprint, then matched Joliffe's own thought with, "Someone stood there to turn the body over, well after she was dead and the blood had ceased to spread."

A servant with a lighted torch came into the garden, followed by one of the household priests and two more servants carrying lighted lanterns. Master Wydeville ordered the torchbearer to stop barely inside the gateway and hold the torch high, to throw as much light as might be over the darkening garden. He gave short answers to the priest's short questions, left the man kneeling to pray near the body, took one of the lanterns from a staring servant, and ordered at Joliffe, "Take the other," before sending both servants to stand outside the gate to keep anyone unneeded from coming in.

"Now," he told Joliffe, "we look carefully all over this garden, to find out anything we can. Come the morning, there'll be search by daylight, but we have to try tonight, too. You understand? Anything, whether you think it matters or not. Start at the gateway and work that half of the garden, back toward the door, while I work this half."

Freed by Lady Jacquetta's and M'dame's going, household folk outside the gate were jostling for better view. No one presumed to ask anything of Master Wydeville, but a few questions were shot at Joliffe, who ignored them, keeping his mind tightly to his search, but when he and Master Wydeville met at the door in the wall, their faces told each other neither had found anything. Joliffe took the chance, though, to say, wanting to hear what Master Wydeville would answer, "It must have been that she let her murderer in."

"He did not need to come through the door to be here," Master Wydeville returned. "Alizon surely came through the garden. So could he."

"But he knew the door is here, to let himself out," Joliffe said. As the blood marks showed he must have. Master Wydeville nodded, beyond doubt thinking the same as Joliffe was—that the murderer must almost surely be someone of the household, to have spent time in this most private garden and so know of the door and how to open it.

"Whichever way he came," Master Wydeville said, "Alizon was expecting him."

"Or her," said Joliffe.

Master Wydeville was silent a moment before granting, "Or her. Although if the kill was made with a sword, we'll have to grant it was done by a man. We'll know more when the body has been properly seen. But, yes, otherwise there's nothing to say a woman could not have done it."

Joliffe's unsaid, unwanted thought was of Perrette. But what reason would Alizon have to meet with Perrette, secretly or otherwise? Or Perrette have reason to kill her? But if there was a reason Alizon had to die, and if it had been Perrette here, how much part in it might Master Wydeville have? Was all this searching and questioning here only a pretense on his part? Smothering a definite terror at that thought, Joliffe shied aside from those questions by saying with forced steadiness, "About the blood on the doorway here. The lower smear looks much as if someone leaned there, bleeding."

"It does," Master Wydeville agreed. "It's fair guess, too, that the lesser smear, higher up, was probably from the same hand that left the print on the fountain's rim. Those two could well be Lady Alizon's blood. This one, though"—he nodded at the lower smear— "gives more the seeming that the man were wounded himself."

That matched Joliffe's own thought, and he asked the question that went with it. "Wounded by whom?" Because Alizon was unlikely to have had any weapon with her; demoiselles did not go armed about the household.

But everything about her death was unlikely, so the unlikely had to be considered possible.

But Master Wydeville seemed to share his own doubt, saying, "I don't see how she could have wounded him, unless she fought him and did it with his own dagger, unlikely though that is against a man. Let us see."

They went back to the body. The priest had been joined by a second priest. Master Wydeville stepped between the two kneeling men—the gravel must be uncomfortable under their knees, Joliffe thought—and lifted first one of Alizon's hands, then the other. Having looked at them in his lantern's light and laid them gently down, he stepped back and several paces away before saying quietly what Joliffe had seen, too. "There are no cuts on her hands as if she had tried to fend off the dagger. My judgment would be she was struck without warning and fell and died, taken completely by surprise. But if so, then how did her murderer come to leave his blood on the door post?"

Master Wydeville was less asking for Joliffe's answer than considering aloud, but Joliffe said, "Then there had to have been a third person here. Someone else who was attacked but not killed. Someone who escaped."

"Or else the murderer wounded himself. Which I doubt. Or he was the one wounded by some third person here." Master Wydeville turned his head toward raised voices outside the gate and spoke more quickly. "That will be the marshal, perhaps the coroner and all. We're done here, you and I. But listen to me. First, say nothing about the blood on the doorpost. Second, someone as hurt as whoever bled there will need some manner of help with a hurt like that. I want you to ask questions among apothecaries and surgeons hereabout, to see if any of them have helped a hurt man tonight. Make up whatever story you need to, to cover why you're asking. Then go to Master Doncaster with what you've learned. Or haven't learned. Go now."

"Now?"

"Now. Take yourself away at your first chance."

"They'll want to ask me questions, as one of the first-finders."

"I'll answer for what was found. They'll be satisfied. You've been overset by seeing this murder and are likely going to slip away to get drunk as possible." Starting toward the three men now coming into the garden, Master Wydeville added in a raised voice and impatiently, "Get hold on yourself, Ripon. Be a man, not a mimsy rag."

Joliffe promptly slumped into John Ripon and began a whining mutter about his stomach.

Master Wydeville snapped at him, voice still raised, "If

you're going to be ill, don't do it in here!" and the three men moved well aside as Joliffe, his free hand pressed over his mouth, scuttled past them with a hasty bow and out the gate, thrusting his lantern into someone's hands among the on-lookers. With shoulders hunched and hand still over his mouth, he shook his head against the questions thrown at him and made heaving sounds that got people out of his way as he stumbled toward the *hôtel*, nor did anyone follow him through the darkening garden, saving him the trouble of feigning worse sickness by way of a finger in his throat.

At the *hôtel* he went in and up by the private stairway but only to the grand chambers. He cut through them and along the long gallery, having the good fortune to meet no one either there or as he went up to the dormer. There he shed his clerk's gown, put on his cloak and hat again, and went down the stairs into the stableyard corner of the fore-yard. From there he had only the outer gateway's guards to satisfy. They proved curious, having caught the word murder from whoever was gone in search of the coroner but knowing no more. Joliffe told them he only knew it was some woman in the garden and he was heading out for a drink because who knew when supper would be tonight.

Fortunately, no order had yet been given to let no one leave. They did not stop him going out, and because rumor had had too little time to spread further, there was no questioning crowd gathered outside the gateway. Once beyond it and among people in the street there, Joliffe was no one. Unfortunately, he was also nowhere, so far as knowing where to go. He had made no study of apothecary shops or surgeons in Rouen. Even if had he, he did not know which way the wounded man—woman?—murderer?—had gone once out the garden's door. Right or left along the path there, yes. But which?

Come to that, he did not even know where the path ran, but he found the nearer end of it by simply asking a pair of children sitting on a doorstep, probably waiting to be called in to their supper. They jumped up and happily took him along the street to where a short alley came out between two houses. He gave them each a small coin in thanks, to their complete delight, just as their mother called them angrily home.

Left looking into the alley's shadows, Joliffe did not much like the thought of going into it, especially to no purpose, and crossed the street instead, to where someone's apprentice was closing the shutter across a shopfront. He asked the youth if he had been there the past hour or two and got the answer, "Freezing my fingers and selling nothing, yes. Could have closed three hours ago, for all the profit there's been."

"Has anyone come out of that alleyway in that while? Someone who came along the stream path there?"

"That's not much used this cold time of year," the youth said scornfully. "There was no one I saw today, anyway, and I did not have much else to look at."

Joliffe gave him two coins and went back to the alley and unwillingly into it. Going now with the last afterglow of sunset was better than in the full dark that was coming, but "better than" was not the same as "good." And what if the wounded man—woman?—had been too hurt to go far, was lying somewhere there in the dark and not grateful to be found and still able to use his dagger?

Not that Joliffe much wanted to stumble on his corpse, either.

He came out the alley's far end onto the open pathway without having encountered anyone or anything and was grateful to see how the path ran with the stream on one side and, on the other, a blank, tall, stone wall—part of Joyeux Repos—giving no hiding places where a hurt murderer might be lurking. He went quickly forward, keeping watch toward the stream for any floating body caught along its edge, on the chance that blood-loss might have made his quarry fall that way. At the same time he tried to watch for any signs, including more blood smeared anywhere on the wall, but the light was too far gone to give him real hope of seeing either that or any other subtle sign about his quarry.

Torch- and lantern-light and voices on the other side of the wall told when he passed the door in wall. Even on this side, where it was not hidden, it was all but invisible in the deepening dark. Joliffe went faster, glad when he came out the path's other end and into another street where there was the welcome warm light of evening lanterns beside doorways. Better than that, not twenty yards away an apothecary shop's sign of a mortar and pestle was hanging over the street, with a line of light around the front window's closed shutter telling someone was there.

Accepting his luck, Joliffe went, knocked, and when someone said, "Come," went in, giving a tipsy sway sideways as he crossed the threshold into a small, candle-lighted room. Shelves crowded with the usual apothecary clutter filled most of the walls, while behind a trestle-and-board table a stout middle-aged man stood grinding at something in a stone mortar. At Joliffe's slight stumble, he looked up with inquiring eyebrows, and Joliffe asked, slurring the words and making his French worse than it was, "I look for my friend. He hurt himself. He went to be helped."

Speaking slowly and somewhat loudly to help the foreigner understand him, the man asked, "Do you mean he was ill?"

"No. No." Joliffe made a poking gesture, as if he were holding a dagger. "A fight. Hurt."

"You do not want me," the man said. He came from the table to take Joliffe by the arm and turn him toward the door. "You want Master Vengier. He is a surgeon. Around the corner from here." He steered Joliffe out of his door. "He would be where your friend is gone. To Master Vengier."

Joliffe let himself be aimed in presumably the right

direction, thanked the man with a happily drunk man's friendly ease, and swayed away along the street.

He had his doubts about the success of this quest Master Wydeville had set him on. How many barber-surgeons and apothecaries might there be in Rouen? How long would it take him to find them all? And the hurt man need not have gone to any of them but to a friend who might be willing to tend his wound and hide him. After all, the wound might be slight.

No, there had been blood enough to think it was more than slight. Still, was it so bad the man would be desperate enough to go for help to the nearest surgeon when report of a murder in the neighborhood was sure to be spreading almost on his heels?

That would depend on how bad was the wound and how desperate the man. And he might not know he had left blood behind him that betrayed he was hurt. He might believe that with the hidden door shut behind him and no immediate outcry of pursuit, he was clear away, with no worry about going to the first help there was.

Or he might make for his home and send for a surgeon to come to him.

Or misjudging his hurt and not sending for help, he might quietly bleed to death somewhere.

Which would be thoughtless and unhelpful of him.

Joliffe let go his seeming drunkenness as he turned the corner from the apothecary's shop; when he knocked at the door under the barber-surgeon's sign he was only a man in worried search for his friend. The woman who soon opened the door to him was short and pleasingly plump, aproned like a busy housewife and, judging by her fine linen head-cloth and the good wool of her gray gown, no servant. She assessed him with a look, standing there on her doorstep in her lantern-light, and said before he had quite opened his mouth, "You're looking for the stabbed man? Good. You can take him back to the garrison. We don't want him."

Joliffe felt his mouth dropping open, stopped it, closed it, swallowed what he had been going to say, gathered his wits, and said, sounding stupid even to himself, "He's here?"

"He's here. Come." The woman turned and started back along the brick-floored passageway. "Shut the door," she added, plainly not thinking he would have the sense to do even that without he was told.

Joliffe meekly followed her inside and shut the door. The house was much like Master Doncaster's, with a kitchen at the far end of the passageway, where warmth and light and supper-smells met Joliffe as he came in, while in the room's middle at a wide wooden table a man was standing bent over and doing something to the bare back of a man seated on the bench there with his face hidden against his crossed arms resting on the tabletop.

The standing man was short and plump like his wife— surely she was his wife; they had that immediate look of a couple—and he said to her as he looked around and saw Joliffe, "You were not to let anyone in!"

Going past the table toward the hearth, she returned, "He is not the watch or angry. He wanted his friend, that's all."

"You were to say no was here!"

The woman sniffed. "He passed you money to say that. He did not pass me money." She stirred at something bubbling in a pot hanging over the fire. "If there's someone to take him away, we don't want to keep him, do we?"

The seated man lifted his head, turned it enough to see Joliffe, and let it sink onto his arms again with a groan.

"Master Durevis," Joliffe said.

Who should not be in Rouen at all, having ridden out with the other household men two weeks ago.

But it was Durevis nonetheless; and he whispered, as if gathering words was almost beyond his strength, "Did you do this?"

"No," Joliffe answered with startled certainty.

Durevis regarded him through pain-taut eyes. "Can you forget you found me?"

"I was sent to find you."

That seemed to startle Durevis in his turn. "How?" But pain cut off his curiosity. He shut his eyes again and muttered, "Stay then."

The plump man grunted and returned to his work. Joliffe circled for better view and saw he was stitching closed a long, ragged slit low down on the right side of Durevis' back. A bowl with a cloth and bloodied water in it sat nearby on the table, beside an open box of various pottery jars. Beside those, another cloth lay with an array of metal implements Joliffe chose not to see too closely. There was also a cup with a little red wine left in it, probably mixed with something to lessen pain, or Durevis would be flinching more than he was to the push and pull of needle and thread through his flesh. As it was, his eyes were squeezed tightly shut, and because there seemed small use in trying to question him now, Joliffe settled onto a joint stool to wait.

The woman swung the pot away from the fire, filled a wooden bowl, sat down with it and a spoon and a large piece of bread at the far end of the table from where her husband worked, and ate her supper while he finished with Durevis. He eventually snipped off the last stitch, set aside the needle and scissors, opened a jar from the box, and with his fingers smeared ointment from it over the length of the wound and its stitches, then set to putting a pad over the wound and a bandage around Durevis to hold the pad in place. He finished as his wife finished her supper, and she said, "See him to the bed. Then come eat your supper." She looked at Joliffe. "You help."

The bed that stood against the wall on the kitchen's far side was only a narrow straw-filled mattress laid on boards kept off the floor by a low frame, plainly there for such as

could go no further after the surgeon had seen to them.
Joliffe, helping the surgeon ease Durevis, groaning, to it,
looked no more closely than he had to at the stains on the
mattress but saw enough to judge they were old, of varied ages, and well-scrubbed more than once. Anyway, the
mattress and the pillow there were clean enough now, and
assuredly Durevis did not care, gasping as much with relief
as pain as he settled onto his unhurt side.

Across the kitchen, the woman had refilled the bowl
from the pot and said at her husband as she brought it
back to the table with more bread, "You eat now. I'll see
to things."

Joliffe stood aside, wondering when he would have
chance at questioning Durevis, as the surgeon obeyed his
wife and she came to the bed, pulled a blanket off the wall-
pole above it, and covered Durevis from toes to chin before giving Joliffe a hard look and saying, "He has to rest
now."

"I have to talk to him." Joliffe looked at Durevis, wondering if it was the drug or feigning that had his eyes so
tightly closed. "While I can. He needs to tell who did this
to him."

The woman lifted one of Durevis' eyelids and peered
at his eye. Durevis made a mixed sound of protest and
groan. The woman let go his eyelid, straightened from the
bed. "You might get a few moments sense out of him," she
said and went back to the table to busy herself with tidying
away her husband's work while he ate.

Joliffe sat down on his heels beside the bed. In his weeks
at Joyeux Repos, few words had ever passed between him
and Remon Durevis. Their places in the world were too
wide apart for much to ever be said. That made it all the
stranger to lean close to him now and say, quiet-voiced but
insistent, "Master Durevis. You have to hear me. You have
to answer me."

The squire opened his eyes, closed them again. More

insistently, Joliffe said, "Durevis, you *have* to answer me. Lady Alizon is dead."

Durevis said thickly, the words blurred, "I know. I found her."

"You didn't kill her?"

"Dead. She was . . . dead. Then . . ." Durevis seemed to be dragging the words from somewhere beyond the drug he had been given against the pain. ". . . he stabbed me. From behind."

Joliffe leaned closer, trying to hold him to his senses at least a while longer. "He stabbed you. Who?"

"Did . . . not . . . see." Whatever the surgeon had given him was gaining on him.

"It was a man, though," Joliffe insisted.

"He ran . . . not in . . . skirts. Out the . . . gate. Behind me."

"But you had come into the garden through the hidden door."

"Um."

That seemed agreement. Joliffe pressed, "Who let you in?"

Durevis slurred, "Alizon."

Joliffe almost pointed out that she was already dead. Then his wits caught up, and he said, spacing the words to give time for each to reach Durevis' fading mind, "She had the door unlatched for you. You were there to meet her. But you found her dead."

"Um," Durevis granted, so faintly that Joliffe thought to have no more from him.

But from a last drift of awareness Durevis whispered, "Lay . . . ja . . . she . . . secrets."

The last word came clearly enough, but it was the last word. Durevis' breath hissed from it into a long sigh, and he was altogether gone into whatever sleeping place the drug had taken him.

Chapter 19

"**H**e said 'secrets,'" Master Wydeville said. "More than one of them. You're sure of that?"

Joliffe was tired, had already answered that several times, and said, "Not to stake my soul on it, no. But sure enough otherwise."

He was, for the first time, in Master Wydeville's own house. When Durevis was fully asleep from the drug and likely to stay that way for several hours, according to the surgeon, he had gone to Master Doncaster's as ordered. The weapon-master must have already had some word from Master Wydeville, because he took what Joliffe told him calmly, then led him upstairs and by way of a stoop-low door behind the wall-hanging into this small, windowless room with its squat, square, empty table, a three-legged stool, and a closed door in the opposite wall.

Left there with a candle, Joliffe had drowsed with his head on the table until jarred awake by the door from Master Doncaster's opening and Master Roussel coming in. At the same time a slow tread up stairs beyond the room's other door brought Master Wydeville, who now stood tapping his fingers on the table and looking as if he wished there were a way to pry more out of Joliffe.

Master Roussel, with a hip hitched on the table's edge across from Master Wydeville, said, "Secrets. Whose secrets? This Alizon's? What secrets would she have that he would want? Her own or someone else's?"

"Secrets worth a secret meeting and murder?" Master Wydville said. "I would have to think they were someone else's."

"Then what else he said at the last—could he have been trying to say 'Lady Jacquetta'?" Master Roussel asked.

That matched one of Joliffe's own thoughts in the time he had had to think about Durevis' final slurred sounds, and wearily Master Wydeville agreed, "That's what I have to fear. That the secrets have to do with Lady Jacquetta."

"Secrets that this Alizon was going to tell to him?" Master Roussel mused. "Or secrets he was going to tell to her? Or was it secrets *for* Lady Jacquetta, that this Alizon was to take to her? Was she killed to stop her telling secrets, or to stop her hearing them?"

"All questions we'll ask Master Durevis when he comes back to his senses," Master Wydeville said. "That and some few other things."

"Questions to be asked of Lady Jacquetta, too?" Master Roussel suggested.

Master Wydeville nodded slowly. "When I know more, yes, she'll have to be asked things, too."

"You've put someone to watch this Durevis where he is?"

"Two men. With order to sleep turn and turn about, and eat and drink nothing given them there. The surgeon could be part of whatever it is, rather than simply the first one Durevis came to."

Joliffe, not liking the feeling he was a tool that had served its purpose and been set aside, to go unnoticed until needed again, asked, "So is Master Durevis somebody's spy?"

"We have to think so," said Master Wydeville. "Whether French or Burgundian we don't know yet." He looked at Master Roussel. "Which is more likely?"

"We can only guess until he says, but my guess would be Burgundian. Did he come with Lady Jacquetta, when she married my lord of Bedford?"

"No. He came a year ago, when some of her people returned to her brother's household and others took their place. There's been no sign he is a spy. Meaning he's a skilled one, if he is."

"He only began to be particularly friendly with Lady Alizon after Shrovetide," Joliffe said.

"True," Master Wydeville said. "Before then, he favored none of the demoiselles more than another."

"Until his quarrel, if that's what it was, with Lady Jacquetta in the garden," Joliffe said.

It came to him belatedly that this was something he might have done well to tell Master Wydeville at the time, but Master Wydeville only nodded now, showing no particular surprise. Because he was not surprised? Joliffe suddenly, sharply, wondered, while Master Roussel asked, "Are we going to suppose, for now, this Durevis has told true what happened in the garden?"

Master Wydeville looked at Joliffe. "You saw his wound. Could he have given it to himself?"

"Not where it was in his back. He might get his arm twisted around to there, but not deliver a dagger-blow like that one."

"It was a dagger?" Master Wydeville asked.

"A narrow-bladed one, I'd say. Assuredly not a sword."

"It was a narrow dagger that was used on Alizon," Master Wydeville said. "I saw the wound with the coroner. But I'd judge it was not used expertly. Not by someone used to such work. It lacked the look of an experienced kill."

"A woman maybe did it?" Master Roussel asked.

"I would doubt it. There was considerable strength behind the strike. But it was not under the ribs and up, not a clean in-and-out." That was the dry judgment of an expert considering a problem, well-removed from the reality of a steel blade driven into a girl's soft, living flesh. "He struck between ribs, and the blade partly cut into a rib, deeply enough that a hard and twisted jerk was needed to wrench it free and have it out. The wound it made was large enough to account for how much she bled in the very few moments it must have taken her to die."

"Master Durevis' wound was likewise poorly done," Joliffe offered.

"So, all in all, what he says and what we saw in the garden fit together. Someone was there before him and killed Alizon, waited for him, stabbed him, and ran away. By way of the gate, he said. Not out the door."

"Yes," Joliffe said. "So whoever it was had to have been waiting outside the gate. The garden has no hiding places."

"Taking a raw chance that the afternoon shadows and the leafless trees at the greensward's end would hide him from someone chancing to look out an upper window," Master Wydeville said grimly. "Which they did."

"We are supposing that this Durevis has not lied, did not bring the other man with him," Master Roussel put in. "Then was betrayed by him."

"Alizon was stabbed some while before he found her," Joliffe said. "Long enough for her blood to have begun to thicken."

"That would not take long. It was a cold afternoon," Master Roussel pointed out.

"It would still take at least a little while," Joliffe returned.

"For now I think we have to follow what he has said happened," Master Wydeville said. His weariness was becoming more marked. "Questions are already started at the *hôtel* of who was where when in the afternoon. There's always hope someone chanced to see something and has not thought about it yet." He rubbed at his face. "That will be for tomorrow, though. Tonight . . ."

"There is still the matter of Tom Kechyn," said Master Roussel.

Master Wydeville dropped his hands with a sound not quite a groan. "Kechyn. I had forgotten. You had him out of Paris easily?"

"No. There was trouble at the end. I'm worried that word came as fast as we did, that there will be watch and search for him here in Rouen."

Master Wydeville swore, but he was thinking while he did because he followed with, "Then best he be away more quickly than they will suppose likely. The *Bonhomme* sails on the dawn tide. He will have to take his own chances at Honfleur, but he should be ahead of pursuit enough by then if he sails now."

"Perrette came in this afternoon. She could see to having him aboard."

"Good," Master Wydeville agreed. "Did it go well with her?"

"So she said, the few words we've had. She'll tell you more later, surely."

Master Wydeville accepted that with a nod. "I haven't asked you, either, how matters go in Paris."

Master Roussel paused before answering tautly, "I would not go back there if I did not have to."

"What of your father?"

"He still thinks there may be hope. I wish he was out of there."

"So do I," Master Wydeville said grimly. The silent pause between the two men then had many unsaid but understood things between them, before Master Wydeville added, "Take Master Ripon to go with Perrette and Kechyn. He can serve to guard their backs."

Something to eat and the chance to lie down and sleep were what Joliffe had been hoping for, but seeing Perrette again would be good, and he dragged himself to his feet as Master Roussel stood up from the tabletop and Master Wydeville left the room. In silence, Master Roussel lighted the small wick in the oil of a shallow clay lamp he had brought with him, put out the candle, and still in silence, led Joliffe out the other way and across Master Doncaster's practice room to where another poorly painted wall-hanging hid another low door that let them into what plainly served the Roussels as a storage chamber. Handing the lamp to Joliffe for a moment, Master Roussel shoved a large and apparently heavy willow-woven hamper to block and hide the door, took back the lamp, and led the way down through the house, first by way of ladder-steep stairs into a bedchamber where no one stirred, either behind the bedcurtains or on the blanket-humped truckle-bed beside it, then across that chamber and down more stairs to a passage and along it to the expected kitchen door. It was shut, and although there was candle-glow along its sill, there were no sounds beyond it. Master Roussel made an uneven pattern of knocks on its wood, paused, then opened it wide, all the way back to the wall.

To be sure of no one behind it, Joliffe thought as he followed Master Roussel into the room's welcome warmth, and wondered what it was like to live a life where you could not be sure of going into your own kitchen safely.

A man unknown to Joliffe sat on the bench near the hearth, leaning wearily forward on his arms. Beyond him, Perrette was turning from the fire with a thick slice of newly-toasted bread on a long-handled fork. Master Roussel's lamp guttered out as he set it beside the candle already burning on the table, and the man straightened, to greet him with, "How does it go? Anything further amiss?"

"You're to sail with the present tide," Master Roussel returned. "The sooner you're in England with what you know, the better. Perrette, will you be able to get him to the *Bonhomme* unnoted, do you think?"

Having closed the door, Joliffe was going toward the table as Perrette slid the toasted bread from the fork onto a wooden cutting board beside a quarter of cheese while answering, frowning, "Yes. Probably. Will they be looking hard for him?"

"I don't know. Possibly."

Rising and going to the table, the man who must be Kechyn drew the board, bread, cheese, and a knife toward himself and said, "If it's Ambroise le Jeusne heading the hunt, they'll be hunting hard."

He had began to cut a piece of cheese, and Perrette asked Master Roussel and Joliffe. "Are you hungry?"

Master Roussel said, "No." Joliffe said, "Yes."

She turned the fork and offered it to him handle first. "So am I. Thank you."

Joliffe took one of the slices of bread lying already cut on the table, speared it on the fork, and went to crouch on his heels beside the low fire, leaving Perrette and Master Roussel to sit down on a bench opposite Kechyn and begin talking of possible ways to have him safely and—for preference secretly—to the ship, to keep the hunt up for him here in Rouen while he was well away. Not knowing who Kechyn was or why he was hunted or by whom, Joliffe only somewhat listened at first, intent on getting food into his hungry stomach. He surrendered the first slice of toast to Perrette. When he came with his own to sit on the bench, Perrette, without turning from her talk, handed him a piece of cheese already cut. He did not interrupt their talk with thanks but settled to eating, finally taking a full look at the man Perrette was expected to get unnoticed to a ship.

His first thought was "small chance" if any kind of watch at all was being kept. To the good, the man was only of average build and probably height, but he was an even-featured, rosy-cheeked Englishman with curly yellow hair.

A hood might serve to cover the hair, but anyone looking for him would be watching for something as obvious as a close-fastened hood; it would merely draw their suspicious heed to his face, and it was an open, easily remembered face.

That was Perrette's thought, too, it seemed. She was arguing they should wait and send him with some pilgrims leaving for Canterbury and other English shrines in a few days, saying, "Better he reach there alive and later than be dead here because of our over-haste."

"If I thought keeping him a few days hidden would better his chances, I would agree," Master Roussel returned. "But I greatly doubt they will. He would have to be moved from here, as well. I've nowhere for him, and neither Wydeville's nor Doncaster's is altogether safe anymore."

Around a mouthful of bread and cheese, Joliffe said, "I know how to get him away."

Master Roussel, Perrette, and Kechyn all looked at him as if he had suddenly appeared from nowhere. Joliffe swallowed the bread and cheese and said, "I'll show you."

It did not take long. Some grease from the pot kept near the hearth for greasing pans served to flatten the man's curls, and ashes combed into it turned his hair a weary gray. Then Joliffe asked for honey, lard, and brown flour. Master Roussel, probably with a wary thought of what his wife would have to say about this rifling of her kitchen, found them and brought them to where Joliffe was now straddling the bench with Kechyn seated facing him. Master Roussel was about to sit down with Perrette on the table's other side to watch whatever Joliffe would do next, but Joliffe asked, "Can you get me some women's clothing?"

"Hai!" Kechyn protested.

"Not for you," Joliffe said and added to Master Roussel, "A gown that will cover me, and a coif and a headkerchief. Very plain if possible."

By the time Master Roussel returned with a faded green

gown, a coif, and headkerchief, Joliffe had almost finished with the man, who now had a round, fat nose, lumpy cheeks and a dull-fleshed face.

Master Roussel, stopped in the doorway with a soft exclaim. Perrette, who was having trouble holding back from laughter, looked around to him and asked, "Yes?"

"Yes!" Master Roussel agreed.

Joliffe stood up and stepped back to judge his work, wiping his hands on a cloth and warning, "It won't hold for long, so we had best leave now. Give me the gown." He was glad to see it would go over his doublet. His cloak would serve, hopefully, to hide the unlikely shape of him in it.

Master Roussel handed him the gown while looking a question to Perrette, who answered, "It seems the fellow had an overly merry last night in Rouen. His two lady-friends are loath to part with him. Or maybe we fear he will not find his way to his ship on his own."

When Joliffe was ready, Kechyn took up a strapped sack he must have brought with him. Led by Perrette, they went out by way of Master Roussel's rear yard into the alley but only a short way along it before she opened a well-oiled gate and led them into a passageway so narrow it was barely there between two houses that joined above it, roofing it into pitchy darkness. Lesser darkness at its further end showed where it ended at a street, partly blocked by another gate at which Perrette ordered in a whisper, "Stand."

Both men obeyed while she opened this other well-oiled gate, thrust her head and shoulders out, looked both ways with over-played care, went out, and—giggling—turned to beckon Joliffe and Kechyn to her. As they joined her, she put a finger to her lips and hissed, "Ssshhhhh!" very loudly, before hooking her arm through Kechyn's and starting to pull him along the street in a tipsy-slipsy way.

Joliffe linked his arm through the man's other arm and copied her, giggling, too. Kechyn did not immediately get into the spirit of the business, at first only staggering because Joliffe and Perrette pulled him into it, even protesting as Perrette turned at the first corner, "This is the wrong way." He started to point. "The harbor is . . ."

Perrette swung herself against him, stopping his arm and heartily kissed him before hissing into his face, "Just do what I do and don't talk if you can't sound drunk."

He lurched a fairly convincing step back from her, giving Joliffe reason to lean hard against him as if to steady him while whispering to Perrette, "No kissing. The masking won't hold." As it was, he was counting on the cold to hold it a while longer than otherwise.

Perrette giggled drunkenly at him and pulled them onward. It was late enough in the night that many of the lanterns hung by doorways had gone out, leaving the streets mostly to shadows and cold starlight. Likewise, it seemed that such of the watch as might have been in the streets were gone, too—Joliffe guessed out of the cold into somewhere warm. Only a few other revelers—probably too drunk to feel the cold—and several skulking lone figures happened into sight as Perrette led them unevenly through Rouen. Kechyn grasped now what she and Joliffe were trying for, joined in their faked argument at a corner of the marketplace on which way they should go from there, and by the time they reached one of the city gateways to the quay, was lurching and singing as well as either of them.

Because tides kept their own time, there was no curfew at the harbor's gates. Lanterns and torches blazed everywhere, there being more than one ship readying to leave on the tide's turn, and the guards made no trouble over a drunken man and his two whores swaying past. Perrette had cut the time fine: men were starting to loose the ropes holding the *Bonhomme* to the quay. At the gang-board, a sailor placed there to keep the unwanted from going aboard demanded to see Kechyn's coins, to show he would be a paying passenger. "But not them," he added with a nod at Perrette and Joliffe.

"No," Perrette agreed with shrill merriment. "Not us." She elbowed Joliffe rudely aside, pulled Kechyn around and to her by his cloak, and gave him a long, hard kiss and a grind of her hips. In his startlement, he let his strapped sack thump to the cobbles. The sailor laughed and said something rude. Giggling, Perrette staggered back from Kechyn and sideways into Joliffe so that they tangled "drunkenly" with each other, staggering away together as Kechyn snatched up his bag and went aboard. Giggling and holding each other up, they waved and watched, making certain none but crew followed Kechyn onto the ship before the gangplank was hauled in and the ship cast off.

They went on leaning on each other and waving farewell until Perrette said, "He's away. If he isn't safe now, that's how the dice rolls and it's beyond our helping it. We're done here. Come."

Still playing the somewhat drunken whores, they lurched back into Rouen, Joliffe letting Perrette choose their way as she threaded them through several back alleys and passageways. They lost their seeming-drunkenness along the way, well before they came into the street where they had started. Joliffe supposed they were bound for Master Roussel's house again, or else Doncaster's or Wydeville's, but as they went careful-footed along the dark slit of the passageway toward the alley, Perrette paused, snicked a latch, opened a door Joliffe had not known was there, and let them into a small room that was—guessing by the barely glowing coals on a small hearth—someone's kitchen. Those should have been covered for the night but were not, which was good or they would have had to make their way blindly to another door and into another small room.

There, with the kitchen door shut behind them, they were in full darkness, and Perrette took him by the hand. She led him across the room, said softly, "Stairs," and set his hand on them. In the darkness he could only tell they were of wood and steep, but he could guess they were probably also narrow, with a wall on one side and nothing on the other.

"Don't stumble on your skirts," Perrette said, still softly, and started up them.

Joliffe bundled his skirts up and out of his way over one arm, used his other hand to feel his way, and more or less crawled up behind her. At their top, Perrette said, "Wait," and he listened as, invisible, she padded away from him, until with a scrape of wood on wood she opened a shutter to the lesser darkness of the night outside, relieving the room's utter blackness but doing nothing to relieve its damnable cold. Able to see at least shapes now, Joliffe guessed by a curtained bed against the further wall that it was a bedchamber.

Crossing to the bed, Perrette pushed aside the nearer curtain, swung her cloak from her shoulders, and spread it over whatever covers were already on the bed. "It's too late—or too early—for you to go elsewhere. I'm inviting you into my bed," she said, a touch of laughter in her voice. "But you might want to take off your gown first."

With a soft laugh of agreement, Joliffe freed himself from his cloak and copied her in laying it over the bed before ridding himself of the headkerchief, coif, and gown, folding them and putting them on a stool he had knocked against on his way to the bed. He was aware of Perrette undressing, too, down to her white undergown, a pale shape in the room's darkness. In the normal way of things, in a house and with a bed, it was usual to go to bed naked, but she went no further, instead moved toward the bed, saying with a weariness that matched his own, "Come sleep now."

Some other time Joliffe would have regretted she did not sound like she was inviting him to more than simply sleep. Just now, though, everything was so far in so many ways from where he had started the day, from what he had thought the day would be, from what the day had become, and he was now so tired, that he seemed to be moving half-brained through a strange dream that seemed to make sense now but might not in the morning when he awoke. Body and mind, he was weary; fumbling out of his doublet and hosen with increasing clumsiness, he wanted nothing so much as what she had offered—sleep.

She was in the bed now, holding the covers open for him. Still in his shirt and braies, he joined her. The sheets were as chill and damp as he had expected they would be. Sheets were always chill and damp this time of year unless there were bed-stones to warm them. And a fire to warm the bed-stones. And, with luck, a servant to warm the bed-stones and put them into the bed. Lacking servant, fire, or bed-stones, Joliffe and Perrette made do with each other— would surely have made more than do, except just then weariness and the need for warmth were stronger than lust, and when they had warmed the bed and each other enough for the shivering to stop, they fell simply to sleep, wrapped tightly together in each other's arms.

Chapter 20

Matters were otherwise in the morning.

Joliffe awoke first and lay for a long moment with his eyes closed, gathering memory of where he was and why, before opening his eyes to the gray light of a cloudy dawn in a strange room. Perrette was no longer in his arms. His body and mind both regretted that, until he found she had only rolled over and a little away from him in her sleep. By her breathing, she still slept, and he shifted to curve himself along the curve of her back, carefully put an arm over her, and stroked lightly at the softness of one breast. Perrette made a small murmur of pleasure and wriggled her body backward, closer to his. Joliffe presumed then to kiss her uppermost shoulder, then gently moved her long hair aside from the back of her neck and shifted his kisses to there. By then she was at least half awake and softly laughing as she rolled over, keeping in the curve of his arm to press the length of her body against his and return his kisses.

What came next came naturally, and afterward they lay,

again wrapped in each other's arms, in utter ease. It was only after a while that Perrette stirred enough to stroke a hand along his jaw and murmur, "You're fortunate to have a pale beard. Even this morning it hardly shows."

"It saves on shaving," Joliffe murmured in return. His own hand began to move along the lovely curve of her hip and thigh.

She shifted slightly to show she liked that and said, teasingly, "You played the woman well last night."

"I've been . . ." Despite himself, Joliffe's hand and answer paused before he finished, "When I was a player traveling with a company and all, we all had to play every part, sooner or later."

Perrette, now running the tip of her forefinger in invisible patterns on his chest, murmured, "You also play the man very well."

By the shift of her hips against him, she gave him to understand she was willing for him to play the man again right now. He was ready in every way and more than willing, and afterward, replete and content, they lay for a long time silent together. Beyond the window, both the day and Rouen were fully awake, and he was so late to his secretary-duties—beyond any good excuse he could make—that he saw no point in hurrying to be out of bed. Perrette seemed to feel the same about wherever she might be supposed to be.

Only necessity finally drove them from the comforts of bed and each other, Perrette saying, "The kitchen will be warmer," as they gathered up their clothing in shivering haste.

In the kitchen, a pottery jar set at the rear of the hearth was full of water still somewhat warm from the fire that had died on the hearth in the night. While Joliffe hurriedly washed and dressed, Perrette readied kindling and slivers of wood on the hearth, took a coal kept alive from yesterday in a small, sealed firepot, and encouraged little flames to dancing life. Then, while she washed and dressed in her turn, Joliffe tended the fire into a sufficient little blaze that they were able to break their fast with toasted bread and honey stiff from its pot.

While they ate, Joliffe had time to note not only how small the room was—narrow and short and low—and how clean—the stone-flagged floor swept; no cobwebs among the ceiling beams—but how bare of comforts. Except for the honey, there were only necessities: the fire and its fuel, a toasting fork, a long-handled spoon, and a short-legged pot hanging beside the hearth, a basin and pail of water with which to wash, a three-legged stool, a wooden box with a lid where the bread and the knife to cut it were kept, along with the honeypot and its spoon, and a lidded jug from which Perrette poured ale into a single wooden cup to share with Joliffe. Joliffe presumed there was at least a bowl in the box, too, but he did not see it. There was not even a table.

Upstairs, he had noted little beyond the comfort of the bed and of Perrette, either last night in the dark or this morning when—once he had slipped from the shelter of the bedcurtains—he had only been in haste to be downstairs; but thinking back, it seemed that room had been as bare as this one was of anything not starkly necessary. If this was Perrette's house, he did not have to wonder if she lived alone: she seemed hardly to live here herself.

Last night and this morning did not give him any right to question her about herself, but while he crouched on his heels to toast another piece of bread, he said easily, "You know something of my past. That I've been a player. But I know nothing of yours."

Perrette, seated on the stool close by, had begun combing her fingers through her hair, readying it to plait and fasten up. Her silence seemed to be all the answer she was going to give him until she said quietly, "I had family once and a home. Then the war happened. Now I have neither. I have my cousin. I have my work. There is no more."

No more that she was going to tell him, anyway. And certainly no more that he had better ask, her silence told him.

There was something that he *had* to ask, though, and uneasily he did, because it was something he should have thought of sooner. "Um. If . . . a child . . . if there's . . ."

"There'll be none," Perrette said, still quietly. "I thank you for asking, though." She stopped combing her hair to take the toasted bread he now offered her. It was the last of the bread and she tore it in half and shared with him.

In the easiness that implied between them, Joliffe tried another question. "The fellow we helped on his way to England last night. What word is he taking to England that's so desperate?"

"I don't know, and you should not ask."

"You don't wonder?"

"I wonder. But it's better not to know."

There seemed nothing else to say. Joliffe ate his share of bread slowly. Perrette ate hers more quickly, plaited her hair, stood up as he finished eating, and said, "Best we go our ways now. We are surely late to our duties."

They surely were, but putting off necessity for the moment, he held out his arms to her. She came to him readily, and they stood together, their arms around each other, the slender length of her body pressed along his, her cheek on his shoulder and his on her head nestled against his neck. For that moment, she was more real than anything else in the world. Was more warm and alive and . . .

Memory of Alizon—deliberately kept at bay for this while—came cold through his mind: Alizon lying dead and empty in the garden, with nothing of warmth or life left to her, with everything gone from her . . .

Joliffe did not know if it was because his body responded to the thought in some way Perrette felt, but from somewhere among her own thoughts, Perrette, with her face still pressed against his shoulder, asked in the same quiet way she had told of herself, "The demoiselle who was killed yesterday, she was the one who was 'Wisdom' in the Shrovetide play? Fair-haired and lovely?"

Keeping his warm, tight hold around her, Joliffe answered softly, "Yes."

"Ah." No more than that small, single sound, but it seemed to Joliffe to carry a world of grieving, not only for Alizon but for all the lovely things that died before they should have.

They stood together a moment longer, until Perrette stepped back from his hold with the firmness of having given as much of herself as she intended to give and became as she had almost always been—quick and assured and needing nothing and no one except herself as she gathered up her cloak and said again, "Best we go our ways now."

Joliffe, picking up his own cloak more slowly, said, "Perrette. One thing. It was not you who was in the garden with Alizon yesterday?"

Perrette stopped in the midst of fastening her cloak at the throat and looked at him. Rather than offense, merriment danced in her eyes. "No," she said. "Was it you?"

"No," he said, no more offended that she seemed to be. It was a fair return-question, after all. But apology seemed needed, too. "I thought I should ask."

"So you should. Although it might have been better to do so before putting yourself at my mercy by falling to sleep. And of course I could be lying to you." Mischief was added to the merriment. "Instead of merely lying *with* you."

"I could be the one who is lying," Joliffe pointed out.

"You could be, and if so, then I am the foolish one." She went to the door into the passageway. "Fortunately, we both survived the night."

Following her, Joliffe protested lightly, "But what was that you said about 'merely' lying with me? There was more than 'merely' about it." He went deliberately sorrowful. "Wasn't there?"

Her only answer was to laugh at him, as he had meant her to do, laughter being a better way than some to return to the world they had let go for a few blessed hours.

Outside, they went separate ways without more farewells, Joliffe taking his straightest way back to Joyeux Repos, save for a stop at an early-opened tavern—although not all that early; the morning was well along toward noon, he found—to make sure his breath smelled of wine. After that, he rumpled his hair and slacked open the collar of his doublet and shirt front, and for good measure, let loose two of the points holding up one of his hosen and was hobble-hopping, trying to tie them again while walking, as he came up to the *hôtel*'s gateway. The guards there were rude-humoured at him, favoring him with their opinion of someone fool enough to disappear after there had been a murder. Still fumbling at his points, Joliffe muttered thickly, "You didn't see her dead. I did. Blood everywhere, and there she was, lying in it, and . . ."

"Clerks," one of the guards grunted. "Can't face anything brighter than ink." He pushed Joliffe, not unfriendly, through the gateway. "Get on with you."

"Best you go straight to Master Wydeville, if you know what's good for you," the other one offered.

Master Wydeville being very much whom Joliffe wanted to see, he took that advice, cutting across the courtyard to the tower door beside the stableyard as quickly as John Ripon's unsteady condition would allow. Nor did he give up his seeming when inside and on the stairs, but went up them with an occasional lurch against the wall and a few groans just loud enough to be heard ahead of him. By the time he shuffled into the office, Master Wydeville was ready for him, glaring. Pierres and Henri were also there, holding various papers and looking uncertain whether to be openly amused or safely disapproving.

Master Wydeville had no such ambiguity. Coldly angry, he said, "Master Ripon."

Joliffe flinched and clutched his head with both hands. "Sir. I. Yesterday. The blood. And all. I."

"Pierres, Henri, we'll finish later," Master Wydeville snapped. "I'd best see to this now."

Both men bowed and retreated. Master Wydeville followed them far enough to be certain the door was closed behind them, saying while he did, "Master Ripon, you're a fool. By disappearing as you did, you've caused trouble where we did not need more trouble. Neither my lady nor I are pleased with you." Turning back from the door, he went on, his voice still stern but too low to be heard beyond the room, "He's safe away?"

His voice even lower than Master Wydeville's, Joliffe said, "Yes."

"Without trouble on the way?"

"None."

"Afterward?"

"None then, either."

"I meant, where have you been?"

"Perrette gave me place to stay. The hour being so late. Then we slept late into this morning."

With no sign of taking other than what the bare words said, Master Wydeville accepted that with a nod but went on, "The misfortune is that, no matter how well you've done, John Ripon has done badly and must suffer for it."

Having been certain of that, Joliffe gave a quick nod of understanding, and took the chance to ask, "How is it with Master Durevis?"

"He still lives. I was able to question him somewhat in the while he was in his senses toward dawn. I let him understand he's in danger of being thought Alizon's murderer. That made him willing to tell what he could, but it's little enough beyond what you already had from him." Master Wydeville was still speaking sternly and now rapidly, because there was only so much time the chamberlain would waste on John Ripon but the spymaster needed to tell as much as need be. "First and foremost, he *is* the duke of Burgundy's man, as we feared."

"He admitted it straight out?"

"Because he hopes to be ransomed rather than hung. He was to learn what he could against Lady Jacquetta, to send it straight to Burgundy to give the duke a lever against her uncles."

"Against her uncles? Not her brother?"

"Her brother, as the count of Saint-Pol, is held, perforce, to playing Burgundy's game, to keep his lands and people safe. Her uncle Sir Jean de Luxembourg is less bound that way, and while he can no longer fight with us against the Armagnacs, neither will he fight against us. He prefers to hold to his past oaths more faithfully than Burgundy does, and Burgundy wants to bring him to heel. As for Bishop Louys, his bishopric is in Burgundy's hands but he's beyond Burgundy's hold. But Burgundy would make use of any infamy proved against Lady Jacquetta to show the bishop has failed in his duty to his niece, disgracing the family."

"There is no infamy, though," Joliffe said.

"That does not mean Durevis could not have twisted something to that end. Lies will serve where truth does not, but they're all the better if built on even the thinnest strand of truth."

"And Alizon was helping him to betray Lady Jacquetta?"

"Not knowingly, if Durevis says true. He thought all she would have to share was merry household talk about what he would have known if he hadn't had to ride out against the Armagnacs."

Joliffe had never heard the word "merry" said so grimly, and if Durevis had been wooing Alizon only for what she might unwittingly betray to him, it seemed a waste of her loveliness. But her loveliness was all wasted now, and he asked a thing he had already wondered about. "What was he doing back here at all?" Raising his voice and turning it into John Ripon's on the last four words for the sake of anyone trying to overhear.

Master Wydville gave a silent "Ha," of approval before answering, "He came back to Rouen two days ago with others of the household men. Because they were to ride out today in guard of more supply wagons, they were kept at the castle, rather than being so briefly here."

His voice low again, Joliffe asked, "When did she promise him 'secrets' then?"

"Before he rode out, she laughed that if what she thought turned out true, she would have two fine secrets when next they met. That's why he troubled, this first time he returned to Rouen, to send her a message to meet him in the garden. He hoped to learn these secrets."

But he had not, because . . . Slowly Joliffe said, "Someone killed Alizon to keep her from telling those secrets? Is that the way of it, do you think? Which means those secrets exist, and Alizon knew them or else that someone believed she did. Or . . . maybe there are no secrets, and she was killed for some other reason entirely."

"Whichever of those is true, we need to find who did it," Master Wydville said. "Questions have to be asked about who was where in the household yesterday afternoon, and when. The marshal and coroner have done that to some degree, but you are nearer it all, will see what they do not, ask questions differently than they can, and be answered differently. You see what I want you to do?"

Joliffe curtly nodded and asked, "What's been learned thus far?"

"Very little. M'dame, who would usually know most, was gone out. An errand for Lady Jacquetta's coming birthday, so that she wanted to go to a goldsmith's shop herself. Lady Jacquetta was in the chapel in prayer. Other than that, there's been too much weeping and wailing among the demoiselles for much sense to be had from them." His voice rose and went irked. "I've let you make excuses enough, Ripon. None of them suffice. Go to your duties for now. No. Where is your gown?"

Pitching his voice into the humiliated John Ripon's carrying whine, Joliffe said his gown was in the dorter.

"Then go dress yourself properly to be seen in my lady's house," Master Wydeville snapped.

Joliffe cringed a bow and left hurriedly. In the dorter, he tossed his cloak onto the bed and shrugged into his black gown, all the while going through what Master Wydeville had told him and he otherwise knew. Durevis had been using Alizon in hope of learning something against Lady Jacquetta. If the killing was not from plain stupidity, then either Alizon had found out such a thing, or else someone feared she had, and that someone had silenced her. Someone who had come to the garden before Durevis. From the *hôtel*, following Alizon—or through the door from the riverside path? From the *hôtel*, most likely. So the someone was likely still here, because it would be too simple if whoever in the household was guilty had simply run off and was openly missing. As he had been, himself, last night. But he was also among those who could not be guilty, because he had his fellow secretaries and clerks to say where he was when Alizon was killed. Just as he knew where they had been—a hands-count of men he did not have to find out about. That only left how many in the household still to go?

Too many.

Begin simply, he told himself. There were a goodly number who almost certainly could not have followed Alizon, would not even have known when she went from the *hôtel*. Anyone of the kitchen could be discounted. Or maybe not. There were knives in plenty in the kitchen. Easy enough to take up one and later return it. Even if not wiped completely clean, a bloodied knife could easily go unremarked in a kitchen if slipped in among others waiting to be cleaned. Master Wydeville had said the killing was done with a dagger but . . .

Joliffe took firm hold on that trail of thought. It was stretching likelihood that someone of the kitchen had chanced to leave there, taking a knife with them, at just the right time to follow Alizon to the garden and kill her, then known to lie in wait for Durevis, and after leaving him for dead, return to the kitchen with never anyone taking note that they had been gone for no good reason. Even if this supposed-someone had made some manner of excuse yesterday of where they had been, after Alizon was found surely some new questions about where they had been would have been roused.

Or perhaps not. People could be curiously incurious about things that should raise a warning.

Still, there were more likely possibilities to be followed first, he thought as he started downstairs again. Beginning with those of the household closest to Lady Jacquetta, and therefore closest to Alizon. Fortunately, that included very few men. Which brought him immediately to Alain. But Alain had been giving heed to Guillemete since Shrovetide. Why should he have followed Alizon to the garden—or cared what she did there? Or, at least, cared enough to kill her? No, this had to be deeper than Alain was.

Or did Guillemete have something to gain from her older sister's death?

There was an ugly thought Joliffe did not want to have.

Downstairs again and aware of John Ripon's disgrace, he slunk with lowered gaze and hunched shoulders through Master Wydeville's office under Pierres' disapproving look. In his own office, silence, save for the scratching of busy pens, was his only greeting among his fellows as he slipped to his desk, except that after a few minutes Henri hissed, "At least fasten your collars."

Having left his shirt and doublet undone so someone could disapprove, Joliffe hurriedly laid down the pen he had just finished sharpening and fumbled them closed. He had pen in hand again when George asked, "So, just what did you see in the garden, that you had to run off and get drunk?"

Henri hissed disapproval at him, while Joliffe again dropped his pen, sank his head onto the desk, and moaned, "Blood. She was lying there in all that blood." He clutched his head between his hands. "Oh, god and the saints! All that blood!"

"Leave it for now," Henri said angrily.

Everyone turned back to his own work, leaving John Ripon to his misery and Joliffe to his thoughts. Among the scratching of pens and the rustling of papers and parchments, he set to fair-copying a letter he had drafted yesterday, his mind going its own way while his hand moved across the paper. Speaking of blood had reminded him that blood was a part of the problem. How much might have got on the murderer? If much, being rid of it would have been troublesome. But that was surely something Master Wydeville at least had thought of and seen to questions among the household—someone with a change of clothing, or bloodied clothing found discarded. And perhaps the murderer had had the good fortune not to be betrayingly blood-bespattered.

The trouble was the murderer seemed to have been altogether too fortunate in too many ways.

Perversely, that made Joliffe think the murder could not have been planned. In life, plans seemed to go awry more often than not. Therefore, given how much seemed to have gone in the murderer's favor, this murder had to have been unplanned.

Joliffe was pursuing that doubtful logic when his untended pen splotted ink across his writing. He sat back, startled into looking at his work, and found the ink had only finished marring what he had already done badly.

Pierres, just come in with papers in his hand. said disgustedly, seeing the mess, "You're useless today, Ripon. Go lie down or something. Just don't go out again or you'll be in worse trouble."

Joliffe muttered John Ripon's shamed thanks, went on muttering with self-pitying misery while he wiped his pen and closed his inkpot and gave a pointless shuffle to his papers, sure by the time he finally left that he had made everyone glad to see him go.

Chapter 21

The trouble was that—released from his desk—where was he to go? Given that he had no overt authority to be wandering through the *hôtel* asking questions, he decided to do, first, simply as Pierres had said. He wanted time to think more. The dorter's long space under the roof seemed still as deserted as it should be at this hour of the day. Joliffe heard no sound of anyone else, anyway, as he went to his stall, pushed his pillow against the wall at the head of his bed and sat, wrapped in his cloak and not particularly comfortable but glad to give over being John Ripon for a time.

Not for the first time, he wondered how much longer he would be kept at this pretence. How much more was he to learn before being loosed from the household?

On the face of it, the desire to be done here and away seemed unreasonable, if not downright foolish. He was presently living far softer than ever anywhere else in his life, with even Lent's penances and fasting eased by wealth and skilled cooks. And yet—

Joliffe had learned to be wary when his mind threw up "and yet." It meant, usually, that he was about to make more of some matter than he wished he would.

And yet—despite the ease of the rich life in Joyeux Repos inside the strong circle of Rouen's walls, he was never truly at ease. He was too aware there were reasons why Rouen's castle kept a full garrison overlooking the town—why there were so many men-at-arms to be seen in Rouen's streets—why nobles and gentlemen of the household had ridden out armed and armored and hoping for brigands to hunt. The peace and safety of Joyeux Repos were real enough, but beyond Rouen's walls was war. The raw warfare that had been tearing France and Normandy to bleeding pieces for more than a generation, with no surety that sometime, anytime, even soon, that warfare would not break through into Rouen, into Joyeux Repos.

Or perhaps, with Alizon's murder, it had already, given Durevis was Burgundy's man.

Except murder was murder, a thing apart from warfare.

Unless the killing that came with warfare was looked at for what it was—murder claimed as a virtue because men did it at the behest of those over them rather than by their own wills.

Although it was by their own wills that they chose to obey and kill.

And the dead were just as dead when it was done.

Was it that their being dead was held not to matter so much? That killing in quantity in a war was a different matter from killing one by one in "peaceful" murders?

Yet each death was a separate death for the person who died.

As near as Joliffe could sort it out, there seemed to be a severance between parts of a man's mind, with no link between them, if he could see single killing as a sin but killing in quantity a virtue so long as your lord or your fellows told you to do it. He hoped that was a severance he would never make.

But none of that brought him nearer to knowing why Alizon had been murdered. Even the how was not firmly determined yet. Stabbed, yes, but beyond that, what was sure? That she had gone to the garden and been killed there by someone before Durevis came, and that that someone then had waited—dangerous though the waiting was—and tried to kill Durevis.

But had this someone gone with her to the garden? Surely not. He—for likelihood's sake, let it be "he" for now—must have followed her. Or he could have been in the garden already, waiting for her. No. If he had been waiting for her, she would not have unlocked the door.

But he could have unlocked it himself after she was dead. Supposing she had told him she was there to meet someone. Although that might be something he had already known.

Or he might have come through the door after she unlocked it for Durevis.

Or over the wall at any time.

And there was always the chance that it was Durevis he had foremost intended to kill, and Alizon been killed simply to have her out of the way. That was something Joliffe had not considered until now—that someone, knowing Alizon was going to meet Durevis, had followed her, killed her to have her out of his way, and then waited for Durevis to come.

But if that was the way of it, why hadn't he made sure of Durevis before running away? Besides, there had to be far better places to waylay Durevis than in the *hôtel*'s garden.

Unless here was the one place the murderer could be sure of finding him.

That gave two clear questions: Who could have been waiting for Alizon in the garden? Or else who could have followed her there?

Or rather, three questions. Had she indeed had secrets she meant to tell Durevis?

Or maybe it was four questions: supposing she had secrets to tell, who would know it?

Or—

Joliffe swung sideways and stood up from the bed, not to escape the increasing questions but because someone was coming along the dorter between the sleeping cells. That in itself was not unreasonable—unusual at this hour, but not unreasonable. After all, Joliffe himself was here. But someone in this *hôtel* was a murderer, and he had not known how deep-set was his unease at that until now, when his instant response to being found here alone was sharp wariness.

It was only with an effort that he made himself sit down again, now on the bed's edge. After all, among Master Doncaster's lessons was how to defend and how to attack from sitting; and he shifted his clerk's robe to clear his dagger, propped his elbows on his knees, and sank his head onto his hands in the seeming that John Ripon might well have just now, but all in a way that kept a clear view of the curtain closing his stall.

Whoever had come along the dorter stopped, shook his curtain, and asked, "Ripon, are you in there?"

Relieved, knowing Foulke's voice, he raised his head. "Yes."

Foulke pushed the curtain aside. Usually a sober-faced man, he was more sober-faced than usual and doubtful as he said, "You weren't at your work. My lady says you're to come to her. But if you're ill . . ."

Joliffe stood up. "I'm not ill. I had a bad night. Yesterday and all. How are you today?"

Foulke went from sober-faced to grim. "Well enough. It's my lady and the others need their minds eased. Are you fit to read to them? M'dame thought it could help."

Joliffe straightened his shoulders and ran his hands backward through his hair. "Do I look fit enough?"

Foulke eyed him with no great approval but said, "You'll do." And added as they went toward the stairs, "They say you're overset by what we saw yesterday."

Tired though he was with John Ripon, Joliffe answered with something of Ripon's whine, "It was the blood and seeing her dead that way. I've never seen anyone dead like that. With blood and all."

"You've not been in France long enough, then," Foulke said without sympathy.

"I don't want to be here long enough for that. And this is Rouen. There shouldn't be killing *here*."

" 'Shouldn't' isn't the same as 'won't be,' " Foulke said over his shoulder as they went down the stairs. "Who would have thought, a year ago this time, that we'd be on the edge of losing Paris. We 'shouldn't' be." He dropped his voice as they came off the stairs and started along the gallery. "But we are."

His own voice as low, Joliffe made Ripon protest, "We can't be. If we lose Paris, what happens to the rest of France?"

"It will probably go, too. For now, anyway. Normandy is otherwise, if that's any comfort to you. Normandy we'll hang onto by tooth and toenail for as long as there's still among us those who think this war is worth the winning."

"Worth the winning? Don't you think it's worth the winning?"

"Oh, I think it's worth the winning," Foulke assured him. "Whether it can be, now Burgundy has turned—" He shrugged.

"Is that what the duke of Bedford thought, too?"

"Bedford?" Foulke's voice warmed, as Joliffe had noted most people's did when speaking of Bedford. "His brother gave him Normandy and France to keep for the young king until the young king could keep it for himself. That was what mattered to Bedford—keeping faith with his brother. He did it, too. Better than any other man could have."

Foulke's voice took on a bitter edge. "The trouble was that others didn't keep faith with him. Now it's time for young King Henry to get himself here and take up what's his to have. Only I don't see him making any move to come. If he doesn't —" Foulke shrugged. "Who knows what will come of it all?"

Foulke might not *know*, but what he *thought* would come was plain enough, and Joliffe's layers of unease thickened.

At Lady Jacquetta's parlor they found that Bishop Louys and one of the household priests had come to discuss Alizon's funeral and were withdrawn with Lady Jacquetta, Guillemete, and M'dame into the bedchamber to talk privately, leaving the other demoiselles to each other's company and—to judge by the reddened eyes among them—shared tears.

"You're to wait, though, Master Ripon," Ydoine said. As tear-marked as the others, she was at least calm-voiced.

Michielle added on a hopeful, tear-edged sniff, "You could read to us meanwhile."

"No," Ydoine said. "We wait for my lady. Would you have some wine while you wait, Master Ripon?"

Joliffe said that he would; was wondering how he could best use this chance to ask questions here without bringing on more tears, when Ydoine came to it first, asking as she handed a filled goblet to him, "Where were you when it happened?"

Startled, Joliffe echoed, "Where was I?"

"It's what we're all asking ourselves," Blanche said from where she sat at the window with Isabelle. "Where . . . what . . ."

She broke off, her tears flowing again, and Ydoine finished for her, "Where were we, what were we doing when Alizon died. All unknowing, what were we doing?"

"Weren't you all here?" Joliffe asked.

"I was gone out with M'dame," said Ydoine.

Marie from where she sat on a cushion on the floor with

one of Lady Jacquetta's little dogs clutched to her breast said, "Michielle and I were with my lady in the chapel. She was praying."

Joliffe supposed she would be, there being little other reason to be in the chapel, but he nodded with solemn approval of that before asking, somewhat with mischief, "Weren't you and Michielle praying, too?"

Marie gave him an unexpectedly stricken—guilty?—look and hid her face against the top of the dog's furry head, while Michielle gave a soft, sobbing gasp and said, "No. We were talking with one of the priests there."

Marie raised her head. "Just outside the chapel," she said in quick defense. "Not inside while my lady was praying." She pressed her face to the dog's head again, muffling, "We shouldn't have been."

"We knew him from when we did the play. There wasn't any reason we couldn't talk with him. We didn't know!" Michielle wailed.

Isabelle at the window said miserably, "You didn't do anything amiss. It's Blanche and I who let her go. We just sat here and let her go. If we hadn't . . ." She broke off and turned her head away, to look out over the gardens.

"You were sitting there?" Joliffe asked, very carefully even-voiced. "At the window?"

Blanche and Isabelle nodded, Blanche gulping on a sob. Joliffe crossed the chamber to stand between them, looking out over the gardens. The little grove of slender trees at the greensward's end obscured the gateway to the enclosed garden, and its walls were too high to see over, even from here, just as he had thought.

"If we had looked we might have seen her going," Blanche mourned. "And seen whoever was with her. Then we'd know who . . . who . . ."

"We would have seen nothing," Isabelle returned, desperately defensive. "They surely went by way of the arbor walk. Even if we had looked, we would not have seen her."

Which was true enough, Joliffe saw. The near end of the arbor walk was out of sight of this window and probably most windows of the *hôtel*, and once into the walk Alizon and whoever else would have gone unseen to the enclosed garden. And, in the murderer's case, come back equally concealed.

"It isn't our fault she went!" Blanche wailed softly and covered her face, well-used handkerchief in hand.

"Of course it is not your fault," Ydoine said with the touch of impatience that told she had said it some several times before now. "Why should you think she'd gone to the garden? You had no reason to think it."

Marie gave an unexpected giggle. "Well—"

"Yes," Ydoine said sharply. "But now it is nothing to laugh at, is it?"

Sudden and stark-sober silence answered that from everyone, until Michielle said in a small voice, "Has anyone found him?"

The women's and girls' heads turned to Foulke still standing at the door. He shook his head. "Not that I have heard, no."

"Who?" Joliffe asked.

"Remon Durevis," Ydoine said with a quelling look at Michielle, as if angry at having to mention his name.

"Master Durevis?" Joliffe echoed, feigning the ignorance people found so hard not to answer if they could.

Marie lifted her cheek from the top of the dog's head. "He and Alizon, they . . . since Shrovetide . . . they . . . liked to be together when they could."

"Now he's missing," Isabelle said "And there's thought . . . some people think . . ."

She started to cry. Marie joined her. Feigning confusion, Joliffe said, "But he's been gone from Rouen these several weeks, with all the others."

"They came back two days ago," Ydoine said. "Or some of them. Only for a little while, without time allowed them to come here. We wouldn't even have known they were, except M'dame and I chanced to meet Sir Richard at the goldsmith's when we were out yesterday."

"M'dame went out to a goldsmith?" Joliffe asked, still playing ignorant. He had what Master Wydeville had told him, but he wanted to hear it from this side. "I would think there's not a goldsmith in Rouen who wouldn't gladly come here with his wares."

"It was about a birthday gift for Lady Jacquetta," Ydoine said. "That could hardly be done here without she knew everything. So M'dame went out. She stopped at a silversmith's, too, and bought four silver spoons to send to a godchild, for excuse."

"Was Sir Richard at the goldsmith's about a birthday gift, too?" Joliffe asked as if only trying to make easy, distracting talk.

"He just happened past and saw us," Ydoine answered. "Then he walked us back to here, but could not come in, which grieved us all. But he had to be back to the castle, he said. He left us at the gate."

"And you came in and found Lady Alizon was missing," Joliffe ventured.

"We came in, and Lady Jacquetta was just back from the chapel, and M'dame showed the spoons she had bought and said we had met Sir Richard. My lady asked how he did, and they talked of that a little, and then . . ." Ydoine looked around to the other women. "That was when M'dame asked where Alizon was, yes?"

"She asked before," Marie said. "When she first came in. Remember? But then she had to show my lady the spoons and didn't have answer until afterward."

"If we'd paid heed earlier and looked for her," Blanche said, choking on tears, "we might have found her before— found her in time to—"

"Would we have?" Ydoine demanded at Joliffe. "Blanche

keeps saying that, but would we have? Wasn't it long too late even before we began to look?"

"It was surely far too late," Joliffe said, and possibly it was, but he was following his thought about whether Sir Richard could have had time to leave M'dame and Ydoine at the *hôtel*'s gate, go up the street and follow the riverside path to the door in the garden's wall that was already unlocked for Durevis's coming, go in, kill Alizon, wait for Durevis, stab him, and be away, with time after that for Durevis to recover enough to leave before Alizon's body was found. It might have been possible. In the chill of the day, Alizon's blood might have congealed even faster than Joliffe guessed that it had. But it all hung on Sir Richard knowing that Alizon and Durevis were going to meet and when the garden door was going to be unlocked.

And on him having a reason to want them both dead.

And why would he have encumbered himself with M'dame and Ydoine? If—as Ydoine said—he happened on them in passing, he could have gone on passing or made excuse not to accompany them back to Joyeux Repos.

But of course Durevis was certain whoever stabbed him had run from the garden toward the house. That would not be Sir Richard.

Supposing Durevis was telling the truth.

"What's thought," Ydoine said, "is that Remon must have sent word to Alizon to meet him secretly. Otherwise why would she have gone to the garden yesterday?"

"And now he's missing and she's dead," Foulke said grimly from the doorway.

"So it's thought he met Lady Alizon and killed her?" Joliffe pursued.

"Yes," Ydoine said as if weary of the question.

"But it was truly too late to save her even before we began searching for her?" Blanche pleaded at him. "Truly it was already too late?"

Joliffe had never noticed her to have many thoughts, and so she must cling tightly to the few she had, he thought. She was surely clinging to this one, and to help her move onward from it, Joliffe said in a deliberately broken voice, "I'm . . . certain, my lady."

Blanche missed it, but Isabelle said instantly, "Oh!" and clamped a hand onto Blanche's wrist. "He saw her. He does not want to remember. Let him be."

"But Lady Jacquetta saw her, too," Blanche protested.

"Would you dare to ask *her* to remember?" Ydoine demanded. "No. Then do not ask him either. Think how you would feel if it were you being asked."

Blanche's eyes widened and her mouth made a silent O as that new thought took hold on her.

Joliffe judged that if the secrets Alizon had been delightedly hoping to tell Durevis did truly exist, Blanche would not be someone likely to suspect them—was unlikely to see a secret even set openly in front of her unless it came with bells and ribbons on it. But others among the demoiselles were sharper—Ydoine for one, certainly. If those secrets did exist, they surely had to do with Lady Jacquetta's household because Alizon was never elsewhere, and now—suddenly and belatedly—Joliffe wondered who else among the demoiselles might know them. Because if Alizon was dead because of them, whoever else knew them could be in like danger. Come to that, in how much danger would he be himself if he came close to them?

Rather than following that thought, he chose instead to play off Blanche's dismay by bowing his head and saying, still brokenly, "I just keep hoping . . . hoping that . . ."

"That she died quickly," said Foulke helpfully from the doorway.

Joliffe held back from giving an irked glance his way. Instead he shook his head and said, "No, not that. I mean, yes, I hope that. But . . . I just keep hoping that she was happy in her last days. Or her last day."

That was crudely done, he knew, but was rewarded as he raised his gaze to see looks passing hither and thither among the demoiselles. There was uncertainty, questioning, some surprise, he thought—but no guilt, no sudden wariness; and when Michielle said, "I suppose she was, yes. She was just as always," a general nodding agreed with her, except that Marie added, "I thought she was very merry yesterday and trying to hide it."

"That was because she had her secret hope of meeting Remon." Blanche sighed.

"It was a fool thing for him to be doing, meeting her like that," Foulke grumbled.

"It was even more foolish to have killed her!" Ydoine flashed back at him.

"Why did he?" Joliffe asked with an edge of anguish meant to draw answers.

"We don't *know*," Isabelle cried back at him, and Marie said, "We've talked and talked it over. We thought at first it might be because—"

She broke off as if away from something that should not be said aloud, but Blanche said, "She was not, though. Lady Jacquetta asked the coroner outright."

"Not with child," Marie explained, on the chance the men had not understood.

"Was there maybe someone jealous of her meeting Master Durevis?" Joliffe tried, trying to watch everyone at once and seeing looks again pass among them but again not as if hiding anything, only silently asking each other what they each thought, before there was a general lifting of shoulders and shaking of heads, and Ydoine said, "No. We would have already told if we thought there was, but there isn't."

They knew each other very well, these demoiselles who shared each other's lives hour by hour through most of every day. Secrets must be very hard to keep from each other, Joliffe thought. What could Alizon have known no one else did? And how had she come by it?

"So it had to be Remon," Isabelle sighed. "We just do not know *why*."

"Or maybe it's that someone has killed him," Marie said rather hopefully. "Then threw his body into the river, and that's why he has not been found. Then they killed Alizon, because she saw them do it. Or . . ."

"If Remon is missing, it's because he's guilty," Alain said angrily, unnoticed in the parlor's outer doorway until he spoke. "He went out from the castle yesterday afternoon and hasn't come back. What else can it be but he killed Lady Alizon and then fled? If ever *I* find him, I'll kill *him*!"

"Oh, *you*," Marie said scornfully.

Alain went red-faced. He started angrily, "I—" but from the bedchamber's doorway across the parlor, M'dame said sternly, "We do not need foolish talk of killing here."

An instant hush took everyone, and at a sharp gesture from M'dame as she stepped aside from the doorway, those not already standing stood up, and everyone together gave deep courtesies to Bishop Louys and a priest coming out of the bedchamber. The bishop swept past, but the priest paused long enough to make the sign of the cross and a murmured blessing over their bowed heads before leaving, too. As the demoiselles rose and Joliffe, Alain, and Foulke straightened, M'dame gestured for the demoiselles to go into the chamber and said, "Master Ripon, my lady is ready to be read to for a time. You may come, too. No one else, Foulke, until my lady says otherwise."

Alain started forward.

"No," M'dame said at him. "Not you either." She turned away into the bedchamber with a single, sharp beckon for Joliffe to follow her, and he did, leaving Alain standing beside Foulke with a stiffened, stricken face.

Chapter 22

In the bedchamber, Joliffe saw that M'dame was undoubtedly right to spare Alain, who would have been both discomfited and probably useless here among the weeping now being shared by Michielle and Blanche and Guillemete, all clinging together in the middle of the room while Marie sniffed heavily as she handed the little dog to Lady Jacquetta sitting on the chest at the bedfoot, the other dog nestled in her skirts. Even Ydoine, gone to pour a goblet of wine at the table beside the wall so that her back was to the room, had a betraying shudder to her shoulders, as if struggling against tears.

"All is decided?" Marie asked faintly.

Lady Jacquetta nodded. Her little dog pressed to the side of her face, she looked to Joliffe, and said, "Read to us, please."

M'dame was already bringing him a book. He had finished *Reynard* and begun an *Alexander* before Lent had brought its different sort of reading, but it was the *Alexander* M'dame now gave him, and he took up the siege of

Porus' city with its walls of gold and palace gates of ivory and ebony. Even if hardly suited with the black misery of the room, at least it was other than the grief and he read strongly and was nonetheless glad when after a time Lady Jacquetta held up a hand to silence him and said, "There is enough for now. My thanks." She looked around at her women. "Our thanks." And added as Joliffe bowed in answer, "Ydoine, give him some wine, that he not go from us thirsty as well as tired."

He had been searching, while reading, for a reason to keep him there, to give him chance to ask more questions, and he took this one gratefully, saying, "Thank you, my lady. I can read more if you like. I'm thirsty, yes, and grieving with you, but not tired."

"Grieving with us," Lady Jacquetta said, taking that up as he had hoped she would. "Yes. More than others may. You were there. You found her. You saw all."

Hoping to keep the talk to yesterday, Joliffe demurred, "I was only one of those who found her. Foulke and Master Queton were there, too."

Lady Jacquetta lifted one hand, dismissing their part in it, saying, "They only saw that she was dead, then left her. You stayed with her."

Joliffe wanted to defend at least Foulke but instead tried, as Ydoine handed him a filled goblet, "I understand there's search for Remon Durevis."

All Lady Jacquetta's ladies became suddenly interested in their laps or hands. Lady Jacquetta flashed a sharp look around at them all and said, her voice suddenly hard, "Yes. I hoped his time gone from here would let passions cool between him and Lady Alizon. M'dame had even spoken to her about it. To no good, it seems."

Guillemete faltered, "My lady, they had talked of betrothal. They . . ."

"Pah! There could be no question of that, and Remon well knew it. So did Alizon, or she was a fool."

"My lady," M'dame reproved, but Lady Jacquetta was already crossing herself, saying a quick prayer for forgiveness for ill-speaking the dead.

Joliffe copied everyone else in echoing her gesture, but asked as they finished, while he still had the chance, "How did she know to meet him, though? Surely there were no open messages between them."

"That has been asked," Lady Jacquetta said. Her accusing look went around her ladies again. "No one seems to know."

Blanche protested, "We don't!" and Isabelle added unhappily, "We've told all we know of it. Truly."

"You should have kept her from going," Michielle said, earning resentful looks as Blanche protested, "We didn't know it would come to this!"

"No," Lady Jacquetta agreed. "You did not know it would come to Alizon's death. But to her disgrace—that you had to know was possible."

"She would not have let herself be used that way. Never!" Guillemete cried from her handkerchief.

But Michielle said, hushed with horror, "That may be why Remon killed her. Because she would not let him . . . use her."

"But we don't know it was Remon who killed her!" Marie protested. "He may have been killed, too, and that could be why Alizon was killed. Because she was with him."

That was a theme Marie had followed in the outer chamber, Joliffe remembered, and for something different he tried—deliberately sounding hapless and hopeless, "Or Master Durevis was killed because *he* was with *her*. But that brings it back to who would have reason to kill her, doesn't it?" He looked around at all of them and finished feebly, "And no one did, did they?" on the chance of catching some betraying look somewhere.

Instead, he caught bewilderment on some faces, several

head-shakes of agreeing denial from others, and a tightening of M'dame's mouth that warned he had maybe pressed too far. But he went on, still working to sound no more than stupidly wondering, "Besides, who would even know she was gone to the garden at all? She would not have told anyone she was going to meet Master Durevis, surely."

Isabelle said, "Even Blanche and I did not know for any certainty where and why she was gone. We only guessed at it. I doubt she would have said more to anyone else."

Blanche nodded ready agreement with that but unwarily added, "Nor would we have told anyone anyway, even had we known."

"And let what came of your silence lesson you against it another time," M'dame snapped.

Everyone momentarily froze. Then Guillemete burst into open sobbing and collapsed sideways, her face into Lady Jacquetta's lap. As Lady Jacquetta bent over her, stroking her hair and murmuring to her, Blanche and Marie broke into matching weeping, and M'dame gave a cold nod of permission at Joliffe, letting him know he could leave.

He did, setting aside on a chest the goblet he had forgotten he still held as he made his escape, glad to leave the weeping but regretting as he closed the door that he had not learned more. Come to it, had he learned much at all or anything of use? Not who besides Blanche and Isabelle had known Alizon had gone out, nor how word had come to Alizon to meet Durevis. Marie at least seemed willing to think he was not the murderer but a victim, too. Was that simply from blind hope, or because she knew something she was not saying? And could he find chance to ask her without others there to hear him? He had not yet fully shaken free of the thought that Alizon might have been killed simply because she was in the way of someone's attempt at Durevis. Did Marie might know something that would help there?

An altogether new thought came to him—that there was nothing to say that the man who had attacked Durevis was the same as whoever stabbed Alizon.

Joliffe gave an inward shudder of refusal against that possibility. Better to keep to the likelihood they were the same man. And if Durevis told truly when he said whoever had stabbed him had run out of the garden as if back to the *hôtel*—always remembering that Durevis and truth might not keep close company much of the time—then the murderer was almost surely someone of either the bishop's or Lady Jacquetta's household. And if—for some reason— this someone needed Durevis dead *now* but had no other likely way to come at him, that could explain the hazard- laden chance they had taken in the garden.

But, again, if Durevis was the intended victim, why not make more certain of his death, instead of taking that single ill-done stab and then fleeing? Someone ruthless enough to kill Alizon to have her out of the way would surely have made sure of Durevis.

No, this had to do with Alizon and, almost to a cer- tainty, with the secrets she had laughingly said she might have to tell. Almost surely she had been killed to keep her from telling any secrets. And Durevis had been killed because . . .

Not because he "was there" when Alizon was killed. He had not been there. Nor had he come so soon afterward that he might have caught her murderer just after the act. By the evidence of the blood, there had been time enough for the murderer to get well away. Why had he risked lingering long enough to kill Durevis? Did he think Alizon had al- ready told these secrets and killed her in punishment, then attempted to kill Durevis for the same reason?

But if the murderer knew enough to know Alizon had learned these secrets, whatever they were, didn't he know she had not yet had chance to tell Durevis? Or had he been uncertain whether she had or not, and so decided that her death would serve either as a sure silencing—or else as punishment?

But why kill Durevis? The questions kept coming back to that. If Alizon had already told him these secrets, he could be expected to have already done with them whatever he meant to do, already told whomever he meant to tell, making killing him a pointless trouble once Alizon was dead, whether for punishment or revenge.

What were these damnable secrets?

Supposing they even existed.

Durevis said Alizon *thought* she would have something to tell him. What if this whole business of "secrets" was not part of the matter at all?

If it was not, then Joliffe was even further than he feared from finding a trail to the murderer. He did not even know the nature of Alizon's supposed secrets. Were they the murderer's, and so he had killed to protect them? Or were they someone else's, and the murderer had killed on that someone's behalf? Estienne as an Armagnac spy might well have secrets he needed to keep. But how would Alizon know anything of his secrets?

No, the secrets were here. In these rooms. Among these women.

But how to learn them?

"Master Ripon?" Foulke asked uneasily.

Joliffe became aware he was standing in the middle of the parlor, staring into air. Alain was gone, but Foulke was standing at the outer doorway, feet apart, hands behind his back in the patient waiting way he spent so much of his time, to be ready when needed, and looking at him worriedly.

Joliffe shook himself and said, going forward, "I was just giving thanks to be out of there."

"How goes it with them?"

"Fairly much as it was when they were out here. They're weeping and wondering, and blaming themselves for letting Alizon go out, and telling each other they aren't to blame."

"I'll warrant M'dame isn't telling them they aren't to blame."

Joliffe gave a short laugh of agreement and almost went on, not wanting to lose the track of his thoughts in talk, but stopped with another thought and asked, "What of you? Is she blaming you?"

"No, for a mercy. There were some heated questions yesterday, but my duty is to keep the unwanted out, not pen the women in. I'd no way to know the girl was going anywhere she shouldn't."

But someone had known and followed her to the garden; and since everyone in a household had duties that set where they should be at most times of any day, who, yesterday, had not been where they should have been? That question alone maybe served to lessen possibilities, because anyone in the bishop's household would have difficulty keeping close enough watch on Alizon to know when she went out, let alone have chance to follow her then and linger in the garden and not be missed. And that narrowed the matter to someone among Lady Jacquetta's people—an ugly thought. But everything about this was ugly.

"We're all wondering why she went out at all," he said.

"Ah, that's known well enough," Foulke said. "It was to meet Master Durevis. The hunt is up for him, no mistake."

"I wonder how he got message to her to meet him. It surely didn't come openly?"

Foulke frowned with thought. "No one's said aught about a message coming for her. You're right, though. She must have heard from him somehow."

Frowning, too, to show John Ripon was thinking deeply, Joliffe tried, "Someone could have passed secret word to her at dinner in the great hall, I suppose."

"My lady and the rest of them dined here, not in the

hall," Foulke said. "Broke their morning fast and had dinner here yesterday."

"In the chapel then, at the morning's Mass."

"Aye, that's possible," Foulke granted.

"Or someone who came here that day, or maybe the day before?" Joliffe ventured.

Foulke considered that with a, "Hm," a pause, and then, "Nobody in particular comes to mind. Not anybody I saw talking to her, anyway. For what that's worth." He named several names of household servants, and then, "There was Master Cauvet in the morning. He came early with some message from her uncle to my lady. He had to wait until she finished dressing. I don't know but what he talked some with Alizon or some other of the women while he waited?"

Foulke did not sound certain of it but Joliffe supposed that, yes, Cauvet might well have done so, with no one thinking twice about it, and easily able to pass a small written message to Alizon secretly. But that would mean . . . regrettable things about Cauvet.

It could also mean that Cauvet might well have known when and where Alizon and Durevis would be.

For appearance's sake, Joliffe gave a regretful shake of his head and said, "None of it makes sense, does it?"

Foulke agreed, and Joliffe went on his way, unsure where to go next with his questions. He would have preferred to stay in talk with Lady Jacquetta's demoiselles. Somewhere among them there had to be things they knew, that, piece by piece, meant little, but if he had the pieces and put them together rightly, they might go well toward answering much. But very likely there were pieces to be had elsewhere in the *hôtel*, too. The trouble was that to find them he had to ask the right questions, and hopefully not bring the murderer's heed around to him while he did.

Something else was twitching at his mind. There was something he should be wondering about, something . . .

As he came to the foot of the stairs from Lady Jac-quetta's rooms, Alain closed on him and demanded, "How is it with Guillemete? You saw her? How is she?"

Resigned to dealing with him, Joliffe said, "She had been crying before I came in, she was crying when I left. Lady Jacquetta was comforting her." He spread his hands apologetically. "I saw no more of her than that."

"I need to see her," Alain said. He was urgent, angry, and sullen. "But M'dame is angry at me and won't let me."

"Angry? About what?" Joliffe said in surprise.

The question, coming from outside his own intense pit of misery, seemed to take Alain by surprise. He fumbled, "I . . . All I did was forget I was . . . to go out with her yesterday. To the goldsmith's. She told me in the morning, but I forgot. I . . . just forgot." He turned bitter. "They were safe enough with Mathei. It didn't matter I didn't go. I waited for them to come back, to make my apology as soon as might be. Before I could, Foulke wanted help looking for Alizon and—" He broke off, grabbed his temples between his hands, and moaned, "I just want to be with Guillemete and she won't let me!"

Joliffe spread his hands in apology again, not sure for what, and went away, down the stairs toward the great hall, thinking that if Alain followed him, he could hope to scrape him off on someone there. To the good, Alain stayed where he was. To the better, he had jarred loose the something that had been twitching at Joliffe's thoughts. Where had Guillemete been when her sister was killed?

All the other demoiselles seemed accounted for. Where had she been?

He had the discouraging thought that he was gathering questions far faster than he was finding answers. If he had been able to ask the outright questions, he might have got useful answers, but as that afternoon went on, all he was able to do was wander apparently aimlessly through the *hôtel*, talking to whom he happened on; and while people were talking of not much else than the murder, what questions he could work into their talk gave him nothing useful.

Even more hindering was that everyone jumped at the chance to ask *him* questions about what he had seen in the garden. Estienne was among the most eager to hear what he could tell, and while Joliffe kept brief what he told, he was at least able to learn in return that Estienne had been among those away from the *hôtel* with Bishop Louys yesterday afternoon.

A pity: Estienne guilty would have caused Joliffe no pain at all.

The best he gained was in talk with Cauvet and several others of the bishop's household when he wondered to them how Alizon had come to be in the garden at all, saying, "What's being said is she was there to meet Master Durevis, and that no one has seen him since. But how did she know he would be there?"

One man ventured on the openly probable. "A message, surely."

"But how did it come to her if nobody knows about it?" Joliffe persisted with John Ripon's insistent ignorance. "My lady's demoiselles surely should not get secret word from men."

That brought laughter among the men. Cauvet said, "They should not. That does not mean they do not," and remembrances followed from one and another of the men of times they had bribed a servant to take a message where it would otherwise not have gone. Only in their foolish younger days, never here, they immediately added.

"Nor will whoever did it yesterday ever confess it now," Cauvet added.

By the afternoon's end, what Joliffe had mostly gleaned was that while it was widely known Remon Durevis was missing and being sought, most people's thoughts were that either he must be the murderer or else that he could not be and was missing for some reason of his own. Not a few favored the murderer being an altogether unknown some-one from outside Joyeux Repos. Only one man pointed out—more with delight at his horror than with fear it was true—that the murderer could be someone among them right now.

Joliffe would have been glad of a chance to talk with Master Wydeville, but heard in passing that he had left the *hôtel* in mid-afternoon. That left the hope that he was gone to question Durevis again and more closely.

For himself, after several probably wasted hours and a Lenten-dull supper, he accepted he had not come much of anywhere pursuing "how" and "who" among the house-hold. That left "why," which almost surely must have to do with the secrets Alizon had laughed about, and because Lady Jacquetta's ladies lived within narrow bounds within the household, the where and how Alizon could have come by secrets was likewise narrow, and narrowed the possi-bilities of whose secrets they were.

With very limited eagerness, he made to return to Lady Jacquetta's chambers, only to be surprised at the foot of their stairs by several men coming down. In the gray twi-light of early evening he took a moment to sort out they were some of the squires and gentlemen who often spent evenings in Lady Jacquetta's rooms, Alain among them, and he bowed and asked "What's toward, sirs?"

"We are not wanted," one of them said. "Last night was no time for us, surely, but Master Cauvet passed word from Bishop Louys that our company might be welcomed tonight."

"But no," another said. "Her grace and her demoiselles keep alone in their mourning."

"It's M'dame's doing," Alain said angrily. "She says they're to keep apart until after the funeral. But it's only to keep me from Guillemete when Guillemete needs me!"

Draping an arm over Alain's shoulders, another squire

said in rough comfort, "Your Guillemete will still need you in two days' time. Come away. If we're not wanted here, there are other places to be."

Alain looked still ready to grumble but let himself be led off toward the great hall. Joliffe waited until they were gone from sight, then took himself up the stairs despite what they had said. Mathei, standing guard, answered his question of whether the ladies might want his reading with, "I've only orders against the bright-eyed youths. There's been a harper let in. Your reading might be welcome, too. If you're willing to dare the dragon, go on."

Joliffe decided to dare and went in. Only the harper— one of the household's musicians—was in the parlor, sitting alone in a single candle's light, rippling soft music from his harpstrings. He and Joliffe exchanged silent nods as Joliffe passed him toward the bedchamber door that stood a little open, probably for the music's sake. Joliffe's soft scratch at the doorframe was answered by M'dame, looking more dragon than ever, ready to deny and defy anyone who might be there, but seeing only him, she asked over her shoulder if he should come in and, at Lady Jacquetta's answer, opened the door to him.

Chapter 23

Unlike the parlor, the bedchamber was full of candlelight, as well as over-warm from a large fire in the fireplace, but sadness hung like a pall in the air. The demoiselles were seated here and there around the room, none crying but none pretending to any task except Michielle at an embroidery frame. Guillemete, her head bent to rest on a cushion she was clutching to her breast with both arms, sat rocking gently side to side on the bench below the shuttered window. Lady Jacquetta, on the long, cushioned chest at the bedfoot, one of her dogs nestled beside her, the other in the folds of her skirt on the floor, was turning over the page of a book lying open on her lap—the *Alexander* again, Joliffe saw as he made his bow to her and she said musingly to him, without looking up, "This is another book my lord of Bedford had made for me, that I might take pleasure in learning English. I think much of the time he saw me more as a daughter to be taught, than a wife to be loved."

M'dame, just sitting down on the far end of the chest, said, "My lady," in a voice layered with warning and other things less easy to read. But Lady Jacquetta answered firmly, "No. It is good to remember him, to talk of him sometimes." She turned another page. "He said once that his first wife told him that if she died, he was to marry someone young and beautiful. He told it to me to please me, you see. But I would never tell my husband such a thing. I would want my husband never to marry again, to live always remembering me or else to die when I died. She must not have loved him, to tell him to marry again." She looked at Joliffe. "Is that not so?"

Joliffe had supposed her lost in her memories and thoughts, and was startled to find himself questioned. He hesitated, then answered, careful of his words, "I think love takes many different forms, my lady."

"That is what a priest would say," Lady Jacquetta returned somewhat sharply. "You are not a priest, are you, Master Ripon?"

"No, my lady."

"Nor have you truly loved, to say such a thing. Do you think Lady Alizon loved Master Durevis?"

"I—have no way to know, my lady."

"She was sadly deceived in him if she did. If he was who killed her. Although one can be deceived without murder following," she added bitterly.

"My lady," M'dame said again.

"Yes," Lady Jacquetta replied impatiently. She thrust the book at Joliffe. "Read to us, Master Ripon. Make our minds think on other things."

Joliffe obeyed, but the over-warm room, thick with all the grief he could not comfort and questions he could not ask, weighed down on him, oppressing his thoughts as it must be oppressing Lady Jacquetta, if her talk was true echo of her thoughts. Last night and this morning with Perrette seemed days away, rather than only hours, and he could not see what good use he could make of being here, now that he was. Even if, somehow, he had chance to talk alone with, say, Guillemete, what was he to say? He could hardly ask outright, "Where were you when your sister died, and do you know what she knew that got her murdered?" Master Wydeville might ask her those things; John Ripon was too much nobody to dare it. He wished he had stayed in the hall or gone out—no, John Ripon was forbidden that—or maybe just gone to bed.

But he read as if none of that was in his mind until eventually Lady Jacquetta said, "Thank you, Master Ripon," held out her hand for the book, and asked just as she had on other, better evenings, "Would you care for wine before you go?"

He was about to refuse when Guillemete said unexpectedly, "I'll bring it."

Silent looks of surprise passed among everyone as she put her cushion aside and hurriedly rose, but Lady Jacquetta said only, mildly, "Thank you, Guillemete."

Joliffe followed as she went to the table where the pitcher and goblets stood. He wondered if he was alone in seeing she needed both hands to steady the pitcher as she poured, while asking him in a desperate whisper, "Please, have you seen Alain?"

Aware from the side of his eye that a gesture from M'dame had set Ydoine moving toward them, he answered, quiet-voiced and quickly as she set the pitcher down and took up the goblet, "He seems to be forever downstairs, hoping for chance to see you. He's miserable that he can't be with you." He took the slightly trembling goblet from her hand. "Has he seen you at all since . . . yesterday?"

Guillemete shook her head and slipped away, back toward the window. Ydoine took her place in front of him, held out a small plate of gingerbread slices as if that had been all her purpose in coming to him and said, "Guillemete is to go home with her sister's body after the funeral."

"That will be hard for her," Joliffe said, then decided

bold was as good a way to go as any and asked, "Where was she when Lady Alizon died?"

"Where was she?" Ydoine echoed, somewhat sharply.

As if not hearing the sharpness, Joliffe said with apparently only ordinary concern, "I wondered that perhaps she feels somehow guilty she was not with her yesterday. You know—that the guilt too often felt for no good reason, only because we're alive when someone else isn't?"

Ydoine accepted that with a sad down-turn of her mouth and a nod. "I think that likely, yes. Blanche has said that after M'dame and I went out, Guillemete slipped away to meet Alain somewhere. Behind M'dame's back, you see. So she may feel doubly guilty."

"Ah." Joliffe nodded his understanding. Alain had said he had forgotten to go with M'dame. It seemed "forgot" had maybe not been quite the way of it. But a thought jarred into his mind from seemingly nowhere. He had been wondering how Durevis had got word to Alizon to meet him in the garden. What he had not wondered was how Durevis knew M'dame would be gone, giving Alizon that chance to meet him; and trying to make it seem an idle question, he asked, "Was it a sudden thing, M'dame choosing to go out yesterday?"

"To me she said nothing until just before dinner. When she first thought of it, I do not know."

Perhaps no sooner than when a message maybe came to her in the chapel that morning. He had already thought of that as a way Alizon could have known to meet Durevis. What if . . .

Ydoine left him with the goblet in one hand, a piece of gingerbread in the other, and a flow of thoughts in his head that he hoped he was keeping from his face. What if at Mass, it was M'dame who received some message that decided her to leave the *hôtel*? There was no way yet to know what such a message might have been, but suppose there had been such a message. No one would much question if she said she was going out that afternoon. It was her place to question what went on around Lady Jacquetta, not to be questioned herself. But once she had said she would be going out, someone in the household, bribed before this to keep Durevis informed of just such a chance, saw to Durevis learning of it. How that was done was something to be found out later. What mattered was that then Durevis must have sent word to Alizon to meet him in the garden and . . .

Or Alizon, when she knew M'dame was going to be gone, had sent word to *him*. Or . . .

It was too tangled. A maze of messages flying secretly in and out of the household were possible, of course, but so many in the small time there seemed to have been for them—that was possible, of course, but "possible" and "likely" were two different things.

Yet Durevis had to have known M'dame was going to be gone, for him to think Alizon would have any chance of coming to meet him secretly. How had he known?

Could he have sent a false message to M'dame, to draw her off? What could such a message have been? Nothing deeply secret, since she had taken Ydoine with her. But if there had been a false message to draw her off, surely she would have said as much to Master Wydeville or someone by now.

He found he had nibbled the gingerbread away and finished the wine. He was about to set the goblet aside and bow his retreat when someone spoke sharply to Mathei at the outer door and started across the parlor with the rapid tread of someone who did not mean to be stopped. Joliffe's first thought was that the young fool Alain had finally decided to force his way to Guillemete, but it was Sir Richard Wydeville who paused in the bedchamber doorway long enough to say over his shoulder to someone, "No. If I'm not needed here, then I'll go. But I'll know for myself. *No*."

That must have been to his father, because Master

Wydeville came in close behind him, no longer trying
to stop him. Lady Jacquetta rose to her feet exclaiming,
"Sir Richard!" at the same moment M'dame, likewise rising, said, sharp with warning, "Sir!" As Lady Jacquetta
held out her hands to Sir Richard in open welcome, Joliffe
saw not only the exchange of looks between M'dame and
Master Wydeville but also the single sideways jerk of his
head that denied or refused something she had not said.
M'dame, perhaps in answer, said crisply, "We'll leave you,
my lady," and ordered at the demoiselles, "Come," nodding
toward the parlor.

They went, although M'dame had to take bewildered
Guillemete by one arm and guide her firmly after the others. Joliffe moved quickly to stand beside the door, bending
in a hurried half-bow while they passed him with a heavy
whispering of skirts that cost him any chance of hearing
whatever Sir Richard was saying, low-voiced, to Lady Jacquetta across the room. Down on one knee in front of her,
he was grasping both her hands, and she was leaning toward him. Master Wydeville moved to where he somewhat
blocked them from view from the other room and with a
gesture silently ordered Joliffe to leave, too. Joliffe did,
and at his back Master Wydeville swung the door closed
enough that nothing could be seen of Lady Jacquetta and
Sir Richard but open enough that she could not be said to
have been left alone with two men.

Her ladies, wide-eyed and confused at the suddenness,
were clustered around Guillemete, who was crying again,
at the parlor's far end, but M'dame was still beside the
door, looking as if she meant to stay there. On guard? Or
simply waiting for a summons from Lady Jacquetta? Or
both?

Pieces were shifting in Joliffe's mind, and he stopped in
front of M'dame, turned so his back was to everyone else,
and said, low-voiced, "M'dame, that day you sent me to
the garden to interrupt whatever was happening between

Master Durevis and Lady Jacquetta—why did you want me in particular?"

M'dame regarded him with unrevealing eyes. "Did I? I think not."

"You said, 'There you are. That saves time.' As if you were seeking me in particular."

"How strange. You are dismissed for this evening, Master Ripon. You should leave."

"You sought me that day because you know that I serve Master Wydeville."

M'dame's brows rose. Somewhat disdainfully, she said, "I thought you served my lady, not her chamberlain."

"You know my meaning."

He was playing it more boldly than he felt, and for a moment under her unwavering, cold stare, he thought he had played it badly, until the barest of possible smiles twitched at M'dame's stern mouth and she said, "Yes."

Greatly relieved behind his front of confidence, Joliffe tried, "You know who he is, beyond being my lady's chamberlain, and who I am in his service. That's why you sought me in particular that day. You work together, you and Master Wydeville, for Lady Jacquetta's safety."

"It would make good sense for us to do so," she granted.

Joliffe would have welcomed a stronger confirmation from her, but supposing he would not get it, he thrust directly on. "Master Durevis and Lady Jacquetta were not friendly together that day. What did he want from her?"

M'dame surprised him more than she already had by answering, "For her to tell him things. He thought he knew something. He wanted to know more. He thought she would tell him. She would not."

"What did he want her to tell him?"

M'dame shook her head, refusing him that.

Joliffe let it go, said instead, "It was after that he began to give heed to Lady Alizon. He wanted from her what he did not get from Lady Jacquetta."

"So we thought," M'dame granted.

Who did that "we" encompass? She and Master Wyde-ville? Lady Jacquetta? Hoping to set her at least a little off balance, he asked sideways, "Yesterday, you planned somewhat suddenly to go to the goldsmith's."

Not set off balance at all, she returned evenly, "Did I?"

Joliffe persisted, "And somehow Master Durevis knew that you would be gone and that Lady Alizon would have her best chance to slip away to the garden while you were away. The question is how he knew you would be out."

Her look at him sharpened.

He kept on. "You said nothing about going out until late morning. It was during the Mass, in the chapel, that someone passed you some message. A message that Mas-ter Durevis had to know of, despite he was not there nor anywhere about Joyeux Repos."

"Messages and messengers can go astray," M'dame said evenly, neither confirming nor denying what he had said.

Given no help with the way he was trying to go, Joliffe said, "Lady Alizon almost surely received her message to meet Master Durevis then, too. That gives two new ques-tions. Why did you have to go out that day so suddenly? And how did Master Durevis know of it so well ahead of the time? Which brings us to two other things that are not questions. Where he was that morning, and who you met while you were out. He has been sharing duty and probably a good deal of company with Sir Richard Wydeville. And it was Sir Richard you met while you were out."

"Sir Richard chanced to be passing the goldsmith's. That is all."

"I think he neither chanced nor was passing. I think it was arranged you would meet him there, a thing Master Durevis could have learned easily enough if he were in-deed making effort to know about Sir Richard's doings, and I think he must have been. I think he was making effort to know because Lady Alizon had told him she might have secrets to tell him. Secrets about something he already suspected."

"Secrets are best left secret," M'dame said, her voice still level.

"There are secrets that won't keep, and someone has already died for them." He paused. He was about to step out over a deep pit, either onto an invisible bridge he was almost sure was there, or else to his doom. Taking a grip on his certainty and with memory of what he had just seen in the bedchamber, he said, "Lady Jacquetta and Sir Richard are lovers."

Michielle chose this moment to turn from the other demoiselles and start across the parlor toward M'dame. Not removing her gaze from Joliffe's face, M'dame raised an abrupt hand toward her. The girl promptly retreated, and M'dame with her gaze still fixed on Joliffe said softly, "They are not lovers. They are married."

Joliffe just barely kept from blurting out his first, idiot thought—To each other?

M'dame continued, flat-voiced, "They were married at Twelfth Night. Here. Secretly."

Twelfth Night, Joliffe thought, picking one clear thought out of his jumble of other ones. That last of the Christmas holidays, when everyone in the household would have been busy, early and late, with their own merriment.

Well before her uncle's return from England.

Long before the king's council had required her oath never to marry without royal permission.

Her oath. She had given her oath to her uncle that day that she would never marry without the king's—or else the council's—consent. No. That was not what she had sworn. She had been refusing to swear that, had summoned Master Wydeville to her with claim she wanted his advice. But what she had truly wanted was his help in escaping an oath she could not honestly give. And he had given her an oath she *could* give—that she would not marry without royal consent *from this time forth*.

Barely able to say it, Joliffe forced out, "Master Wyde-ville knows this, too."

M'dame granted that with the smallest of small inclinations of her head, watching his face all the while.

"Who else?" he asked.

"The priest who took their vows. None other."

"But her women suspect. Surely they must suspect."

"Lady Alizon surely did. Now you know it for certain *and* what you have to keep secret while you ask your questions about her death. But we have been in talk over-long. You should leave." And a little raising her voice, she finished, "Thank you, Master Ripon. I will consider it."

He took that dismissal gladly, bowed first to her, then toward the demoiselles, and escaped without looking toward the bedchamber as he went. Deeply in need of a chance to re-gather his thoughts and sort them, he was not sure where he was going and was very unpleased to come on Alain in the long gallery—and even less pleased when Alain hurried at him saying furiously, "M'dame allowed you in and then Sir Richard. Why you and him and not me?"

"All I know is that Lady Jacquetta allowed it. I read aloud for a while, that's all. Sir Richard"—Joliffe shrugged—" he was with his father, not there on his own."

"But why them and no one else?" Alain demanded in agony.

Rather than try for a lie that might divert him, Joliffe offered, "Guillemete made chance to ask after you."

Very satisfactorily diverted, Alain cried, "How is she?"

"Sorrowing. She's to accompany her sister's body home after the funeral."

"I have to see her before then! I have to talk to her!"

Did he ever do more than demand and exclaim? Joliffe wondered. He did not want the bother of Alain just now, but at the same time could not help but pity him and said, "Alain, I'll put your plea to M'dame."

Alain grasped his arm. "Will you? Now?"

"Not now. After the Wydevilles leave."

"But tonight?"

"I was dismissed for the night. I will in the morning." He loosed Alain's grip from his arm. "What you have to do is go down to the hall, find a game to gamble in and something to drink." A lot to drink, he thought to himself. "If I have word with Guillemete before you do, is there anything I should say for you?"

"Tell her . . . No. Tell her . . . No." Alain shook his head helplessly. "Tell her to wait until we have talked. Tell her that."

"To wait until you have talked. Yes." He turned Alain toward the downward stairs. "Now go to the hall and join the others. That will be better than waiting here."

The advice was good and Alain took it. Joliffe did not. The long gallery was cold and mostly dark except for a lantern by the stairs at each end. He had it to himself as he paced its length and back, then paced it again. He wished he had his cloak, but the need to speak to Master Wydeville was stronger than his urge to comfort, and after all it was not so very long before he and Sir Richard came, their voices ahead of them sounding as if they were in a low-voiced argument.

If they were, they broke it off at sight of him. Sir Richard swore, mostly under his breath. His father, more calmly, said, "Master Ripon. Good. There's need we speak together. Richard, there's no more to be done here. Return to the castle for now."

Sir Richard started to protest that.

Master Wydeville cut him off with "But, yes, you're in the right about the other thing. We've come to the end of it."

Sir Richard's mouth snapped closed, apparently with

surprise, before he gathered himself and said, "You see it has to be that way?"

"The whole world will be seeing it before long," Master Wydeville said curtly. "Best we not wait for that. For now, go."

Sir Richard went, not hallward but toward the narrow twist of stairs down to the corner of the foreyard.

"As if that will keep his coming here a secret," Master Wydeville said somewhat bitterly when he was beyond being heard. He turned his look on Joliffe. "M'dame told you they're married."

"Yes."

"Besides that," Master Wydeville said grimly, "Lady Jacquetta is with child. Something I've only now been told."

"Then those," Joliffe said slowly, covering the race of his thoughts, "would be the secrets Lady Alizon thought she would learn and was going to tell to Durevis." Two grave secrets. Even the first was dark enough. For a common-born knight to marry the nobly born widow of a royal duke disparaged both her *and* her family. That she was childing, too. . .

The duke of Burgundy, cheated of using Lady Jacquetta to his own ends in some marriage, would surely find ways for making ill-use of the scandal.

Slowly, wary of the words, Joliffe said, "You knew of the marriage. M'dame said you witnessed it."

"As my lord of Bedford would have wished me to do," Master Wydeville answered steadily.

"He would have wished your son to marry his widow?"

Despite Joliffe's try, he failed to keep disbelief and accusation altogether out of his voice, but Master Wydeville answered evenly, "My lord of Bedford knew that after his death she would of necessity be married again, being too useful and now too wealthy to be left a widow. He married her to keep her safe from the duke of Burgundy. Her brother is already being pressed by Burgundy to demand she come back to her family, meaning into Burgundy's reach again. This marriage forestalls that. She will go to England, out of his reach forever."

"She could have gone to England without the marriage."

"Where she would have been used in some marriage chosen for her by the royal council and the king. My lord of Bedford was used by king and royal council all his life. At the end he did not want her to spend her life as such another pawn."

"So you provided your son."

"No," Master Wydeville said curtly. "Anyone but a fool could foresee what would likely come of a fair-faced youth and a beautiful girl being together in a household. My lord of Bedford was no fool, but when he did not send my son away, I told him that he should, before anything could even begin. He told me he chose not to, that he trusted them both, and I'll grant that he had the right of it. While he lived there was a great liking but nothing dishonorable between them. Then, when he was deathly ill, when he knew that he would die, he told me I was to let matters go the way they would, that Lady Jacquetta, for good or ill, was to make her own choice for her life. She has. She has chosen my son, and I am not happy for it. There are too many ills too likely to come of this marriage." He said it with the sternly controlled displeasure of a man indeed not pleased by what others would see as his son's great good fortune; and in the same controlled voice, he went flatly on, "But whatever comes will be for them to deal with. Once I've seen them away to England, I'll have done all I could. I would rather not have told you any of this, but you've done well at guessing much, and having it all may help you toward finding Lady Alizon's murderer. So, what have you learned toward that end?"

With an effort, Joliffe pulled his mind around from the marriage and told as briefly as he could what he had so far pieced together. In the telling it did not seem much, and he ended with his own question. "Has Master Durevis had any more to say?"

"He's carefully admitting nothing more. He's still hoping to be ransomed back to Burgundy."

"I'll warrant he at least suspected more," Joliffe said. "Have you asked her about what passed between them in the garden that day?"

"She claims he was trying to lure her into telling him any secret he might find useful by pretending to know more than he did."

"And all she did was turn angry at him," Joliffe said, "and that set him to winning Lady Alizon, in hope of what *she* might tell him."

"It would seem so."

"Will he be ransomed back to Burgundy?"

"Very likely. Despite he'll take with him the settled thought that it was Lady Jacquetta who ordered Lady Alizon's murder and his."

That startled Joliffe into saying, "Did she?"

"Not so far as we've yet learned," Master Wydeville said evenly. Which was uncomfortably far from a firm "no."

Joliffe stared past him at an empty wall without really seeing it, wondering just how much of a fool he would have to be to ask the next question. A fairly great fool, he determined, and returned his gaze to Master Wydeville and asked it anyway. "What of M'dame? Did *she* order it?"

As evenly as before, Master Wydeville said, "She says not."

Another infirm answer.

He waited for Joliffe to ask more, but Joliffe, already knowing more than felt safe to know, found there was nothing else he wanted—or was it dared?—to ask just then, and he settled for, "It might be helpful if Master Durevis would tell how he knew M'dame would be out, and how he got word to Alizon to meet him."

Master Wydeville nodded. "Well thought. If he hasn't been asked, he will be."

Footfall and voices on the hallward stairs said people were coming. Joliffe, out of things he wanted to ask or say, welcomed the reason to escape, bowed and said clearly enough to be overheard, "Sir, by your leave, if there's no more?"

In kind, Master Wydeville responded, "There's no more. You may go." And added sternly for the benefit of whoever was coming, "But see you're at your desk in good time to-morrow morning, to make up for today, Master Ripon. No one is pleased with you."

Chapter 24

The past two days had been long enough and last night short enough that, once lain down on his bed, Joliffe simply slept, immediately and soundly, with no dreams left over to trouble him when he awoke in the dark sometime before anyone else was rousing for the morning. He did not rouse either, but stayed warm where he was. His mind, though, unfortunately began to churn as soon as he was awake enough for thoughts. The after-troubling of a dream would have been better, because it would have had the good grace to fade once he left his bed and took on the day. Unlike his thoughts. And he found his first and strongest thought was that . . . he was afraid.

Probably with good reason, but there was no comfort in that. He was gone far beyond any familiar depth. The things that served in the making of all people's lives and choices—loves, angers, lusts, hatreds, kindnesses, greeds—were as real here as anywhere else, but were all tangled here into worse by the overlay of high matters among powerful men, the ambitions of great lords, and the secret workings of men who lived by lies in the service of those great lords. Men like Remon Durevis.

And Master Wydeville.

And himself these past months.

Joliffe shifted uncomfortably on a mattress that seemed suddenly lumped with rocks. There were too many layers here that he understood not enough. He could understand a secret marriage between two people with more passion than sense, but this marriage went beyond that because it would be objected to by very many people for very many reasons, all of which Lady Jacquetta and Sir Richard surely knew, beginning with the high scandal of the disparaging distance between their places in the world, but beyond that—and even more likely to bring fury down on the pair—was that a pawn had presumed to take herself out of political play. None of the several sides that had wanted to use her were going to be pleased at the loss, and their displeasure could be fierce.

Why, then, had those who should have guarded most strongly against the marriage allowed it? He had Master Wydeville's reason, for what that might or might not be worth. M'dame's reason he was never likely to have, not being so foolish-bold as ever to ask it of her.

So.

This was a marriage that was going to make a great many powerful people very unhappy when they came to know of it, and they would likely do what they could in return to make the couple equally unhappy for it. For good measure, there were surely also some—such as the Armagnacs supporting the Dauphin—who would not care about the marriage itself, having nothing to lose or gain by it one way or the other, but be pleased for the trouble it made among their foes, while the duke of Burgundy would make what political use he could of the scandal.

There were reasons enough, then, to keep this marriage a secret as long as might be. But if Lady Jacquetta was indeed childing, the secret could not be kept much longer, come what may, nor the marriage be undone, no matter what angers there were.

Therefore there was no deep reason to kill to keep the secret.

Or was there? Why kill to keep a secret that would shortly, inevitably, not be a secret anymore? Perhaps the murderer did not know about the child. Or there was a reason why the secret had to be kept just the little while longer that it could be—some reason behind reasons, buried in the layers of ambitions and contentions among the powerful that he had only glimpsed or guessed at and maybe had no hope of understanding.

Joliffe turned back to what he did know. The narrow time in which Alizon's murder and the attack on Remon had happened might be his surest way to the murderer. Whoever had done it must be someone of either the bishop's household or Lady Jacquetta's, because he had gone back to the *hôtel* after stabbing Durevis, and he had to have had a reason to kill both Alizon and Durevis when simply silencing Alizon would have been enough.

Or would silencing Alizon have been enough? Had she died for some other reason than Lady Jacquetta's secrets? But if not because of those, then what? And why need Durevis dead, too? For revenge on him for being a spy willing to betray Lady Jacquetta? That was possible. And Alizon's death seen as justified because of her intended foolish betrayal, even if she had not understood just how much of a betrayal it was, not knowing Durevis was a Burgundian spy?

But how would the murderer have known all of that about them? And how much more was playing out here behind what there was for everyone to see? The reason for Alizon's death might well be hidden there. And if it was, how was he ever to come to it?

* * *

When the day had truly got under way for the household,
he went to his desk after breaking fast and even made an
outward effort at work until dinnertime took him and his
fellows down to the hall for a Lenten-plain meal made
the more subdued by the pall of waiting for the funeral
that would come that afternoon. That might have been
sooner in the day, but for a courtesy to his niece, Bishop
Louys was to do it and could not until he had finished
with some meeting of the council at the castle, and with
no word yet of when the bishop would return, Joliffe was
standing in talk with Cauvet and Henri in the hall before
going their ways back to their duties, when Alain came
up to them, nodded with vague respect and greeting at
Cauvet and Henri, and begged at Joliffe, "Please, you
must go and ask how Lady Guillemete does. I truly need
to know."

Henri said, "By the arrow in Saint Sebastian's big toe,
they will not kill you just for asking. Do it yourself. Master
Ripon has his right duties."

"I'm turned away at the door!" Alain cried. "No one
will tell me anything!"

"Then there must be nothing you should know," Cauvet
suggested.

Plainly, Joliffe was not alone in being irked by Alain's
ways but he said, trying to sound resigned and pitying together, "I'll go."

"You belong at your desk," Henri warned.

"I know," Joliffe agreed and went anyway.

He made Alain stop in the long gallery and left him there,
which proved a good thing because Foulke, on duty outside
the parlor door, greeted him with a mock glower and, "At
least you're not that fool Alain. I've sworn I'll throw him
down the stairs if he comes bothering me again."

"I've come on his behalf."

Foulke rolled his eyes. "He's not set you to plead with
Lady Guillemete to see him."

"He'll settle now for knowing how she does. Although I can't see the harm in him seeing her."

"Ask M'dame. It's on her orders no one goes in. Not that anyone with sense would want to. Near as I can hear, it's a pit of weeping in there."

"I have to tell the poor fool that I at least asked about her."

"Your funeral," Foulke said, then winced and added, "Or not." His light scratching at the door was answered by Marie barely opening it and saying through the small gap, "What is it?"

"Master Ripon is here to ask how Lady Guillemete does," Foulke said.

Marie paused, glanced over her shoulder, then opened the door a little more and beckoned to Joliffe. He had to slide in sideways, and she put out a hand to stop him until she had shut the door with great care. That gave him time to see Guillemete sitting at the window between Blanche and Michielle, twisting a handkerchief in her hands and staring at him piteously, before Marie, with a look toward the closed bedchamber door, whispered, "No one is to be here, but if you can tell Guillemete anything of Alain, do it quickly and be away before M'dame knows. Maybe it will help."

Joliffe nodded that he understood, crossed the parlor, went down on one knee in front of Guillemete, and said, quickly and quietly, "My lady, Master Queton is desperate to know how you are. No one will tell him, so I have come in his stead."

"Oh," Guillemete gasped. She pressed her handkerchief-clutching hands against her breast, somewhere near her heart. "I want so much to see him. I *need* to see him, but M'dame will not let me. He *does* want to see me?"

"He's been haunting outside the door, hoping for the chance," Joliffe assured her.

Guillemete half-rose, as if to go on the instant. "I could

go out to him now. I could go and be back before M'dame knew. I . . ."

Michielle grabbed her arm and pulled her back down, whispering fiercely, "You do not dare. Not now. After the funeral perhaps, but not now."

Guillemete began to cry again. Blanche put her arms around her and said, comforting, "At least you had your time together the other day."

For an instant Guillemete stared at her, at first confused, then stricken into a great sob of misery and even harder crying, burying her face in her handkerchief.

"*Idiot*," Michiele hissed at Blanche.

"You'd best go now," Marie said urgently to Joliffe, pulling on his arm.

More than willing to escape Guillemete's tears, Joliffe stood up and let Marie herd him toward the door, but whispered as he went, "Is all this because M'dame is still angry at Alain for not going with her the other day when she went out?"

"What?" Marie said confusedly. "He went. Or if he did not, M'dame said nothing about it, was not angry at him." She gave a fearful look toward the bedchamber and pleaded, "*Please*."

He gladly slid out of the room, and she shut the door quickly at his back. Foulke, openly grinning, said, "Not eaten, then."

"Not this time," Joliffe said, overplaying relief. "But I wouldn't care to chance it again."

Foulke laughed and Joliffe went to satisfy Alain as best he could, finding him pacing the long gallery but breaking off and coming toward him demanding, "Did you see her? Did you speak with her? Did you tell her . . ."

"I saw her. I told her you are longing to see her. She longs to see you, too, and would come to you if they would let her."

"If *M'dame* would let her," Alain said bitterly.

Joliffe tried, "Things will ease after the funeral, surely."

Alain granted sullenly, "I suppose," and turned away without thanks.

Being rid of him was thanks enough for Joliffe, who went willingly back to his desk, even though questions old and new nagged through his mind. Always questions, never answers, he thought. If he could find answers as readily as he found questions, he would be further along by now, instead of still helplessly lost. When Alizon died, how many people had known M'dame was going out that afternoon? Had Master Wydeville had chance to have Durevis asked who had given Alizon word to meet him in the garden? Was it possible the demoiselles were all—or some—lying to him about which of them was where when Alizon slipped away to the garden? They were young; one of them might be strong enough to have stabbed her. But where would one of them have come by a dagger so readily, to have it to hand just when needed? Besides, Durevis had been certain it was a man who ran away after stabbing him. But what if he had been stabbed by someone else, not the same person who stabbed Alizon?

Joliffe gave a sharp shake of his head against that. That latter thought kept coming and he kept shoving it away, because if that was the way of it, then everything was even more twisted around and knotted. Let him get answers to the straightest questions and forget the more twisted ones until—Saint Genesius forbid—the more twisted were the only way left to go.

he accomplished little at his desk then, before time came to gather in the long gallery with others of Lady Jacquetta's household and follow their lady and her demoiselles to the *hôtel*'s chapel for Lady Alizon's funeral. What sun there had been in the morning was gone, leaving a heavily gray day well-suited to a funeral, Joliffe thought. The only brightness in the chapel's gloom were the candles on their stands and the torches around Alizon's bier, until even those were dimmed by the wreathing incense clouds thickening as the Mass went on.

He was not high enough in the household to have better place than among those crowded just inside the chapel's door. Standing there, he could hear enough of what passed around the bier and at the altar but see only some of it, which suited him, but with most of his view blocked by the men around him, he only knew something untoward had happened when unexpected movement spasmed among the people somewhere toward the altar and Bishop Louys' voice briefly broke off in the middle of a prayer. Another man's voice rose, demanding, "Let me pass. Let me out!" and there began a shifting of people that went on even as Bishop Louys took up the interrupted prayer, until a moment later Joliffe was able to see Sir Richard Wydeville was shouldering his way toward the doorway, still ordering, "Let me pass. It's too much for her. Let me pass," carrying Lady Jacquetta in his arms.

She had not altogether fainted; her arms were tight around his neck, her face hidden against his shoulder, but assuredly she must have swooned at least somewhat, with the incense and torch-smoke to blame, Joliffe thought.

That—and that she was with child.

Her long skirts, trailing over Sir Richard's arms to the floor, were hindering him as much as the press of people, too close-packed to shift readily out of his way. Joliffe, since he was near the door, took on himself to push people aside from it, first inside the chapel and then outside, where Foulke and Mathei joined him in making a way through the outer crowd of household folk until finally in the wider air of the great hall Joliffe, Foulke, and Mathei paused, and Sir Richard shoved past them and kept going.

Foulke and Mathei, guessing he was bound for Lady

Jacquetta's rooms, ran ahead to have doors open. Joliffe, from naked curiosity, followed among the perhaps half-dozen others, including Estienne, who were choosing curiosity over piety. They had reached the long gallery when Lady Jacquetta stirred in Sir Richard's arms and must have said something because he said, "Of course, my lady," and instead of toward her stairs, went to one of the windows and set her carefully on her feet but kept an arm around her waist while he unlatched and swung a window open. Lady Jacquetta, her eyes closed, leaned gratefully into the cold rush of clear air, breathing deeply.

Without looking away from her, Sir Richard swung his free arm, silently ordering everyone else to keep back. They did but were staring and talking with the excitement of it when M'dame, at last escaped from the crowded chapel, came in a grim rush, Ydoine and Isabelle behind her.

"Sir Richard," she ordered, "help her to her rooms. Master Ripon, run to have the door open, and the window in her bedchamber, and stir up the fire there. The others of you are not needed."

Joliffe elbowed away from the dismissed men and ran, met Foulke coming back down the stairs to find what had happened to everyone, turned him back with quick words, left him and Mathei ready at the parlor's outer door to turn back the persistent curious, hasted to obey his own orders, and was kneeling at the bedchamber's hearth, encouraging the fire into a blaze, when Sir Richard carried in Lady Jacquetta. Rather than to the bed, he took her to the window, lowered her gently onto the seat there, then sat beside her, leaning close in concern while at the outer parlor door M'dame firmly told those who had presumed to follow that far, "It was the incense. The too many people. Her grief. Go back. You should not have left the funeral."

Joliffe heard Foulke and Mathei take over herding them away, but stayed kneeling at the hearth, tending the fire that no longer needed him, while he watched Isabelle fluttering with concern at Lady Jacquetta and being waved back by Sir Richard. Ydoine, ever the more practical among the demoiselles, had been pouring wine, and was just turning to take it to Lady Jacquetta when M'dame came in from the parlor and snapped, more with demand than concern, "My lady?"

Lady Jacquetta whispered, "The air is helping," without opening her eyes or lifting her head from Sir Richard's shoulder.

Taking the goblet from Ydoine, M'dame advanced on her. "So will this. Sir Richard, you should go."

Lady Jacquetta's eyes flew open and she clutched at him. "No!"

Warningly, M'dame began, "My lady—"

Sir Richard said soothingly, holding out his free hand for the goblet, "The wine will help, my lady. Here."

M'dame grimly gave him the goblet, and at his gentle encouraging Lady Jacquetta was drinking a little when Marie, Michielle, and Blanche shepherded weeping Guillemete into the room. They were all crying at least a little, Marie perhaps the least as she said, "It's done. The funeral. Oh, M'dame, Alain is . . ."

She did not have to finish about Alain. He was there in the bedchamber doorway, with Foulke catching him by the arm from behind, saying, "Here. You're not wanted now. Come away."

M'dame started toward him, ordering, "Out!"

Alain cast her a glare and twisted to be free of Foulke, openly intent on reaching Guillemete, who would have gone to him if Marie, Michielle, and Blanche had not been all around her.

Sharply M'dame ordered, "Master Ripon, help Foulke."

Joliffe obeyed, he and Foulke together having Alain out of the room before he could much resist, but in the parlor he made to struggle against their holds on his arms until

Joliffe warned, "Stop it. She'll call guards to take you. You know she will."

Alain went slack in their hold with a despairing gasp. Looking back over his shoulder, he demanded, sounding close to angry tears, "Why? Why another Englishman? *Why?*"

"Because he happened to reach her first in the chapel," Foulke said. "That's all. Come away now."

"He's nobody," Alain groaned. "Nobody. My lord of Bedford was at least noble. English, yes, but royal-blooded. This one—he's nobody—he's common."

"He happened to be nearest her," Joliffe insisted. "That's all."

Foulke, out of patience, said grimly, "You come, sir, or M'dame will have the hair off both of us." He still held one of Alain's arms and now gave it a twist behind his back. Alain gasped and was abruptly ready to do what he was told, so that Joliffe let go his own hold and turned back to the bedchamber, to be met just inside its door by Ydoine who handed him wine while looking past him at the departing Alain.

"Poor boy," she said sadly, too low for M'dame across the room to hear. "Poor Guillemete."

Agreeing with her, sorry for them both and grateful for the wine, Joliffe said, "Surely M'dame could forgive him by now. It might a little ease Lady Guillemete if they could at least speak together."

Ydoine looked at him, seeming confused. "Forgive him? For what?"

Confused in turn, Joliffe said, "For not going with her that day. To the goldsmith's."

Ydoine shook her head as if not understanding him. "Go with her? She told him he need not come."

"No, he forgot," Joliffe said. Well, forgot on purpose, for a chance to be alone with Guillemete, but—unsettled by Ydoine's certainty, he asked, suddenly doubtful, "Didn't he?"

"No," Ydoine said, quite certain. "He was not there when we were ready to leave. I asked should I send Mathei to find him. M'dame said there was no need, he wasn't to come after all."

"He wasn't?" Joliffe echoed, sounding stupid even to himself.

Certainly Ydoine looked at him as if wondering about his wits. "No," she insisted. "He wasn't. M'dame had told him he was not needed." Still looking doubtful of his wits, she left him, going to attend to the wine.

That was . . . strange, Joliffe thought. Alain had said M'dame was angry at him because he had forgotten to go with her. Then yesterday Ydoine had said—no, Ydoine had said *Blanche* said he and Guillemete had taken the chance of M'dame being gone to be secretly together, which made Alain's "forgot" into a lie, but a small one, presumably meant to protect Guillemete.

But if what Ydoine had just said was right, "forgot" was even less the truth than Joliffe had thought it was. If what Ydoine had said was true, Alain's "forgot" was a large, outright, and unneeded lie. But why?

With an itch of unease and a careful eye toward M'dame lest she send him out as firmly as she had sent Alain—but she was in close talk with Lady Jacquetta and Sir Richard, heeding nothing else—he sidled around the room's edge, to where Guillemete sat on the chest at the bedfoot between Blanche and Michielle. Their mutual tears were worn out for at least a while, but Guillemete was drooping sideways, her head leaning on Michielle's shoulder, while Michielle held and patted one of her hands and Blanche the other. She looked a worn out child, and Joliffe thought that for mercy's sake she should be given a sleeping draught and put to bed to sleep for as long as might be. But he said quietly, "Lady Guillemete."

She opened her grief-rimmed eyes without lifting her head and looked at him as if nothing would ever matter to her again. Feeling ever worse at what he was doing, he said with all the gentleness he could, "When you were with Master Queton the other day—the day when—the other day—when M'dame was out." As if not saying "the day your sister died" would make it better. It did not; Guillemete drew a trembling breath toward new tears, and Joliffe said quickly, "When you and Master Queton were together that day, that afternoon, you . . ."

"We weren't," Guillemete quavered. She lifted her head from Michielle's shoulder. "We were supposed to be, but I waited and waited, and he never came. That's what makes it all so worse. I should have been with Alizon, because then she wouldn't have gone out and then nothing would have happened to her. But I wasn't!" Weeping overtook her again. Michielle and Blanche wrapped their arms around her in a tangle of comforting, but she sobbed on, "I waited and waited until I couldn't wait longer, and then Alizon was dead and everything is terrible!"

She covered her tear-wracked face. Michielle made a small shooing gesture at Joliffe, but with careful quiet, he asked, "Lady Guillemete, where did you wait for Master Queton?"

The fast-flowing tears escaping from her tightly shut eyes, Guillemete choked out, "The minstrels' gallery. He said no one is there that time of day. He said he would 'forget' to go with M'dame, even if it put him into trouble. He said we would have at least that little time all to each other. But he had to go with M'dame after all, but I didn't know, and I waited until I had to come back here, and . . . and . . ." Sobbing completely overwhelmed her.

Marie, coming to join Michielle and Blanche in trying to comfort her, glared at him. His thoughts racing far away from Guillemete's grief, he backed away, retreated to the hearth, and knelt down to make a show of adding wood to the fire. He had thought Guillemete and Alain accounted for each other through the time when Alizon was killed and Durevis stabbed. Now it seemed they did not. And if what Ydoine said was true—that M'dame had released Alain from going with her—then Alain had lied when he said he had forgotten to go with her. Why? The lie had made sense when Joliffe supposed it was to hide he had been secretly meeting Guillemete, but Guillemete said he had never come to the minstrels' gallery.

But there was only Guillemete's word that they had been supposed to meet at all.

But Guillemete surely, *surely*, had not killed her sister.

But why would Alain? And why attack Durevis afterward?

Joliffe had rarely been satisfied with knowing merely the *what* of things. The *why* was what drew him, and mixed in with the *why* was always *who*, because *who* explained *why*—or else *why* explained *who*—nearly every time. Part of the trouble these past days was that with both *who* and *why* unknown, his foremost questions had been about *how*.

Now he was come on a knot made by someone's lying, and the *why* of that lie had to lead somewhere.

He took himself slowly through it again. Alain said he forgot to go with M'dame and that was why she was angry at him. Yet Ydoine said M'dame had told him he need not come with her. And while Guillemete said Alain had never meant to go with M'dame, she also said he had failed to meet her as he said he would, despite he had not gone with M'dame.

Of course Guillemete might be lying to protect herself, not understanding it were better she and Alain could say where both were at the time Alizon died. Or she could be lying about ever meaning to meet Alain, her claim to have waited for him in the minstrels' gallery false. Or Ydoine might be lying when she said M'dame had excused Alain from going with her.

But was Guillemete sharp-witted enough to lie that

thoroughly and hold to it so believably? And why would Ydoine lie about what M'dame had said? And why would M'dame tell Ydoine she had told Alain he need not come with her, if she had not indeed told him he need not come? Alain's claim to have forgotten looked more and more to be an outright lie.

But why say he had forgotten, if the simple truth was that M'dame had freed him from going? And why not meet Guillemete in the gallery? Always supposing Guillemete was telling the truth about not meeting him there, and almost surely she was. Where had he been if not with M'dame and not with Guillemete? Where had he been when it seemed he was not anywhere he should have been?

The thought that had to come was that he had been with Alizon in the garden.

But why?

Why be there? Why kill her? Why try to kill Durevis? *Why?*

Chapter 25

Joliffe would have gone in search of Alain with those questions—or perhaps to Master Wydeville, but as he stood up and turned from the fireplace, he saw Alain was yet again in the bedchamber doorway, staring angrily, stubbornly around the chamber.

Silently damning Foulke for not having got better rid of him, Joliffe started toward him, hoping to have him away before either M'dame—busy over Lady Jacquetta—or Guillemete—now weeping on Michielle's lap—knew he was there. And because he was moving toward him, Joliffe saw the backward jerk of his head as if he had been brutally slapped, saw his eyes widen, his mouth twist open in—disbelief? denial?—or just plain rage, because in the next moment a suffusion of blood darkened Alain's face and his mouth clamped shut in what could only be read as rage and outrage.

Joliffe flashed a look to where he was staring, saw that M'dame was just moving aside from where Sir Richard still sat with Lady Jacquetta, holding her close to him with one arm curved around her waist while his free hand lay on her skirts over her stomach in a gesture of care and worry and familiarity.

A gesture of possession too plain to be mistaken.

Sir Richard leaned to whisper something very near in Lady Jacquetta's ear, and Alain started toward them, rage raw as madness on his face, drawing his dagger as he went.

Even had Sir Richard seen him coming and instantly believed what he was seeing, there would have been too little time for him to move away from Lady Jacquetta, to rise and draw his own dagger in defense. But he did not see.

It was M'dame, turning away as she was at that moment, who saw and understood and, weaponless though she was, made to come into Alain's way.

And Joliffe, who only understood because his just-past thoughts had already wide-awakened his suspicions, likewise saw and moved almost all in a single instant, throwing open his loose clerk's gown to come at his own dagger— John Ripon's jest of a dagger but a dagger nonetheless— wrenching it from the sheath at his doublet's belt as he flung forward, reaching M'dame a bare, gasped instant before Alain did, shouldering her violently aside as he grabbed leftward, seizing Alain's dagger-wrist in the way Master Doncaster had made him do and do again in practice. Alain twisted, trying to lunge past him, past M'dame, to come at Sir Richard, maybe at Lady Jacquetta, but Joliffe, still holding his dagger-wrist, had followed through with his own dagger, driving it in low and deep below Alain's ribs—again just as Master Doncaster had made him do again and yet again until there was no seeming thought to it, only reaction to action.

Except that this time it was not wooden blade jarring against padded jerkin but sharpened steel sinking through clothing and into a man's flesh. Into a man's guts.

For the time of short-held breath Joliffe and Alain stood

frozen, staring into each other's eyes, almost as close as lovers, both equally disbelieving what was done.

Then Joliffe let go of his dagger and Alain's wrist, and Alain staggered a backward step, let fall his dagger, buckled at his knees, and sagged to the floor, to kneel there, his arms slack at his sides, his head bent forward to stare down at the dagger hilt sticking so strangely out from his doublet's front.

Somewhere in the room someone began to scream.

Then there was much screaming and suddenly far more people in the chamber than there had been—Foulke and Mathei and other men—and M'dame was giving sharp orders that had Foulke lifting Alain under the arms, another man taking his legs, to carry him from the room while Mathei saw to crowding the other men out, freeing her to turn on Sir Richard, held where he was by Lady Jacquetta clinging to him, crying wildly against him, and say, "Keep her here. Let her see nothing more," before ordering at everyone else, "Isabelle, help him with her. Wine. The oil of lavender. Valerian. Michielle, stand at the door. Close it behind me. Let no one in. Guillemete, that's screaming enough. Marie, take her out. Not through the parlor, fool! By the corner stairs. Somewhere away until she gathers her wits. Blanche, you and your wailing go with them. Ydoine, bring water, cloths, wine." Turning finally on Joliffe still standing frozen, rigid-legged, in the middle of it all.

"Come," she said. "You need tending."

Joliffe, still feeling in repeating horror the thrust of his blade into Alain's flesh, did not know what she meant. Only when she took his right arm and drew him forward did he feel the pain and, surprised, jerk a look down at his left arm where a long slit in the upper sleeve of his black gown was darkly wet with apparently his own blood. He made a strangled sound and let M'dame draw him from the bedchamber into the parlor and to the window. There she ordered him to sit.

With his legs gone suddenly shaking under him, he did, an appalled part of his mind trying all the while to refuse sight of Alain across the room. Trying but failing.

The squire had been put into a chair; was sitting braced at a rigid backward slant against its tall back, gripping the arms with white-knuckled strength and no longer staring at the dagger hilt still standing out from his doublet but up at Bishop Louys bending over him.

Joliffe vaguely supposed that was where all the men in the bedchamber had suddenly come from. The bishop, after changing from his funeral vestments, must have been coming to see how his niece did and had walked in on this. His men were now jammed together at the parlor's outer doorway, kept there by Foulke and Mathei, but someone among them would have gone for a doctor by now, Joliffe thought. He was trying to think of anything but his arm's increasing pain. Of anything but the pain and Alain. Of anything but . . . He made to fumble open his gown one-handed. M'dame put his hand aside and deftly undid it for him, then his doublet. Cauvet and Foulke appeared beside her and together helped ease gown and doublet off him, baring his shirt with its blood-soaked sleeve. Using the tear already in it, M'dame ripped it wide, baring his arm. Joliffe took one look at the slantwise slice across the flesh of his upper arm and turned his head away, sickened.

Foulke, on the other hand, said approvingly, "It's not deep. With a good cleaning and some stitches, you should mend fine. Be stiff for a while, that's all." Then to M'dame more than to Joliffe, "What happened in there?"

"Master Queton went mad and came at me with his dagger." She met Joliffe's sudden look at her with a straight stare that defied him to say otherwise. "Master Ripon stopped him."

Cauvet said, "You needed those lessons after all, Ripon. Well done."

"I doubt Master Doncaster will be pleased," Joliffe

said, making a shaky jest of it. "I think he intended I go unwounded."

"Better wounded than dead." Foulke sent a sobered look toward Alain. "You've done for him, anyway."

Ydoine appeared with water-filled basin, a perilously held pitcher of wine, and clean cloths. M'dame told her to set them down beside Joliffe on the window seat, told her to see what help Lady Jacquetta might need, and sent Cauvet and Foulke away with thanks and, "People will want to hear from you what happened." With them gone, she said to Joliffe, "I will only clean this and bind this for now. The surgeon can see to the stitching."

Joliffe accepted that with a silent nod and made teeth-gritted readiness for what would come, as across the room Bishop Louys' voice rose, insistent at Alain.

"You must confess. You are going to die. If you do not confess, I cannot shrive you and save your soul. Do you understand? You *must* confess."

Alain, braced in the chair as if trying to back away from the pain in him, said, his own voice rising, choked and wild, following his own thoughts as if unhearing Bishop Louys, "I said she was lying. She laughed. She said it would be no secret soon enough. She said she was going to tell him. She laughed." He writhed and gasped out, "Oh, God. *Pain.*" He seemed unable to get air enough into his lungs but panted, "She was going . . . to . . . tell him. It. Hurts. It . . ."

He made to grab the dagger's hilt. Bishop Louys caught his hand and held it in a firm grip, demanding, "Who? Who was going to tell? Tell what to whom?"

M'dame pressed a wine-soaked cloth to Joliffe's cut, ordered, "Hold that there," and left him, going rapidly to Bishop Louys and saying something close to his ear.

He gave her a sharp and startled look. She returned a stare that he met for a long moment before he swung around and ordered at the men still at the parlor doorway,

"Out. Everyone. Let in the surgeon when he comes. No one else. Out."

They went. Alain had come enough back from wherever he was going to glare at M'dame and choke out, short-breathed, "*You*. You told me. I was to stop her. You said. She shouldn't. Tell Remon anything."

"You only had to keep her from meeting him," M'dame said coldly. "I did not tell you to kill her."

"She went. Before I could stop her. She was going to tell him. Even after I followed her. There. That lie. Those lies. She. Said I was a fool. That Lady Jacquetta . . . Lady Jacquetta . . ." He coughed, gasped with the pain of it, coughed again, and blood came out of his mouth.

Urgently, Bishop Louys said, still gripping his hand, "You have to confess. You have to make contrition. Then I can absolve you. Do you understand? You are going to die. I'm trying to save your soul."

Alain, laboring for breath, stared at him as if unable to make sense of that until a spasm of pain stiffened him. Braced back in the chair again, he gasped, "I killed. Her. Because she was. Lying. But she wasn't. In there. I saw. She." Tears rose and spilled and washed down his face to mingle with his blood beside his mouth. Struggling for air enough for words, he gasped, "My lovely. My lovely. Lady. How could. She. With him. How . . ."

He coughed and more blood came, strangling off his words. Bishop Louys, maybe taking what he had said for sufficient confession and contrition, set to steadily praying, signing the cross again and again over him.

M'dame returned to Joliffe, took the cloth, put his hand aside, and set to cleaning the wound. Fighting to keep his words steady, he asked, low-voiced, "Was that the way of it? You set him simply to keep Lady Alizon from Master Durevis?"

"I told him to keep her from going to him," M'dame said, going steadily on at his arm. "That was all. He failed at it.

So he followed her to the garden. Angry at him for that, she foolishly told him what he did not want to hear about Lady Jacquetta. Then she mocked at him for doubting it. He lost his head and in his own anger killed her. Then he waited to kill Master Durevis, too, because to his mind it was Master Durevis' fault he had killed Lady Alizon."

"How long have you known all this?"

"He told me that day."

"But you told no one." Not even Master Wydeville? he did not ask.

"There were still Lady Jacquetta's secrets to keep."

"They can't be kept much longer."

"But for as long as they can be, they must. When there was no more need for silence, I would have told, if he was not found out before."

Only the slightest tremble in M'dame's voice betrayed she was not as steady as she outwardly showed, and somewhat less harshly than he might have, Joliffe said, "Meantime you meant to keep him from Guillemete."

"He could not see why he should not talk with her, despite he had killed her sister. I could not allow that."

She covered the wound with a folded pad of clean cloth and began to bind it in place with a strip of other cloth. The pain of that welcomely distracted Joliffe from Alain's increasingly desperate struggle to breathe, but it also kept him from more questions before a bustle at the outer door brought in a man who must be the surgeon, carrying a box that would have his implements, and a priest from the chapel, carrying another box that would have the things necessary for the Last Rites. But from somewhere else Master Wydeville was also suddenly there, gripping Joliffe by his unhurt arm and lifting him to his feet, saying, "Best you be out of here. M'dame, too."

Both obeyed, M'dame gathering up Joliffe's doublet and gown and following as Master Wydeville took him back into the bedchamber.

Lady Jacquetta was now on the bed, propped up on pillows, with Sir Richard sitting beside her, his arms around her as she sobbed against his shoulder. It was a quiet sobbing, though, and Ydoine and Michielle stood by, ready with a damp cloth and a goblet. A glance must have satisfied M'dame that she was not immediately needed there, because she asked Master Wydeville, "What now?" with a look at Joliffe.

"I'm sending him to my house. Best to have him well out of the way for now." Master Wydeville nodded at Joliffe's doublet and gown. "Let's have those on him as best we may. Master Ripon, you will keep to your feet, no matter how much you feel like falling down. Do you understand?"

Joliffe understood but did not know if he answered except by staying upright. Nothing around him seemed fully real. He found he had begun to shiver and could not stop and let them dress him, making small effort to help them nor resisting when Master Wydeville led him to the corner stairway and down it all the way to the garden, where he was given over to Pierres, who somehow was waiting there, and took him from Master Wydeville and away.

Without Joliffe being quite clear about any of it; they came to Master Wydeville's house. There, he was grateful beyond measure when allowed to lie down on a bed in a room that turned slowly around and around him while Pierres piled blankets over him and brought a fire-warmed brick to put in the bed beside him. The shivering, that had been coming and going, stopped, and Joliffe, cradling his arm that now ached rather than outright pained, would have welcomed sleep's oblivion as escape from what he kept seeing in his mind, but a surgeon came instead of sleep, and he had to sit up and be undressed again and the wound unbandaged for the surgeon to see. The man, after a little prodding that reawakened all the pain, pronounced the wound well-cleaned and stitched it closed, bandaged

it again, told him to use the arm as little as might be for a
few days, gave him a draught to dull the pain, and left him
to Pierres, who put him under the blankets again with a
newly-warmed brick.

"Sleep," Pierres said.

Whatever the surgeon had given him to drink made that
order easy to obey, Joliffe vaguely hoping as he slipped
away that when he awakened, all this nightmare would
somehow never have happened.

Chapter 26

Despite the surgeon's draught, Joliffe's sleep was unquiet and shallow, and he awoke from it to find Master Wydeville standing over him, a lighted candle in his hand and darkness beyond the chamber's window.

The thought with which Joliffe had gone to sleep was the first that came to him as he came awake, and he asked, "Is he dead?"

Master Wydeville set the candle down on a chest beside the bed. "He's dead. The surgeon said there was no hope. So when Bishop Louys had finished with him, they took the dagger out and he died."

Joliffe did not know what he felt and tried to hide he was feeling anything by struggling to sit up. Protecting his hurt arm made him awkward, and Master Wydeville helped him, shifted the pillow to behind his back, then said, stepping away but watching his face, "You have not killed a man before this."

"No. I never have." And wanted never to do it again, wanted to say it had happened without he meant it to, that he had simply done what Master Doncaster's lessons had taught him to do.

But he had known those lessons were for that. Their whole purpose had been how to kill and keep from being killed. Now he had done as he had been taught, and all he wanted was to be rid of memory of it.

But that was hardly something he was going to say to Master Wydeville, and he said instead, "It shouldn't have come to killing him. If I had sorted out sooner that it had to have been Alain in the garden, it wouldn't have come to my killing him."

"Could you have sorted it out sooner?"

Joliffe had to stretch his mind to think back across the wide gulf between then and now before he was able to answer slowly, "The last piece, the one that told everything, I only had and fitted to the others just before he came into the bedchamber."

"Then I would say that you sorted it out in good time. Would you have understood so quickly what Alain meant to do and moved in time to stop him, if you had not worked your way to knowing his guilt? And remember it would not have come to killing him if he had not chosen to play the utter fool there. Because he meant to kill again, didn't he?"

Sharp-edged memory flashed in Joliffe's mind. Yes, at that moment Alain had assuredly meant to kill. Against whom he had been set was less sure, whether Sir Richard or Lady Jacquetta or maybe both of them if he could, but yes, he had been intent on killing, and no matter what Joliffe felt about having killed him instead, it was better than living with having failed to stop him.

That was what Master Wydville wanted him to see, and he did and accepted it but could not help saying bitterly, "M'dame knew. She knew all the while what he had done."

"So she has told me, now. Do you understand why she kept it secret?"

"To protect Lady Jacquetta. To protect your son. Even though their marriage can't be secret much longer."

As if he did not hear the accusation in Joliffe's voice, Master Wydeville answered evenly, "Gain of even a little more time helps."

"Helps what?"

"To have things in order for their leaving here. They've known all along they cannot stay in France, that it will have to be England for them. Now, with the child coming, they will have to go very soon."

"Did Bishop Louys know their secret before today?"

"No. Nor does he fully know it now."

"How could he not? Alain's babbling surely gave it all away?"

"As you say, it was babbling. I have since made suggestion to my lord bishop that, for this time being, he might do well to let it go at that."

"He accepted that?"

Only after a noticeable pause did Master Wydeville answer, his gaze steady on Joliffe, "My lord bishop and I have worked together a long while. He was willing to take my advice that present ignorance could serve him well in future trouble. Master Ripon, Alain Queton was a fool. He chose to live by his passions, forgoing reasoned choices. He killed Lady Alizon for no good reason. He tried to kill Remon Durevis with even less reason. Today he meant to kill again if he could, simply because he could not bear his passions nor bother to think through what he intended. He was a fool and he died for it, and if you had not killed him, he would have died just as surely but more slowly at his execution. Let him go from your mind."

Because the simplest answer—and perhaps the best— was agreement, Joliffe gave it with a silent nod.

"Good," Master Wydeville said. "Food will be brought soon. Then you should sleep again. You're at some surgeon's place, not here. Your wound is being given out as worse than it is, which is why no one has come to question you. Instead, it's being accepted that you told M'dame, while she tended to you, that you saw Alain start forward with the dagger and moved to stop him. That you know no more than that about anything."

Joliffe nodded again, again because agreeing was easiest. But he could not help, "One other question, if you'll grant it."

Master Wydeville made a small gesture of permission.

"How did M'dame know to set Alain on to watch Alizon that day?"

"Sir Richard, in his message to her that arranged they meet at the goldsmith's to exchange his letter and Lady Jacquetta's, warned he thought Durevis hoped to somehow meet with Alizon. He wrote that if M'dame thought Alizon knew or had guessed too much and might tell, they should be kept from each other. So she set Alain to watch her."

And Alain had "played the fool" that day as badly as he had today, Joliffe thought and was abruptly tired beyond words with the hurting in his mind and his arm. He closed his eyes and gratefully listened to Master Wydeville leave; but he was equally grateful when Pierres came in soon afterward with food and drink.

Joliffe ate and drank because his body wanted food and drink. Worn out by the effort of that, he slept, that seeming the most useful thing to do, and awoke in daylight to find more food and drink had been left for him beside the bed. Awkward with his hurt arm and no one to help him, he ate and drank and slept again, and awoke in what had to be late afternoon to find Perrette sitting at the window, sewing— mending his doublet, Joliffe realized in the moment before she said, without looking up from her work, "These have been washed. I've finished with your clerk's gown and am nearly done with this. There is a new shirt for you. Your other was beyond hope."

"Perrette." The word croaked from his dry throat. He

took up the cup waiting by the bed and drank and said again, because she had gone on sewing and not looked at him, "Perrette."

Her hands went quiet, and she lifted and turned her head to him. The day's light was behind her, keeping her face in shadow.

He held out his hand. "Perrette, come sit beside me."

She put his doublet aside and came, sat down on the bed, and let him take her hand, all silently. With her there, Joliffe after all did not know what to say and simply held her hand a while before finally asking, "Perrette, how much do you know of this?"

"What happened in the Lady Jacquetta's chamber yesterday and something of why. Although not all of it, I think."

Joliffe made to say something. Perrette raised her free hand, stopping him. "Nor should you tell me more."

No, probably not. Not without Master Wydeville's leave. He shifted away from what he might have said and said instead, hoping the words were right, "Perrette, Lady Jacquetta will be going to England soon and not returning. All her household will go with her. I will be going with her." And glad he would be of it. "Perrette, come with me."

Perrette curved her free hand gently around his that held her other one and said quietly, "No."

He had been expecting that refusal and so had an answer ready for it, saying quickly, "Perrette, there's peace in England. There isn't war and death hanging over everything. There . . ."

"Death is everywhere."

"Yes. Well. Yes. But it clusters more thickly some places than others. Here, if not now, then soon. In England you would be safe from that. We could be together. We—"

"My life is here," she said, the words flat.

"It doesn't have to be. You—"

"It has to be. My life is my penance. It has to be lived here."

"Your penance?" he blurted. "For what?"

"For being still alive."

Joliffe lay still, with no answer to make to that and no question he dared to ask that he thought she would answer. She met his gaze for a long moment more, then took her hands from him, stood up from the bed, and went back to the window and her sewing.

Neither of them spoke again, and when she had finished and folded the doublet and laid it on his gown on a stool at the bedfoot, she came to him one last time and, still silent, kissed him long and lingeringly on the lips. In answer, he briefly took hold on her hand again, but there still seemed no words worth saying between them, and she again took her hand from his and left the room, closing the door silently behind her.

It was another day before he returned to Joyeux Repos, and by then he was restlessly more than ready. The surgeon had briefly seen him in the morning and pronounced the wound free of infection and healing well, and long before Pierres came for him in the late afternoon he had struggled into his shirt and doublet and was trying to be used to the leather strap looped from his neck to hold his hurt arm. Pierres helped him put on his gown, leaving the left sleeve hanging loose, and laid his cloak around his shoulders, something nearly impossible to do one-armed, Joliffe realized.

Eager though he was to be away from Master Wydeville's, the walk back to the *hôtel* tired him more than he wanted it to, and the stairs up to the offices nearly finished him, so that he was glad to sit down at his desk and put up with the jibing and careful back-slapping that served for welcome from George, Henri, Jacques, and Bernard. There was jesting about Sir Richard having to be saved from "mad Alain" by a secretary, but nothing that showed anything was guessed at about Lady Jacquetta. Joliffe answered questions with what Master Wydeville had said he was to say. In return, he was told the search for Remon Durevis had been given up, that he was presumed killed by Alain and shoved into the river, and that Lady Guillemete had left that morning, taking her sister's body home as intended.

No one said what had become of Alain's body, and Joliffe did not ask.

That evening, when he would rather have taken to his bed, he made himself go to the great hall for supper, supposing it best to get done with whatever more jesting, jibing, and questions might come his way there, only to find word had come that afternoon and was excitedly spreading through both households that there was no more doubt the duke of Burgundy had preparations well forward for an attack on Calais. Word was that the duke of Gloucester would lead an army out of England to counter him, which was to the good for Normandy, since it meant most effort here could be turned to whatever the Armagnacs, led by the *comte de* Richemont, were set to do. Talk was loud and split between whether that would be the long-expected attack on Normandy in force or else the long-feared attempt to reach and take Paris.

In all the loud talk and much swearing, the happenings of two days ago seemed near to forgotten, for which Joliffe was greatly grateful. Only Cauvet and Estienne said anything at length to him about what had happened—what they knew of it, anyway—and he was able to answer Cauvet's sympathy and Estienne's curiosity without saying anything he should not. His hope was to go gratefully to his bed as soon as supper was done, but a servant found him while he was still in the hall and said he was summoned to Lady Jacquetta. Wearily, his arm paining him, he went.

As on so many of the other evenings he had been summoned to her, she was in her candle-lighted bedchamber, her ladies around her, her dogs curled against her skirts, but tonight there were too few demoiselles, and no youths in bright talk with them, and no laughter. Nor did Lady Jacquetta ask him to read to her but beckoned him forward to kneel in front of her where she sat on the cushioned chest at the bedfoot. In her widow's wimple and black veil, she was paler even than usual, but had no sign of lately crying, and her voice was steady as she said, "You know you have my very great thanks, Master Ripon. My thanks and those of Sir Richard. This is but outward and poor token of what we owe you."

She held out a small, drawstringed purse. It was of silk, embroidered with the Luxembourg lion, and weighed heavily in Joliffe's hand as he took it from her. He thanked her, kissed the hand she held out to him, and understood—by the way M'dame moved forward from beyond the bed—that nothing more was wanted of him here. Glad of that, he stood up, bowed deeply to Lady Jacquetta, and let M'dame show him from the chamber, expecting her to see him only to the door, but she followed him into the parlor, shut the door behind her, and said, levelly and quietly, "I equally owe you thanks, Master Ripon. I would have not been able to stop him from reaching my lady."

Joliffe bowed his head, acknowledging her thanks, not knowing what other answer to make. No right words coming to mind, he gave up and asked, "Would you answer me one thing, M'dame?"

"If I may," she said, austerely as ever.

"This marriage. Your given duty is to guard Lady Jacquetta. This is a rash thing she's done, yet instead of stopping her, you stood witness to it, in despite of all your duty. Why?"

"My duty is to my lady," M'dame said. "I am here not to be her gaoler but to guard and guide her. I warned her of everything there is to be feared for her in this marriage. When she then made her choice despite it all, my duty was to guard her and her secret. That I have done and will do for the while until it is no longer a secret."

Joliffe bowed, able to say nothing in answer to that. She gave him a short nod in return and turned back to the bedchamber and her duty.

For his part, more tired than ever and his arm aching, he returned to the dormer, slipped his arm from its sling, and sat on his bed, cradling it. The dormer's silence around him was welcome. He only wished his thoughts were as silent, but like his arm's aching, they went on.

The blazing talk of the war had spared him questions in the hall that evening, and against all the deaths in the fighting past and to come, Alizon's was surely only a little death, and Alain's an even lesser one, and both already disappearing from men's minds; but they were deaths nonetheless and not disappearing from his mind. All the living Alizon might have had was stolen from her, and Alain was dead along with all his wild, unthinking desires and hopes—dead and perhaps damned, with no chance to become the man he might have steadied into being.

And Guillemete. She lived, but how deep were the scars she would bear in her heart through the rest of her life?

All because of a secret marriage that, will or nill, could not be a secret for much longer, and when the scandal and the angers about it had faded, when the marriage had become simply a marriage and there was the child and in the inevitable way of things probably more children—Alizon and Alain would still be dead.

Joliffe found he was rocking gently forward and back, partly to comfort his arm's ache, partly to comfort the ache in his mind, and maybe to comfort the thought that if, in that desperate moment in the bedchamber, he had been ill-fortuned or only a little less skilled, he would be among the dead now.

He was glad that in barely a few weeks he would be back in England.

* * *

The next day, with his strength increasingly come back to him, he went to thank Master Doncaster. As expected, the weapon-master responded, "You're *supposed* to kill without taking hurt yourself," before adding, grimly approving, "Nevertheless, well done."

It was the day after that when Master Wydeville stopped him at the afternoon's end, as he was leaving his desk. With everyone else gone, he took the duke of Orleans' silver bowl that Master Wydeville offered him and drank and was all the while wary of why he was there, and for no good reason all the more wary when Master Wydeville said, "It's set that Lady Jacquetta will sail for England in two weeks time. You've perhaps thought you will go with her."

"I had thought it likely, yes," Joliffe granted carefully.

"As part of her household, you surely would have, but you are to leave her service and go into the bishop of Therouanne's household. Tomorrow."

"Tomorrow? The bishop's household?" Joliffe echoed, both wariness and protest open in his voice.

"You've proven yourself too valuable to let go simply back to England. Nor do I think Bishop Beaufort wants you there yet. So you will now serve Bishop Louys." Master Wydeville paused, his gaze steady on Joliffe's face, as he finished, "Which means that four days from now you will be among those who go with him to Paris, where he will do what can be done there against the *comte de* Richemont's coming."

Joliffe's stomach did a slow knot around on itself. "To Paris," he said, trying to make the words mean something else.

"To Paris," Master Wydeville agreed.

Author's Note

There are a number of historical people serving as characters in this book, including Lady Jacquetta and her uncle Louys de Luxembourg, bishop of Therouanne. Historical, too, are Master Richard Wydeville and his son Sir Richard, who are rather too frequently confused with one another in modern historical accounts, but are well worth while keeping separate because they followed quite different careers. That Master Wydeville was the duke of Bedford's spymaster is my own choice, but what we know of his career does not preclude the possibility. The political situation as detailed here is as it actually was in the dangerous year of 1436. Many details have had to be left out or skimmed over, but nothing has been distorted or "made convenient" for the story, and while many incidents specific to the story are imagined, Lady Jacquetta was indeed required to swear not to marry without the royal council's or king's consent at a time when she was either already secretly married or soon would be.

Likewise, there is record from early in that year of a

female spy for the English reporting the Bretons would
soon attack Normandy. It's one of those frustratingly tiny
pieces of information about which one would like to know
so much more but probably never will.

As for the books read to the duchess and her ladies, a
version of Reynard the Fox's adventures that might be close
to what they heard can be had in *The History of Reynard
the Fox,* translated from the Dutch original by William
Caxton and edited by N. F. Blake for the Early English
Text Society, 1970. There are numerous medieval works
about Alexander the Great; the one they heard here could
be related to *The Prose Life of Alexander*, edited by J. S.
Blake for the Early English Text Society, 1913. The poem
Joliffe was reading in Chapter 2 is by Thomas Hoccleve (or
Occleve) who was writing poetry in Middle English in the
early part of the 1400s. There are various editions of his
works, and selections of his poetry can be found in various
anthologies of Middle English poetry.

The maps Joliffe is set to memorizing would hardly be
recognizable by modern eyes as guides to anywhere, but
medieval maps are a delightful study, revealing a relation-
ship to the world sufficiently different from our own that
the shift in thinking needed to move from our modern
perception of geography to a medieval one is an excellent
exercise in seeing what different ways there are for relating
to the world around us.

The detailed examination of the murder victim's body
is not an anachronism. Medieval coroners were advised
not only to make close observation of crime scenes but of
wounds and any other circumstances around a murder that
would give details toward understanding what had happened. In fact, according to the Oxford English Diction-
ary, the word *investigation* was used as early as 1436 in the
sense of "making search or inquiry, systematic examination, careful and minute search."

On a minor note, the university at Caen, mentioned in

Chapter 13, was indeed founded by John, duke of Bedford, and still exists, the one thing that has lasted from his long struggle to bring peace and return prosperity to war-destroyed Normandy.

As for what came of the scandal-marriage between the duchess of Bedford and Sir Richard Wydeville—or Woodville, as it is often spelled now—first was a heavy fine to the English government for marrying without permission, then at least thirteen children, and eventually a secret, royal marriage that made their eldest daughter queen of England, a grandson briefly king of England, a granddaughter queen to the first of the Tudor kings, and a great-grandchild into King Henry VIII.